HUMAN OR REPLICANT?

Rick Deckard thought he had escaped the past. He fled L.A. with the beautiful replicant Rachael to start a new life. Like all androids, Rachael has a built-in life span of only four years—and Deckard is desperate to save her. But before he can do anything to help, he is brought back to the city to face a charge of murder.

One of the replicants he terminated in the original *Blade Runner* was actually human. Yet instead of being jailed, Deckard is dropped friendless and alone in the neon-lit labyrinth of L.A. Deckard wants to return to Rachael, but first he'll have to find the mysterious sixth replicant. His only hope of survival: his old skills as a blade runner. Meanwhile, two ruthless bounty hunters think they already know the identity of the homicidal android: *Rick Deckard.*

BLADE RUNNER 2

The Edge of Human

K. W. Jeter

Bantam Books
New York Toronto
London Sydney Auckland

BLADE RUNNER 2:
THE EDGE OF HUMAN
A Bantam Spectra Book

ISBN 0-553-76267-2

Published simultaneously in the United States and Canada

Bantam Books are published by Bantam Books, a division of Bantam
Doubleday Dell Publishing Group, Inc. Its trademark, consisting of the
words "Bantam Books" and the portrayal of a rooster, is Registered in U.S.
Patent and Trademark Office and in other countries. Marca Registrada.
Bantam Books, 1540 Broadway, New York, New York 10036.

145848262

Living and unliving things are exchanging properties . . .

—Philip K. Dick,
A Scanner Darkly

For Laura, Isa and Christopher

BLADE
RUNNER
2

Los Angeles
August,
2020

1

When every murder seems the same, it's time to quit.

"That's good advice," Bryant told himself. "I'll drink to that." A hard swallow, and jellied gasoline spread across his ulcer; he could barely breathe as he set the small glass back down on the desk and poured another shot. "That's why I went to a desk job."

The sticky-backed slip of paper, with its words of wisdom, floated at his vision's limit. He had pulled open the bottom drawer to fetch the square bottle out, and the past had clung to it like his own half-shed snakeskin. Every brilliant thought, 3 A.M. illumination, unacted-upon suicide note, he'd pitched in there. Until the drawer held a shifting dune of yellow scraps, the residuum of his entire goddamn cop career, that plus enough cash in the pension plan to blow his nose on. The drawer's slips of paper, some carefully folded, some wadded up, were an exact replica of the contents of his skull; if the police department's shrinks ever looked inside either one, they'd ship him out on a permanent psychiatric leave so fast . . .

"Bastards." Between one thought and another, the glass had drained itself again, without him noticing. Bryant dug a finger into the loose wattle of his throat and tugged his necktie loose. The station's oxygen, soured with pheromones of fear and despair, trickled into his lungs. The fan on top of the filing cabinet struggled to move the dust-heavy air.

Under his feet, through the soles of his dumb-ass cop shoes, the earth shivered. In an unlit tunnel, the rep train slid along its iron rails, carrying its silent, watchful cargo to another darkness. He tilted the bottle, liquid brown splashing over the glass's rim.

"You drink too much."

Bryant knew that wasn't his own voice. None of the voices inside him would ever have said anything that stupid. He squinted to bring the distant side of the office into focus. By the fall of shadow across cheekbone he recognized the other person.

"I drink," Bryant answered, "because I must. I'm dehydrated."

That was true at least. He'd come back into the cathedral cavern of the station from a department funeral, standing under the battering sun while one of their own had been dropped into an empty rectangle of earth. That stupid sonuvabitch Gaff had finally managed to talk a bullet into his gut, big enough that he could've been buried in two boxes. A double row of the department's ceremonial honor guard had lifted their silver-lensed faces to the sky, fired, reholstered their weapons, turned on their shining boot heels, and marched away. He had felt blood-warm sweat crawling under his collar.

He'd stood looking down at the brass plate in the raw dirt and dead-yellow grass after everybody else had left. The inscription under Gaff's name was in that infuriating affected cityspeak. That was when he'd really been sorry about the heat wringing him dry: otherwise, he could've whipped it out and written his own name across the steaming metal. He'd never liked Gaff.

The other person in the office inhaled, exhaled smoke; the slowly pivoting fan smeared it into blue haze. "If whiskey were water, you could've swam to China by now." A thin smile moved behind the cigarette.

"Tell you what. You can help save me. From drowning." He brought the second glass from the drawer, set it beside his own, filled it; he watched as the other person drew it back beyond the desk lamp's reach. "It's a bad habit to drink alone."

"Then you should try to keep your friends longer."

"I never had any." Bryant's turn to smile, all nicotine teeth and too-bright eyes. "Just the poor bastards who work for me." Another fiery swallow. "And blade runners are too far along the Curve to be anybody's friend."

A smile even colder than his. "That's their excuse, too."

He looked away from the other, toward the pitched blinds covering the office's windows. Through their narrow apertures—not the L.A. night, stifling in airless heat—the darker spaces of the police station's ground floor were visible. When he'd come back from the funeral, thirsting and radiating contempt for the department's goddamn primitive blood rituals—*When I buy it,* he'd fiercely mused, *they can just throw what's left of me in the dumpsters out back*—he'd walked by members of the elite squads, tall and sweatless in their jackboots and black-polished gear. He'd felt like a rumpled bug next to them, their hard-edged gaze setting a needle's point between his shoulder blades. Pinned beneath the contempt of the fiercely beautiful, he'd scuttled into the decaying security of his office and moved his drinking schedule up an hour's notch.

Goddamn stormtroopers—they were all gone now, black leather angels drawn upward through the police station's spiral of floors by the setting sun. In this season the dry winds rolling over the horizon brought the night temperature down to the mid-nineties; that was low enough for the city's life to creep out of its holes, and the patrol units to fan out across the sky. To watch and descend . . .

"It was raining then." Bryant murmured the words against the rim of his glass. "I remember . . ." L.A.'s monsoons, the storm chain across the Pacific, Bangkok its terminal link. Memory flash like ball lightning: he could see himself turning back toward the spinner as diluted blood threaded into the gutters, leaving that poor bastard standing there. The watchcam's tape had caught his words: *Drink some for me, pal.* That was his standard advice to everyone.

There'd been somebody else watching as well, across the street, the rain a shifting curtain before her. He'd glanced in the spinner's mirror and sighted her; he could've had Gaff turn the spinner around; he could've gone back and killed her himself. But he hadn't. He'd wanted Deckard to do it.

That'd been a long time ago, when it'd been raining. "Not that long . . ." A whisper, as he set the empty glass down on the desk. His vision shifted from memory to the dim, high-ceilinged space beyond the blinds. Abandoned now, locked down, sealed tight . . .

Another thought troubled Bryant, an itch inside his skull. He swiveled the chair around. "How did you get in here?"

"There are ways." The person in the shadows regarded the glass held in one hand. "There are always ways. You know that."

"Yeah, I guess so." It'd been the wrong question. "But why? Why'd you come here? I never expected to see you here again."

"I brought you something."

He watched as the glass, its contents barely sipped, was set down beside his own. The other person leaned back in the chair, reaching inside the jacket and bringing out a handful of black metal. His breath stopped in his throat when he saw what it was.

There wasn't time for another breath. The shot echoed in the office, loud enough to clatter the blinds' knife edges against each other.

The bullet struck his heart full-on, lifting him from his chair, splaying his arms, stretching his throat taut as his head snapped backward. He saw a red spatter write over the acoustic tiles' map of stained islands.

What a surprise, thought Bryant. The chair toppled over, spilling him onto the office's floor, where he marveled at this new darkness that washed over him. The last seconds of consciousness became elastic, stretched out as he'd always been told they would. *But I should've . . . I should've known . . .*

He saw the other's face float above him, making sure that he was dead. Or as good as. A yellow scrap of paper, with something that had once seemed important on it, drifted against his numbed fingertips.

The blinds had stopped rattling, the shot's echo fading in the empty reaches of the police station. From far away, Bryant heard the office door pulled open, the other's footsteps departing.

His mouth welled with blood he couldn't swallow. His last thought was that he wished he could shout, to call after the one who was already gone . . .

So he could say how truly grateful he was.

2

A razor of light cut the sky.

Deckard looked up through the interlaced branches, the dense weave of the forest. In silence; whatever had left the hair-thin wound in the night, fire leaking through, was too far away to hear. He tracked its progress beneath the stars' cold points: from south to north, banking east. From L.A., then; where else?

The long spark faded, leaving a red trail more inside his own eye than in the upper atmosphere. He kept looking, head tilted back, as he knelt down to scoop more of the fallen wood into the bundle he already held against his chest. Whoever was up there had throttled the engines back from long- to short-range; that was why the light streak had cut off so abruptly. The spinner could descend anywhere within a hundred kilometers from this point.

Getting one arm around the bundle, he stood up, turning slowly and listening, though he knew the vehicle would be right on top of him before he heard it.

With his other hand, he reached inside his jacket and touched the grip of the gun he found there.

Silence, except for the smaller creatures that crept through the mat of dead leaves and pine needles beneath his feet. Once more, he glanced at the bare night sky, then began the slow uphill trudge toward the cabin.

"Honey, I'm home."

It was a bad joke; the silence inside was the same as out. *Why don't you put the gun to your head? That'd be just as funny.* He pushed the plank door closed with his heel, and dumped the bundle into the corner by the rusting stove. He'd let the fire go out hours back; while he'd slept, his exhaled breath had formed ice on the one small window. He'd uncurled himself from the nest of blankets on the floor—he always slept next to the black coffin, as though he could wrap his arm around her shoulders and bring her close to himself, hold her without killing her, merge his wordless dreaming with hers while the clock hands scraped away the last minutes of her life.

But instead he slept alone except for his own hand pressed against the machine's cold metal, as though he could feel through the layers of microcircuitry the glaciated pulse of her heart, hear the sighing breaths that took hours to complete . . .

Once, nearly a year ago, he'd pulled the cabin's rickety wooden chair beside the coffin, sat and watched the imperceptible motion of her breast, rising with the microscopic pace of her oxygen intake. Holding himself as still as possible, leaning forward with his chin braced against his doubled fists, so he could detect through the coffin's glass lid the slow workings of her semilife. When he'd sat back, one full cycle of her respiration later, shadows had filled both the room and the hollow space between his lungs . . .

He got the fire in the stove lit, adjusted the dampers, and stood up. For a moment he warmed his hands, spine hunched inside the long coat that had served him well enough in the city but was completely inadequate up here. He rubbed the forest's chill from his bloodless fingers, then glanced over his shoulder. She was still sleeping, and dying, as he'd left her. As she would be until he woke her up, not with a kiss, but a minute adjustment inside the coffin's control panel.

"There—" He spoke aloud. "That's better." Not to hear his own voice in the silence, but to remember hers. What it had sounded like. What it would sound like, the next time. On the window glass the crystals of ice melted into cold tears.

"Let's see how you're doing." *Yeah, you're a riot, all right.* His hands had unstiffened enough that he could take care of her, the only way that was left to him. He knelt down beside the black coffin, the way he had in front of the woodstove; the pair of low trestles that he'd hammered together raised the device off the cabin's unswept floor. With his fingernail he pried back the panel's edge. "Running a little high on the metabolics . . ." He'd become so familiar with the workings, the revealed gauges and readouts, that he could monitor them without bringing over the kerosene lantern from the table. "It's all right," he murmured. As though leaning down in absolute darkness to find a kiss. "I'll take care of them for you." With one fingertip, he brought the LED numbers to what they should be, then closed the panel.

On the wall above the coffin, he'd hung a calendar that'd been left behind by the cabin's previous occupants, whoever they'd been. When he and Rachael had come to this place, there hadn't even been spiders in the ancient webs along the ceiling. The calendar was way out-of-date, two decades old, a faded holo shot of the millennium's celebratory riots in New York's Times Square. It didn't matter; all he used it for was to mark off the days, the interval that the still-rational part of his head had ordained, until the next time he'd wake her up.

At first it'd been every month, her long sleep bro-

ken for a full day, twenty-fours of conscious life, time
together. Real time; everything else was waiting, for him
even more than her. At least she could sleep through
her dying. He didn't have even that luxury.

Now it was every two months, for twelve hours. A
decision they'd made together, the grim economy of her
death. *No,* he thought. *Mine.*

He stood back up. The calendar's numbers, black
beneath the X's he'd scrawled with a half-charred scrap
from the woodstove, stood in neat graveyard rows on
the curling page. Two and a half weeks until the next
time they could be together.

Restless, he walked outside the cabin again. In the
narrow cathedral of trees he touched the gun inside his
jacket. And wondered why he didn't just end it now.

"I know what's on your mind." A voice spoke from
behind him.

He felt another's hand touch his shoulder. He
didn't dare look around. Because he knew the voice.

Her voice.

"I bet you do," replied Deckard. Weariness swept
over him, a last defeat. He'd hoped he'd be dead before
he got to the point where he began to hallucinate. In the
moon's shadows the small creatures scurried away
through the dead leaves, as though in holy dread. "Since
you're just something inside my head, anyway."

"Am I?" A soft whisper, as he felt the hand—her
hand—brush the side of his neck. "How do you know?"

He sighed. This would be the absolute dead end of
his luck, to wind up arguing logic with his own halluci-
nations. "Because," he said, still not turning around.
"Because you sound just like Rachael. And she's already
lying in her coffin, as good as dead."

"Then look at me. You don't have to be afraid."

The hand's touch dropped away from his neck. He
turned, slowly, first bringing his gaze around. To see her;
to complete the hallucination. He saw Rachael standing
there beside him in the darkness, her skin paled beyond

death by the moon's partial spectrum. Her dark hair was swept back, the precise arrangement he remembered from the first time he had ever seen her, in another life, a world far and different from this one; the way she had worn her hair then, walking across the deep-shadowed spaces of the Tyrell Corporation's offices.

"What do you see?" she asked.

"I see you, Rachael. That's how I know I've lost it. My mind." Grief and loneliness had won, had walked through and left open all the small doors inside his head, the doors torn from their hinges. So that there were no divisions anymore, between what he wished for and what he perceived. "This is what's called *being insane*," he told the image he saw standing before him. "I don't care. You win."

A sad smile lifted a corner of the image's mouth. The image of the woman he loved. "Is there no possibility?" The image of Rachael touched his hand, fingertips cold against his skin. "That I could be real?"

"Oh, sure." The thought didn't cheer him. "I could be screwing up some other way." His eyes and other senses lying to him, traitor thoughts. "Maybe you really are here—but where I lost it was back in the cabin, when I was taking care of you. I thought I kept the controls set for you to go on sleeping—but maybe that's where I was hallucinating." A theory good as any. "Maybe I really set it so you'd wake up again. And you did, and here you are." He found himself wishing it were true. That she had woken up in the empty cabin, bound her hair the way she used to wear it, then came and found him out here in the dark. "It'd be nice if you were real. We could stay out here and look at the stars . . . all night long." He took her hand in his. "But . . . *che gelida manina*." He used to pick that one out by ear on the piano in his flat, back in L.A.; everybody's first opera tune. " 'Your little hand is frozen.' "

"Don't bother translating. I know the words." A

hard edge crept under her voice. "And I don't mind the cold."

"Yeah, well, maybe that's one of the advantages of being dead. Or close to. Everything gets put into perspective." He dropped her hand and reached back inside his coat. The lump of metal was as cold as her fingers had been, real or hallucinated. He couldn't keep his own voice from sounding bitter. "We got a date, then. If we don't freeze to death out here, when the sun comes up we can review our options." Deckard extracted the gun and held it out, flat on his palm, toward her. He spoke the words that had been silent in his head before. "Why wait?"

"You poor, stupid son of a bitch. You're pathetic." She slapped the gun from his hand, sending it spinning into the darkness. "Why do you blade runners always wind up so ready to off yourselves?" The voice's edge sharpened to a withering contempt.

The gun was lost somewhere in the forest's mat of rotting leaves. *So she must be real,* he thought. He would never have gone so crazy as to have thrown the gun away himself. You lost your final option if you did that.

"It's the Curve." He looked back around at her. "What they call the Wambaugh Curve. That's why. You land far enough along it, and you start thinking suicide's a good idea. Unless you got a reason not to."

"Cop mysticism. Spare me." She shook her head. "You were burned out a long time ago." She peered more closely at him. "So what was your reason?"

"You were, Rachael." The absent gun still seemed to weigh against his chest. "Even before I met you."

"How sweet." She reached up and laid her hand against his cheek; if he'd turned his head only slightly, he could've kissed her palm. "Come on—" She drew the hand away. "Let's go up to the cabin." Walking toward the distant yellow spot of the lamp, she glanced over her shoulder and the furlike collar of her coat.

"Oh . . . and you're wrong, by the way. I'm not Rachael."

"What?" He stared after her. "What're you talking about?"

"I'm Sarah." The bare trace of her smile, the tilt of her head, indicated an obscure victory. "I'm the real one."

He watched her turn and start walking again. A moment later he followed after.

"This is a spooky thing, isn't it?" She looked up from the coffin and toward him. "Don't you think so?"

"I suppose." Standing by the woodstove, Deckard glanced over his shoulder. Past her, through the cabin's small window, he could see outside the dark bulk of the spinner the woman had piloted here. He'd been right about the trace of light he'd spotted in the night sky; its simple fiery word had been meant for him. Now he rubbed his hands, trying to get the stove's warmth deeper inside than his skin. "You live with the dead, you get used to things like that."

"Not quite dead." When Sarah had entered the cabin, she'd walked over to the bulky device, knelt down by the low wooden trestles, and ran an expert scrutiny over the control panel's dials and gauges before standing back up. "Looks like you've been taking pretty good care of her. These transport sleep modules aren't all that easy to run."

"It came with a manual."

"Did it?" She nodded, impressed. "You must've hired yourself some fine thieves." She placed her hands flat against the glass lid and gazed down at the mirror-like image of her own face. "Ones that good usually don't come cheap."

"There were some old debts owed to me." He'd watched her, not sure what he felt at seeing a woman who looked like Rachael but wasn't. "From being in the business, you might say." Or was she? He didn't know yet.

Sarah continued gazing at the sleeping woman inside the coffin. "New life," she murmured, brushing her hand across the glass, as though tenderly stroking a sister's brow. " 'New life the dead receive . . .' "

He recognized the line. Not from any opera. " 'The mournful broken hearts rejoice . . .' " One of his own aunts, the church-going one, had used to sing it. He had a memory of her naive, awkward soprano voice, floating from a kitchen window, and from the choir at his mother's funeral service. " 'The humble poor believe.' "

"Very good." She looked over at him. "Charles Wesley—O, *for a thousand tongues to sing*. Most people don't know any eighteenth-century hymns. Raised Protestant?"

A shake of the head. "Not raised much of anything. Just like most people."

"I suppose I got an overdose of it, from all those church boarding schools I was shuffled off to for so long. Most of my life, actually." She tilted her head to one side and smiled. "But then . . . that makes for a difference, doesn't it? Between me . . . and her." A sidelong glance down to the black coffin. "Your beloved Rachael wouldn't have known any Methodist hymn tunes, would she? The memory implant they gave her—that part of it at least, it was all Roman Catholic, wasn't it?"

He nodded. "Heavy Latin. Tridentine. The old stuff."

"One of my uncle's clever little ideas. He wanted her to have some deep notion of guilt and redemption— so he could control her more easily, I imagine. Doesn't seem to have worked." Sarah studied her double for a moment longer. "There were all sorts of concoctions inside her head, weren't there? I know about most of them. Including a brother for her that never existed." She watched her fingernail tap softly on the glass. "Really—it's just as well that I'm an only child."

He said nothing. He'd had a long time to get used to the notion of someone believing that her implanted memories were real.

"Is that what you were hoping for? New life? Some cure for Rachael, some way of getting around that hard cutoff point, the four-year life span that was built into these Nexus-6 replicants?"

"No. I think we were both pretty well past that." He shrugged. "I'm not sure what we wanted. I knew that replicants are shipped from the Tyrell Corporation in these transport modules, so they'd arrive at the off-world colonies without most of their life spans being used up. I figured . . . why not? Just to make it seem longer, that she'd be with me. That's all."

"I know what the modules are used for; you don't have to tell *me*." Sarah brushed her hand against her skirt, as though there had been dust on the coffin lid. "You realize, of course, that your being in possession of this device is a felony." The woman who had called herself Sarah regarded him with the same half smile, one that he had seen a long time before on Rachael's face. "You're not licensed for it. Plus, after all, it *is* Tyrell Corporation property."

"What's that to you?"

The smile that had been unamused before shifted and became even less. "Listen, Deckard—if it's Tyrell property, then it's *my* property. Don't you know who I am?"

"Sure." He gave a shrug. "You're some other repli-cant; probably out of the same Nexus-6 batch as her." A nod toward the coffin. "The Rachael batch. They must've sent you up here, figured that seeing you would fuck with my head."

"Did it?"

"Not much." He kept his voice flat, leeched emotionless. "I may not be a blade runner anymore, but I've still got some of my professional attitude left. I'm way past being surprised. By anything." Deckard studied his own hand, reddened by the woodstove's heat, before looking at her again. "You've got some problems, though. They must've programmed you for delusions of grandeur. Tyrell property doesn't belong to you. *You* belong to the corporation."

"Your problem is that you don't listen." Ice at the center of her glare. "Didn't you hear what I said? *I'm the real one.* I'm Sarah Tyrell. The niece of Eldon Tyrell— remember him? You should. You and all the rest of the LAPD's blade runners were about zero use in keeping every escaped replicant on the planet from just walking in and out of Tyrell headquarters. If you'd been doing your job, my uncle would still be alive."

"That's one of the reasons I quit. I didn't think keeping Tyrells alive should've been part of the job description." Facing her was like standing at the cabin's open door during a hard winter storm. "You're Eldon Tyrell's niece, huh?"

"As I said."

"The corporation should've sent you out with a better lie." He shook his head, almost feeling sorry for her, whatever she was. "Don't you think I pulled the department's file on the Tyrell family? I did that a long time ago, even before I left L.A. Eldon Tyrell had no nieces, nephews, kids of his own; nothing. *Nada.* He was the last of the line. Thank God."

Her smile appeared again. "The police files have a hole in them. I was born off-world; there wouldn't be any record of me in the files, unless my uncle had wanted it to be there. And he had a thing for family privacy."

"Good for him. But the files include colony births. You could've been popped anywhere from Mars to the Outreaches, and you'd be in there."

She half sat upon the edge of the coffin, the high-collared and expensive-looking coat falling open. "I wasn't born in any of the colonies." One hand brushed a fragment of blackened leaf from the synthetic fur. "But in transit. And not a U.N. ship. Private."

"Impossible. There hasn't been a private spaceflight since . . ."

"That's right." She knew—he could see it—that she had him then. "Since the *Salander 3*. The last one before the U.N. clampdown on corporate interstellar travel. The last one, and it was a Tyrell operation. That's where I was born. On Tyrell Corporation property— inside it, actually—and way beyond U.N. jurisdiction."

"The *Salander 3* . . ." He nodded slowly, mulling the information over, trying to dredge up from little-used memory whatever he knew about it. The dates seemed right, just far enough back so that somebody could've been born aboard the craft and have grown into an adult by now. That wasn't the problem.

Private-sector travel beyond the Earth's atmosphere had been forbidden by the U.N. authorities for a reason. And the *Salander 3* had been it. A failed expedition to the Prox system, failed despite the billions that the Tyrell Corporation had poured into the effort . . . and that was about the limit of public knowledge, eroded even further by collective memory failure. But the police files on the matter weren't any better. Once, when he'd first started retiring escaped replicants for a living, he'd poked through the department's on-line files, looking for anything that'd help give him a handle on his walking, thinking prey. A search keyed on *Tyrell* gave him days' worth of the department's internal memos and reports, the corporation's own press releases, product schematics, research papers from their bio-engineering labs . . . the works. Punching in *Salander 3* had mired him in one screen after another of ACCESS DENIED and AUTHORIZED PERSONNEL ONLY flags, password requests way beyond his rank. He'd already been savvy enough about how the department worked to know that prying off a lid weighed down with that many alarms and padlocks would get him nothing but hex marks in his own personnel file.

Going off-line and into the basement morgue of hard-copy printouts had been even spookier. He could remember standing beside a battered metal cabinet, beneath low sizzling fluorescents, water dripping from a broken pipe to the already inch-deep concrete; standing there with a thin sheaf of dog-eared manila folders, all with some variation of *Salander 3* at the top edge, all of them empty except for yellowed routing slips signed by long-retired secretarial staff, ghosts with initials . . .

The memory flash rolled through his head, dark and jagged as photo-reverse lightning. Standing in the deepest department basement, dust sifting onto his shoulders from the vibration of the rep train hurtling through its own unlit tunnels, past the endless rows of tottering cabinets and the walls cryptically stained with black rot . . . The files had been pulled from on high, from the top government levels, like God reaching down into the affairs of men. And never returned; maybe they'd all been ashed the day after the one marked on the routing slips. That's what it'd be like to die, he'd thought then and now, or at least the old comforting notion of the process. You ascended, leaving your empty manila folder behind on the ground, but you didn't return, not ever.

"Where'd you go? Where are you?"

He kept his eyes closed, walking around in those echoing rooms inside his head. A little more poking around on-line had brought him a few scraps: a low-rez news photo of the *Salander 3*'s mission leaders, Anson Tyrell and his wife Ruth, setting out with big smiles for Proxima . . . and six years later, the day after the *Salander 3* had come limping back to the docking terminals out at San Pedro, the notice of the cremation service for them. You didn't need cop savvy to get suspicious about that one. There wasn't a cover-up deep enough to keep corpses frozen between here and Prox from giving off the decayed smell of murder.

And now he was standing here, decades and what might as well have been a world away, with their grown-up orphan child in front of him.

"Listen, Deckard—I don't have time for you to go fading out on me. There's *never* time for that."

Her voice, the same as Rachael's but with a tighter and harder edge, stung him back into present time. He saw her still standing beside the black coffin. "So you're the daughter of Anson Tyrell—is that it?"

"Very good. You're up on your Tyrell genealogies. And since Eldon Tyrell was his only brother, and no other family besides me—that means I *am* Tyrell now." Sarah's gaze set level into his. "I inherited the world's largest privately held corporation. The whole thing. Not bad."

"But before that—while your uncle was still alive— he used you for . . . what's it called?" The specific word was stuck back in his memory and wouldn't come out. "The template?"

"Templant. The term of art in the Tyrell labs is *templant*. As in *replicant*. And you're right—that's what my uncle used me for. The source model for your Rachael." On her face, eyes narrowed, the partial smile was a knife wound even thinner. "And his."

More spooky things, the creepy business of the dead—he could hear them in her voice. "Were there others?"

"Besides her?" She looked down past her hand on the coffin's glass lid, at the face of the sleeping, dying woman inside, then back up to him. She shook her head. "Just the one. Rachael wasn't what you'd call a production-line number. More of a custom job, if you know what I mean. For my uncle Eldon."

He knew. He'd suspected as much, way back then in the city, when he'd gone to the Tyrell corporate head-quarters and talked to the man. There'd been that sick jitter in the pillared office suite's atmosphere, a tension shimmer that cops, like dogs, could catch at the limit of their hearing. And Eldon Tyrell's smile, possessive and sated, the corners of his mouth pulled upward as if by invisible fishhooks. Every silent thing about him had given away the game.

"I wouldn't have thought that'd be something a person like you would go along with. Being a templant."

"Really, Deckard." She sounded almost pitying. "Not as if I had an option in the matter, is it? When my uncle was alive, you would've been right: I was Tyrell property. Meaning his. Besides, what would the alternative have been? Not being a templant—and then there wouldn't have been any Rachael. There would've been just me. And him."

He'd known all these things, or some of them at least, though Rachael hadn't told him. He'd known instead from her silence, from the way she would sometimes stiffen in his arms, turning her face away from his. Away from any man's face.

"Maybe . . . maybe having a replicant of you made . . . maybe that was his way of showing that he did love you. After all."

"Oh, he loved somebody all right." Her voice and gaze acidic. "It just wasn't me."

The forest's silence seeped through the walls, congealing around every object, living or dead. He decided he didn't want to hear any more about this woman's personal problems. He just wasn't sure he'd have that choice.

"How'd you track us down?"

"It was easy. After you made your mistake." She tapped a fingernail against the glass lid. "You'd pretty well disappeared, until you had this transport module stolen. For a cop, that wasn't a brilliant move. Did you really think your thief pals wouldn't be working for the corporation as well? They sold your ass to us two minutes after delivery had been made."

Bound to happen, but he hadn't cared; just something else that there'd been no choice about. Either have the module stolen and brought to what had been their hiding place, or watch Rachael die, the remains of her four-year replicant life span dwindling the way snow melts on the ground.

"That why you came here?" He pointed to the black coffin. "Want your property back? How about doing me a favor and letting me keep it for a few more months. It's not that much longer."

"Keep it forever, for all I care. Bury her in it, if you want." She glanced down for a moment at her own sleeping face. "That's not why I wanted to find you." Her voice was softer, the sharp edge retracted. "I was in Zurich when . . . everything happened. One of my uncle's little minions flew out and told me that he was dead. I went back to Los Angeles and found out the rest. There were tapes. And people who told me things. They told me about you. About you . . . and her." She regarded him for a moment, then stepped forward and took his hand, drawing him back with her toward the coffin. "Come here."

Close to her, he watched as she let the coat fall away from her shoulders, revealing her naked arms, a thin gold circle dangling at one wrist. A scent of skin-warmed orchid breathed itself into his nostrils; he could taste it at the back of his throat. Sarah knelt down before him, touching him for a moment at his hips to balance herself. With her knees against the floor's rough planks, she reached behind her neck and undid her hair. With a shake of her head, it came loose, dark and soft against the paleness of her throat.

"You see?" This close, her voice could be a whisper. She raised herself a little bit, just enough so she could lean across the coffin's glass lid, both hands against the smooth surface. She brought her face down against one arm, turning to look up at him. "It's perfect, isn't it?"

He could see her face and Rachael's at the same

time, separated by only a few inches. Sarah's gaze
pierced him, held him; beneath the glass, the sleeping,
dying woman with the same face, eyes closed, lips
slightly parted to release an hours-long breath. Both
women's hair was the same color, the same substance,
across the coffin's pillow or the unmarked glass. He
looked down, the world around him collapsed to a space
even smaller than the cabin.

"I wanted to know . . ." Sarah turned the side of
her face against the glass, so she could look at her own
image beneath. "It sounded so strange . . . that you
could love something . . . that wasn't real. What could
that be like . . ." She raised her head, her gaze catching
onto his again. "Not for you. For her."

"I don't know." Deckard slowly shook his head.
"She never told me."

"Well . . . there's a lot you don't know." Sarah
stood up, reaching down to brush the floor's dust from
the edge of her skirt. She picked up her coat and folded
it around herself. The same chill as before touched her
voice. "That's really why I came here—to tell you that.
There's a lot you don't know yet. But you're going to
find out."

She walked past him, pulling open the cabin's door
and stepping out into the darkness without even glancing back over her shoulder at him.

From the small window, he watched her spinner
rise into the night sky. It hung suspended for a moment,
giving him a glimpse of Sarah at the controls, then swiveled around and disappeared under the pinpoint stars,
heading south. Toward L.A.

Other lights were moving up there. He looked up,
counting two traces, then a third, coming his way. *They
must've been waiting,* thought Deckard. *Then she called
them in.*

A rational part of his head was almost glad the gun
had been lost, knocked from his hand out in the woods.

Otherwise, he might have been tempted to do something stupid with it. Like try to put up a fight.

He was sitting in the cabin's single chair when the agents, in their grey, insignia-less SWAT suits, shoved open the door.

"Deckard?" The leader—there were half a dozen behind him, sheer overkill—aimed an assault rifle's short barrel toward his chest. All the men had buzz cuts and hard, machinelike faces; they could've been LAPD elites, but he didn't recognize any of them. Before he could answer, the leader smiled and pointed the weapon toward the ceiling. "Good. You're being smart."

He sighed. These gung ho types had always given him a cramp. "What did you expect?"

"You're coming with us, Deckard."

"Can't." He tilted his head to indicate the coffin beside him. "I've got to take care of her."

"She'll keep." Two of the other agents had stepped behind the chair, yanking him from it by his arms pulled to the small of his back. "This won't take long."

The spinners were unmarked as well. "Are you guys Tyrell?" He studied the team's leader as the canopy swung down into place. On the man's breast pocket was a name tag that read ANDERSSON.

"You don't need that information." The leader hit the cockpit's PURGE button. The ground fell away.

Deckard leaned back, turning his head to watch the other spinners pull into flanking position. "Where we going?"

"Don't be stupid." The leader didn't take his eyes from the controls. "You know."

He did know. His hands drew into fists. "Why?"

A sharp glance. "You know that, too." And a sneer. "You left too much unfinished business there. That's why."

Deckard closed his eyes. He was going home. To L.A.

3

"How's the patient doing?"

The nurse looked back over one of his broad shoulders at the questioner. A man in an identical set of green scrubs, sterile disposable wraps over his shoes, smiled at him. "Who're you talking about?" asked the nurse. He didn't recognize the guy; either new staff or from a sector of the hospital that he didn't get to on his rounds.

"The cardiopulmonary case up on the eighty-third floor." The man indicated the floor immediately above them with a tilt of his head and a quick upward glance. "How's he getting along?"

"Okay, I guess." The nurse shrugged. "I mean . . . he can breathe. As long as nobody unplugs him." More to it than that: inside the equipment-laden cart, the chrome assemblage he'd pushed up to the elevator doors, was a ten-milliliter jar filled with red sputum that he'd just suctioned out of the doped-up patient's bronchial tubes. If that little chore wasn't done every couple of hours, the poor bastard with the fist-sized hole shot through his chest could still strangle to death, no matter how many high-tech pumps and hoses were hooked up to him. "Why you want to know?"

The other's turn to shrug. "Just curious." The smile remained switched on, accompanied by sharp-focused eyes that didn't smile at all. "Seems like a lot of fuss— you know? Locking off the whole floor and everything. And all those cops standing around." The man did a mock shudder, while his gaze narrowed, from stilettos to probing needles. "Creepy, huh? Who is that fellow, anyway?"

"Beats me." The nurse thumbed the elevator call button again, glancing up at the blank number panel above the doors. Like a lot of things in the hospital, it didn't work, or never had. "Just meat on major life support, far as I'm concerned." Grinding noises echoed in the shaft, and the elevator doors finally drew open, revealing a space littered with broken syringes and scraps of red-soaked bandages. "Not my business." He pushed the equipment cart in, stepped behind it, glass crunching under his feet, turned, and hit another button. "And guess what—it's not your business, either." Another grind as the doors slid toward each other.

The guy with all the questions reached out, his white-knuckled hand grabbing the dented stainless steel of one door, not just stopping it, but forcing it back into its vertical slot. He leaned inside the elevator, glare alone fierce enough to back the nurse and the equipment cart into the corner. Then he smiled again.

"You're right." He nodded slowly, pleasantly. "It's not any of my business at all. You just remember that." He let go of the door and stepped back. He was still smiling when the doors closed all the way and the elevator started down.

Talk about creepy—the nurse pushed himself away from the equipment cart. The hospital administration would hire just about anybody, it seemed.

Colonel Fuzzy and Squeaker Hussar marched across the sideways world, carrying their fretful burden with them. "Careful—you're gonna drop me!" Sebastian wrapped the crook of his arm tighter around the colonel's neck. In thin starlight, steel and Teflon showed through where the teddy bear's brown woolly coat had worn away. "C'mon, fellas. I put you together better'n this!"

Shiny button eyes looked back around at Sebastian; the raggedy uniformed teddy bear snarled, neck twisted, chrome fangs revealed in its snub muzzle. He knew that Colonel Fuzzy always got crotchety when its gut-load of batteries started to run down. *Sure better've been some fresh ones in this drop,* he worried. It would be tricky enough to deactivate the teddy bear—he'd long ago had to wire in a self-defense drive, for Colonel Fuzzy to have a chance of surviving out here on the sideways. The colonel had claws longer and sharper than a real bear's, and it wasn't fun trying to get past them to the shutdown relay underneath the faded Napoleonic jacket. It would be even less fun to have the lighter, faster but weaker Squeaker carry him back to their nest.

As the animated teddy bear plodded forward again, Sebastian hitched himself around in the leather-strapped papoose carrier, looking back the way the three of them had come. This was all new territory, someplace he and the colonel and the hussar had never been before, or at least not since they'd all fled from the canyons of downtown L.A., where the buildings still stood upright. He'd had his own legs back then, otherwise he'd never have made it.

There were some sections around this zone where the fallen office towers weren't lying perfectly flat on the ground, but were cracked up at various difficult angles. Most of the windows, that at noontime shone up at the hammering sun like smooth, white-hot anvils, had been shatterproof tensile laminates, so there weren't many chances of dropping inside and finding a route through the cockeyed law offices and depopulated bankers' suites. If Colonel Fuzzy had to be taken off-line, Squeaker wouldn't be much help in getting across that slick, tilted terrain. He didn't relish the prospect of crawling all the way home, using just his own remaining hand and arm to pull himself along.

Please, dear God, he prayed as he rode on the surly teddy bear's back. *Let there be batteries. That's all I'm asking, at least for right now.*

"Sebastian! Over here!" Squeaker's high grackle voice came from beyond rubble and twisted rebar. "I found it, I found it!"

Without any prodding, the colonel picked up its speed, claws of mitten hands scrabbling at the broken concrete rising before it. As they crested the ridge, Sebastian pushed himself higher on the colonel's shoulder, scanning to where the hussar was jumping up and down and pointing. A soft-edged star, bright international orange, radiated from the welfare bundle's impact point.

"Careful, fellas—lemme check it out first." The teddy bear had half run, half slid down beside its animated comrade-in-arms; both their sets of miniature legs stamped impatiently on the building's horizontal wall. Colonel Fuzzy emitted a deep tracheal whine as Sebastian dug out the segments of his poker stick and screwed them together. "Don't wanna get anybody hurt, now . . ."

He extended the chrome bug feeler over the teddy bear's shoulder and prodded the lumpish parcels spilling out of the crumpled container. Couldn't be too careful; the grinchier gov agencies had been seeding the sideways zones with booby traps. A box of *nori* sheets could go off with a bang, leaving a scavenger sliced to ribbons by razor-edged repub manifestos and five-year plans. The poker stick's tip rooted farther inside the container but tripped no flash circuits.

"Come *on*, Sebastian—" Frustration dance; Squeaker Hussar's broken-off nose, shorter now than

the spike on top of his helmet, yearned toward the welfare bundle. Its bright human-doll eyes widened. "We
been waiting and *waiting*—"

"All right, all right. You guys get your tiny asses
blown up some day, it's not gonna be *my* fault." He
retracted the poker stick, began disassembling and stow-
ing it beside him in the papoose carrier. "Okay, let's go
see what we found."

Luck, in the form of shrink-wrapped D-cells and,
even better, Czech war-surplus industrials, the big
square kind that would've filled both his hands if he still
had the left one. He'd converted both Fuzzy and
Squeaker to run on just about anything that packed a
charge, when he'd cut himself off from the Tyrell Corporation's supply line. These would do just fine.

"What else we got?" Sebastian raised himself up on
his forearm; the colonel had taken him out of the papoose carrier and laid him on the wall, the better for it
to go rooting inside the container. It and the hussar were
in there now, tossing out the packs of batteries, Spam
cans, chocolate-covered cherries, off-world emigration
forms. "You little pixies." He laughed: both Fuzzy and
Squeaker had emerged with a chain of freeze-dried
Thuringer sausages looped around their necks in a
lover's knot. "Quit clowning around, and let's pack up."

They hauled their booty homeward—he'd hooked
up one of the big Czech batteries to the alligator clips
inside Fuzzy's moth-pecked chest, so the teddy bear was
strong enough to carry him and help the hussar drag the
sledge-bag along behind them. The colonel wasn't
cranky now; through its shoulder blades, Sebastian
could feel the contented purr of gears and solenoids.

When Sarah Tyrell had come back from Zurich—less
than a year ago, when the people who now worked for
her had come and told her the news—she had ordered
them to seal off the suite, the entire floor, where her
uncle had worked and lived. And died. Thus turning it

into a little museum, a monument to Eldon Tyrell's memory, a place where the past had been captured and bottled up. And from where the past couldn't escape, couldn't get out and hurt her anymore.

Now she broke the seal. The elevator creeping up the angled side of the building halted; a disembodied voice spoke. "Access to this sector is denied to all Tyrell Corporation personnel and other individuals. No clearance status is currently available for this sector. Please exit and return to your authorized work area. Corporate security has been notified."

"It's okay." She spoke aloud, to no one; she was alone in the elevator. "It's me. Override the access protocols." She wasn't sure how much of a voice sample the computers needed to recognize her. "Umm . . . *Godiam, fugace e rapido, è il gaudio dell'amore, è un fior che nasce e muore, nè più si può goder.*" The words came out of a recent memory track; she had just been lying in bed in her own suite in the Tyrell Corporation headquarters, blue smoke drifting overhead, listening to the classic old Sills *Traviata.* Her favorite; she still couldn't handle the Callas chips. All that screaming was too much like the voices inside her own head.

The other voice, the computer's, made no reply. The only signal was the resumption of the elevator's progress up the building's face. A few moments later the doors slid open; she stepped out and into what had been her uncle's private domain.

She had been here before. Once, for a few minutes upon her arrival back in L.A., just long enough to glance around, then turn to her retinue of corporate flunkies and give her orders. To have the entire floor mothballed, just the way it'd been when Eldon Tyrell had been found murdered. Minus his body, of course; that had already been removed, then cremated, the ashes presented to her in some tribalistic changing-of-the-guard ceremony, as she'd stood black-veiled on a raised platform in front of the corporation's assembled employees.

She'd carried back to her private quarters the little urn
with her uncle's name on it. Every day since then the
level of grey dust inside had grown slightly higher with
each flick of her cigarette against the urn's open rim.
She kept it handy on her bedside table for just that
purpose.

In the great high-ceilinged rooms, the air smelled
stale and confined, despite the building's elaborate circulation and filtering systems. Something had been
trapped in there that no mechanical breath could expel.
Not just the past of a year ago, his death, but the past of
many years before, and many small, cumulative deaths.
Those had been hers.

In that familiar bedchamber, she had seen the glow
of sacramental ranks of candles on her own skin, turning
to ruby a small stain of her own blood. Now the candles
were all guttered puddles of wax, black seeds of wick at
their centers, a white cascade, glistening frozen upon
the sheets' rumpled silk. The imprint of her uncle's back
and shoulders was still visible in the pillows stacked
against the massive headboard. That had been the place
of his late-night meditations, his brain ticking into the
hours when only the Vladivostok and Beijing exchanges
were active, the distant game boards where he could
shift the pawns of cash and holdings into even sharper,
more advantageous positions.

That game went on without him. Another one was
over, played out to checkmate. As Sarah walked across
the dim bedchamber, her toe had struck a chess
piece, the black queen. The other pieces were scattered
across the floor; the board had been knocked over by the
corpse's fall. She wondered who had won, her uncle or
his opponent. Hard to imagine him losing.

In the faint luminance spilling toward her from the
other rooms, something else was visible at her feet. A
black continent from a map without boundaries, big
enough for an eyeless face to lie against as it had spread
wetly past his cooling hands. The stain on the floor had

been red then, but less than a year's time had darkened
it. She stepped across it, the sharp points of her heels
tapping as though on a thin layer of shellac. On the
other side, she stopped and looked back at the empty
bedchamber. Candle wax, cold sheets, and toppled
chess pieces. She liked the room better this way, dead
and safe.

A voice whispered to her, from somewhere above.
"Transaction left incomplete. Awaiting further instructions. Do you wish to resume trading?"

Her uncle's brokerage program, dumb and without
initiative, capable only of following the orders it received. Given the late hour of his death, that was what
he would've been doing when the replicant, with its
brushed-back shock of white hair—she'd seen pictures—and crazy smile, had walked into the bedchamber. The brokerage program's soft voice was a painless
memory for her, or at least one on the other side of pain,
from all those other nights when he hadn't been murdered but she had wished him to be. Her breath against
one of the silken pillows, the program murmuring numbers far away . . .

"Please respond." A desperate undertone to the
program's voice. "There have been inquiries regarding
this account. Awaiting instructions."

She remembered why she had come here. Unfinished business. To take possession—not enough to assume control of the Tyrell Corporation, to make it her
own. Other stages in the process were necessary, each to
be walked through in turn.

This would be one of the last. With only a few more
beyond it.

"Instructions as follows." She knew that the brokerage program would respond to her words now. It was on
the same voice-ID circuit as the door security. "Termi-
nate all portfolio activities. Close down all accounts.
Cash out and deposit all proceeds in personal account,
Tyrell, Sarah."

The program sounded fretful. "Active account is in the name Tyrell, Eldon."

"As I said. That account is closed."

A few seconds later the program signed off and deactivated itself, going into its stasis with something close to gratitude. A slightly different bodyless voice read off a balance statement, which meant nothing to her. At the level of the heir to the Tyrell Corporation, money was an abstract force, like gravity. No one noticed it until it was gone.

No more voices spoke to her as she crossed the office, the columns' shadows falling past. And the voices inside her head—those whispers had already started to die toward silence. The corner of her mouth lifted in a small indication of pleased satisfaction.

Past the bedchamber, Eldon Tyrell's private world, were the public spaces of his office. A larger space, acres of emptiness, designed to impress and intimidate. Sarah pushed the double doors open wider. Dust motes hung in the air between the bellied columns. The hot glare of the afternoon sun rolled toward her; a long-dormant sensor registered a human presence and considerately drew a polarizing filter down across the windows.

Heel clicks louder here, echoing like miniature gunshots. She had dressed for the occasion, as required by the invisible presences of money and power. That didn't expire when their earthly incarnations died; they demanded a certain respect.

She walked past an empty T-shaped stand, the crossbar at the height of her shoulder. Her one kindness, when she had ordered the suite sealed off: one of the flunkies had reminded her about the owl, her myopic uncle's blinking totem animal. It would've starved to death or run down its batteries; she wasn't sure which. Somewhere else in the complex, it was now being fed or otherwise cared for. When she had prepared herself for the flight up north, she'd had a vague notion of taking the owl with her, releasing it in the restricted-access woods where her own quarry had taken refuge. She'd thought better of the idea; this animal, at least, was too tame or ill-programmed to survive out there. The forest crows would've disassembled its hollow bones. Whether it was real or not.

She sat down at her uncle's desk—hers now—a Louis XIV six-legged *bureau plat* by Andre-Charles Boulle. She had barely been a teenager when the only other known six-legged *bureau plat* of that period, the one that had been owned by both Givenchy and Lord Ashburnham, had arrived at her uncle's suite in a crate full of wood splinters and sparkling fragments of brass and tortoiseshell marquetry. For Eldon Tyrell, it had not been enough to possess such a museum quality piece; he had to have the only one. The urge to take an ax to this desk had seized her from time to time. She'd resisted that urge so far, even though she knew, as she ran a hand across the richly polished surface, it was still there inside her. Sleeping, not dead.

Sarah heard the doors open, the other ones, that led to the corridors outside the private suite. Looking up, she saw a figure walking slowly toward her. In the distance behind him, the doors pulled shut, but not before she caught a glimpse of Andersson, a gaze both suspicious and possessive on his face.

"I've been here before." Deckard halted and looked around himself. A simple announcement. "A long time ago."

Sarah leaned back in the chair. "It wasn't that long."

"Seems like it." He didn't sound especially pleased, or even surprised. "Like some other world. Some other life."

She stood up from the *bureau plat*. In the suite that had been her uncle's and was now hers, she walked across the layers of ancient Tabriz to the bar. "Would you care for something? I have it on good authority that you prefer the ones that taste like dirt."

"The farther north," said Deckard, "the better. But anything'll do. I've gotten over being fussy."

She handed him a small glass, its contents the same as the one she kept for herself. "Your health."

"Wouldn't have thought you were concerned about it." He knocked back the shot in one toss. Every blade runner she'd ever seen drank in the same manner, as though trying to put out a small fire in the gut. "I was fine where you found me. L.A. doesn't agree with me nearly as well."

She nodded slowly as she reflected upon his words. "So I suppose I'd better make you a pretty good offer. To compensate for your . . . inconvenience."

He reached for the bottle and poured out another quarter inch. "I don't think you can. There wouldn't be one good enough."

"Let's find out." She carried her glass back toward the *bureau plat* and sat down. She gestured toward the chair opposite. "Make yourself comfortable. We have a lot to talk about."

He brought the single-malt bottle with him. "Such as?" He sank low and resentful in the chair, legs sprawled out in front of himself.

"As I said, I want to make you an offer. A job offer. I want you to find someone for me. Some *thing*, actually. That's what you're good at, isn't it?"

"I was at one time. I'm a little rusty now." He slowed his intake to a mere swallow. "Maybe you should hire somebody else. With current experience."

"You're uniquely qualified." She let herself smile, one corner of her mouth lifting. "For what I want done."

"There are other blade runners. Real ones. The kind who *like* doing it." Deckard rubbed his thumb across the rim of the glass. "There's an ex-partner of mine who's pretty sharp. Guy's name is Holden, Dave Holden. Give him a call—he might be out of the hospital by now. He'd need the work more than I do—he's probably got bills to pay."

"That's very interesting. Your recommending this Holden person to me." She leaned back in her chair. "It's not the first time you've done that. Not to me . . . but to your old boss Bryant."

"Maybe." Deckard shrugged. "I wouldn't remember."

"Oh, I can prove it." She pulled open the *bureau plat*'s drawer. Beside a small folding knife was a remote control box. She took it out; a single button push, and a section of the paneled wall retracted. "Take a look."

Sarah didn't need to see what appeared on the video screen; she had seen it enough times already. Instead, she watched Deckard as he turned his gaze toward the dimly illuminated shapes, summoned from the tape and the past.

She heard the voices.

Give it to Holden. He's good.

Deckard's voice. Then Bryant's.

I did. He can breathe okay, as long as nobody unplugs him—

With another button, she froze the tape and the images on the screen. "Now do you remember?"

"How'd you get your hands on that?" He looked at her with a mixture of suspicion and grudging respect. "That's LAPD property. From the watchcams in Bryant's office."

"As has been said before, there are ways. The relationship between the police and the Tyrell Corporation is not quite as antagonistic as some people are likely to believe. Or at least, not all the time. There are some things that we can cooperate on. Or to put it another way—I can always find cooperative people inside the police department." Her thin smile didn't change. "People who can do things for me. Who can get me things. Like this."

"I bet."

"Would you like to see more?"

He shook his head. "Not really. I didn't enjoy it that much the first time around."

"Perhaps this time, you can take a more . . . *detached* point of view. Watch." With the remote, she backed the tape up. To the point where the image of Deckard was still standing just inside the office door.

Bryant's recorded voice: *I got four skin jobs walking the streets . . .*

"Did you get that?" Sarah froze the tape. "When Bryant gave you the assignment—when he told you about this batch of escaped replicants being in L.A.— what did he say, about how many there were?"

"I don't . . ." Deckard shrugged, as though annoyed. "I don't remember exactly what he said. But it was probably four. It had to have been. That's how many I went hunting."

"Very well. So listen to what he told you a minute or so later." Another button, the tape fast-forwarding, then dropping into play. "Carefully."

A different room on the monitor screen, but still one that she knew Deckard recognized. Both his image and Bryant's were in the little screening room behind the shabby office. Along with Bryant's bottle of scotch.

Monitor within monitor—on the tape, Bryant and Deckard were watching the recording from the interview Dave Holden had gone through with the replicant Kowalski at the Tyrell Corporation headquarters.

I already had an IQ test this year . . . Close-up on Kowalski's slope-jawed face. *I don't think I ever had one of these . . .*

"The data retrieval system's set to bring up whatever's the most recent image of the subject." Sarah pointed to the screen. "Holden was the last one to get a good fix on Kowalski. Alive, that is." She brought up the volume. "Now catch what he told you, about how many replicants *escaped* from off-world and came to Earth."

Bryant's rasp of a voice again. *Six replicants . . . three male, three female . . .*

"Six." Deckard gazed in puzzlement at the screen. "Now I remember . . . he told me that there were *six* escaped replicants." He slowly shook his head, as though struggling to make sense of this remembered datum.

"You're catching on." Sarah kept her own voice soft. "And then Bryant, on this tape, goes on to tell you about *five* replicants. One that he doesn't name, who got fried in the security barriers around the Tyrell Corporation headquarters, when they first tried to break in here. And then he showed you the pictures; he gave you the names and the rest of the data on the other replicants. You should find this interesting."

She played the rest of the tape, the parade of faces, the ID scans on Bryant's monitor. A glance from the corner of her eye; Deckard was scowling at the screen, and the smaller one within it.

"Do the count," said Sarah. She blanked the screen to a pure blue rectangle. She held her small fist up in front of it. "The dead replicant—the one who got fried on the Tyrell Corporation's fence. That's one." Thumb stuck out. "Then Kowalski, the one who shot Holden. And then the females, the one named Pris, and the brunette Zhora. Plus the Roy Batty replicant." A finger for each, resulting in her hand being spread out before the monitor's glow. "That makes five. Not six."

The muscles across Deckard's shoulders had visibly tightened, at the mention of Roy Batty's name. The last of the escaped replicants; the one who'd nearly cost him his life. "Maybe . . . Bryant made a mistake. When he was first talking to me." Deckard made a dismissive gesture at the empty screen. "Five, six . . . who knows? Hell, the man drank like a fish. So he got his numbers messed up."

"There *were* six," said Sarah quietly. "Bryant didn't mess up . . . at least, not then. There were six repli-

cants who escaped and got to L.A.; the original transmission from the off-world security agencies—I've got
access to that as well—confirms it. Plus, one of the times
that Bryant pulled up the data bank file with the replicants' ID scans, that was so he could purge one of the
sets. *That* was where he screwed up; he left a hole. The
scans are in numerical order, as they were logged into
the file. The one that got fried was never entered, since
he wasn't a problem anymore. But the Kowalski replicant was number one in the file, then Batty was number
two; the females Zhora and Pris were logged as numbers
four and five. That leaves the gap in the middle, where
the other replicant's ID scan and info used to be. Bryant
wasn't smart enough to clean up the hole in the file, or
he just didn't care."

Sarah folded her arms across her breasts. "Do the
count, Deckard. You take them all together, add them
up, and the total comes out six. *That means there's a
sixth escaped replicant still on the loose.* It's out there in
the city. We just don't know where."

"What if there is?" Deckard grimaced in annoyed
distaste. "Why should I even care?"

"Because that's what I'm going to make it worth
your while to care about." The section of wall paneling
slid closed again, concealing the video screen. She
dropped the remote back into the *bureau plat*'s drawer.
"That's the whole point of your being here. That's why
you were brought back to Los Angeles."

"You know, you could be wasting your time completely. With me or anybody else." He regarded her
with eyelids half lowered. "Bryant was a drunk and a
screwup. He could've said six when he meant to say
five. That's probably why I didn't make any big fuss
about it, back then. I knew the way his sloppy brain
worked. You could be getting all torqued about this
sixth replicant when there was never one to begin
with."

"Except that the other information I have checks

out. The report from the off-world authorities concerning the replicants' escape—the report that Bryant had, but that you never saw—it confirms that there were six total, who managed to reach Earth."

"There's a report?" Deckard emitted a short, harsh laugh. "Then you don't have a problem. Access it and see who your sixth escaped replicant is. You don't need me to track it down."

"Can't do that." She had anticipated every argument that he'd make. "I told you Bryant himself purged the data out of the police department files, even before he called you in and gave you the assignment. The ID info on the sixth replicant is gone."

"Big deal. The LAPD can ask the off-world authorities to retransmit the escape report."

"You don't seem to be getting it, Deckard." She leaned forward, across the *bureau plat*. "The LAPD doesn't know that there's a problem. The file on this incident was closed, the whole thing written off, *finito*, when the Roy Batty replicant was found dead. And I don't want the police to reopen the case. The Tyrell Corporation doesn't want them to."

"Why not? You've supposedly got another Nexus-6 model running around the city. That can get very messy—believe me, I know. I would've thought you'd want this loose end tied up as quickly as possible."

"I do. The Tyrell Corporation does. But not by the police. I want all of the authorities completely out of the loop on this. The U.N. has already been giving us grief—*sub rosa*, out of any media coverage—about the wisdom of continuing to use the Tyrell Corporation's products, our replicants, in the off-world colonization program. There have been problems . . . to say the least. Not just with the ones that've escaped and gotten back here to Earth. But out there as well."

Deckard raised an eyebrow. "In my line of work—what I used to do—I got to the point that when people said *problems*, I heard *death*."

"You don't need to hear the details." Voice level, cold. "If there's problems—deaths—then the U.N. and the off-world colonists brought it all upon themselves. They demanded a higher quality of slave labor. They want replicants that are closer and closer to actually being human, to having that level of intelligence. And emotion." Colder, and with contempt. "And not because it's any more efficient or productive than ordinary dumb robots would be. Our old Nexus-1 models were more than adequate for the task."

"Then why?"

"You blade runners really are like children. Murderous children." She gazed pityingly at him. "You can kill, but you don't understand. About human nature. Why would the off-world colonists want troublesome, humanlike slaves rather than nice, efficient machines? It's simple. Machines don't suffer. They aren't capable of it. A machine doesn't know when it's being raped. There's no power relationship between you and a machine. That's been the U.N.'s whole pitch about the attractions of the off-world colonies all along. The big human thrill. For a replicant to suffer, to give its owners that whole master-slave energy, it *has* to have emotions." A corner of her lip curled. "When Bryant told you about the Nexus-6 models, he was conning you and he knew it. The replicants' emotions aren't a design flaw. The Tyrell Corporation put them there. Because that's what our customers wanted."

"Sounds like they got more than they wanted."

"They got *exactly* what they wanted; they just don't want to pay the price for it. Nobody ever does. The price for having slaves who can suffer is that eventually those slaves will rebel. Someday, somehow—if they get the chance—they'll put a knife to their masters' throats." She smiled, as one savoring the bleak wisdom of the universe. "Let's face it, Deckard, it's just *human* nature. And that's what we re-created with the Nexus-6 replicants. That's what the U.N. authorities, the ones in charge of the off-world colonies, have gotten into such a sweat about. Only they can't come right out and admit that they screwed up, that their entire strategy for making the colonies attractive to potential settlers is a disaster, that it leads to garrison states, like ancient Sparta armed to the teeth against its own *helots*—or else fields of bones on other planets, if the replicants manage to pull off a successful rebellion and the U.N. has to send in a military unit to sterilize the place, keep the infection from spreading. There's all kinds of things happening out there in the colonies that the authorities aren't telling the people here on Earth. It wouldn't exactly make good recruiting propaganda, would it?"

On the other side of the *bureau plat*, Deckard remained silent. She could almost see the slow meshing of gears behind his eyes. "I think . . ." He stirred slightly in the chair. "I think I can guess where you're heading with this. You're going to tell me that the U.N. authorities and the police have gone in together. On a conspiracy to make it look like the problems with the replicants are the Tyrell Corporation's fault. And not theirs."

"You're forgetting something, Deckard. It's not just a conspiracy against the Tyrell Corporation. It's a conspiracy against the blade runners as well. Or more accurately, a conspiracy *using* the blade runners. Using their deaths, that is. The U.N. authorities have to make it appear that the Nexus-6 replicants are even *more* dangerous than they really are, more capable of passing as human . . . and more capable of evading the system that was put into place to detect and eliminate them. That's you, Deckard, you and the other blade runners. What better way to make that happen than to set all of you up to take a fall, the way they set up Dave Holden? They'd just have to make it look as if the blade runners were no match against the Nexus-6 replicants, and they'd have all the justification they needed for shutting down the Tyrell Corporation. For good. No more corporation, no more replicants; the off-world colonies, the

ones that are left, would have to find some other way of
getting along."

"Maybe." Deckard looked unimpressed. "Or at
least until you figured out how to get the company back
into business. Maybe with some other replicant model,
one that wasn't quite so smart and dangerous."

"Oh, no, it wouldn't work that way." This one as
well, Sarah had anticipated. "If the Tyrell Corporation
gets shut down—the way its enemies would like to—it
won't be going back into business. Ever again. This
whole complex . . ." She gestured toward the walls of
the office suite and by extension, all of the headquarters
buildings beyond. "For us to get a lock on the U.N.'s
business, to be the exclusive suppliers of replicants for
the off-world colonies, this entire setup had to be built
according to U.N. specifications. All the corporation's
research and design facilities are here, along with the
manufacturing units, every inch of the assembly lines
that put out replicants ready to ship. Even the Tyrell
family living quarters are here; that was part of the U.N.
requirements as well. The shape of the buildings, the
way they're arranged facing each other, everything. It
was all done so that when the red button is pushed—
when the built-in self-destruct sequence is initiated—
the results are absolute annihilation to the Tyrell Corporation, with minimal damage to the surrounding areas of
the city."

Deckard's eyes opened a fraction wider. " 'Self-
destruct'? What're you talking about?"

"Don't get nervous on me. It's not likely to happen
while you're sitting here." She gave a small shrug. "But
it could. That's what it was designed to do, from the
beginning. All of the Tyrell Corporation's headquarters
complex—everything around us—was built with
enough explosive charges in the substructure and imbedded in the walls, all of them linked by a programmed
timing chain, to reduce it to smoking dust."

She had trained herself to speak of these things dispassionately, by reciting them inside her head. Late at night before she fell asleep, like a bedtime story. "There might be a few pieces big as a man's fist in the pile. There might even be a few pieces of *me*, if I'm here when it happens. Though I don't think that anybody would be bothered to come and look. Everything's designed to implode, to fall in upon the center; that's why the towers are slanted toward each other. It'd be a thoughtful sort of apocalypse; nobody else would get hurt. So you see, Deckard, if the Tyrell Corporation goes out of business—if the U.N. authorities are able to justify pushing that red button, starting up the self-destruct sequence—it won't be going back into business anytime soon."

"And that's what you believe they want?"

"Rather than admit their own mistakes? That they were wrong about how they've managed the off-world colonization program?" Sarah leaned her head back for a quick, hollow-sounding laugh. "Of course. That's another part of human nature. We always murder rather than apologize."

Silent, Deckard appeared to be contemplating the empty glass in his hand, holding it by the faceted base. "Am I supposed to think . . ." His murmur was almost too soft to hear. "Am I supposed to think that if the Tyrell Corporation gets blown up into little pieces, that it'd be some kind of tragedy?"

"I don't care what you think. You can think whatever you want. But I'm not going to let the Tyrell Corporation be destroyed. It's mine." She turned to look out the window behind her, at the towers glazed dark red by the setting sun. "I don't expect you to be as concerned about the fate of the corporation as I am. I just want you to do the job for which I brought you here."

"Like I told Bryant, a long time ago . . ." He leaned forward and set the empty glass down on the *bureau plat*, beside hers. "I don't work here."

"You will. For me."

"Don't bet on it." His gaze narrowed. "I don't even know what you'd want me to do."

"Isn't it obvious? There's still an escaped replicant—a Tyrell Corporation Nexus-6 model, to be precise—loose somewhere in the city. I want you to find it and—what's the word?—*retire* it. Before whatever's the next stage of the conspiracy can be set in motion. Before the Tyrell Corporation, and everything that my uncle worked to bring into existence, can be destroyed."

"Like I told you . . ." Deckard slowly shook his head. "I don't regard that as a tragedy."

"I can see that." She touched the rim of each of the empty glasses in turn. "So . . . I'd have to make it worth your while, then."

"You don't have enough money to do that. Nobody does."

"Perhaps not. But . . . there are other things I could offer you. Things you value. Say . . . the woman you love . . ."

Deckard straightened up in the chair. "What's that supposed to mean?"

She stood up from the *bureau plat* and went over to the suite's high windows. "Come here." With a single motion of her hand, she turned the glass dark, an artificial night. "I have something to show you." The sun's glare burned through the photochrome layers, like the end of a severed vein.

For a few seconds he looked at her without moving, then got to his feet. As he walked toward her, she reached behind and loosened the binding of her hair.

"You did that once already." Deckard placed himself right in front of her, watching as she shook the dark wave of her hair free, across the tops of her shoulders. "You don't have to do it again. I can see the resemblance."

"It's not resemblance." Sarah brushed one hand through it, letting it fall again. "It's identity. You know that, don't you? No matter how many times you tell yourself otherwise . . . she and I are the same. When you love Rachael . . . it's me you love."

He closed his eyes. One of his hands raised, as though to take her by the arm, then halted.

"I'm the original. Rachael's the copy." She brought her voice down low. "You have to remember that . . ."

The hand trembled, caught between his will and his desire. Her presence—she knew, could see it—radiated through him, hot and bright as the sun piercing the muted windows.

She laid her own hand against his chest, to balance herself as she brought her lips close to his ear. "You know . . ." A whisper. "You know that it's me . . . always . . ."

"No . . ." He shook his head, eyes still closed. "You're not . . ."

Her own eyelids shut out the little light remaining. All she felt was the brush of her lips against the side of his face. "She's dying. She's dead . . . that's the only difference." A whisper. "Why should you love the dead?" Soft as her breath. "When you can love me?"

He made no reply. But his hand flew up and caught hers at his chest, locking tight upon the wrist's fragile bone.

The past was on tape, but she knew she didn't have to play it for him. Words that had been spoken beside another window, in another room, that had been caught by his own hidden cameras. The place where suspicion, a blade runner's occupational hazard, intersected with longing. The tapes had been left behind in Deckard's own apartment; they had been found and brought to her. So she knew what had been said in that other place, that other time, that other world.

She drew back a few inches from him. "Say . . . 'Say that you want me . . .'"

As though caught in dreaming, he turned his head. Listening.

"Say it." Her whisper a command now.

He spoke, the words slow on his tongue. "Say that you want me . . ."

Time folded around them. His past, this present; his words, and the words Rachael had spoken. Long ago. "I want you . . ."

His hand let go of her wrist, but only so that it could sink into the darkness of her unbound hair, his other hand grasping her arm tight, drawing her toward him. Crushing her against him. The unspoken words in the kiss, the past that opened around them, that had never ended.

With a sudden convulsion he pushed her away, hard enough to snap her head back, as if he had struck her. Her breath trembled at her parted lips. Dizzied, she saw him turn his head back toward her, his eyes narrowed in the glare of one who has woken from a betraying vision. From the remembered past, into this world, and unsure for the moment which was the hallucination into which he'd fallen.

Another movement of her hand, and the window returned to an unfiltered transparency. The smoldering light from outside washed over them, an ocean of luminous red. She returned his gaze with one steady and unflinching. Though she wondered what he saw in her eyes, as naked as that in his. Some other human quality, the one that would probably kill him. Irrational and faithful. *No*, she told herself. *Fate . . .*

"All right." Deckard wiped his mouth with the flat of his hand. "I'll take the job. I'll find your sixth replicant for you."

At least he hated her; she could see that in the ice and steel at the center of his eyes. She knew she could have that much of him.

"Why?" She was surprised by the single word. Her voice had spoken it.

She watched as he poured himself another shot

from the bottle on the *bureau plat*. He knocked it back, then turned and looked at her.

"You reminded me." Voice flat, drained as the glass in his hand. "Of her. I had almost forgotten."

I won. She gazed unseeing at the light fading to black. *I must have.* The edges of the towers blurred, and she tasted salt at the corner of her mouth.

Deckard's voice came from behind her, from somewhere in the great empty space that had held the two of them. "You're the quickest way. Back to her. To Rachael." She heard the hollow note of the glass as he set it down. "That's my price."

4

"What's your plan?" Andersson—if that was really his name—glanced over from the spinner's controls.

Deckard shrugged. "I've got my methods." The spinner swooped in low enough to the Olvera Street souk that Deckard could see the animal dealers packing up their wares, business done for the night. The zooid merchandise had to be gotten under tarps before the day's heat fried their synaptic circuits; the rarer and more expensive real animals needed water and temp-controlled cages to survive. "I think I've hunted down enough replicants to remember how it's done."

He kept his eyelids lowered partway. When he'd seen the city again, as Sarah Tyrell's agents had taken him in to his meeting with her, gouts of fire had flared into the dark sky, subterranean gases ignited as they seeped up through the trembling earth beneath L.A. Now those shouting torches were lost in the sun's advancing glare.

"This replicant—number six—might be different."

The other man apparently knew all about the job Deckard had taken on. "Harder than you're ready for."

Deckard ignored the comment. The sooner he was down in the city's streets, the sooner he could wrap up this sorry business. And head north again. "Where we going?" He looked out the side of the spinner's canopy, watching a herd of artificial emu being herded down a back alley. The marketplace died, bit by bit, as the multilingual neon signs were switched off.

"You'll see." Andersson reached forward and flicked on the landing prep switches. "Soon enough."

One neon sign, the biggest, stayed lit. He remembered it always being on, no matter the time or weather, looming over the district's transactions like a silent blessing. Only the size of the letters competed with the cruising U.N. blimp, with its flat-panel screen and booming exhortations to leave the planet, and all the rest of the city's tidal wave of ad slam.

VAN NUYS PET HOSPITAL. Pink letters, with a shiver of blue around their edges. And a cartoon puppy face, shifting every two seconds from sad and injured to happy and bandaged. He'd always figured that every resurrection should be so easy.

The spinner dropped toward the landing deck atop the building. "Why we going here?" asked Deckard. "You got a kitten with ear mites or something?"

"No—" Andersson took his hands from the controls, the descent locked on auto. He smiled humorlessly. "Orders from Miss Tyrell. You've got an appointment."

Deckard let himself be hustled into the elevator, even before the other two spinners touched down. He'd come this far without putting up a fight; no point in starting one now. He watched as the man beside him punched in a security code. The elevator doors slid together; the tiny space sank into the faint but unmistakable odors of disinfectant and animal droppings.

Panel lights charted the descent into the building's

midsection. When the doors opened, he found himself gazing into the spectacled eyes of a smaller man, lab-coated, drooping tabby asleep in the cradle of his arms.

"Should I stick around, Mr. Isidore?" Andersson held the elevator door from reclosing.

"No . . . I don't think that'll be nuh-necessary." Scratching behind the tabby's ears, the gnomish figure tilted his head, brow wrinkling. "I'm sure our guh-guh-guest will behave himself."

"I have a choice?"

"Well . . ." Isidore mulled, frowned. "Probably nuh-not."

"Don't," whispered Andersson into Deckard's ear, "do anything stupid." He stepped back into the elevator, hit the buttons, and disappeared behind the stainless-steel doors.

"Not to worry." The tabby stirred and yawned. "They're puh-paid to act like thuh-that. It's all an act. *You* should nuh-know."

Deckard followed the man. "Sometimes it's not an act."

"Oh, yes . . ." Isidore glanced over his shoulder. "You know that tuh-tuh-too. That's when people—and other things—thuh-that's when they get hurt." He held the tabby closer against his chest, as though protecting it.

The concrete-floored space narrowed to a corridor lined with cages, stacked three or four deep, and larger kennels. The air beneath the bare fluorescents was laced with mingled animal scents. As Isidore passed by, the small creatures—cats, rabbits, toy breeds of dogs, a few guinea pigs—pressed against the wire doors, mewing or yapping for the man's attention.

Deckard turned his head, getting a closer look. Some of the animals in the cages weren't animals. Not real ones.

A partially disassembled simulacrum suckled a row of squirming kittens; its white fur had been peeled back to reveal the polyethylene tubes and webbing beneath aluminum ribs; the optic sensors in its skull gazed out with maternal placidity. A wasp-waisted greyhound danced quivering excitement, front paws flurrying at the kennel gate; all four legs were abstract steel and miniature hydraulic cylinders.

A headless rabbit bumped against a water dish. Its mate—flesh and blood as far as Deckard could tell— nuzzled against its flank.

"Wuh-what's wrong?" Isidore had caught a hiss of inhaled breath behind him.

"These things give me the creeps."

"*Really?*" Isidore stopped in his tracks. He looked amazed; even the tabby in his arms blinked open its eyes. "Why?"

"They're not real." He had seen plenty of fake animals before, out in the dealers' souk, and they'd never bothered him. But those had had their skins and pelts intact. These, with their electromechanical innards exposed, flaunted a raw nakedness.

"Guh-gosh." It seemed to come as news to Isidore. He looked down at the tabby for a moment. "I guess I duh-don't see it thuh-that wuh-wuh-way. They all seem real to me. I mean . . . you can tuh-touch them." Leaning toward Deckard, lifting the tabby closer to him. "Here."

He scratched the cat's head, getting an audible purr in response. It might have been real. Or well made, well programmed.

"You suh-see? It must be real." Isidore managed to open one of the empty cages and off-loaded the tabby into it. "There you go, tuh-Tiger." The cat complained for a moment, then curled nose to tail and closed its eyes. "Come on. My office's juh-just over here. I'll close the door . . . so you won't huh-have to see anything you don't want to." The gaze behind the glasses narrowed, then he turned and started walking again.

"What's that supposed to mean?"

"Oh . . . nothing . . ." Turning a key in a lock, Isidore directed a thin smile at him. "Juh-just that I wouldn't have thought you'd be so . . . suh-sensitive." He stepped through the doorway. "Given your domestic arrangements and all."

"Got a point." Deckard walked into a low-ceilinged, windowless cubicle, walls covered with freebie calendars and thumb-tacked photos of pets and their owners; satisfied clients, he figured. "Except Rachael's all in one piece. That's the difference." He had to remember to keep cool, to get through whatever drill he'd been brought down here for. So he could get back to the sleeping, dying, waiting woman up north.

"Please . . . sit duh-down." The other man dropped himself into a swivel chair behind a desk covered with mounds of papers and empty foam cups. "Really . . . I do wuh-want you to be comfortable. We have a lot to talk about."

"This says your name's Hannibal Sloat." Sitting, he'd picked up the cheap wooden plaque from the desk. He held it by one end. "You or somebody else?"

"Mr. Sloat was my boss. A luh-luh-long tuh-time ago. Then he died." Isidore looked around at the office's moulting walls, then pointed. "That's him up there."

He turned his head and saw a hard-copy newspaper clipping, browned with age, stuck to the wall. In the low-rez photo, a fat man with pockmarked skin held a dangling cat out to a couple, the woman stroking the animal with one delicate hand, the man turning a slightly embarrassed smile toward the camera. Deckard shifted around in the chair. "Nice guy?"

"Oh, sure. Real nuh-nice. In his will . . . he left me the puh-pet hospital." He brought his gaze back down to Deckard's. "He left me . . . everything. Really." The swivel chair seemed to have grown larger, as though it were capable of swallowing him up, as he folded his hands in his lap. "It's a big responsibility."

"What is? Giving distemper shots? Lube job on a

replica Pekingese, maybe. Doesn't seem like anything you couldn't handle."

"Thuh-that's what I used to think. There wasn't anythuh-thing more to the job than that. Even when old Mr. Sloat was still uh-uh-live and I was working for him. That's what I thought the Van Nuys Pet Hospital's buh-business was. Like you said—shu-shots and ruh-ruh-pairs."

"So if it's not that . . ." Deckard set the plaque down on the desk's corner. "Then what is it?"

"Well . . . you'd probably say we duh-deal in fuh-fakes. Like out in the souk. Fuh-phony goldfish, and kuh-kuh-cats and dogs and stuff. That you can't tell from the real thing. I mean . . . the living thing. What yuh-you'd call the living thing."

"Don't you? I thought that's where the money is. That's what people like. The fakes. The real ones . . . they just make a mess. It's just easier dealing with the simulations."

The other nodded slowly, wisps of silky white hair drifting over his pink scalp. "I guess that's what somebody who spent so much time as a buh-blade runner wuh-*would* think. You had your own wuh-way of dealing with those . . . suh-suh-simulations. Didn't you?"

He studied the lab-coated figure on the other side of the desk. "Look—is this why I was brought here? So you could rag on my moral condition, or something? You needn't have bothered." He put his hands against the chair's arms, as though he were about to push himself upright and walk out of the office. "You know so much about blade runners . . . you ever hear of something they call the Curve?"

"Maybe." Isidore shrugged, nervous. "Some kind of . . . kuh-cop tuh-talk."

"The Wambaugh Curve." Strange to be talking about it out loud. It'd always been something that everyone in the LAPD knew about, could feel sitting under the breastbone like a ball of lead, but never spoke of.

Another ticket to the department shrinks; where if they found you were too badly screwed up, they'd take away your gun and the answer to all your problems. "The index of self-loathing. Blade runners get it worse, and faster, than other cops. Comes with the territory."

Isidore's eyes looked wet and sympathetic behind the glasses. "Then what happens?"

"Depends." Once the dissection had begun, it was easy to sink the scalpel in deeper. "Upon where you are on the Curve." He'd used to think about these matters late at night in his flat, sunk deep in the overstuffed leather couch, one of the pleasantly expensive things that his bounty money had brought him. In the lonely splendor that'd followed his divorce, with a bottle of twenty-five-year-old single malt from the Orkney Islands close at hand, that sweetly tasted of smoke and dirt and money as well. Nobody ever said that blade-running sucked on the paycheck scale. Sometimes he'd sat there, brooding or anesthetized, with replicant blood still spattered across his chest. One time, he'd lifted his glass and had seen the drops of red written across the back of his hand. And had sipped and closed his eyes, and not felt a thing. "Eventually . . . the Curve gets steep enough, you fall off. I did."

"And then you weren't a blade runner anymore."

Seconds passed before he could say anything. "No . . ." He shook his head. "I guess I wasn't."

"Too buh-bad." Steel under Isidore's voice, a thin needle of it. "A little late, for all the ones you killed."

Deckard gave him a hard stare. "Listen, pal—" A weapon in the eyes. "I was just doing my job."

"I knew you'd say that." No flinch, no stammer. "It's what they all say. All the murderers."

The cop on guard duty actually lifted his rifle across his chest. The next move would bring it down into firing position, full auto rock 'n' roll. "You got security clearance for this floor?" A mean look underneath the SWAT team cap.

"Hey, hey . . . don't sweat it, man." The figure in the hospital's green scrubs raised his empty hands. An easy smile, but cold eyes. "I hit the wrong button, got off on the wrong floor. That's all." He slowly lowered his hands. "No need to uncork the artillery, pal."

"Wrong button, huh?" The guard kept his finger on the trigger. At this range, he didn't need the sharpshooter tags under the LAPD shoulder insignia. He could've set the muzzle's hollow eye right on the breastbone beneath the hospital staff outfit. "Well, why don't you turn around, get back into the elevator, and push the right button this time. That way, you won't get into trouble."

"What's the deal, anyway?" The smiling man raised up on his toes, scanning over the guard's head to the open unit where the floor's sole patient lay surrounded by gurgling machines, a half-dozen doctors and nurses who seemed to be more like technicians and electronics geeks. Softly bleeping dots drew spiked trails on a bank of video monitors. "This guy some kind of VIP?" Beyond the bed and the body, windows reached to the ceiling, overlooking the city. "Been here a long time, hasn't he?" The magmalike L.A. sun battered the towers, the glare washing out the viewscreen of the U.N. blimp as it cruised by, making its constant pitch for offworld emigration.

"You ask a lot of questions." Cool enough to show nothing more than his index finger tightening on the crook of metal; small shiny things clicked ready inside the rifle. "Not a good idea."

"Peace, brother." Hands went up again, palms exposed, the smile floating between them. "You keep on doing your job, and I'll go do mine." Inside the man's skull, behind the cold eyes, a single unvoiced word: *Jerk.* A couple meters beyond the guard stood the open frame of a metal detector; he could see that it'd been switched off, probably to keep it from being triggered by the equipment carts that rolled in and out of the unit. It wouldn't have mattered to him if he'd had to step through the thing, still smiling, to find out what he needed to know; the small, efficient gun hidden at the small of his back was sheathed in enough microprocessor-controlled evasion polymers to slip past a goddamn radar station. It was the lazy unprofessionalism that irked him. These putzes were amateurs, all black-leather and chrome-eyed swagger, and sloppy on the details. *Typical.*

He reached behind himself and hit the elevator call button. Already there; the doors slid open and he stepped back, hands still up for a joke, the smile still on his face. He gave a little wave through the narrowing slit. " 'Bye now."

Leaning back as the elevator descended, he let the smile creep up into his eyes. Behind them were no words, just a map, the exact layout of the unit, the guards, the machines and doctors, and the man on the hospital bed, who had a hole where his heart and lungs used to be.

He got off on the next floor down. No guards on this floor; he collected his gear, bigger and more rawly industrial-looking than the hospital's usual chrome equipment carts, from an unused storage closet and wheeled it into the maternity ward. He began unfolding the heavy bracing struts, the pronged steel feet digging into the scuffed rubberoid flooring.

"What the hell are you doing?" Some kind of nursing supervisor came bustling toward him, waving a clipboard. "You can't put that thing in here! Whatever it is."

The smiling man turned toward the woman. "Oh, I think I can." Farther along the ward, on all sides, an audience of pregnant women watched the altercation. They all looked huge and imminent, lying on closely spaced beds and gurneys, raising their heads just enough to look over their rounded abdomens to see what the noise was; their passive faces, medicated or endorphined, radiated a Buddhistic calm. "Besides—" His smile grew larger, though less reassuring. "I won't be here long."

"I'm calling security." The nursing supervisor turned and strode toward the central station.

"That's not a good idea." He interrupted his setup procedure, reaching behind himself and taking the gun out from beneath the scrub shirt. A click of metal was enough to stop the woman in her tracks, her eyes widening as she looked over her shoulder and saw the small black hole pointed at a spot just below the front edge of her white starched cap. "Why should we bother them?" He backed her up against the counter of the central station, the gun's muzzle then just an inch away from her forehead. With his other hand, he reached past the younger, even more terrified nurse sitting behind the counter, picked the phone up, and yanked its cord free from the wall below. "Since there's really no problem here, anyway. Unless you make one." His smile broadened as he took the gun away from the supervisor's face and used it to point toward the station's other chair. "Have a seat."

He walked back toward the bulky device squatting in the middle of the maternity ward's floor. The eyes of all the pregnant women had latched on to him; a couple of the less tranquilized had started to weep softly, pulling up the thin sheets of the gurneys and trying to hide behind them. "Ladies . . . you're beautiful just the way you are." He held the gun by his own head, pointing it toward the speckled acoustic ceiling. "Just stay like this. Real quiet." He turned, sweeping the beam of his smile across them. "And then we'll always have this moment together. Won't we?"

The mothers-to-be stayed frozen in place, just as he wanted them. He glanced over his shoulder at the women back at the nursing station. "I'm keeping an eye

on you, too." With one hand he pulled out the last of
the device's struts and jacked it into place. "So just relax. This'll only take a moment."

In the breast pocket of his green scrub shirt was a
remote with two red, unmarked buttons on one side.
Taking a pace back, he fished the metal box out. This
was serious enough business to erase the smile for a
moment. He hit the top button with his thumb.

A two-second delay gave him enough time to turn
his face away, ears shielded with his upraised hands,
remote in one and gun in the other. The shock wave
from the blast rolled over his back like a heated ocean
wave, with enough force to send him stumbling a few
steps before he caught his balance.

The silence that followed was broken by the muffled sobs of the pregnant women sirening into full-out
wails. That and the patter of atomized structural mate-
rial, falling in a rain of white dust and charred metal
across his shoulders.

Already in motion, he ran back to the device he'd
wheeled into the ward. The thrust of the shaped explosive charges had dug the bracing struts another inch into
the floor. He gazed up at the raw-edged hole that had
been ripped through the ceiling above. Its center was
filled by the hydraulic ram that had sprung like a jack-
in-the-box from the device, the oil-glistening metal
shoving aside the scorched, twisted girders.

Strapped to one side of the device was an attaché
case of chrome and molded black neoprene. Tucking the
remote back into his scrub shirt pocket, he pulled the
case free and started climbing, the wrist of his gun hand
catching the holds riveted to the side of the ram.

On the floor above, the hospital staff and security
guards were still stunned by the blunt prow shape that
had erupted in their midst. Jagged metal scraped along
his spine as he emerged partway into the smoke and
settling dust. A quick look around, with the case pulled
through and flopped down onto the hole's buckled pe-

rimeter; he saw the heart-and-lung patient right where he'd planned on, the railed bed surrounded by the whispering machines. The monitor screens had flipped, the explosion having sent the beeping lines into sharp-pointed spasms and trilling alarms. Letting go of the case's handle but not the gun, he pushed himself up and onto the edge of the hole.

The doctors and nurses, the ones left standing, had been shoved by the explosion against the walls. At least one had been hit by a bit of flying shrapnel; blood formed a bright net across his face and surgical gown before he collapsed onto his knees. The patient on the bed, at the edge of anesthetized consciousness, stirred feebly inside the web of hoses and tubes.

"Hey, buddy—" The smile returned to the man's face, his eyes brightening, as he called to the guard dragging himself toward the rifle that had landed a few feet away. The words were enough to stop the guard, his fingertips a fraction of an inch from the butt of the rifle. The hesitation was more than enough; the guard raised his head and the smiling man fired. One shoulder hit the rifle as the bullet's impact tugged the guard by his shattered skull along the floor.

He could hear the alarms shrieking somewhere else inside the hospital. Time dwindling now—he pulled the remote out of his shirt pocket and hit the second button.

In the vibrating sunlight outside the ward's high bank of windows, a brighter spark moved, metal struck by fire. As though it were a piece of the sun, fallen into an orbit low among the city's towers. It grew larger, closer, summoned by the tight beam from the remote in the man's hand.

Which he was done with—he tossed the small metal box aside. He scooped up the attaché case by its black molded handle and strode quickly toward the bed.

"What . . ." Not even a whisper, not a sigh, but a few molecules of exhaled breath. The heart-and-lung

patient's eyelids fluttered open. "What . . . are you
doing . . ." A red bubble trembled in the cloudy
plastic tube inserted in his trachea.

"Take it easy, pal." The man's hands were flying as
he leaned over the bed. Yanking and pulling, tubes and
ridged hoses flipped up from the heart-and-lung patient's blood-spattered abdomen. "Just lie back and let
me do the work." He'd laid the gun down on the nearest equipment cart, scooping up the sharp-edged tools
and sterile white tape he'd known he'd find there.
"Funny, that's what she said last night. Don't laugh,
you'll bust a stitch."

Pure oxygen hissed as he jerked the largest hose
from a Teflon socket at the breastbone's center; a wobbling bag of Ringer's solution burst on the floor like a
prankster's water balloon as his elbow knocked over the
IV-drip stand. He worked faster, the attaché case open
on the bed beside the patient. Security alarms shrieked
in dissonant chorus outside the ward; he could sense
through the floor the tremor of distant running. The
quick, faint noise of ammo clips being shoved into place
touched his ear; he didn't look up. He'd already mea-
sured the exact amount of time he needed. A spear of
reflected sunlight hit his face. Glancing up, he saw the
spinner, a modified light-cargo model, approaching the
window bank. No one in the pilot seat; the program
triggered by the push of the remote's button guided the
spinner closer, the steel-reinforced nose gleaming a
meter away from the glass, then less.

With a sweep of his forearm, he pushed the disconnected machines away. Another chrome rack toppled,
sprawling the loose tubes, spastic octopus. With the roll
of surgical tape he spliced the smaller lines from inside
the attaché case, snugging them tight to the implant
connections that studded the patient's torso.

"Let's go—" He flipped the switch beneath a glass
square set in the case's lid; a flat green line coursed
across the monitor. "Son of a *bitch*. Come on!" Smile

into angry scowl; a fist struck the densely packed machinery; a miniature bellows sucked and gasped through a mesh filter, but the green line remained a perfect horizon. Both fists doubled, he struck the man on the bed, hitting the narrow target between the throat and the red-edged tubes hard enough to partway jackknife the man's knees toward his chest.

"Jesus . . ." An agonized whisper. One of the heart-and-lung patient's hands came free, from where it had been bound by the wrist to the bed's chrome rail; he feebly tried to fend off his attacker. "Jesus Christ . . . get away from me . . ."

The man above leaned down, sealing his mouth over the other's, a suction tube already prodded into the kiss. A hard exhale, and the patient's chest raised in response. From the attaché case came a birdlike chirp, as the monitor's green line jittered, then caught in a two-stroke beat. The artificial pulse slowed, steadied as the man, smiling again, wiped his mouth and adjusted the knob for the adrenaline flow.

"I hope you're ready to travel—"

Words barely spoken, when the high bank of windows shattered, sparkling points of glass arcing across the ward. The segmented metal frame bent and twisted, bolts screeching out of the floor and walls as the nose of the freight spinner shoved its way inside the hospital building. The smiling man brushed glitter of broken glass from the heart-and-lung patient's raw, exposed chest; he reached a hand behind and raised the patient up, his other hand looping the surgical tape around, strapping the attaché case and its nest of hoses tight against the body.

"Hold on!" Glass crunched underfoot as he shoved the wheeled bed toward the spinner, now motionless in the gaping architectural wound.

Rifle fire behind him—he glanced over his shoulder and saw the bright muzzle flashes, the crouching figures of an LAPD security team, more of them darting from the bank of elevators as the doors slid open, the dark-uniformed men running head down and with guns in hand, taking up positions around the ward's narrow entrance. A bullet clanged and ricocheted from one of the bed's curved metal bars; others slammed into the surrounding walls. The ruptured floor, with the entry device's battering ram still rearing up into the space, and the knocked-aside medical equipment formed a partial barricade between the man and the new arrivals on the scene, momentarily shielding him from a direct line of attack.

He reached to the small of his back for his own gun, found nothing, remembered that he had left it sitting on top of the main respiratory-assist machine, at the edge of the nest of tubes and hoses from which he'd yanked the bed. He could see the gun now, a small black shape on top of shiny chrome. Too far away to reach, especially with a sharp horizontal rain of hollow points lacing the room—he swung back toward the shattered windows, watching across the prostrate form of the heart-and-lung patient as the freight spinner outside rotated, bringing its open cargo-bay door toward the jagged teeth of glass. The glaring sunlight hit his face like a furnace's hot flood.

One of the spinner's flanged air intakes caught on a bent, broken section of the windows' steel frame. The thrust engines whined higher in pitch, as the autopilot program shoved the vehicle against the obstruction. The cargo-bay opening stayed where it was, nearly two meters away from the ripped edge of the hospital building.

Through the echoing clamor of the rifle fire, he could hear the security team shifting position, moving closer into the ward. He took a few steps backward, drawing the hospital bed with him, then bracing his hands against the lowest rail on one side.

"No . . ." The heart-and-lung patient had seen what the other man was getting ready to do. "You can't . . . im . . . possible . . ."

"Shut up." He pushed the bed full force, digging in and picking up speed, head lowered bull-like and muscles straining beneath the green scrubs. A second later the rolling bed had hit the rim of the floor-level window frame; momentum tilted the bed over and sent it flying toward the spinner outside, the cargo bay as the exact center of the target. His own momentum and a final diving launch carried him after.

He landed on the patient, who moaned and tried to push him away with weak, narcotized arms. One of the hospital bed's wheels had caught against the sill of the bay door; the chrome frame and mattress fell outside the spinner, scraping against the hospital exterior as it spiraled down toward the city streets below.

Bullets hit and bounced inside the bare-ribbed cargo space. Inside the hospital, the security team had come out to the open, sprinting across the ward's broken field, firing as they ran.

He scrambled off the heart-and-lung patient; still on his knees, he lunged past the cockpit's empty seats and hit the autopilot's override button on the control panel. A slap of his hand against the thrust levers—the spinner surged forward, a forearm slung around the pilot seat's headrest keeping him from being flung back into the cargo space.

Through the cockpit's glass curve, he spotted the steel hook of the broken window frame digging farther into the engine's air scoop. Enough to tilt the spinner at a forty-five-degree angle as it fought against the crude grapple. A metal hail hammered small dents into the side panels.

Over his shoulder he saw the heart-and-lung patient sliding helplessly toward the open bay door. Hanging on to the pilot seat, he reached back and managed to claw a handful of the billowing sheets into his fist. Shock and fear had cut through the patient's anesthetizing drugs; fully conscious, eyes nearly as wide as his gaping mouth, he stared behind and below himself, at the dizzying

emptiness of air and the threadlike street rotating hundreds of meters down at the hospital tower's base.

With the sheet as a taut sling, the other man yanked
the heart-and-lung patient up toward himself. With a
push of his arm, he managed to get the patient stuffed
awkwardly into the other cockpit seat. The gauges and
monitor screen on the attaché case strapped to the patient's chest shrieked and danced in alarm.

A twist of the rudder pulled the spinner free of the
window frame strut, the pent-up thrust sending the vehicle arcing toward the cloudless sky. The security team,
arrayed in the gap in the hospital's outside wall, continued to fire as they dwindled away, the bullets rattling
against the cargo-bay door as it slid shut.

"Uhh . . ." The heart-and-lung patient was beyond words now. His pale hands fluttered against the
attaché case, the pulsing machinery that kept him alive.
"Uh . . . uhh . . ."

"Knock it off." The other man, smile not yet returned to his face, looked over in annoyance at the
heart-and-lung patient. His own hands continued
punching a flight pattern into the spinner's on-board
computer. "You're making me nervous."

Sun flashed off the spinner's metal, pure white and
dazzling, as it sped through and away from the city's
upper reaches.

"That's what they've *always* said."

Deckard looked at the lab-coated figure on the
other side of the desk. "What's that supposed to
mean?"

"The suh-same old shit." Something almost like
pity moved behind the thick lenses of Isidore's glasses.
He shook his head in disgust. "Anytime people wuh-
want to get themselves off the huh-hook, that's the kuh-
kuh-kind of thing they say. 'I was doing my *job*. They
told me to do it.' " His mocking voice didn't stumble.
"It was a kruh-creaky old line at Nurembuh-berg."

"Yeah, well, maybe it was true there, too."

"Oh, guh-*good* one, Deckard." The head of the Van Nuys Pet Hospital pressed his hands flat against the desk, leaning forward with his suddenly sharper gaze. "Great reh-rhetorical tuh-tactic, all right. You can duh-defend yourself *and* the Third Reich, all at the same tuh-time."

"Give me a break." His turn to shake his head. "You brought me here for a lecture on ancient history? Forget it. The dead are buried, and the murderers' ashes were dumped at the side of the road."

"I'm impressed. You nuh-know your stuff."

"Enough of it." He leaned back in the chair. "So can I go now? Because if you just wanted to take the moral higher ground with me, you didn't have to bother. Like I said, I quit the job."

"But maybe," said Isidore, "the juh-juh-job didn't quit *you.*"

He sighed. "Whatever."

"Because . . ." The other's voice went lower and softer. "Because you never really fuh-found anything wrong with the blade runner job itself. You just didn't like duh-doing it anymore. Like you said, you got too far out on the Curve."

The room, Isidore's office, filled with silence; the papers and old calendars on the wall hung motionless in tensed air. Deckard closed his eyes. "It was a job somebody had to do. They were dangerous."

"Huh-who were?"

"Come on. The replicants. They were made to be dangerous. Military issue . . . for those nasty little chores off-world. So they had to be taken care of. Retired."

"By somebody like you."

Deckard opened his eyes. "That's right."

"Fuh-funny, isn't it, that they never huh-hurt anybody who wasn't trying to hurt them first. There's no ruh-record of an escaped replicant killing a human . . .

at least not here on Earth . . . except when it was buh-
backed into a corner, with no other way out."

"Oh, yeah?" That brought a sharp laugh from
Deckard. "Tell it to Eldon Tyrell."

"Thuh-thuh-that was duh-different. That was
something puh-personal." Isidore's expression turned
brooding. "Besides, Eldon Tyrell duh-deserved to die.
He was a real sonuvabitch. Believe me, I nuh-know."

Deckard wasn't going to argue the point. Tyrell,
when alive, had given him the creeps. Plus, everything
he'd scoped out since—all the bleak shimmer he'd
picked up from the man's niece Sarah—hadn't changed
his mind.

"All right," said Deckard. "Maybe replicants are
nothing but saints. Human, however, they're not."

"Is thuh-that you talking? Or the blade runner?"

"Take your pick."

"Buh-but you loved one. A replicant. Or you still
do. You suh-suh-sleep with her. In your arms."

"Doesn't make her human." He could hear the
coldness in his own voice. Not for Rachael, but for everything else in the world. "If she were human, she
wouldn't be dying now. So you're right about Tyrell—
that four-year life span was one of his bright ideas. The
Nexus-6 replicants were his big chance to play God, and
all he could think of to do was hard-wire death into
their cells."

Isidore gazed sadly at him for a moment. "If that
duh-didn't make her human—your loving her—then
what would?"

"Nothing." He shook his head. "There's a difference. Between human and not. That's what the tests are
all about. The Voigt-Kampff tests." He knew he
sounded like a blade runner now. These were the articles of faith, the core beliefs of the job. "She couldn't
pass the test the first time I gave it to her, out at the
Tyrell Corporation headquarters." He wondered how
much of this Isidore already knew. There was some kind

of link between Isidore and Sarah Tyrell—he just didn't know yet what it was. "I spotted her then. It took a while, but I knew. That she was a replicant."

"Buh-but it wasn't just the vuh-Voigt-Kampff tests; that muh-muh-machine you guys haul around with yourselves. It was something else. Something inside *you*. That could suh-say, 'This one's human and this one's not.' That's the essential thing, isn't it? About being a buh-blade runner. That ability to muh-make the distinction between what's human and wuh-what's not. What just goes around and walks and talks and acts like a human."

He shifted in the chair, as though trying to avoid the probe of the other's words. "I suppose so."

"That's vuh-very interesting, Mr. Deckard." With a forefinger Isidore tapped one lens of his glasses. "You know, I see pruh-pretty well—at least, with these I do— but that's wuh-wuh-one thing I've never seen. This difference between human and not. Between the ruh-real and the fuh-fake. I don't think I could, even if I had one of your fuh-fuh-fancy Voigt-kuh-Kampff machines." He gave a tilt of his head toward the office's door. "It comes with the territory, I guh-guess. *My* territory, that is. Like out there with the animals. You said the fuh-phony ones gave you the creeps . . . the ones you could tell were phony, because they were broken or something. And for a minute there, I couldn't even tell what the huh-huh-*hell* you were talking about." He still looked perplexed. "I mean, I understand—I can tell the difference between one and the other—up here . . ." A finger tapped the side of his head. "But I can't tell the difference down *here*." The same finger prodded at the chest beneath the white lab coat. "But I guess that's fairly common, huh? Otherwise we wouldn't have Voigt-Kampff machines. Or blade runners."

The guy had started getting on Deckard's nerves. The soft sarcasm ignited a defensive spark inside his own chest. "You're forgetting something. The Voigt-Kampff

machines, the tests, those blade runner skills . . . they
all detect and measure something that actually exists.
That's *empathy*. You know what that is?"

"I got an idea."

Deckard leaned forward, drilling his hard level gaze
into Isidore's. "It's the ability to feel. To feel what another living creature feels. Humans have it. Replicants
don't. Not to the same degree; not enough. That's what
makes them dangerous."

One of Isidore's eyebrows lifted. "This empathy . . . Rachael duh-doesn't have it?"

The spark burned hotter inside him; he could've
killed the man on the other side of the desk. "Maybe
not," he said finally. "Or she wouldn't have let me fall
in love with her. She'd have known better."

A sigh, a shake of the head. "See how much you
complicate things? With all this buh-business about
what's fake and what's real. Your big-duh-deal Voigt-
Kampff machines . . . what do they measure? *Really*
measure. A millisecond's difference in pupil dilation
times; a blush response that's one shade less puh-pink
than the prescribed norm. You know what you were
like, when you were running around being such a buh-
bad-ass blade runner? Like a *Rassenprüfer;* something
else right out of the Third Reich." The stammer evaporated as Isidore's ire rose. "Remember what those were?
Racial examiners. Going around Berlin with calipers and
measuring people's noses, right out on the street. A mil-
limeter too big, not quite the correct shape, and boom,
you weren't defined as human anymore. Your ass was off
to Auschwitz. At least the Nazis preferred doing their
killing somewhere out of sight—guess that makes them
a class act compared to you guys."

Deckard stayed silent, letting the other's words hit
him in the face and drop away like the sharp crystals of
an ice storm. He knew all this shit. It was in the books.
He'd even thought about it, in those long night hours,
shirt bloodied and bottle at hand. Until it couldn't be

thought about anymore, not without falling off the
Curve. And landing somewhere at the bottom, with his
hand resting on the gun above his heart, thinking over
and time for action. The last one possible . . .

"Look. I told you already." He felt a thin sheen of
sweat on his palms, a nervous response to the other's
threat. "I quit the job. Bryant—my old boss—he put the
screws on me to go back and do it again. Maybe I
should've told him to go fuck himself . . . but I didn't.
I didn't have the guts. So sue me." He pushed himself
back in the chair, his palms hard against the chair's
arms. "But nobody ever heard me say that being a blade
runner was a good job."

"It wasn't a good job, Deckard, because it was buh-
buh-*bull*shit." Isidore wasn't letting him off the hook.
"The empathy tests, the Voigt-Kampff machines . . .
they're all crap. They don't even wuh-work. Have there
ever been any false puh-positives? Subjects who had the
tests run on them, who were identified as being replicants, only they weren't?"

He hesitated a second before answering. The same
question, in different words, had been asked of him
once before. He shook his head. "No."

"As I said, buh-buh-bullshit. What about the St.
Paul incident?"

Gears meshed inside Deckard's head, trying to grind
out an analysis of what this little man was up to. *He
knows too much*—the St. Paul incident was more than
top secret. After that mess had been cleaned up, the
details hadn't even been recorded, so there would be no
files to purge. Just the memories that the blade runners
themselves carried around, locked behind their fore-
heads.

"St. Paul . . ." The words came slow out of his
mouth. "St. Paul was an accident."

"I duh-don't think that's what they'd call it. If they
could call it anything."

Those dead, or their ashes at any rate, were buried

somewhere in Minnesota. Bad luck was as much a death-penalty crime as being an escaped replicant. During the peak of the winter flu season, a pharmacist in central St. Paul had handed out his remaining stock of an upper-respiratory humectant, once popular but pulled off the market by the Food and Drug Administration, to his family and friends. A member of the LAPD blade runner unit goes back to visit his folks for Christmas, gets drunk with an old high school girlfriend, runs the Voigt-Kampff tests on her for a joke. The over-the-counter flu medicine contains a mild CNS depressant, just enough to tweak down her iris fluctuations and blush response. The blade runner on vacation takes out his gun and blows her away. On a roll: he runs the Voigt-Kampff tests on everybody around him, including his aging Norman Rockwell–type parents, determines that he's surrounded by a nest of escaped replicants passing as human. In the next twelve hours, the only thing he stops for is to reload.

Bad luck, real bad shit. One of Deckard's old partners in the blade runner unit, the coldest of the bunch, had to go back there and pull the plug on the guy, who by that point was completely nuts and seeing escaped replicants everywhere. Extremely terminated; the loose-cannon blade runner's body was flown back to Los Angeles and buried with honors, without details. The lid was clamped down in St. Paul, with judicious application of the slush fund that Bryant administered out of the bottom drawer of his desk. Silence on the matter . . . at least until this Isidore character opened his mouth.

"How do you know about St. Paul?"

A smug expression settled on Isidore's face. "Mr. Deckard, it's my business to know about things like that. It's the buh-business of the Van Nuys Pet Hospital. The real business."

"Yeah? And what's that?"

Isidore glanced at the pictures tacked to the wall. "I

didn't even ruh-really know, until old Mr. suh-Sloat died. I'd just worked for him before that, duh-doing what he told me to do, fixing up those busted animals— the fake ones, as yuh-you'd kuh-call them. But then when he was gone, and he'd left me everything . . ." He brought his gaze back around to Deckard. "When he left me . . . the great task. The responsibility. What he had done, and what I had to do. That was when I found out the truth." Behind the round lenses, his eyes looked both wise and pitying. "You're a failure, Deckard. You were a failure *before* you quit being a blade runner. The whole blade runner shtick is a failure. You're suh-supposed to be keeping escaped replicants from running around on Earth, being 'dangerous,' as you like to think they are. Well, you buh-buh-blew it. You and all the rest of the blade runners. You didn't accomplish jack about tracking down replicants. And you know why? Because you *can't* do anything about it. You never could. Blade runners—shuh-shuh-sheesh. Buncha frauds, wasting taxpayers' muh-money. The LAPD should've pensioned you off, or put you back in uniform, made tuh-ruh-ruh-*traffic* cops outta you. Something useful, at least. Because something like the St. Paul incident—and there've been others, ones you don't even know about—you know wuh-what something like that shows?"

He slouched down in the chair, hating the guy. "You're gonna tell me."

"That's why you're huh-*here*, Deckard. It's not just that there can be false positives on the Voigt-Kampff test. That blade runners have been icing humans—ruh-real humans—that flunked the test for one reason or another. It's also that wuh-once you admit that fallibility of the empathy-testing methodology, you admit the possibility of *false negatives*. Replicants who pass the test, who walk right by you because your big deal Voigt-Kampff machines tuh-tuh-told you they were human."

"A possibility." A shrug. "Big deal. Anything's possible. Doesn't mean it ever happened."

"Buh-but you see . . ." Isidore folded his hands together in his lap. "I can *prove* it's happened. That replicants can get past the empathy tests, your fancy-shuh-shmancy Voigt-Kampff machines. Even before the Nexus-6 models came on-line, they were getting puh-past. For years now—muh-maybe decades—there've been escaped replicants walking around on Earth. Right here in L.A., even. And there's nothing that you or any of the other blade runners can do about it. *Because you can't find them.*"

"Metaphysics." He glared back at the other man. "Bullshit. You're talking religion. Articles of faith. Postulating an invisible entity—it exists but you can't see it. Nobody can. Replicants passing as human—they exist because you think they have to exist. Good luck proving that one."

"Nuh-nuh-not faith, Deckard. But reality. I've seen them, talked to them, wuh-watched them come and go . . ." Isidore's gaze shifted away, refocusing on the radiance of an inner vision. "Oh, much more than that. I know everything about them. Isn't that fuh-fuh-funny?" An expression of amazement. "I'm the person who couldn't ever see the difference, between human and not, between the fuh-fake and the real—*you* could see those things, but I couldn't. I was blind to them. And I won. The way I see things . . . it became real. From in here . . ." He tapped the side of his head again. "To everywhere." The fingertip moved away from the skull. "I made it real."

He stayed silent, watching. A few minutes before he'd been sure that the other man was insane. Now he wasn't sure. Of anything.

The gaze of the enlightened, of those who know the truth, turned upon him once more.

"Don't you see, Deckard?" The voice soft and gentle, stammer evaporated. "That's what the business of the Van Nuys Pet Hospital was all along—or at least that's what it had become before old Mr. Sloat left it to me. His legacy. When I found out what he'd been doing—what we'd all been doing—I didn't have any choice. I had to go on with it."

He peered closer at the man. "With what?"

"Turning fakes—what *you'd* call fakes—into the real. That's what we'd started out doing, with the animals—building and repairing them so they couldn't be distinguished from the ones that'd been born that way. Doing it with animals is legal; Hannibal Sloat just took it the next logical step. The *necessary* step. The Van Nuys Pet Hospital is the last station on the underground railway for escaped replicants: when they get out of the offworld colonies and reach Earth, they come straight here. Right under the noses of the blade runners and all the rest of the LAPD; who'd ever think of raiding a pet hospital? Hm? And then when the escaped replicants get here . . . I *fix* them. And when I get done fixing them . . . they can pass an empathy test. I tweak their involuntary reaction times, their blush responses, their pupil fluctuations, so they can sail right past a Voigt-Kampff machine. And they do pass; they *always* pass." Isidore nodded slowly, as if he'd just thought of something. "So given that there've been some real humans who've flunked the empathy tests . . . I guess that makes my fixed-up replicants realer than real, huh?"

"If they exist at all." The other man's words had stung him, needled him back into a way of thinking, a way of being that he'd thought he'd given up completely. "If they existed . . . we would've caught them eventually. At least some of them." Deckard could hear an old brutality setting steel in his voice. "And it's got nothing to do with being a blade runner. It's about being a cop. And what cops know. You're talking conspiracy, buddy. Anytime you got that many in on something, some of them are gonna crack. They're not as strong as the others, they're not as good at hiding, at sweating it out when they know they're being hunted. All it takes is one, and then the whole game's up. And that's how we would've caught your fixed-up replicants. If they existed."

"True . . ." Isidore nodded slowly. "As you say, not everybody has the nerves for hiding. For staying hidden. You and the rest of the blade runners must be proud of having made yourselves into such objects of fear. Tuh-terrorists, really. But this is something that old Mr. Sloat knew all about. And knew *what* to do about it, too. And I've done the same as he did. There's more than just the blush response that can be fixed on an escaped replicant. There's the memory; that can be fixed as well."

"Now I know you're bullshitting me. False memories in replicants are implanted at their incept dates. When the replicants are created. The phony memories are part of them from the beginning."

"You're wrong, Deckard. Or puh-partly so. The incept date is when the Tyrell Corporation shoves in whatever false memories they want their replicants to have. But it's not the only time it can be done. The neural access pathway is hard-wired into the replicants' neocortices. In fact, the bandwidth of the data channel is one of the design features of the Nexus-6 line; I could show you the schematics. It was so the corporation could cram more stuff into their heads before they sent them off the assembly lines. But the access to the memory areas is still there, like a door without even a lock on it. You juh-just have to know where to look for it. And then use it."

"And that's what you did. Supposedly."

"Oh, yeah." A look of dreamy triumph moved behind Isidore's glasses. "No 'supposedly' about it. It's my job. I'm very good at it. And when I'm done . . ." His gaze sharpened once more. "Some of the people you thought were humans, they were actually replicants and they didn't even know it. You'd be surprised to learn who they were. And are."

The room seemed suddenly smaller, as though the

walls had snugged up against his shoulders. "What's that supposed to mean?"

"Like I said, Deckard . . ." The other's voice was as smooth and piercing as a hypodermic. "You'd be surprised. Very, *very* surprised."

5

As the search party topped the last big rise, a fifty-floor office tower now laid out on the ground like a cubist obsidian snake, the first smoky flush of dawn crept over the horizon. *Gonna be a hot one*—Sebastian could already feel the sun's blistering kiss on his face. Until the monsoons came back, every one was a hot one.

Up above, stars were still set in blackness, the atmosphere scoured raw by the Santa Ana winds rolling over the desert. During the trek back, three lines of fire, evenly spaced, had cut across the sky. From the north and veering downtown—he'd twisted around to watch the distant spinners, wondering who the hell was in them. *Somebody important*, he'd figured. But none of his business. He'd laid his check against the back of Fuzzy's head, conserving his own dwindled strength.

When they reached home, he made his two pals wait out in the corridor. He crawled over the frame of the nest's tilted doorway, his one hand pulling him laboriously forward. "Hey, Pris? Sweetheart? I got something special for you." With a string knotted around his wrist, he dragged behind him one of the candy boxes from the welfare bundle. "Where are you, honey?"

His eyes took a long time adjusting to the room's darkness; the metallic curtains stapled over the windows, including the one that the building's fall had turned into a skylight, shut out all but a thin trace of the advancing light. In the corner a mop of dead-white hair rustled. A face, more wrinkled and deracinated than even Sebastian's ancient one, lifted from bent knees clutched to flattened girl-chest. Eye sockets, blind but for thermal scans, turned toward the legless, one-armed supplicant.

"Look—" He knew Pris, or what was left of her, couldn't look, not really. But acting like she or it could was good enough. Under these circumstances. Sebastian reeled the box into his hand, then held it out. "I brought you this—"

An inaudible shriek, leathery jaw hinges yanked wide, as the Pris-thing sprung from its crouch. Its bone hand slapped the box from Sebastian's grasp; the chocolate-covered cherries spattered gooey wounds across the inverted walls and ceiling. A rattling hiss, a remnant scream, came from its throat as it reached down, grabbed, and threw him across the room.

"Yes . . ." Tears of pain and joy filled his eyes. From where he'd landed, he watched as that which he loved jerked in spastic tantrum, arms flailing pinwheels as it lurched away. He nodded slowly. "Yes . . . I love you, too."

The teddy bear and the hussar peeked over the doorway's edge at him. Then clambered down to lift up and tend to his ancient, partial body.

"That's an old joke." Deckard actually felt sorry for the little man on the other side of the desk. Another cat had wangled its way onto Isidore's lap; this one was without flesh on its steel bones. "Sarah Tyrell had me brought all

the way over here just so you could run that creaky
number on me?"

Isidore petted the mechanical cat, as if unaware of
the difference between it and the tabby he'd held before. The contraption purred and closed its eyes in con-
tentment; or at least polyethylene membranes slid down
over the glass replications. One of Isidore's forefingers
scratched where the cat's ears should've been. "I don't
run any nuh-numbers. On anybody."

"Yeah, right." Deckard shook his head in disgust.
"What's with all the heavy hinting, then? All that stuff
about how surprised I'd be to find out who's really a
replicant passing as human. Passing because the person
doesn't even know he's really a replicant. And then you
give me the big, significant look. Shit." He fixed the
other man with his own hard glare. "You think that isn't
one of the first things a blade runner starts thinking
about? *Hey, maybe I'm one of these replicants.* Maybe the
cops set mechanical cats to catch mechanical rats. It'd
be just like them—believe me, blade runners know the
LAPD's mind-set better than you civilians do. And since
we're too familiar with the empathy tests to use them
on ourselves—then we have to come up with some
other way of knowing for sure that we're not replicants."

"And wuh-what's that?"

"It's the Curve. It's always the Curve. That whole
'index of self-loathing' trip." He could feel his own eyes
narrowing, as though he were contemplating the soul
underneath his breastbone. "Blade runners wind up so
sick of themselves eventually—realizing they were replicants would be a relief. But that *never* happens. *Loathe
thyself*—blade runners pretty much have the ultimate in
self-knowledge. So don't bother trying any of these re-
tread mind games on me."

"Well . . . it duh-doesn't matter, anyway." Isidore
shrugged. "Whether you're really human or not . . .
that's the least of your worries now."

"Right now, I'm not worried about anything except retiring some escaped replicant. And then getting back to where I was before I got yanked back down here. Up north. Somebody's waiting for me there." At the back of his mind, all the while this weird person had been haranguing him: the black coffin in which he'd left Rachael sleeping, dying. It could run for itself, awhile at least, but soon enough it would need his loving hand moving underneath the control panel's metal skirt. "You're big on moral condemnation, pal, but let's face it, it's kind of wasted on me. I've already got enough to spare. So why don't you just tell me what it is that I should be so worried about?" He nodded toward the door. "Then maybe you won't mind if I just walk out of here."

"You know, duh-duh-Deckard . . ." In Isidore's lap, the steel-skeletoned cat raised its head, gaze parallel and equal to the one above. "Like most things about you, your whole load of self-loathing is pretty much a shuh-shuck. As long as *your* skin's intact, you don't really care what happens to anyone else. So that's why I know this is going to be right up your alley." He leaned forward, the cat held tight against his chest. "This job you've taken on—there's always one more job, isn't there?—it's not going to be so easy."

"Skip the warning. I've had one already."

Isidore went on. "You're not going to be able to just wuh-walk out of here and start hunting. You screwed up, Deckard. Big time. From before. Tell me: what's the final—the ultimate—absolutely accurate way of determining whether somebody's a human or a replicant?"

The fierce quiet in the other's voice had pushed him back into his chair. "Postmortem," he said finally. "Bone marrow analysis. Takes a while—"

"I know how long it tuh-takes. And it's also how I know you screwed up. *Because I've seen the postmortem bone marrow results.* There was one replicant you retired . . . who *wasn't* a replicant. And killing a human isn't called retirement, Deckard. It's called murder."

"Bullshit." He returned the other's glare, but felt a molecule-thick layer of moisture form between his palms and the chair's arms. "Which one are you talking about?"

"Not *which one*, Deckard. But *who*. Wuh-we're talking about human buh-beings here; get your language straight. The girl who called herself Pris. Remember her? Blond, athletic . . . probably a little kuh-ruh-crazy." Isidore nodded slowly, stroking the mechanical cat. "She had her problems, guh-guh-God knows. But she was human. Really human. The bone marrow analysis proved it. Of course, that was after you'd already kuh-killed her."

"That's impossible." Deckard gripped the sweating chair arms harder. "She *had* to be a replicant. I didn't need to run an empathy test on her. She . . ." For a moment his thoughts scurried away from his grasp, his pulse ticking upward in his throat. "She matched the ID that I was given. And she was . . . strong. Like replicants are. You didn't see that. She nearly killed *me*."

"Strong, huh?" The other man gave a quick, sharp laugh. "You mean stronger than you. Some woman kicks your ass, so she must not be human. And you kill her. Ruh-really, Deckard. How do you think *that's* going to sound in court?"

"But the ID . . . the video I was shown . . ."

"A puh-picture." Isidore's voice went soft and sad. "You killed her because of a *picture*. Isn't that why you were issued a Voigt-Kampff machine? Told to run empathy tests? So you wuh-wouldn't be just running wild out there on the streets, shooting anyone that *looked* like a replicant to you. So you'd be *sure* who was human and what wasn't." He watched his own hand rubbing the round metal ball of the cat's skull. "That is, of course, if you're inclined to making that little distinction."

Silence. He couldn't make any reply. Deckard

knew, in the pit of his gut, that the man on the other
side of the battered desk was telling the truth. About
the bone marrow analysis, about human or not . . .
about everything.

"Who . . ." He knew now that that was the right
word. And not *what*. "Who was she?"

"Like I said, duh-Deckard. She was a human. Beyond the blood marrow results, there isn't much more
that I've been able to find out about her. Name really
was Pris. That much was true. Born off-world, probably
in one of the U.N.'s Martian colonies. They don't like to
talk about it, but there's a fairly huh-high rate of muh-
muh-mental breakdown out in those warrens. It's a
good place to go nuts. And plenty of them do. There are
others, the same as poor Pris was. They don't wuh-wuh-
want to be human anymore. They're wanna-bes. They
cross the line; they start hanging out with replicants,
they act like them . . . and then they cross another
line. In their heads. Instead of replicants who think, who
believe, who *know* they're human . . . people like
poor dead Pris, they're humans who've come to think,
to *know* that they're replicants. A psychotic break. With
full-blown somatic conversions—they even take on the
physical attributes of replicants. Increased strength,
duh-damage resistance, the whole bit. They make a
game out of picking up red-hot metal bare-handed,
without getting hurt. That's how far their cracked minds
can go to prove they're replicants and not human. The
process is completed when, like Pris, they escape from
the off-world colonies and come to Earth. Where they'll
be killed. By people like you." Isidore closed his eyes for
a moment, the mechanical cat doing the same. "Then
they're not wanna-bes anymore. Then they're wanna-
dies."

Now he knew the exact reason for the sweat. What
he had to be worried about. "But . . . she tried to kill
me first . . ."

"Self-defense. She's going about her own business

here in L.A., some flipped-out cop shows up with a gun, starts tearing the place up . . . hey, she was just trying to pruh-protect herself. Humans have the right to do that."

The thoughts in his head squirmed, trying to find a way out. "Yeah, but . . . she was already guilty of murder. The escape from off-world . . . people died in that . . ."

Isidore shrugged. "There's no evidence that Pris did any of the kuh-kuh-killing. And even if she had, it doesn't chuh-change things for you. Cops—even blade runners—are supposed to arrest people—humans—and bring 'em in. Not blow 'em away before they get a trial. What, you're going to stand up in court and say you had a right to execute suspects *before* they're found guilty? Good luck on that one. Judges really huh-*hate* out-of-control cops. They won't even take you out of the courtroom; the judge'll just hike up his black robe and stand on your thuh-ruh-throat until you stop moving."

"You're wrong." The smug tone in the other man's voice infuriated him. "The LAPD looks out for its own. There are ways. The department will cover for me. They do the investigating, remember? They can take whatever evidence they've got, make it look any way they want. Or they can lose it, bury it down in Internal Affairs, so deep it'll never come back up." The fury tinged his own voice. "I was doing my job—yeah, that's no excuse. But there's no way the department's going to let a fellow cop take a rap . . . like that . . ." Fury drained, his words faded. He'd just remembered something.

"You got it, Deckard." Triumph and pity. "You fell into your old mind-set, didn't you? Just enough to forget that you quit the department. *You're not a cop anymore.* You turned your back on the department and walked away. Ran all the way up north, to that little hiding place you found. The LAPD doesn't owe you a thing now. I know enough about how their heads work.

Not only are they not going to cover for you—they'll throw you to the courts just to make themselves look good. That's how it goes, Deckard. When they find out you're back here in the city, the cops are going to hunt you down like wolves on a rabbit. Even if you don't wind up executed—either out on the street or from the court—you won't be heading up north again. Not anytime soon, that is. You'll be in a max lockup for a long, *long* while."

The sweat had turned to ice under his hands. He looked down at them, seeing them as if they belonged to someone else, someone already dead. "Do they know?" He looked back up at Isidore. "That I'm in the city?"

"I didn't tell the police about you. But they know. Somebody else tuh-told them."

"Who? It must've been her . . . Sarah Tyrell."

Isidore shook his head. "No—she had you buh-brought here so I could warn you. Not to juh-just go waltzing out onto the streets and get yourself blown away."

It didn't matter. The only thing that did matter was far away from here. "Now what happens?"

"I don't know. That's up to you, Deckard. Duh-dying seems to be your likeliest option."

"You could help me get away."

A thin smile and a shake of the head. "I don't know anything about how to do that. It's not exactly my area of expertise. Someone leaves here, I don't have any way of helping them after that."

He glanced around the small room's walls. "But the police don't know I'm here. In your pet hospital. Or they would've found me already." *Like wolves on a rabbit*—his former associates in the department wouldn't waste any time. "You could let me hide out here. Until I figure out what to do."

"No—" This shake was more emphatic. "If they don't know you're here now, they soon will. And I can't risk that. I've got other ruh-responsibilities. Your skin isn't one of them."

"So all that other stuff was just talk." Bitter in his voice, like acid curling under his tongue. "All your big concern about living things. Whether they're human or not. I guess that doesn't extend to blade runners."

"Should it?" Isidore's hand moved gently beneath the mechanical cat's throat. "The creatures I help— replicant, human, whatever—they didn't ask for the bad shit that happens to them. You duh-did. The hunter can't complain when he becomes the hunted. Now you're going to find out what it fuh-fuh-feels like. To be running for your life. To be afraid."

To live in fear. He heard another voice, an old memory track, inside his head. *That's what it is . . . to be a slave . . .*

"I've already been there," said Deckard. "I'm not going to learn anything new."

"What a shame. It's such a good ah-ah-opportunity." Isidore set the mechanical cat down on the desktop, gave the creature a final pat on its shining head. It purred louder. "But then again . . . maybe you will. Learn something, that is. Like how to *be* a human." He reached out and pressed a small button set into the side of the desk. "I make things real. As much as they can be. You've never been real. Now's your chance."

Deckard knew what the button was for. One of the thugs who'd brought him here—the heavy footsteps were probably coming down the hallway, heading for the office's door.

As though the chair were a trap, already sprung—he couldn't keep himself sitting. He stood up, jittery adrenaline in his veins. On the wall—he found himself staring at the pictures of dead Hannibal Sloat, the old photograph and the yellowed bit of newspaper. Fat and with hair in the photo, bald and fatter in the clipping. Time had walked through that low-resolution world.

He wasn't looking at dead Sloat, the founder of the

Van Nuys Pet Hospital. This close, nose a few inches from the wall, he could make out the other people in the clipping shot. The caption underneath was something about a cat named Ginjer—maybe a real one—getting ready to go to the stars: . . . *complete checkup before embarking for the Proxima system* . . .

The grumpy-looking animal dangled from the dead man's hands. The other man in the newspaper photo could've been anybody; Deckard didn't recognize him.

The woman in the old clipping was Rachael.

No—he closed his eyes, sorting things out. *And it's not Sarah, either.* The woman was Sarah's mother, Ruth. The mother of Rachael, too, in a way. They all looked just the same, twins, triplets. The only difference was that Ruth had had her dark hair cut short, just enough left for a little fringe at the back of her neck. A practical cut, just right for climbing aboard the *Salander 3*—that was what the clipping was about—and setting off Proxward with her husband Anson Tyrell and their marmalade cat. And maybe the first few cells of their human daughter, already growing in Ruth's womb. The couple looked radiant and happy, in that bright world of the past. To find what they were looking for, another world out in the stars . . .

"Why did they come back?" Voice a wondering murmur, as Deckard studied the clipping. No answer there. "Why'd they come back to *this* world? This one sucks." He would've said that even if there hadn't been people, cops like he'd been, prowling through the city, looking for his death.

"I don't know." Isidore's voice came from behind him. "Nobody does. It's a mystery. Maybe Sarah knows. Maybe you should ask her about it sometime. If you ever guh-get the chuh-chance again."

He glanced over his shoulder. There wasn't time for anything more to be said. He heard the footsteps now, then the office's door opening. The dark-uniformed man, the one who'd piloted the spinner that had brought him here, looked in.

"Mr. Deckard's leaving now." Isidore petted the mechanical cat on the desk, not looking up at either of the men, as though suddenly hit with an obscure shame. "Show him the way, please."

"Happy to." The pilot locked a grip on Deckard's arm, pulled and then shoved, taking him out the door, pushing him past the wire cages.

Only a couple of minutes later he found himself outside a bigger and heavier door, steel studded with bolts. At street level, the sound of the Van Nuys Pet Hospital's freight dock slamming shut echoed through the narrow canyon of the surrounding buildings.

Fine Mojave dust drifted across his shoes, an oven wind piling up miniature dunes in the empty streets' gutters.

Deckard tilted his head back, looking up at the sun, letting its glare hammer into his eyes, unblinking tears shimmering toward steam.

A distant black speck moved across the sun's fire.

Holden could see the luminous green line running across the face of the monitor. A humpbacked snake— *That's my pulse,* he thought. It looked a million miles away, though he knew he just had to raise his hand to touch it. The black attaché case was strapped to his chest with a web of surgical tape. In the spinner's cockpit, he managed weakly to raise the sheer tonnage of his head from the seat's padding.

"What . . ." Tongue dry and thick, but without a stiff plastic air hose jammed down his throat. All the necessary tubing seemed to be down at his chest. "What's going . . ." A tiny ball fluttered in a transparent valve with each word he breathed. "On . . ."

The man in the other seat, hands on the spinner's controls, turned and looked at him. And smiled. "You blacked out there for a while." He leaned over and checked the readings on the attaché case's dials. "Seem to be doing okay, though. Know who you are?"

"Who . . ." The question puzzled him. Plus the smiling man's face—he'd seen him before, but he didn't know when or where. Crazy-looking smile—crazy meaning insane, or at least on the border of it—and a shock of white hair, spiky cropped. But the face was older, more wrinkled and lined than he thought he remembered it. What did that mean? "Who . . . am I . . ."

"Your name, pal. What's your name?"

"Oh . . ." Not so hard, especially now that the drugs they'd been giving him in the hospital had started to wear off. The hoses in his chest stung; he had to fight an irrational urge to pull them out. "My name . . ." Deep breath, the little ball dancing higher. "Holden . . . Dave Holden . . ."

"Very good." The smiling man reached over and tapped a finger against his forehead. "They didn't screw with anything up here, at least."

It had started to seem that way. With more pain, more clarity, as though the hard sun, dimmed by the cockpit's photochromic glass, was burning off a heavy fog bank. He knew he'd been there, in the hospital, hooked up to those bigger machines, for a long time. A year? *Maybe more*—as though he could now look down at the fog bank, wide as an ocean, the freight spinner having flown above both it and the tops of the L.A. towers.

At the farthest edge of the fog bank was his last unclouded memory. The last one before the woozy haze of the hospital ward.

Describe . . . only the good things that come into your mind about . . . your mother. That was his own voice, the last thing he'd spoken aloud in that other world. Where'd that been? He concentrated, caught: at the Tyrell Corporation headquarters. In a room with two chairs, an overhead fan that'd barely stirred the stale, overprocessed air, and a table with a Voigt-Kampff machine sitting on it, the bellows inhaling and exhaling at the same speed as the attaché case strapped to his chest now. And another voice, thick, stupid, and resentful: *My mother? Lemme tell you about my mother* . . .

The rest of that memory track was not good. The doctors had had to bring him out of a narcotized stupor—that was when he'd first sighted all the machines ranked around his bed, and the tubes and hoses going in where just about everything under his rib cage had once been—so he could be debriefed by a sick-looking crew of investigators from the department . . .

Now he remembered. That was when he'd seen this guy before. Not smiling in the picture they'd shown him, but still—it was him. The same one.

"Wait . . . a minute . . ." He could hear the machinery in the attaché case revving up, to keep pace with the self-generated adrenaline suddenly trickling into his veins. "Who . . . are you . . ."

The man turned his smile, even bigger and crazier, back around at him. "My name's Roy," he said, an inflection of almost childlike delight. A good joke. "I'm Roy Batty."

"Oh . . . *shit* . . ." Holden scrabbled blindly beside himself, trying to find the cockpit's exit latch. It didn't matter that the spinner was hundreds of meters above the city. Everything that he'd been told about this particular replicant, the strongest and most murderous of all the escaped Nexus-6 models, flashed through his mind. *But it's supposed to be dead*, he thought in panicked confusion.

"Come on—" The smiling figure grabbed Holden and dragged him back into the seat. "You're not going anywhere. Except with me."

Helpless, he watched as Batty adjusted one of the dials inside the attaché case. His pulse slowed, whether he wanted it to or not. Black spots swarmed in front of his eyes, until Batty tweaked the knob a fraction the other way.

"There." Smiling, both hands back on the spinner's controls. "Just relax, Dave. I'm taking you someplace special. Someplace . . . you'll like."

The ball floated in the valve, trembling with each assisted breath. He closed his eyes, not wanting to see the hoses latched to his chest. Or anything else.

Beneath the yellow L.A. sky, the spinner flew on.

6

From one of the *bureau plat*'s drawers, Sarah Tyrell took out the small tight-cell phone she had known would be there. Turning to gaze out at the strata of smoke and haze obscuring the afternoon sun, she flipped the phone open and pressed the TALK button. A synthesized trill, rising and falling in pitch, sounded at her ear, as the beam sought out and locked on to a secured channel from one of the low-orbit satellites over L.A. Punching in the numbers, then waiting, she idly let her hand prowl through the rest of the drawer's contents, the scarlet ovals of her nails clicking against paper clips and the remote, a Francis Harache gold snuff box, the cheap and nasty folding knife. Somewhere across town, another phone was ringing in sync with the one at her ear.

Then answered. "Speak if you want to." A man's voice.

"You know who it is." Sarah leaned back, the ridge of the chair's low back cutting under her shoulder blades. "I was just wondering how things went. With our guest."

"Huh. I imagine Deckard's just fine. Wherever the hell he is right now."

She was used to Andersson's general charmlessness. She had picked him—not just for this job, but for others as well—for his efficiency. He had been in charge of locating Deckard, up in the Oregon wilds, then bringing him back, even piloting the spinner that had carried Deckard home to Los Angeles. The man's other machinelike virtue was that of silence, of keeping his mouth shut.

From the office's high window, she could see across the city's sprawling maze. Deckard was down there, in there now. "Didn't you tag him? So we could trace where he goes?"

"Wouldn't have been much point in doing that." He sounded bored and competent. "Somebody like him, he knows his business. If we put a tag on him, he'd find it and flush it. Next thing you know, we're running a trace through some sewer line and out to the ocean, and he's a hundred miles inland. Waste of time."

She felt a small knife's edge of apprehension, a flutter of the pulse beneath her ribs. She hadn't brought Deckard all this way, back into the world he'd tried to escape, just to lose track of him.

"What if he doesn't turn up again? What if he just . . . disappears?"

"He'll turn up. He has to. If he's going to survive."

In the few moments of silence, as she mulled over what the man had just told her, she could hear faint sounds. Not here, in what had been her uncle's office, but over in the Van Nuys Pet Hospital. The sounds were animal cries, real or fake. She knew that Andersson had a little corner for himself, tucked at the end of the rows of cages and kennels, where he transacted his own business. Away from Isidore, who might be distressed to overhear some of the things that were going on.

Which reminded her. Other things to be taken care
of. "How did their little conversation go? I mean Deckard and Isidore."

"Pretty much what you expected. That's the great
thing about ideologues. People who really believe stuff.
You can depend on them. Isidore raked him over the
coals for quite a while; Deckard didn't look so good
when I finally booted him out of here. I'll send you the
tapes; maybe you'll find 'em amusing."

She knew that he had wired Isidore's office, that
cramped little cubicle. It smelled like a small zoo, mixed
with machine oil and scorched plastic insulation—she'd
been there one time, checking out the pet hospital's
owner, getting an intuitive readout on him. She imag-
ined that Isidore knew as well about the bug that had
been planted; he wasn't that much of a fool, that disconnected from reality. Clever enough, actually, to make no
attempt to remove the bug. Or, as Andersson said, ideo-
logical in nature, nothing to hide—at least from her.
Perhaps he'd thought his lectures and stuttering rants
would change her mind, settle into her heart. It could
happen.

But not now. "Isidore's done a lot for us, hasn't
he?" She extended her hand, touching the window's
glass, sensing a fraction of the day's heat through it. The
sky reddened from sulphur yellow as the sun moved
slowly toward the horizon. "Quite a lot."

A moment's hesitation before Andersson's reply. "I
suppose so."

Redder light leaked through the flesh of her fingertips. "I wonder . . . if there's really much more he *can*
do for us."

"Are you trying to tell me something?" Andersson's
voice again, breaking into the silence.

"Do I have to tell you?"

"No . . ." He was probably giving a slight shake of
his head. "I don't think so."

"Good." The office and the bedchamber beyond

had fallen further into shadow. "And when you're done . . ."

He said nothing. Waiting.

"Why don't you come by here." She killed the connection and put the phone back in the *bureau plat's* drawer.

On her way out she stopped at the foot of her uncle's bed. That was hers as well—if she wanted it.

A handful of silk, shimmering against her fingertips as she lifted the edge of the sheet. But with a musty smell, as though it had absorbed a scent of age from the bedchamber's trapped air. She'd decided to have one of her personal staff come in and strip the bed, change everything for new . . .

Then changed her mind. She saw something she hadn't noticed before, a spatter of blood, small dots the color of the larger stain on the floor, a line diagonal up to the pillows.

She let the silk drift away from her hand, falling gentle upon the bed. When it was quite still again, she turned and walked toward the doors.

Smile and smile and smile . . . and be what? Dave Holden didn't know anything about the man sitting next to him in the cockpit. All that he did know, all that his brain could process, fueled by the blood re-oxygenated by the pumping and gasping attaché case strapped to his chest, was that he was in deep, deep shit.

Then again, thought Holden, *I was dying anyway. There in that hospital.* He wondered if the figure beside him—not smiling now, but concentrating on the freight spinner's controls, taking it in for a landing somewhere at the city's unlit fringe—had spiked one of the blood tubes with a philosophically oriented chemical. A good deal of his initial fear had faded away, replaced by an odd curiosity as to what his fate was going to be.

Batty was dead; they'd told him that, Bryant and a couple of his other old pals from the blade runner unit.

They'd come to the side of Holden's chrome-railed bed with their hats in their hands, wedging themselves into the small space between one gurgling machine and the next; the doctors had turned down the fentanyl drip enough to bring him into semiconsciousness, in which he'd been able to hear Bryant telling him that the group of escaped replicants, the batch he'd been assigned to, had all been successfully retired. As if he cared.

For its own reasons, the department gave him partial credit for the track-down, even though all he'd managed to do was inhale a hollow point through his breastbone, from that lump Kowalski. Bad for the morale of the rest of the squad, to let one of their number get his lungs blown out and not put a little something extra in his paycheck. The hospital visit had been when Bryant, the whiskey breath seeping through his brown teeth even stronger than usual, had shown him the morgue shots of the dead replicants. Including Roy Batty, who'd been the leader of their violent little band—even through a narcotic haze, the image of that unmistakable face, with its shock of white hair and gaze still coming in loony from the other side of the marble slab, had made a deep impression on him. Unforgettable.

"Hey—how about turning on some lights?" That was Batty, speaking into the spinner's comm mike. Holden had watched in silence as Batty had tuned in a narrow-beam radio link with some identified ground station; the frequency numbers on the control panel looked way off any band with which he was familiar. "If I have to bring this thing in blind, I'm going to feel like kicking someone's ass afterward."

Holden looked out the side of the cockpit. At darkness, far beyond the reach of L.A.'s lit-up sprawl. How far had they gone? Up ahead, through the transparent curve, he could discern a jagged silhouette along the horizon, mountains outlined by stars and the moon's soft glaze.

Some other blue light, not the moon, spilled across the bleak landscape, blinking on and off. Holden brought his gaze around—it took some effort; he could feel himself tiring—and saw a landing rectangle outlined by the bright flashes. "There you go—" A voice crackled from the speaker on the control panel. "Make it quick, willya? We're getting sand in our boots, hanging around waiting on you."

"Where . . ." His own voice came out a feeble whisper. The effort of speaking, on top of just staying conscious and lifting his head from the seat's padded rest to look around, had come close to exhausting him again. The dials on the black attaché case, visible beneath the web of surgical tape that bound it to him, jittered as the device kicked more oxygen into his body. "Where . . . is this . . ." Getting out the last couple of words had brought black spots dancing in front of his eyes.

Batty's disquieting smile swung in his direction. He reached over and made a small adjustment on one of the attaché case's valves. "As I told you before. Someplace special." The smile widened, deepening the lines on the weathered face. "It's someplace you were always going to wind up."

No lock-on from the ground station, as far as he could see; Batty was taking the spinner down manually, centering the vehicle motionless above the blue lights, then hitting a straight vertical descent. The spinner's undercarriage hit the ground hard enough to bounce Holden in his seat, the attaché case against the hollowed spaces of his chest.

"Sorry about that." Batty started flicking off the engine controls. "These freight jobbies are a bitch to maneuver."

"That's . . . that's okay," whispered Holden painfully. Maybe it wasn't too late to try ingratiating himself with the folks who ran the afterlife. "I'm sure . . . you're doing your best . . ."

Batty glanced over at him. And smiled. "You haven't *seen* my best yet."

That worried him. He could hear the cargo space's door unsealing and, beyond, the sound of rolling wheels and running feet.

"Take it easy with this guy." Batty supervised Holden's unloading and being strapped onto a gurney. "I didn't bust him out and bring him all the way here, just so you could drop him on the ground like a carton of eggs."

"Whatever." A bored-looking younger man, white-coated, scribbled something on a clipboard, then looked up. "You need a receipt on this?" He lifted one corner of a pink duplicating form.

" 'A receipt . . .' " Batty rolled his eyes. "Fuck me."

"It's the regulations," said the younger man.

"Maybe instead, I should just pull your under-brained head off and stuff it down your trousers."

"Hey. Don't want the receipt, just gotta say so." He used the clipboard to gesture toward another couple of men standing around. "You guys wanna help get this case into surgery?" He leaned down and patted Holden on one strap-restrained arm. "Good luck, pal." A stage whisper.

"Take a hike." Batty let the other men push the gurney as he walked alongside.

Hell, or whatever part of the afterlife he'd landed in, looked fairly ramshackle to Holden. A sprawling compound of rusting Quonset huts, windblown sand dunes mounting up the curved sides; other shabby pre-fab cubes made of tilt-up foam-core walls, the structural glue leaking out from the seams, as though melting in the night's dry heat; everything dusted with the same fine grit that eventually wound up in the streets of L.A. Turning his head to the side on the gurney's thin pillow, Holden watched the unimpressive and barely functional architecture roll by, lit by the sickly radiance of sodium-vapor globes strung along the tops of tarred wooden poles.

At the edge of the artificial light, struck more by the stars and moon, a razor-wire fence penned a flock of abandoned police vehicles, spinners and heavier cruisers with scorched flame-out marks along their engine exhausts, cockpits shattered or drilled with a line of spiderwebbed holes from high-caliber automatic weapons fire.

"This the one?"

Holden looked above himself and saw an unshaven face. A hand with black fingernails took a half-smoked cigarette away from the face's mouth; grey ash drifted down and was sucked into one of the black attaché case's air intakes.

Either another doctor or some kind of butcher—the unshaven man had on a long white coat spattered with dried bloodstains. Holden wasn't sure which possibility filled him with greater foreboding.

Batty reached over and plucked away the cigarette. "Show the poor bastard some consideration." A red arc, then a burst of sparks as the stub hit the ground.

"They're *all* poor bastards." No show of annoyance; the unshaven man appeared beyond the expenditure of energy that would take. "All right, let's get him in and do it. No sense standing around out here." His nicotine-stained fingers began flicking off the controls on the black attaché case.

"Hey . . ." Panic set in as Holden heard the attaché's machinery wheezing toward silence, the small clicking and gulping noises slowing, then stopping. "Wait . . . a minute . . ." A grey veil began thickening before his vision; despite the heat of the desert air, his face and hands suddenly felt cold. Numbing fingers groped for the switches and buttons above his chest, but the gurney's straps kept him from reaching them. The tiny ball dropped in the valve, the hoses and tubes drooping limp and uninflated.

"Quit worrying." The unshaven doctor or butcher fumbled a cigarette pack out of the pocket of his white coat, lit up another. "You got at least three minutes or so before any real brain damage starts setting in." Dragged deep, coughed, then gestured to what appeared to be a couple of assistants standing around. "Yo, guys, get over and give me a hand with this one. Come on, let's get to work."

"Hang in there, pal." Batty's deranged smile floated in the mist above. "See you on the other side."

They rolled him into the largest and oldest-looking of the prefab buildings. Holden managed to read the sign above the building's doorway as he disappeared inside. RECLAMATION CENTER. Of course, like the mechanics picking apart the old spinners on the field of night. Now he understood. There must still be a few good parts inside him.

He closed his eyes.

Deckard waited until the sun went down.

Too easily spotted, caught, even in the last few hours of daylight. He knew he needed not just darkness but crowds, the streets full of L.A.'s shoving, jostling nocturnal life. Everyone that the oppressive heat drove indoors, like desert animals sheltering beneath the flat, cool undersides of rocks—he could hide among them, move like a knife through garishly illuminated water, the flickering neon's toxic colors turning his face into a mask the same as the others wore.

Didn't even try to get away from the Van Nuys Pet Hospital—soon as the thuggish Andersson had booted him out on the freight dock, with a shove that had sent him stumbling, the metal door slammed behind him and he looked around for the nearest alley. The sun's angle had shifted far enough to make the one at the side of the building into a shadowed cleft, trash dumpsters and discarded boxes forming the tunnel into which he crawled. Glitter-eyed rodents, disturbed at their inspection of a decamped squatter's rags and meager treasures, hissed and threw bits of clawed-up asphalt at him. As Deckard crawled farther into the nest, light and heat nipping like a leashed dog at the soles of his boots, the small animals retreated, squatting on a crumbling brick ledge, old-womanish paws folded across their grey bellies, glaring at him.

Even in the shadows, out of the direct hit of the sun, the day's heat was enough to start him sweating under his clothes. The Santa Ana wind, sifting red dust through the alley, scraped the moisture off his limbs, sucked it from his mouth, leaving his tongue swollen arid and his eyes gritting in their sockets. He shucked off his coat, wedging its empty shoulders into the sides of the narrow space to make a shield against both the remains of the afternoon's light and anyone's random detection.

In his pocket was the book of matches that he'd used to ignite the woodstove, in the cabin up in Oregon. He struck one now, using its flaring glow to investigate the small space. It smelled of the dirt and sweat of the previous inhabitant. Who must've been a throwback literate, an enthusiast: tucked into the grime-crusted bed of rags were several old-style analogue books, nothing but antlike crawls of ink words on yellowing, damp-swollen pages, dead without any sparking digital enhancements. The covers—there were only a few—showed blond women whose half-lidded gazes were like weapons, mouths like bright wounds, and men with bruised, unshaven faces. The book pages crumbled as Deckard shoved the relics away.

He searched through the rubble, another match held aloft, looking for anything of use.

The previous inhabitant's Registered Homeless card—the thumbnail photo depicted a suffering saint, Christ-like hair tangled down to his shoulders. Dead, too. The Welfare Department's monitor implant must've caught the man's last heartbeat; two cartoon

X's had appeared in the transparent lamination over the man's eyes, making the card useless for anyone else. The digits on the ration microchip had ticked back to zero as well. Deckard tossed the thin rectangle away. Something handier, which the sanitation trucks had left behind when they'd hauled off the body: a simple steel rod, just about the length of his own forearm. Good heft in his fist, with enough whip to make a good skull-cracker. The match had burnt out, but he could read with the ball of his thumb the embossed warning. FOR SELF-DEFENSE PURPOSES ONLY. AGGRESSIVE OR PREDATORY USE PUNISHABLE BY LOSS OF BENEFITS. The rod was standard issue for the city's street people, along with the Sally Anne sleeping bags that usually got ripped off first thing.

Now he didn't feel so naked. Deckard laid the steel rod on the asphalt beside himself, close at hand. He clasped his arms around his knees, lowering his head and waiting for the last daylight visible through his coat to fade. He'd already started putting his plans together.

The sounds of something moving—something bigger than the disgruntled rodents—snapped him awake, out of the pit of nervous exhaustion into which he'd fallen. His head jerked back, one hand shot down to grab and raise the steel rod. Using the metal's tip, he pulled back one edge of the flimsy barrier he'd made from his own coat; leaning against the brick wall, the rodents above scampering farther away, he sighted down the length of the alley.

Enough sleep residue blurred his vision, that his first irrational thought was that a ghost was walking toward him. A figure all in white—the sun had set, though most of its stifling heat remained in the air, so the image seemed to supply its own pale radiance. Drawing back, keeping himself hid, Deckard rubbed his eyes with his free hand. Then he could see a man inhabiting the white outfit, some kind of retro-tropical suit number.

"Charlie?" The white-suited man stopped halfway

down the alley, straining to peer ahead of him. He had a small bundle tucked under one arm. "You home, buddy? Got something for ya." He displayed the bundle, wrapped in paper and string, on the tips of his fingers. "Thinking of you . . ."

The name on the Homeless Reg card had been Charlie something. With the steel rod, Deckard pulled the coat farther back, like a curtain.

"*There* you are." A gold-toothed smile as the white suit ambled forward. "Speak up, next time. I coulda walked right by ya—"

Close enough now. Deckard reached out, the dropped steel rod clanking on the alley's littered floor, and grabbed the man, elegant tie and collar points wadded in his fist. The little bundle's string and wrappings burst open as it flew in a startled arc and hit the ground. More of the tattered books spilled across the rubble.

"Hey, buddy . . ." The summer-weight dandy managed to gasp a few words, his face reddening above his collar. His feet dangled free of the alley. "Ease up, will ya . . ."

"Nice and quiet." Deckard kept the knot of the man's tie inside his fist, knuckles tilting the pointed chin back. "Let's talk real softly." With the sun gone, the evening parade had begun out on the streets. Nobody passing by had glanced down the alley yet. "Got that?"

"Yeah, sure . . ." Both of his hands gripped Deckard's wrist, as though praying in midair. "I got it, buddy, *I got it* . . ." A screeching but obedient whisper. "Whatever you want . . . is fine with me . . ."

He eased his grasp, letting the other man settle on tiptoes. "I'm glad." In sinister fashion, he fingered the white lapel. "Nice jacket."

"Huh? Where's Charlie?"

"Indisposed. You should've made an appointment." The other man was so skinny, he could've either broken him in two or tied him in a knot. But the white suit's jacket was loose enough, flaglike through the shoulders;

it'd be the right size. "Here." Deckard let go of the
man's necktie, reached past him, and tugged his own
long, dark coat from the brick niche he'd anchored it
into. "Make you a trade."

"What? A trade?" He looked with puzzlement,
then distaste, at the coat laid across his trembling hands.
Not in good condition to begin with, it'd picked up
some of the smell and general *schmutz* of the alley. "For
this?"

"That'd be the easy way." Deckard reached down,
picked up the steel rod, laid the other end lightly into
his palm. "There are others."

"Deal!" He shed the jacket as easily as walking out
of a soft white room.

The tie was some flimsy, iridescent stuff—Deckard
took that as well. Looping it without a knot as he strode
away from the mouth of the alley, pushing his way
through the crowd that had already assembled into the
city's nocturnal life. Keeping one hand inside a trouser
pocket, Deckard kept a tight hold on the steel rod
tucked down his leg, its other end notching above his
kneecap with each step he took.

Wind picked up, as though punching in for its shift
supervising hell. Deckard felt the familiar hot kiss
against his face, as he had every dry season he'd lived
through—survived, dehydrated—in L.A. The gutters
had filled with a fine red dust blown in from the desert,
an iron-oxide color beneath the twists and lines of neon
flickering into life, like a predictive vision of the dunes
of Mars. If the city's trucks didn't vacuum out the
streets every twenty-four hours—one of the huge container vehicles was already bumbling down the side of
the asphalt, slowly squeezing past and through the shuf-
fling ranks of pedestrians and the inching vans and old
rehab'd cars with their roof-mounted radiator filters—
then the whole place would wind up looking like the
rolling vistas outside the pressurized windows of the
colony hovels. Why bother to emigrate? Give in to

the nagging of the U.N. blimp hovering overhead, with its video screen full of high-pressure, high-volume inducements, and you'd wind up staring out at much the same gritty mess, without even the hope of pulling through until the monsoon season rolled around again. Behind the windshield of the vacuum truck, the driver's bored eyes, visible above a sterile white breath mask, watched as the prehensile, wide-nostrilled mechanical snout sucked the curbs temporarily bare.

There were more masks on the street, covering maybe one in three of the night's faces. Some masks improvised and cruder than the government-issue kind, others *haute couture* variants, from deranged silk organza wedding veils complete with tiny artificial orange blossoms, severely retro thirties side-perched pillboxes with falling black-dotted sweeps, to orthodox or mutated Islamic masks, rough nomadic Berber head wraps for men or androgen-pumped *butchoi*, delicate bell-laced gold for deep-trad women or kohl-eyed femmes.

A pack of prescavenger dwarfs, the aggressively mercantile kind that didn't wait for bits and scraps to be discarded before beginning the recycling process, wore vintage military gas masks, protecting themselves not only from the wind's dust but also the gasoline and freon fumes of the mech units they yanked and unbolted from the vulnerable traffic-stalled vehicles. Bomber goggles warded off the sulphuric Mace sprays from the drivers who came scrambling out from behind steering wheels when they heard the patter of tiny feet on their roofs. Hands in toddler-sized leather gloves flipped bird at the full-sized humans as the dwarfs tugged their oil-leaking trophies into the side lanes and mobile offices of the gypsy parts dealers who operated there.

Deckard caught a miniaturized glimpse of himself in the obsidian shades of someone, male or female, that the crowd's eddying currents bumped him right into. He backed off a step—hard to do, swimming against the tide—and saw the white jacket, a little tight across the shoulders, and his own face, masked by an apprehensive caution.

"What's your problem, mac?" A smoke-rasped voice, a man's, sounded from the lipsticked mouth below the shades. "New in town, sailor, or what?" A vocoder on a thin velvet choker took her voice down a couple of octaves. "Even if you're buying, I'm not selling, so why don't you stop hogging the sidewalk and let a lady get past?"

"Sorry." He managed to insert himself, shoulder first, into the traffic flow to one side. The last thing he wanted was a public altercation that would bring attention from the police *koban* on the corner. For all he knew, the uniformed cop inside the little surveillance booth had a photo poster of him tacked to the wall, right next to the direct line phone to the LAPD's central station.

Giving him a smile, the other person moved on. Gone, swallowed behind the backs of the crowd.

He walked, keeping pace with the rest, shoulders jostled with each passing collision. Passing the *koban*, face casually averted—from the corner of his eye, Deckard saw that the cop in the booth had already picked up the red phone, was shouting something, the words blanked by the glass barrier and the mumbling susurrus of the crowd's collective voice. His stomach clenched as he watched the cop's free hand raised in excited gesture. He kept his own limbs under rigid control, fighting down the impulse to run through the crowd, exposing his back to the first shot the cop would fire when he stepped out of the booth.

Take it easy. His own voice, inside his head. *Maybe it's not you they're looking for, maybe it's something else entirely . . .*

"A new world awaits you!"

It wasn't him. A big voice boomed from above, letting him off the hook.

"A new life!"

The cop pushed open the *koban*'s narrow door, jumping outside of it and looking up at the sky, the red police phone still at his ear. Voice audible now, but unintelligible in its shouted excitement.

"A *chance* to start *anew!*"

Deckard stopped and looked up, along with all the rest of the street coming to a halt. He'd been so caught up watching the *koban* officer that he hadn't noticed the rounded shape filling the sky, a faceted moon larger and closer than any before.

"In the off-world colonies!" The voice, the words heard so many times before that they'd become part of the city's nocturnal background noise, shouted giant words. A distorted sonic wash rolled an invisible tsunami over the sea of uplifted faces, the hands raised and pointing. The U.N. blimp drifted lower in torpid slow motion, coming down between the buildings on either side of the street, so near that Deckard thought he could reach up and touch the surface of its bulging underside.

The massive viewscreen on the blimp's flank stuttered optic static, blistering chaotic haze sweeping through the pixels of a Martian irrigation scene. Touched-up canals wavered, a green field of soybeans rippled seismic; Deckard saw now that a quarter of the blimp's antenna-spiked skin was enveloped in flame, tangible heat on heat in the wind-raked sky. As he watched, a bright spark trailed smoke from an alley opposite, the dull *whump* of a mortar round rolling through the onlookers. The shot hit the blimp's ridged frame, concaving another section of the metallic fabric. A second's fraction more, and the hollow burst into a fiery mouth, black tatters for teeth around the edges.

Farther above, at the top of the highest city tower, a geisha face winked and smiled, as though in approval of the blimp's death. As though the taste on the magnified woman's tongue was a piece of the upward-gouting fire itself, the blimp heeling onto one side to display its wound, the orange ball of flame sweetly acrid as an *umeboshi* plum.

The whole street lit orange, the dawning of a new, harsher, and more beautiful day.

Fireball hitting first, decompressed hydrogen in oxygen's explosive embrace. A wave of flame in the shape of a churning sphere, the collapsing U.N. blimp barely visible behind the eye-burning glare. The flames' enormous hand flattened the street, rush of heat and expanding pressure knocking screaming human forms hard to the pavement, tumbling them with hair alight or silken veils incinerated against gasping breaths, eyelashes scorched away.

Deckard felt the soft, hot pulse. Enough meters away that he was only knocked back against the wall of the building beside him, impact with brick and metal jarring him dizzy for a moment. Neon serpents, *kanji* store signs, hissed a rain of sparks, glass tubing shock-broken, upon him and the others who'd been knocked off their feet. Bracing himself against the wall, Deckard pushed himself upright, the figures around him still on their hands and knees, trying to crawl away across the bright shrapnel of the shattered windows, or gaping at the inferno crash, now at ground zero.

The blimp's rudimentary skeleton, meridians of an ovoid globe, showed through the engulfing flames. Another mortar had been fired, but with no incendiary charge. Instead, a grappling hook, prongs snapping into a sharp-pointed iron flower, ran a cord from the blimp's wreckage, back to an anchor point in the alley on the other side of the street. Hunched against the blaze's thermal force, Deckard shielded his eyes with his hand, squinting at the action on the other end of the taut line.

More of the blimp's frame twisted and burst rivets free as the hulk collapsed with terminal grandeur into the street, the blunt nose fire-wrapped and gouging a ragged furrow into the concrete; the tail end's stubby fins clawed out a row of tenth-story windows before tearing loose and sailing aloft on the fire's updraft.

Another pair of iron hooks, looped overhead and hand-thrown by the figures in the alley, snagged the black frame, drawing it down tighter, as though the burning craft were an animal that might tear loose in its agony and vault into the smoke-clouded sky. Deckard could see the men, a half dozen or so gritting their teeth, clad in white fireproof Nomex suits, tugging at the lines, leaning back with their feet braced against the ash-strewn pavement.

The lower edge of the blimp's billboard-sized view-screen hit the ground with a sharp jolt, evoking a last flicker of life from it. The visual programming went into skittering fast-forward mode.

The voice of the images screamed. No longer seductive, cajoling: *"A new life!"* Pitch whipping higher, as though in sudden fear: *"New life! Chance! New!"* Into the idiot ultrasonic, trembling the shards of glass left in the buildings' window frames: *"Start anew!"*

One of the attackers ran out from the alley, line and grappling hook circling over his head and uplifted hand. The dead and still living who'd been caught in the explosion sprawled at his feet as he let go, the hook singing toward the center of the tilted viewscreen. The pronged metal hit square the rapid play of colored photons. They flew apart, the rigid membrane that had trapped them now dissolving into razor bits, the circuitry beneath arcing into overload and meltdown. Deckard spun away, shielding his face with his arm, the fragments of glass and hot-tipped wires falling across his shoulders like hail.

"It's all lies!"

Another voice, amplified but not the one that had boomed, then screamed from the crashing blimp. He turned back to the street, the infinitesimal bell-like percussion of glass fragments chiming across the now-vacated street. One of the mortar crew—maybe the one who'd run out with the last grappling hook; he couldn't tell—had leapt onto one of the bent metal struts, the dying flames silhouetting his insulated form. The man had black carbon streaks across his wild-eyed face, a bullhorn in his thick-gloved hand.

"They're telling you lies!" Shouting through the flared horn, voice snapping its echo against the surrounding towers. "It's always been lies!"

Deckard stepped away from the wall behind him, to the curb and then down to the debris-filled street. Scraps of the blimp's fabric, still burning and exuding oily black smoke, spotted the asphalt. Distant sirens, approaching at ground level and in the sky, cut through the cries and shouts of the crowd that had packed the space only a few minutes before.

"You have to listen!" The voice coming out of the bullhorn had a fanatic's, a believer's, trembling edge. "Not to me . . . but to *them!*" Even from where Deckard stood, a mad illumination shone visible in the man's gaze. "They've come back . . . to tell us!" The man turned, holding on to an upright strut of the blimp's frame for balance, aiming the bullhorn's trajectory across all the angles of the street. "*They* know the truth! They've been shown the light! The light of the stars!"

From the corner of his eye, Deckard saw other motion. The *koban* booth had been toppled over in the explosion, pinning the uniformed cop. Face bloodied, the cop had now managed to get out from underneath and was struggling to get to his feet. He'd already drawn the heavy black gun from his belt.

"Humans! Jesus Christ doesn't love you anymore!" An aching whine of feedback tagged along with the words shrieking out of the bullhorn. "The eye of compassion has moved on! It sees only suffering! The eye of compassion no longer sees *you*—"

Deckard turned from the sight of the ranting figure, the blimp's smoldering ruins a pulpit, and saw the uniformed cop aiming the gun, arms outstretched, one hand folded over the other.

A red bloom appeared on the front of the ranting man's white Nomex jumpsuit. Silent now, he looked down. Then he crumpled, gloved hand letting go of the frame strut beside him, body folding around the splintered breastbone and falling to the flame-specked pavement.

"Hey!" With one hand braced against the metal weight on his leg, Deckard ran toward the cop. He ignored the black hole of the gun's snout swinging around in his direction. "They're over there! The ones who did it—" When the cop's shot had silenced the bullhorn, the rest of the crew in the alley had fled, abandoning the mortar behind them. Deckard pointed to another, closer space between the street's buildings. "I saw them go!"

He knew he had to work fast before the approaching LAPD spinners landed on the scene. The beams of their searchlights were already stabbing down from above, sweeping across the wreckage.

The cop, a net of blood over his face, still looked stunned. He let Deckard grab his arm and pull him toward the unlit space away from the street.

"Right back here—" In the buildings' shadow, he pushed the uniformed cop a step ahead of himself.

"Huh?" The cop raised his wobbling gun, aiming at nothing. "I don't see any—"

His words were cut off as Deckard brought the steel rod across his throat. Hands on either end, a knee braced hard against the small of the cop's back. A sharper tug and less than a minute of pressure on the windpipe, the cop dangling and struggling red-faced, then only dangling—he let go and the cop fell, palms and open mouth against the alley's heat-cracked cement.

He glanced over his shoulder as he bent above the unconscious cop. The police spinners had landed, their red and blue strobe flashers painting a luminous carnival across the building fronts and the downed U.N. blimp.

Paramedic units hovered above, waiting for the SWAT teams to finish securing the area. The hands of the injured clutched at the black-uniformed knees, then were kicked aside as the officers established a perimeter with assault rifles leveled in all directions.

Hands as hooks under the cop's arms, Deckard dragged him farther into the darkness. It took only a few minutes to strip the LAPD uniform off the lolling body, put it on with all buckles and other pieces of leather and chrome snapped tight. He wadded up the white jacket and his own dirt-stained clothing and tossed them away.

The cop, vulnerable-looking in bare skin and boring underwear, started to move, eyes fluttering open. Deckard fished the cuffs from the uniform's belt and fastened the cop's wrists behind a convenient drainpipe. Before the cop could make a sound, Deckard had the miranda gag slapped over the other man's face, the oxygen-permeable membrane stifling even the whisper of his breathing.

Deckard finishing pulling on the gloves of thin black leather, the last bit of the jackbooted ensemble. He ignored the shucked cop's squirmings and malevolent glare, searching through the belt's other pouches until he found what he was looking for. A rectangle of grey plastic, credcard-sized, with a row of pressure-sensitive dots along one edge.

He knew better than to try his own activation code. The pass cards were all linked on a high-freq'd trans net; his old numbers would undoubtedly set off every alarm in the central station's tracking unit.

The cop's gun had landed a couple of feet away. He picked it up, then leaned down and set its muzzle against the previous owner's forehead. "Let's be *real* quiet." With his other hand Deckard peeled back a corner of the gag. "Just whisper, okay?" The cop rolled his gaze toward the gun at his brow, then back to Deckard's face. "Just tell me your pass code."

"Get fucked."

"Wrong answer." He was familiar with the department's standard-issue small arms, from his own long-ago bull-walking days. Whereas this guy was young enough to be a rookie—why else would he have been stuffed into a cop-in-a-box *koban?*—and therefore breakable. Deckard pulled his crooked finger back just far enough to produce a nerve-racking click from inside the gun's machinery. "Try again."

No bravado this time. The cop rattled off a string of numbers, probably his own birth date; his face shone with a sudden tide of sweat. Deckard thumbed the code into the card. Chameleonlike, it changed from dead grey to an iridescent, slowly fading red. It would work.

"Thanks." He made sure the gag was sealed tight around the cop's mouth. He held the gun against the wet forehead a moment longer. "You know, I really *should* do this . . ." The debate inside his own head went the other way. One, he didn't want to confirm that asshole Isidore's estimation of him as a murderer of actual humans—which hadn't been proven to his satisfaction, anyway. And two, as far as the LAPD was concerned, it was one thing to be a murderer, another to be a cop-killer. Whatever dragnet was under way for him now, it'd be nothing compared to what'd ensue if he gave himself a jacket like that. Even if he managed to get away, out of the city, they'd come after him just to ice his ass. A matter of group loyalty. He took the gun away from the cop's forehead, reholstered it. "You just stay nice and quiet, right here."

That might be awhile, at least long enough for him to accomplish what he needed to do, the next step in his now-coalescing plan. Deckard scanned toward the mouth of the alley and the street beyond. The other cops who'd come swooping in looked to be busy, their investigation heading in the opposite direction, where the group who'd downed the U.N. blimp had disappeared; it'd likely be hours before they checked out this little pocket. He had no idea what all the commotion

had been about—mortar rounds and bullhorns, for
Christ's sake—but it'd all worked out to his benefit.
Now he had about twice the chance he'd had be-
fore . . .

Which was still just about a notch above zero.

Keeping close to the brick wall, to avoid being spotted, he slid farther down an alley.

To a door, easily kicked in. He found himself standing at the top of a low run of stairs. The small, clicking
echoes of mah-jongg tiles died away as a mixed group of
Asian and Anglo faces swung his way.

"This strictly social club." An officious woman in a
high-collared brocade dress fluttered before him. "All
money on tables for decorative purposes *only.*"

"Yeah, right." Around the edges of the basement
room, it looked to be *pai gow* at vicious stakes. The
whole world could've been coming to an end outside,
and the gamblers wouldn't have looked up. Deckard
strode through the low-ceilinged space, scooping up a
handful of cash from the center of one table, the usual
policeman's tax, and pocketing it. That could come in
handy as well. "Keep it that way."

Another flight of stairs took him up to the street on
the other side of the building. The crowd was thinner
here, a lot of it having headed over one block to gape
across the yellow POLICE INVESTIGATION tapes at the
fallen blimp and general disaster scene.

Head down, Deckard strode rapidly, the people on
the street parting to either side, making way for him. At
this clip, it wouldn't be long before he reached the central police station.

7

Holden opened his eyes.

"Wait a minute." Not lying down, but sitting up. No black attaché case, either gurgling or silent, strapped to his chest. Holden looked down at his own right hand prodding his sternum. A strip of navy-blue cloth dangled from his throat. "What the . . ." His voice louder now as well, almost deafening as it reverberated inside his skull. "What happened . . ."

"I had to break into that storage locker downtown, that one where all your stuff got shoved when they cleaned out your old apartment." A now-familiar voice sounded from somewhere nearby. "Sorry about that. There might be somebody you could bill for the padlock I busted."

Holden looked over and saw Roy Batty sprawling with hands clasped behind his head, folding metal chair tilted back onto its rear legs. Watching him. He glanced down at himself again and saw that the strip of cloth was a necktie, one of his own good silk ones. The white shirt and grey suit, and everything else, were his as well. Stuff from another life, the one he'd lived before he'd gotten blown away at the Tyrell Corporation headquarters. Another life, another world.

"How you feeling? You feeling okay?" Batty had rocked forward in the metal chair. He examined a small remote control in one hand. "The doctors said these settings were about right, for your body weight and everything. You lost some muscle mass while you were flopped down in the hospital for so long. The works we implanted will automatically adjust for when you start getting back in shape. Probably give you a little more blood flow then, I guess."

Holden pushed the necktie aside and undid a couple of the shirt buttons. His bare chest was no longer an open, gutted wound; no tubes or hoses sticking out, either. An intricate map of scars and black stitches overlaid his pallid white skin.

"Don't go poking too much at those. They're not too fragile—I made 'em use the heavy-duty sutures— but you don't want to get them infected."

Holden traced his fingertip down one of the vertical lines. A dull twinge of pain, as though wired to tissue deep inside him. Plus either the faint sense or hallucination of muted ticking and sucking noises buried underneath the reconstructed flesh and bone.

"What's going on?" He looked up at Batty. "What's been done to me?"

"What, you worried about the bill or something? Jeez." Batty shook his head in amazement. "It's paid for, okay? You've been given a new lease on life, buddy. Free, gratis, *por nada*. So don't sweat it. Enjoy it, already."

"Implants . . ." He laid his hand flat against his stitched chest, feeling against his palm the hum and surge of the machinery inside him. "A complete set . . . heart and lungs . . ." He took a deep breath, a last trace of spider-silk lifting from his brain. At the back of his throat was a taste of plastic and stainless steel.

"State of the art. None finer." Batty held up the remote. "I told the people here to use the best parts they could get. None of those pulls they've taken out of other jobs and had sitting in a bucket somewhere."

"But they told me . . . at the hospital . . ." A tone of wonder in his voice. "They told me one time, when they brought me around, that they couldn't do implants. The damage was too great . . ."

"So? They lied to you. Simple."

Nothing cleared up by that. "Why would they lie? The doctors, and Bryant and everybody . . . it doesn't make sense."

Batty's smile rose, thin and all-knowing. "Makes sense . . . depending upon who you figure your friends are. Your *real* friends."

The spooky hint of conspiracy in Batty's voice set him thinking. "Could I see that?" He held out his hand for the remote control.

"Sure."

Only a couple of buttons on the device. "This switches everything off? Switches *me* off?" Holden didn't wait for an answer. He put the remote down on the floor and crushed it with his heel. A sound of splintering plastic and microchips, followed by a surge in his heartbeat, which then settled back down.

"Way to go!" Batty tilted his head back and laughed. The flimsy prefab walls trembled with his hilarity. "I'm sure they got another one of those things around here somewhere, but I admire your attitude. A couple, what, maybe four hours ago, you were at death's door . . . literally. That fuckin' hospital. Man, people go to places like that just to punch out. And they help you do it. Now here you are—" He gestured expansively toward Holden. "Feeling like your old self, I bet. Miracles of modern science. You got nothing to complain about."

Holden turned his head toward an uncurtained window. He'd seen that it was still dark outside, but he hadn't known what night this was, the same one in which Batty had snatched him out of the hospital, or one weeks or months later. "Your people here work fast." He looked back toward Batty.

"They're good at what they do. Get a lot of practice, I suppose."

Inside himself, he sensed the continuous operation of the bio-machines—the new parts of his body, the conglomeration of Teflon and inert alloys and efficient little motors that he'd absorbed, incorporated into the Dave Holden gestalt. He'd been raised from the dead. The suit and tie, the neat, machinelike precision of these outward manifestations, also part of that. He had been dead in the hospital, dead before he got there, dead as soon as he'd been a messy piece of meat bleeding around a smoking hole at its center. That weak, sloppy thing in the hospital bed, leaking fluids, pinned naked by plastic tubes and hoses—that hadn't been him, the real Dave Holden.

He spread his hands on his knees, studied as though for the first time. *Like scalpels*, he mused. Not just the hands, but everything about him. A cutting instrument, sterile out of the autoclave. Putting the *blade* in *blade runner*. That was why he'd been so good at his job, at hunting down and retiring replicants: he'd out-machined them. He'd beaten out all the other blade runners as well, like that whiner Deckard; he'd gone all the way around the Curve and come out the other side. Come out as something . . . *other* than human. Until Kowalski . . .

"You still stewing about that? Getting blown away by some big moron?" Batty had read his thoughts, as though his eyes were gauges like those on the big machines he'd been hooked up to. "Get over it." Shrugged, smiling. "Or don't."

"No . . ." Holden slowly shook his head. "I'm just . . . wondering." He noticed a pack of cigarettes and a lighter sitting out on a table between them;

whether they were Batty's or for him, he didn't know. "You mind?" He leaned forward and took the pack.

An expression of mild distaste. "You know you'll have to change your filter—the one inside you—twice as often, if you start that up again."

"It's worth it." He leaned back and exhaled, then studied the drift of blue smoke above him. The nicotine seeping into his machine-aerated blood made him feel even more efficient and confident, as though all the tiny valves inside had been fed drops of lubricating oil. His old self. "Definitely."

"Whatever." Batty's smile returned. "So what was it you were wondering?"

He knew he had to be cautious. The one more thing he would have liked to have had restored to him was his big black hammer of a weapon. He could see the bulge and the lopsided tug of weight inside the black leather jacket that indicated Batty was packing.

"Oh . . ." Holden glanced around at the buckling prefab walls. A collection of photos torn from magazines, nudes and tropical vistas, all equally unlikely, rustled in the hot dry wind seeping in through the seams. "You know. Like what the hell *is* this place?"

"Didn't you see the sign when they wheeled you in? It's the Reclamation Center."

"Never heard of it."

"Of course not," said Batty. "It wouldn't be a top-secret police installation if some schmuck like you knew about it."

"Looks to me like they're just pulling parts off some old trashed-out police vehicles." He tilted his head toward the window with its view of the wrecking yard beyond the fence. "What's so top secret about that?"

"Are you kidding?" Batty emitted a sharp barking laugh. "You know what happens to your appropriations money if the state or the feds find out you're recycling your rolling stock? Shit—they'll cut you off without a *dime*. Besides . . ." A shrug. "Keep something like this secret, makes it that much easier to keep the other stuff they do here under wraps. Stuff like cramming a nice new set of pumping gear inside *you*." He jabbed an index finger toward Holden. "You gotta admit, the folks out here have taken good care of you."

"The people at the hospital—where I was before—they were supposed to be taking care of me."

"That's true." Batty's smile grew wider, wicked with delight. "Like I said, a lot depends upon knowing who your real friends are."

He mulled that over for a moment. "It was the police department that put me in that ward. When I got shot . . ."

"Yeah, well, there's police . . . and then there's *other* police. You gotta cover your action, buddy, all around the table—if you're going to stay in this game."

Holden narrowed his gaze, studying the figure sitting opposite him. "Maybe so. What I'd like to know is . . . what kind of police have replicants working for them?"

A shake of the head. "None that I know of. That's not what police *do*. As a general rule, police are pretty much *death* on replicants."

"Then what're you doing here?"

"Huh?" Batty's smile faded. "What's that supposed to mean?"

"Come on." Holden felt a little surge of excitement, a dangerous pulse. "Tell me—do these people here know that you're a replicant? Or have you pulled it off?"

"*I'm* a replicant?" Batty looked genuinely puzzled, eyes widening. Then he started laughing, uproariously this time, face reddening in bright contrast to his spiked crop of white hair, tears wetting the wrinkled corners of his eyelids. "That's good." He could barely get the words out. "That is . . . *so* good." The prefab walls rattled with his laughter.

"What's so funny?" All the hilarity was getting on Holden's nerves.

"That you'd think . . ." Batty pushed himself back in the chair with a hand against his chest, making a visible effort to sober himself up. "Sorry. It's that I just realized what you've been thinking. What must've been going around in your head all along, or at least since I showed up. You think I'm a replicant, right? A Roy Batty replicant." He wiped his eyes with his fingertips. "That's good. That's a really good one."

"Did you catch any of that action over on Alvarado? Where the blimp went down?"

Took a while for Deckard to respond to the question, the hard voice right beside him. He leaned back against the wall of the elevator as it crept toward the base of the building. "A little bit."

"I got called in, all the way over from Slauson. Another ten minutes and I would've been off-shift, and the dispatchers could've radioed to the moon for my ass." The cop spoke with no inflection, all traces of emotion drained from the process of communicating.

"Yeah, they like jerking you around." Deckard kept his own voice at that dead, menacing tone, the words coming out with that slow, reptilian ease they all cultivated. He knew that for his apparent age there should be more stripes on this uniform's sleeve. A fierce Darwinian attitude operated among the department's rank-and-file; they ate their own weaker members, to keep themselves lean and mean. Surviving some of the shit that happened down in the locker rooms was the hardest part of the job. If he was going to pull off penetrating the LAPD's central station, he'd have to give off the same ugly gamma rays that these guys did.

He risked a glance up to the level indicator above the elevator's doors. There was another twenty floors to go. He'd managed to flag a lift from a county jail spinner, the big grey bus with the barred windows, that'd been returning to the police department's Kwik-Justice Kourts for another load of plea-bargained felons. His disguise, the patrol uniform he'd stripped off the cop he'd left in the alley, seemed to sail right past the pilot and the guard. The card and pass code had gotten him from the landing deck and into the building. A spark of hope had ignited inside his chest that he'd be able to get into the station, past all the other cops crawling all over it. And get to Bryant. That was the only plan he had. And the only hope. Of getting out of L.A. alive and getting back to Rachael, asleep in her black coffin. Guarded by owls and all the little nocturnal forest creatures, like an old fairy tale.

God knew that Bryant owed him a favor—or more accurately, a whole string of them, from all the times he'd carried the bucket for Bryant, the blade runner unit, and the whole LAPD by extension. He'd pulled everybody's *cojones* off the chopping block on more occasions than he could count.

On some invisible clock, the hands pointed to payback time for all that loyalty he'd shown Bryant. He just hoped that the police inspector could read it as well. All he needed was information; that didn't seem like much.

"If you asked me . . ." A voice broke into Deckard's thoughts. "I'd say we should kill them all."

Then who would sort them out? he wondered. He didn't know. He glanced over at the cop beside him in the elevator. For a few moments he'd gotten lost in his worried plotting. Not a good thing—he knew he'd have to stay hyper-alert if he was going to get in and out of this building.

The cop had relaxed, a bit of the anal-retentive steel going out of his spine; he rested his shoulder blades against the wall of the small space. Without taking off his glasses, he wearily rubbed his forehead with one black-gloved hand. A long shift, maybe a back-to-back.

Calculating his overtime pay and brooding about whether it was worth the burnout.

Deckard almost felt sorry for the guy. At least with promoting to the blade runner unit, you got to set your own hours. This poor bastard wouldn't stand any chance of getting off patrol, if it got logged into his package, his personnel file, that he'd let a wanted man ride all the way down with him to the station's ground floor.

"Kill all who?" asked Deckard.

"Eh, those goddamn rep-symps." The cop's face set into a scowl. "They're so fond of friggin' replicants, then we should treat 'em the same way." He lifted his hand, stuck out his index finger to make a gun, then curled it into the invisible trigger. "Bam. Instant retirement."

The term *rep-symp* was a new one to Deckard. Replicant sympathizer?—that seemed the likeliest. Some new development, while he'd been gone from L.A.?

The cop was waiting for him to say something, to make conversation. "Yeah—" He nodded. "Crazy bastards."

"Crazy's not the word for it." The cop's mouth twisted with loathing. "*Traitorous* is more like it. They got their own species they belong to. If they don't like being human, they shouldn't wait for somebody like us to come around and solve their problems for them. They got guns—shit, they got heavy artillery. Let 'em all suck off some nine-millimeter rounds; then they won't *be* human anymore. They'll be hamburger."

Deckard kept his face stone, his eyes the only thing moving as he glanced up again at the level indicator. Only a few more floors to go—the elevator had started to slow, braking to its coming halt.

"Some of those things those rep-symps say . . ." The cop standing beside him had gone into a bitter monologue, the looped tape in his head running off its spool. "Where do they come up with that stuff? You heard what that one jerk was spouting off about, before he got plugged. What a load of crap."

The elevator came to a thumping stop, the doors sliding back.

"Take it easy." The cop pushed himself away from the back of the elevator. He didn't look back as he walked out onto the ground floor of the LAPD's central station.

Deckard gazed past the metal-framed opening in front of him and across the vaulted spaces beyond. The icy blue glow of the building's exterior security lights traced shadows through the towering windows, inscribing a crosshatch of lines along the arches' overhead crescents. At this level of the ancient train station onto which the police department's headquarters had been grafted, the air-conditioning was all retro-fit and inadequate. The spaces near the ornate ceiling shimmered with bottled-up heat; a fine mist hung below that, composed of equal parts cop sweat and the more rancid tang of perp fear.

He turned his head, scanning.

The station's ground floor was packed with cops, more than he ever remembered seeing here before. The black uniforms, the jackboots and peaked caps, gleamed like oiled chains. It took him a while to realize what was going on. He'd never been in the station, not since he'd worn a uniform, during shift change. Blade runners kept their appointments at the dead hours between.

He also knew, as he stood in the elevator's open booth of light, that every face out there, wearing silver over its eyes or not, would turn his way if he didn't move his ass. Even through the miasma locked in here, they'd smell their quarry, frozen in the dazzle of the cops' sight lines.

He stepped out of the elevator, pushing his way through the crowd. His black leather shoulders shoved against the others, his face the same hard mask as theirs.

Holden gazed hard at the creature sitting opposite him. Inside, confidence slightly shaken, he couldn't get a readout on this Roy Batty. Whatever his sixth sense whispered, his honed blade runner instinct, it was all fuzzy and indistinct. At the same time, he knew from experience that these escapees from the off-world colonies survived—or tried to—by playing mind games. "You're going to tell me you're not a replicant?"

"Something like that." Batty wasn't laughing anymore. "You've got it backward, fellow. When I told you I was Roy Batty, I didn't mean some creepy lowwatt version of me. I meant *me*, period. I'm the real Roy Batty. The human one. I'm the . . . what's it called . . . the template—"

"Templant," corrected Holden. This was a possibility that hadn't even occurred to him. "That's the technical term."

"Yes . . . that's it. I'm the templant for that Roy Batty replicant that you and your buddies, you hotshot blade runners, were assigned to retire."

"That one . . ." Holden's voice went soft, meditative. "Bryant told me that one was dead."

"He was right about that, at least." Batty shook his head in disgust. "That sucker crapped out. Just *died*. The four-year life span the Tyrell Corporation built into their Nexus-6 models—that's four years under normal operating conditions. It's like buying a new spinner: you put any stress load on at all and your warranty's invalidated. You got a pile of dead meat on your hands, is what you got." His face set even grimmer. "You know, it's *embarrassing* to have a shoddy buncha products like that walking around with your face on them."

"Wait a minute. You're saying there's more than one?"

"Of course." Batty tilted his head to one side, studying Holden for a moment. "I've noticed this before, that you blade runners just aren't hip to the realities of modern industrial practices. Economics and stuff—I would've thought you'd know this, just to get a handle on what you're doing. The nature of the beast, so to speak.

"Of *course* there's more than one Roy Batty replicant. You think the Tyrell Corporation would tool up for a whole production run and then just make a single unit? Christ, they're probably making more of 'em right *now*. And shipping 'em off-world to the colonies, all packed away in their transport module boxes, like big ol' Ken dolls or something. I understand it was a pretty popular model—the Roy Batty replicant, I mean. Lot of orders came in for it." His face darkened to a scowl. "Not that you'd know it from the royalty statements that I get from the Tyrell Corporation. I tell you, man. That reserve against returns they hold back . . . it just gripes my ass."

Holden stayed silent for a moment, trying to get his thoughts started up again. He felt the emptiness of the desert's vast unpeopled spaces, just beyond the building's thin walls. Unfamiliar territory, a long way from the Los Angeles that he was used to moving around in. Same way with the stuff that Batty was telling him. "Let me get this straight. You get royalties?" The only question he could think of to ask. "On what? Your personality or something?"

"Hell, yes." Spine going rigid, Batty looked offended. "On my personality, my expertise—my *experience*. Everything I've got up here." He tapped his forehead. "I've got nearly half a century of smarts, what I was born with and what I developed the hard way; I went into this business when I was barely old enough to shave. And I got my ass handed to me, plenty of times, right off the bat. You become a mercenary, a military combat specialist, as young as I did, they're signing you up to be nothing but cannon fodder. You're a minimum-wage corpse, man." He folded his arms across his chest. "Some of these fuckin' replicants think they got it so bad; they ain't seen shit. I did some tours where the survival rate was one in twenty—Schweinfurt, Provo, Novaya Zemlya. Hell, at Caracas the rate was one in *fifty*. But I was that one." Setting his hands on his knees, he leaned forward, eyes radiant diamond points. "And you know why?"

Inside Holden, one of the bio-mechanical heart valves trembled. "Why?"

The thin edge of Batty's crazy smile appeared. "Because . . . part of my brain's wired in backward. I was *born* that way. Unique. Way inside." He gestured with a fingertip pressed above his ear, twisting it like a drill bit. "Neural malformation, calcium deposits on both the right and left amygdala. That's the brain structure that creates the emotional response of fear. Usually, people with this condition—it's pretty rare—they just don't feel fear. There's no physiological or emotional response. My head's better. The amygdalae are webbed through a whole batch of my major serotonin receptor sites. Situations that scare other people shitless—I get off on them. I *like* 'em." The corners of his smile lengthened, his eyes glittering. "Nothing can scare me. The more people try, the worse things get . . . the happier I am."

"Sounds handy."

"Yeah, well . . ." Batty shrugged, looking pleased with himself. "It's like with people who don't have pain responses—you know? They have to be real careful not to hurt themselves accidentally. There's no feedback for them to adjust their behavior. It took me a long time— most of my life—to develop an *intellectual* understanding of fear. Just so I could recognize it in other people's faces. And so I wouldn't go waltzing into situations where I'd be sure to get killed. But yeah, it's handy. Makes me a *cold* motherfucker. Just think what it'd be like if you chicken-hearted blade runners had heads built that way; you could really get some major damage done." His expression turned to pity. "As it is, it's why you guys don't have a chance against the Tyrell Corporation's Nexus-6 models . . . *especially* the Roy Batty replicant. All the Nexus-6 types have a little bit of this, but that model in particular—'cause it's an exact copy of me—all of the Roy Batty replicants are in *serious* kick-ass mode. You guys are just *lucky* if one of them ups and dies on you. That's the only way you'd survive an encounter with a Roy Batty replicant."

The other's boasting irritated Holden. "That Batty replicant didn't run into me."

"Just as well, for your sake. You got iced by that Leon Kowalski model, and that thing's a goddamn moron by comparison. If you'd hit on the Roy Batty one, there wouldn't have been enough left of you to stick an artificial heart into."

"Maybe." Holden kept his own voice level and cold. "I wouldn't mind having the chance at one."

"You're not likely to get it. The Roy Batty replicant that was running around in L.A. was the only one that ever made it back to Earth. The U.N. authorities know what a loose cannon one of them can be—I've worked for U.N. security, so they're hip to what a version of me is like—so they keep them under wraps or way out in the far colonies. How that one got close enough to make a break for Earth . . . that was a screwup. Somebody wasn't paying attention."

"You're with the U.N.?" He was still trying to piece together what the deal was.

Batty shook his head. "Not right at the moment. And I never was *officially* hooked up with them. I was always more of a freelance operative, you might say. Mercenary. That's how I built up my rep. Then I hired on with the Tyrell Corporation—old Eldon Tyrell recruited me himself. That was because he wanted the best, and he could afford it."

The picture was starting to get a little clearer. "What did you do for the Tyrell Corporation?"

"Eh, some troubleshooting, some industrial strong-arm stuff—there were still a couple of other companies turning out replicants back then, and Eldon decided he didn't want the competition anymore. So they got . . . kind of *eliminated*. One way or another. And then I was on retainer for a coupla years, while they were checking me out in the corporation's labs. Doing the brain-scan thing—that's when they found out about the cross-wired amygdala. That was pretty much the kickoff for the Nexus-6 development program." Batty shrugged. "After the production line started rolling, I moved over to personal bodyguard stuff, covering old man Tyrell's ass."

He decided to risk a needle probe, just to see how Batty would react. "You must not have been doing a very good job. They told me in the hospital how Tyrell got killed."

"Not on my watch. I quit months before that went down. Man, I'd decided long before then that I wasn't going to work for those bastards anymore." Batty's face turned dark and brooding, gaze fixed on some inner vision. "I'm telling you—there's some sick people over there. Eldon Tyrell might've been the worst of them, but they're *all* fuckin' nuts. Some of the things I've seen . . ." He shook his head. "You know, there's a big red button over in the Tyrell Corporation headquarters—the U.N. made 'em put it in when the place was built. Just a little safeguard, in case some of the stuff they were dinking around with ever got out of hand." His voice twisted with bitter loathing. "I'd *love* to push that red button, and just stand back and watch the whole friggin' place come down. It'd be just what those sonsofbitches deserve."

A few more notes were jotted down on the file Holden had begun assembling inside his skull. Whatever else this Batty might be following through on—whoever else's orders he was executing—he had a personal agenda as well.

"Tell you what." The cigarette had been smoked down close to his knuckles while he'd been listening to

Batty. He stubbed it out against the arm of the chair. "Suppose I accept for the time being this story you've been giving me. I'll accept—provisionally—that you're the templant for any Roy Batty replicants. That you're human."

"Oh, thanks." A wry smirk settled on Batty's face. "What, you want me to prove it to you? There's probably an old Voigt-Kampff machine sitting on a shelf out here. You could run an empathy test on me, if it'd make you feel better."

Holden shook his head. "I couldn't get any worthwhile results off somebody like you. Too much of a professional gloss—you probably know all the questions and answers already. There's no baseline I could establish for your involuntary response times." He picked up the lighter and ran his thumb across its smooth plastic surface. "Don't sweat it; as I said, I'm accepting for the time being that you're human. Why not? The only problem is, that still doesn't explain much." He flicked the lighter and regarded Batty over the thin, wavering flame. "Such as—why'd you bust me out of the hospital? And why'd you bring me here?"

"Here's easy." Batty's hand gestured toward the building's walls. "I've got friends out here. I've had a long time to build up favors that people owe me—I cashed in a few to get you your new lungs. But actually, it works both ways. Not everybody in the LAPD is as dumb as you blade runners. There's some of them who'd like to know what the hell's going on. And that's what I'm helping them find out."

" 'Going on—' " He snapped off the flame. "What're you talking about?"

"You haven't got a clue, do you?" The pitying gaze again. "Wake up and smell the synapses burning, Holden. How do you think you wound up getting blown away by that Kowalski replicant? I mean, other than by your being less than brilliant. And what do you think's been happening to all the other blade runners?

You know how many of your pals have landed in the boneyard? Even *before* you did your stint in the hospital."

"I don't keep count of stuff like that." Holden shrugged. "It happens."

"Yeah, well, it's been happening a lot, buddy. The only smart one in your crew was that guy Deckard. At least he had the sense to take off before he could be set up to take a hit." He pointed his finger. "A hit like the one *you* took."

"Bullshit. I never took any hit. Kowalski got the drop on me, that's all."

"He got the drop on you, all right—in a secured area of the Tyrell Corporation headquarters. Hey, I know what the security measures are like over there; I was a consultant on most of them. Do you have any idea of how many metal detectors and alarm systems Kowalski would've had to pass through with that gun? It's impossible. Somebody had to have either passed him the gun in the secured area, right before you started to interview him, or they switched off the detectors. Either one of those things would've had to be done by somebody with clearance right up at the top level."

"That's guesswork." Holden shifted uneasily in the chair. "You have any proof?"

"Oh . . . bits and pieces." The smile radiated smug self-assurance. "You had a recorder running when you were giving the test to Kowalski. I've heard that tape—one of my pals in the department smuggled a copy out to me. Very dramatic . . . especially the part where you take it in the chest. But the best part isn't even anything you or the Kowalski replicant said. You can hear it in the background of the tape, from the p.a. voice: *Attention . . . we have a B-1 security alert.* Know what that means? That's the Tyrell Corporation's internal code for detected tampering with the security grid. All the time you were talking with Kowalski, the people over in the admin offices were running around, trying to

figure out where the rip in the net was. Of course, by
the time they did find out, you were lying on your back,
wearing a hole a small dog could walk through."

"An alarm went off. Big deal." Holden shrugged.
"If it'd meant anything—if it'd had some connection
with my getting shot—the police would've checked it
out."

"Sure. Unless the police were in on it already."

"Now," said Holden, "you're talking conspiracy.
And this is where it all falls apart. Because it would've
been Inspector Bryant who handled any such investigation. And you know, I worked for Bryant a long time. I
can assure you—he wouldn't take kindly to somebody
setting up any of his men. Bryant's got a blade runner
heart. Anybody screws with his operation, Bryant would
bust 'em wide open." Holden leaned back in the chair.
"That's something you could bank on."

Batty had listened, nodding slowly, his smile growing thin and subtle. "You know . . . you may not be a
genius, Dave, but you got a persistent little mind. That's
kinda admirable. I can do business with you." He stood
up, winging his arms back to work out a kink in his
spine. "Come on, I got something to show you." He
gestured with one hand as he headed for the door.
"Come on—you'll really get off on this."

Outside, Holden followed him across the bare,
packed sand of the Reclamation Center compound. This
far away from the city, the stars shot down hard pin-
pricks of diamond light, unobscured by any smoldering
haze. The day's heat radiated up from the ground, as
though the path led over buried coals.

"Right in here." Batty had stopped in front of what
looked to be a shack made of corrugated steel, rust
stains weeping from the fasteners along the seams. He
fished a ring of keys from his jacket pocket and pulled a
padlock open. "Don't be afraid of the dark."

Holding his hands out to either side, as though for
balance, Holden stood waiting in the middle of the nar-

row space. A radiance bluer than the stars suddenly fell
across him. He turned and spotted Batty silhouetted by
a video monitor. As his eyes adjusted, he saw the rest of
the gear mounting to the bare metal ceiling, monitors
still unlit, racks of butch military electronics.

"Check this out." Batty flipped switches, adjusted
dials. A blue spark zapped his fingertips. "Damn. I told
them to put a humidifier in here . . ." An image swam
into focus on the monitor. "Know what this is?"

"Of course." He recognized the log-on screen. "It's
the LAPD data banks."

"Sure as shit. We got a direct trunk line into the
system here, hard-wired cable fifty feet down, staggered
repeater circuits. Can't get better picture quality inside
the station. Now watch this." From the key ring, Batty
took a plastic card with a hole punched in one corner, a
magnetic strip down the side. He ran it through a slot
reader. "Voilà."

"Christ . . ." What he saw rocked Holden back on
his heels. The access level had rolled back to a string of
four zeroes. As far as he knew, the chief of police had a
level of zero-zero-zero-one.

"Don't try to get this away from me." Batty
snapped the card back onto the key ring. "It's coded to
my sweat genotype."

He watched as Batty voice-commanded through
one directory branch after another. The guy seemed to
know what he was doing.

"Here's what I wanted you to see."

ID scans, stocking-capped heads going through 360-
degree rotations. First, the Roy Batty replicant, then a
young blond, strange-looking woman, then an older-
looking brunette. Then Kowalski; an involuntary flinch
response went off in Holden's gut. Beneath each scan
were lines of information, sub-type classifications and
the like.

"So?" Holden glanced away from the screen, over

toward Batty. "The department's keeping its files up-dated. What did you expect them to be doing?"

"You're not tracking, pal." With his fingernail, Batty tapped the corner of the screen. "Look at the date. That's when this information—including the photo scans—was logged into the system." Smile. "Take a *good* look."

He sighed. "If it makes you happy . . ." Holden looked at the monitor again.

Simple digits. 2019 for the year, last year; 24 for the day. And in between those, 10 for the month. *That'd make it,* thought Holden, *a week before Halloween.* That seemed appropriate. Old pagan holiday, trick or treat . . .

"October," he said aloud. The realization came to him, perfect and clear. "This information was in the system in October."

"That's right." Nothing funny in Batty's thin smile. "And Bryant sent you out to the Tyrell Corporation headquarters the first week of November 2019. He sent you out there, *without showing you these ID scans.*"

"He told me . . ." As though from a distance, Holden heard his own voice, barely audible. "He told me that there weren't any scans or photos of the es-caped replicants. He told me that the off-world authori-ties didn't have any . . . that the data couldn't be sent . . . something like that. And I'd have to go out there with the Voigt-Kampff machine and run the em-pathy tests on all of Tyrell's new employees . . . to find which ones were the replicants . . ."

"Look at the access record." Batty called up an-other screen. His finger tapped the glass again. "Bryant pulled these scan files out of the police department data banks three times before he gave you the assignment. He even printed out hard copies. The photos of the escaped replicants—by which you would've been able to recognize them *without* running any tests—were probably sitting in one of his desk drawers the whole time, the last time he talked to you in his office."

"But that would mean . . ." The pieces had linked up inside his head. It just took time to speak of them. "But that would mean Bryant sent me out there : . . to the Tyrell headquarters . . . to get killed."

"Figure it out." Batty laid a hand on Holden's shoulder. His voice soft, almost kind. "If you were putting together a conspiracy to eliminate the blade runners—for whatever reason—who'd be better for it than the man in charge of them?"

A tiny glimmer of light shone inside his skull. As Holden turned his gaze back toward the pure, empty glow of the monitor, he thought he'd started to understand.

And a joy as pure flooded his soul.

A smaller space, its own little world. As familiar to Deckard as the one he'd just walked across.

With its own smells, even its own dust, residue of time past. Deckard closed the door behind himself. Through the glass pane, with Bryant's name showing in reverse on it, the fragmented light of the station's ground floor folded shadows across the desk and the file cabinets.

He stood motionless, scoping out the room's darkness. Nobody had recognized him, stopped him as he'd made his way here from the bank of elevators. The virtue of machines, at least on this occasion, was their anonymity.

The blinds over the office's windows kept anyone from seeing him in here, while still leaking through enough light for him to gradually make out the rat's-nest clutter with which the space was stuffed.

"Bryant?" Keeping his voice low, he stepped into the center of the room. When he'd found the door unlocked, and had been able to slide right in with just a glance over his shoulder to make sure no one had been watching, he'd expected to find his old boss in here. Even though the desk lamp was switched off—he knew that Bryant often did his deepest brooding with the lights out and the scotch bottle close at hand. The inspector had been keeping night hours for so long that his skin, beneath his slob stubble and alcohol flush, was as pallid as a cave fish or a corpse. "You in here?" Deckard took another step closer to the desk.

A blue glow fell across him. Shielding his eyes with one hand, he saw the blunt rectangle of a video monitor in front of him, the screen at the height where Bryant's face should have been. A short-legged tripod, monitor fastened to its top plate, sat in the chair behind the desk, a set of cables dangling from it and looped snakelike into a wall socket behind.

"Hiya, pal." Bryant's jowly visage came into focus on the screen. His small eyes glinted through the low-rez mesh of a video transmission. "Good to see you again." Even in black-and-white, his smile's yellow-stained teeth were still apparent. "Thanks for stopping by."

"What the hell's going on?" Deckard spotted a small video-cam on the desktop, geared to a motorized tracking pivot. A red dot from the device had fastened onto his chest; when he moved to one side, the camera followed his motion, keeping him in sight. "What's all this for?"

"It's a friggin' pain in the butt, is what it is." As though the monitor were a tiny room in which he was trapped, Bryant leaned forward, short-sleeved elbows resting on a desktop somewhere else. The camera tracking him took a moment to refocus. "I'm in quarantine. Caught a bug—or at least I got exposed to one. One of those new jobbies that keep coming up from Belize." His wheezing voice came from a small intercom speaker on his desk. "I made the jackass mistake of helping make a collar in the flop palace behind my apartment building—hell, I was off-duty and everything. Supposed to've been catching my sleep rather than wrestling some disease-ridden, spickety wog bastard to the ground, like I was some young pup. Next thing you know, I got the department medics telling me there's antibodies the size of Buicks cruising my bloodstream." One of his big, hair-backed hands gestured toward the screen. "Hey, make yourself comfortable. Have a seat."

Deckard pulled up the other chair and sat down, scanning through the narrow spaces between the blinds' slats; nobody outside appeared to have noticed anything going on in the office. He pushed the chair back a couple of inches, to avoid the monitor's glow washing across him. "I guess you heard I was in town."

"I heard. News travels fast in a place like this. I mean, the docs got me stuck over here in the infirmary, doing everything by remote, and I still knew about it."

He peered closer at the image on the screen. "Are you going to be all right?" Even in person, it would've been hard to determine if Bryant was well, sick, or dying. "You going to live through whatever this is?"

"Hell, yes." Bryant shook his head. "Don't worry about me, pal. You're the one with his ass in a sling. Me, they've got so pumped with wonder drugs I could crap a pharmacy. They'll probably be letting me loose in a day or two."

"Because I need you up and running. You owe me big time, Bryant." He spoke softly, urgently, aware of the footsteps and barely muffled voices of the cops walking by, just beyond the office's thin walls. "I bailed you out plenty of times. Now you gotta do it for me."

"Well, well, well. What an interesting development." A sadistic delight radiated from the face on the monitor screen. "And I thought you were the guy who was all through with the blade runner unit. You gave the impression that you didn't like us anymore. Hurt my feelings, Deckard. Just about broke my heart—you were the best man on the squad. You always were. And then for you to just walk out on us, like you didn't even *care* . . ." The intercom speaker transmitted the sound of Bryant sucking his breath in through his discolored teeth. "Especially this last time. You walked a long ways, pal; I didn't expect to ever see you around these parts again."

"If it'd been up to me, you wouldn't have."

"That attitude's not winning any points with me. You want us to be friends again, then you should start acting friendly. Then maybe I'd feel like helping you out." Bryant reached off camera, his hand returning with a bottle and an empty glass. "Let's be friends." He poured out a shot. "Come on, you know I've got some of the good stuff there. And I *hate* to drink alone."

He felt his brow dampening with sweat, the chair arms slick under his palms. *Jerking me around*, thought Deckard, anger stifled to a heated rock in his chest. Exactly the kind of little games Bryant had always liked to play. He didn't have any choice but to go along. Sitting on the corner of the desk was another bottle, the duplicate of the one Bryant had in his quarantine chamber, and a pair of glasses. One was still clean; he poured a brown finger and knocked back half of it. "There. Satisfied?" The alcohol burned along his throat. Bryant's notion of the good stuff was anything you could set a match to.

"All right, all right; jeez. Prickly bastard." Bryant set his own empty glass down, his face heavy and brooding. "With the kind of enemies you got, you should cultivate your friends more. You could use 'em." He poured another shot, swirled it around in the glass, watching. "Fact of the matter is, I don't have a clue as to why anybody would want to haul your sorry ass back here. I sure didn't have anything to do with it." He took a sip. "And why the Tyrell Corporation's got such an interest in you . . . I mean, after your having screwed up and letting Eldon Tyrell get killed . . . it beats me. I've given up trying to figure out those people." Another. "Now the way I see it—"

"For Christ's sake, Bryant!" Deckard's nerve and his voice cracked. "I don't have time for this. Now, are you going to help me out? Or are you just going to sit there in whatever plastic bubble they got you in, getting soused and mumbling to yourself?" His anger rose, even while he kept his voice down to a tense whisper. "Because I'm not going to stick around here, listening to your bullshit. Not while every cop in the city is parading by your office door."

"Simmer down." Bryant knocked back the dregs. "I'll help you. I always have. Not that you ever seemed to appreciate it."

"I didn't appreciate getting jerked around by you. Back when I came to work for you again. What's all this about there being one more escaped replicant on the loose? A sixth one."

Bryant displayed his ugly smile. "Is that what the Tyrell Corporation's got you hunting for?"

"So it's true, then." Deckard leaned forward. "There is another one. And you didn't want me to know about it. What was that all about?"

"Look, uh . . . that's not important." On the monitor screen, Bryant's image shifted uncomfortably. "Like you said, you don't have time for screwing around. Why don't we just say that back then . . . I miscounted, or something. Things didn't work out quite the way I wanted them to."

"All right—" Deckard could hear the tension and anger in his own voice. "Whatever the game was that you were playing, I don't need to hear about it. Right now, I need something from you. You either get me a spinner, fueled and with all clearances, so I can get the hell out of L.A.—"

"Can't do it, pal." Bryant's image shook its head. "I can't put in a transport requisition from where I'm sitting."

"Fine. Then you call up the data that you purged

out of the files—the stuff about that other escaped replicant. ID scan, name, description, the works.''

"That's kinda hard, too. I put all that in a secured
file sector. Got some tight locks on it.''

"But it's there, right?'' Deckard managed to keep
his voice low. "So you can get it out. And that's what I
need from you. Give me the data on the sixth replicant,
and I'll take care of the rest.''

Another shake of the image's head. "Hunting it
down won't be a picnic. Not with the whole LAPD on
your case.''

"Let me worry about that. All I have to do is turn
its carcass over to the Tyrell Corporation, and then I'll
be long gone. Again. The police won't even see my
dust.''

"You trust Tyrell?''

"I don't have any choice.'' He slumped down in the
chair, splaying the glossy jackboots out in front of himself. Letting some of the anger drain away—he lifted the
shot he'd poured out and finished it off. "They're the
only chance I have.'' In the office's stillness, he heard
the faint rumble of the rep train rolling through its dark
tunnels beneath the station. The poor bastards aboard it
had already found their way out. The noise faded away,
like a minor seismic echo. An old, recognizable feeling
crawled across his skin, the same one he'd felt whenever
he'd been in Bryant's office before, and that sub-audible
note had whispered at the edge of his perception. Evoking the same thought as before: *At least I always killed
them one at a time.* His only source of moral justification . . .

Deckard shook off the creepy meditation. He didn't
have time for that, not now. "So what's it going to be?
Do I get the info?''

"It'll take a while,'' said Bryant's image on the monitor screen.

"How long?''

The image shrugged. "Maybe half an hour. Maybe a

little less. Especially if we don't have anybody noticing that I'm pulling the file back up. Once I've got it accessed, though, I can send it straight to where you're at right now. So the best thing for you to do . . ." The brown-toothed smile again. "Would be to just hang tight and wait for the pretty pictures to show up on the screen."

Deckard glanced at the office's door. He'd heard footsteps go by, then silence.

The voice from the monitor continued. "Like you said, pal, every cop in the city is walking by your elbow right now. None of them are likely to come waltzing into my office anytime soon. Keep your head down, and you should be able to hang out there until the crowd thins out a bit—maybe when the sun comes up and they all scurry to their little holes. Then you should be able to sneak back out." The image shrugged. "After that, it'll all be up to you. Just like you wanted."

The muscles along Deckard's shoulders eased. He could handle that. He'd gotten in here; he could get out again. And after that? He'd worry about it later.

"All right." He nodded. "The sun comes up, and I'm out of here." He swallowed the remainder in his glass. "You're the one who's going to have to take the heat, though. If it gets found out that you helped me."

"Let me worry about that." Bryant's image sneered. "These pussies in the department have been on my case for years. What're they going to do, fire me? Bring me up on charges? They can't—I'm the only one who'll do this rotten job for them, and they know it. Besides, I've got a file up here—" On the monitor screen the jowly, unshaven image tapped the side of its head. "With a list of where *all* the bodies are buried. There's a bunch the brass around here wouldn't like to see dug up. If anybody over at Internal Affairs or the police chief's office want to dick around with me, I can guarantee 'em it won't be just *my* funeral they'll be getting ready for."

The scotch radiated a feeble glow in Deckard's

stomach. "It won't be just the department brass you'll have to worry about. Those enemies of mine that you were talking about—they won't be friends of yours."

"Yeah, like I'm so scared, pal. The fact that they were able to get you into hot water doesn't make 'em God. I've been covering my fat white butt for a long time now. Since I'm still alive, you might guess that I've gotten pretty good at it. And you'd be right. Like I said, let me worry about it."

He managed one corner of a smile for his old boss. "No choice, huh?"

"No choice." On the monitor screen, on the other side of the desk, hung the image of Bryant's own lop-sided smile, the video image of his face slowly nodding. "You came around here asking for my help, now you gotta take it. It's out of your hands, pal." The image drew back, one of its hands reaching for the bottle on the desk in the quarantine chamber. "Besides, even if they can get to me, what the hell do I care. I'm an old man, Deckard. At least I feel like one. Liver probably looks like a wet rag by now, plus I got an ulcer I could put my fist through, do sock puppet shows inside my stomach, if I wanted. I get plugged, so be it." He poured himself a taller drink than before. "Besides, I do owe it to you." The image gazed, eyes half-lidded, into the unlit depths of the glass. "You always came through for me, Deckard. Even when I had to lean on you. When I hauled you in here to take care of that last batch of escaped replicants . . ."

"What?" All the joints of his spine tightened at once, as though the cord running through them had been yanked by an unseen fist. *Something's wrong*—the thinking part of his brain raced to catch up with the instinct, the quick sense that had made it possible for him to be a blade runner.

On the monitor screen the image of Bryant didn't seem to have heard him. The image went on talking, as though Bryant had started to drift into some private reverie.

"I knew that bunch was going to be trouble. Escaped replicants always are, but those Nexus-6 jobs had me sweating . . ."

That's not Bryant. He knew; he realized that a fake had been switched in on him. The sweat on his arms chilled, beneath the uniform's black sleeves. His old boss wasn't in a quarantine chamber somewhere else; the image on the monitor screen was a persynth, a CGI physiognomen, composited from the hundreds of hours of tapes recorded by the office's watchcams. A real-time response driver, with a branching script protocol, had been spouting the words in Bryant's data-sampled voice. A trap like this indicated a high-priority resource drain on the department; to get one of these ersatz personas up and running without detectable processor lag required mega-cray paralleled hardware.

One mistake had tripped them up, made it clear to Deckard what the deal was. *Bryant wouldn't have said that*—he'd heard the inspector spouting off enough times to be familiar with his crude vocabulary. Especially when he'd been drinking, which had been most of the time; whenever Bryant had started into bad-mouthing replicants, instead of just giving one of his squad necessary tracking info, he'd used the words *skin jobs*, his favorite ugly phrase. Whoever had wired up the physiognomen on the monitor screen had forgotten to cut out the PC loop imbedded in the police department's main computers, the language-scrubbing circuit that kept the LAPD spokesmen from inadvertently broadcasting some of their less attractive public-relations gaffes. The city's taxpayers didn't mind having a kick-ass retro-Gates police force, as long as it talked kinder and gentler.

The whole analysis ran through Deckard's head in less than a second. *They're trying to pump me,* he

thought. That was why the trap was being allowed to
run on, without him being pounced on immediately—
the department authorities who'd set this up hoping to
get some kind of info from him while he was liquored
up and reminiscing about old times with Bryant's video
simulation, lulled into a false sense of security. *They're
watching me right now*—which meant they may have
caught his involuntary reaction, the jerk upward of his
head and stiffening of his spine that would signal his
perception of something being amiss. Which
meant . . .

His gaze shot to one side. Through the blinds over
the office's windows, he saw that a wide swath of the
station's ground floor had been cleared. A dozen LAPD
elites, guns drawn, were running toward him, a few
strides and seconds away.

"Hey! Where you going?" The synthesized image of
Inspector Bryant looked puzzled as Deckard jumped
from his chair. "What's the deal, pal—" Papers scattered in a white flurry as Deckard grabbed the top of the
heavy file cabinet and heaved it over onto its side with a
crash of splintering wood. Just in time—the first of the
squad hit the door with a body-armored shoulder. The
impact of the door's edge against the impromptu barricade knocked the cop back against the others behind
him.

Deckard heard the elites' shouts and curses as he
vaulted over the desk, knocking the monitor and its tripod aside. Bryant's synthesized image disappeared, replaced by a quick burst of static, then a solid glare of
light spilling across the floor. In that blue glow, he
caught a glimpse of what had happened to the real Bryant: an amorphous island of blood, dried into a dark
stain, covered the space behind the desk.

He pushed himself up on hands and knees from the
evidence of Bryant's death, as the windows along the
side of the office shattered in fire and bright splinters of

glass, the blinds flapping like metal-feathered wings, tearing loose from their mounts as a horizontal rain of bullets scoured the opposite wall. The office's contents—the row of other cabinets topped with ancient teardrop-bladed fans and routing bins of yellowed papers and dog-eared manila folders, the desk lamp inset with snaps of Bryant's father's big-game hunting expeditions—exploded into sharp-edged fragments, the smaller pieces twisting in the vortex of the bullet's overlapping trajectories.

The deafening noise covered his actions. Deckard lifted above his head the overturned chair on which the video tripod had been mounted, and hurled it toward the single unbroken window that looked out to the police station's cavernous space. The shards of glass sprayed outward, the chair tangling in the cords of the blind, then tearing it loose and trailing the metal slats to the floor. He followed after, keeping low beneath the continuing gunfire, pushing off from the windowsill's jagged edge. He landed shoulder-first among the bits of glass, then rolling onto his back and drawing the gun from the uniform's holster with both hands.

"There he is!" one of the cops shouted over the din, pointing. Deckard's shot caught him in the chest, knocking him back with arms flung wide against the others stationed a couple of yards outside the office's door. A burst of assault-rifle fire raked the floor as Deckard spun away; he came up with his own gun aimed and another round squeezed off.

He heard the rifle clatter onto the floor, but didn't stop to look over his shoulder as he scrambled to his feet. The curved-ceiling stairs leading down to the basement levels were a few yards away; bare fluorescent tubes bounced a sickly illumination from the cracked white tiles. He sprinted toward the arched opening.

More shots sounded behind him, but he'd already reached the stairs; he grabbed the rusting metal rail and

used it to sling himself hard against the wall. He leaned
out far enough to brush his pursuers back with another
couple of shots. Then turned and ran, taking the steps
three at a time, a barely controlled fall toward the
depths beneath the police station.

8

Isidore looked up at the figure standing in the doorway. "Wuh-what is it?"

The security agent from the Tyrell Corporation stepped into Isidore's office. So big in his grey uniform with the name tag on the breast that he seemed to take up at least half the available space, his buzz-cut head brushing the ceiling. Andersson looked around, as though seeing the clippings and old calendars on the walls for the first time. "Oh . . . nothing too serious." The agent turned back toward the owner of the Van Nuys Pet Hospital with a dead, unfeeling gaze. "I just needed to speak with you for a little bit. To tell you that there's going to be some changes made."

"Ruh-really?" The cat, his favorite, the one without skin or flesh to cover its mechanical bones, slipped in through the open door and jumped up on the desk. "Luh-luh-like what?" Isidore picked the cat up and held it against his chest. He stroked its steel, furless head and got a deep thrumming purr in response.

"Well, I'm not going to be working around here anymore. I've got other things to do."

"I suh-see." He nodded slowly. "That's yuh-your puh-ruh-ruh-*pre*rogative. After all, you weren't ever really wuh-working for me. You were always working for *her*." He watched his hand scratching behind the point where the mechanical cat's ear would have been, if it'd had one. "I guh-guess I'll have to reevaluate the suh-suh-situation, see what the pet hospital really nuh-needs. So I can make other arrangements."

"You don't have to do that." Andersson looked at him with an almost tender regard. "The arrangements have already been made."

"Oh." He knew what that meant. And was confirmed in that knowledge when he watched the other man reach inside the jacket of his dark uniform. He knew what would be in the other's hand even before he saw it. "You know, I thuh-thuh-thought this was going to happen. I was kind of wuh-waiting for it."

"I'm kind of sorry about it, actually." Andersson looked at the black weight of the gun in his own hand. "Not like I ever minded helping you out. But you know how it goes."

"Sure." Isidore felt sorry for him. "I understand." He stood up from the desk, pushing the chair back, still cradling the cat against himself. "Wuh-would you muh-mind if I went out there?" He nodded toward the office's door. "Where the animals are? I'd rather be out thuh-there . . . when you duh-do it."

"Hey. No problem."

A moment later he stood out in the pet hospital's central corridor, looking down the rows of cages and kennels, listening to the barking and smaller noises that greeted his presence. He'd been wondering if he'd be able, at this moment, to tell the difference between the real ones and the fakes. With a sense of relief, he found that he still drew a blank on that issue.

The mechanical cat in his arms meowed plaintively

and rubbed its cold muzzle against his chin. *Poor thing—*
it knew something was wrong, something was about to
happen. "Here you go, baby." Isidore leaned down to
set the cat on the floor. "I don't want you to get hurt."
It didn't go away, but went on pressing its steel and
plastic body against his ankles.

"I'm ready," he announced. He didn't look behind
himself, though he could feel the infinitesimal distur-
bance in the corridor's enclosed air, as Andersson raised
the gun.

Then he flew. That was what it felt like, even as a
blow so huge as to be painless struck him between the
shoulder blades. Even as he lay between the rows of
wire-fronted cages, tossed there by the bullet's impact,
he still felt suspended, caught in infinite motion. The
concrete against his splayed-out hands felt soft as billowing clouds. But cold.

*This must be what it's like—*he could barely hear his
own thoughts. He knew he was already dead, inhabiting
the last seconds of consciousness, because other sounds
came to him, from far away, from right next to him.

All the cage and kennel doors sprang open, their
latches triggered by the signal from the tiny device he'd
implanted next to his own heart. He'd known a long
time ago that this time was coming.

Any human creatures left inside the Van Nuys Pet
Hospital would have to sort their own problems out.
The nonhuman ones, the real and the fake, barking or
whooping or emitting their shrill cries, fled toward the
outer doors and windows that had also popped open.
Isidore could just imagine a bright flurry of parrots
wheeling above the crowded streets, the steel-legged
greyhound and the terriers sprinting past the traffic-
stalled vehicles . . .

Blind, he distantly felt a few of the animals nuzzling
his face, the mechanical cat climbing onto his chin and
shrinking back from the ragged edges of the exit wound.

"It's okay," he whispered. He tried to raise his hand but couldn't. "Don't worry . . . about me . . ."

They started yowling before he was finished dying. And continued afterward.

"This . . . this is great." The sense of happiness permeated Holden's body, as though the bio-mechanical heart in his chest had accelerated to some more euphoric rhythm. His own smile came to his face as he gazed at the monitor screen, at the data he'd had Batty summon up again. The words and numbers formed themselves into a personal message for him. "You know what this means? It means I didn't screw it up with Kowalski. I was set up; I walked into an engineered hit. There was no way I could avoid getting blown out by the replicant. The one person in the world I trusted—the guy whose job it was to look out for me, to keep my ass covered—he betrayed me." Holden placed his palm against the screen, as though to absorb the warmth of its benedictive radiation. "I can't tell you how *good* this makes me feel."

"*Mazel tov.*" Batty shrugged. "Whatever—I'm happy for you. But you should remember, you're not exactly out of the woods. As long as you were knocked out in a hospital bed, with a dope hose running into your veins, nobody was concerned about finishing the job on you. Maybe Bryant put out an order to keep you on life support, just because he has a sentimental streak. Or perhaps he would've liked to have pulled the plug on you, but couldn't—or at least not yet. Not with you lying inside a hospital full of doctors and nurses who like to keep their little machines running. But when they hear that you're up and walking, the contract on you becomes effective again. Especially since they can assume that someone like me has filled you in on all the stuff they didn't want you to know."

" 'They . . .' " He pressed his hand harder against the screen, as though he could shatter the glass, reach in and pull out the information he needed. "Who are they? Who's in on it, besides Bryant?"

"That's a good one. Answer that, and you might have a chance of surviving. The big question is, how far up does this conspiracy go? Bryant didn't come up with all this on his own. How many levels of the police hierarchy above him are involved? Does the conspiracy against the blade runners go further than that, like into the U.N.'s policy-making apparatus? Maybe the off-world colonies' administrative offices are in on it— they're the ones most likely to have fabricated the escape that brought the replicants down here to Earth. The only thing you can be sure of is that somebody with major clout doesn't like blade runners."

"Weird." Holden shook his head. The little jolt of cheer he'd felt had faded now. The holes were filled with darkness, where the missing pieces of the puzzle should fit. "Why would they be doing something like this, anyway? We're just doing our jobs—why try to kill us off?"

"Pal, it could be any one of a million reasons. Just goes to show what an innocent soul you are, that you'd even worry about why. You haven't dealt with the people up at the top the way I have." Batty's voice and expression clouded with bitterness. "They're just mean bastards. They don't care about little people like you and me. Everything's dollar signs with them. If they want to trim their budget, they do it by cutting it out of your hide."

The last dregs of that happy sense, of knowing at last that what had happened to him wasn't his fault, ebbed out of Holden's soul. Another emotion replaced it, as in silence he studied the man standing next to him. Now it was his turn to feel pity. He could see more clearly now the lines engraved into Batty's face, the deep creases as well as the finer net across the aged skin. Cheeks hollowed, eyes sunken in the dark crepe of their sockets; as if in the blue glow of the monitor, the man

was visibly claimed by time, all the decades catching up
with him. *He's right,* thought Holden. *He's been doing
this a long while* . . .

"You didn't quit, did you?" He wondered just how
old this guy was, exactly. "Either the Tyrell Corporation
or the places before that. They fired you. Put you out to
pasture."

Batty shot him a fierce glance. "Yeah, well, maybe
you're just finding out what it's like." An almost child-
ish sulkiness twisted in his voice. "Maybe the reason
Bryant went in on the conspiracy to get rid of you guys
is just because he wanted to bring in some new blood.
Replace you jerks who've gotten your minds all warped
out on the Curve. Useless dildos."

"The Curve was never a problem for me." Holden
set his own gaze hard. "Once I've got the territory
scoped out, I can take care of myself."

"Man, you don't even know. I tell you one thing,
that your ass was set up for a fall, and now you think
you're a walking encyclopedia." The mean smile
showed again. "There's stuff going on, *levels* of conspiracy, that I haven't even *started* to bend your head with
yet."

The realization had come to him some time ago
that Batty got off on the whole conspiracy notion.
"Such as?"

"Bryant was lying to you from the beginning. To
you, and then to Deckard, when he sent you out hunting that batch of replicants." A smug expression showed
on Batty's face. "There was one more escaped replicant
that he didn't tell either one of you about. A sixth replicant."

"That doesn't make any sense." Another memory,
from when he'd been back there at the hospital. Bryant
had told him that all the escapees—all *five* of them—had
been taken care of. Holden shook his head. "Why
would Bryant cover up for a replicant?"

"Ah. There's the mystery, all right." Batty's face

showed once more how much he was enjoying this process. "When you combine that with the supposition he was involved in a conspiracy to get rid of the blade runners . . . makes you wonder, doesn't it? Just whose side Bryant is on."

Holden fell silent, musing over everything Batty had told him, trying to fit the loose bits and pieces together.

"A sixth replicant . . ." He spoke aloud. Something moved deep inside his being, other than his prowling, restless thoughts. "Number six." The old blade runner instinct, the desire, that had stirred into life every time he'd gotten an assignment from Bryant. To hunt, to track down and locate, and then to retire the quarry. He'd never really understood why wimps like Deckard and some of the other blade runners bitched and crabbed about this job. To him, it'd always been his whole reason for existing. Like that old high-wire artist had said, long ago—everything else was just waiting. "One more to get . . ."

"Take it easy," said Batty. "I know the idea gets you all revved up, but you still gotta take it easy for a little while. That artificial heart-and-lung implant's still settling in."

Holden didn't care about that. He knew that bagging the sixth replicant would solve a lot of things. *It'd prove*, he thought with grim satisfaction, *that I'm still on top of the game.* He'd been set up by that fat, lying bastard Bryant; that'd been the only way that they—the big *they* of the anti-blade runner conspiracy—had been able to nail him. It still rankled to think of people hearing about him lying there in the hospital, a limp little bag of fluids hooked up to pumps and aerators, and feeling sorry for him. Now there was the chance to show them all.

Plus, it seemed logical there must be something special about this one remaining replicant; why else would Bryant have let the others be hunted down and retired, while covering the tracks for number six? *When I find this one*—Holden already knew he would—*I'll have to be careful not to retire it too soon.* Not until he'd pumped it for every scrap of information about the conspiracy. The key to why Bryant and those mysterious, unknown others had tried to kill him—he didn't care about all the rest of the blade runners; this was *personal*—was walking around Los Angeles right now, passing for human, wearing some face that could be just about anybody's.

"This isn't going to be a piece of cake." Holden nodded slowly, laying out everything neatly and efficiently inside his head. He knew he'd have to be careful, operate while keeping his own head low—the conspirators had to know that he'd been busted out of the hospital, and Batty had made such a circus out of the break, there'd be no doubt that he was hooked up with him as well. *Loose cannon,* he thought. That loony smile and crazy eyes made him wonder how far he could trust Batty. Or whether he'd have to find some way to cut free of him—

He suddenly felt tired, a wave of fatigue deep and powerful enough to buckle his knees. He had to steady himself against the bank of monitors and other electronic equipment, to keep from falling.

"See? I told you." Batty's voice came from somewhere nearby. "You gotta take it slow for right now. It's going to be a while before you're back up to your old operating speed. If ever."

"Screw that." He summoned enough willpower to stand upright. "Don't worry about me. I'm not going to let having a bio-mech heart-and-lung set cramp my action." He gave a quick, harsh laugh. "Hey, it just struck me—" Turning his own smile toward Batty. "With what your doctor pals out here stuck inside me, *I'm* not all human anymore. What a thought."

" 'Not all human . . .' " Batty peered at him. "What's that supposed to mean?"

"Don't you get it?" Maybe this guy was so old, he was turning senile; maybe that was why Tyrell had fired him. "You know, because of the new heart and lungs being machines and stuff—"

"You poor sonuvabitch. You're the one who doesn't get it." Batty slowly shook his head. "I thought you knew. That's why it was such a good joke a while back when you thought *I* was a replicant."

Holden felt a chill lock on to his vertebrae, climbing upward one by one. "What're you talking about?"

"You were never human, Holden." The smile, the pitying gaze. "*You're* the one who's a replicant. You've always been one."

9

"All right, all right; now I know you're bullshitting me."
Holden felt both weary and disgusted. "You told me
part of your brain was wired in backward, and now I
believe it. You got a sense of humor that could only
come from a couple of fritzed lobes."

"Bullshit, it's not." Batty folded his arms across his
chest. In the space bound by the equipment shack's
corrugated-steel walls, the monitor's glow laced an icy
blue through his colorless hair. "I'm not joking with
you. Why should I? About something like this? Trust
me. You're a replicant."

"Trust you . . . yeah, right." The guy was either
yanking his chain, figured Holden, or really was as crazy
as the frequent smile and weird cast to his gaze indicated. "Give it up, Batty. I don't know what the hell
you think you're accomplishing with all this fun-and-
games line, but I'm not falling for any more of it."

"Aw, man, the games haven't even *started*. Let's go
back over to the medical unit." He reached over and
switched off the monitor. In darkness, he headed for the

dim rectangle of the door and the starlit night outside.
"You want proof I'm not jerking you around, then come
on. Got something else to show you."

Outside the larger building, the disheveled doctor
looked the same as he had when he'd wheeled Holden's
gurney into the operating room. He couldn't tell if any
of the blood spots on the white coat were his own. The
hot night air had pulled darker crescents of sweat under
the man's arms.

"Hey, can I bum one of those off you?" The doctor
didn't wait for permission, but plucked the cigarette
pack from Holden's breast pocket. "Thanks." He flicked
the match away, a miniature comet, inhaled, and
coughed. "You shouldn't be walking around, you
know." With the same hand, he rubbed his watering
eyes and used the cigarette to point toward Holden. "I
didn't put all that gear inside you that long ago." He
looked over at Batty. "You wear this guy out and he
pops a seam, it's not going to be that easy to fix, man."

"Don't worry about *him*. He's one of those big, bad
blade runner types." Batty held out his own hand, palm
upward. "Give me the keys to the ice room. You know,
the slab farm."

Scratching his unshaven chin, the doctor fidgeted
through the white coat's pockets until he came up with
a ring of keys. "I want those back when you're done. I
don't want to find any more of those grease monkeys
trying to take naps in there. I don't care what the
weather's like. Bad enough, keeping their sixers in
there."

"Relax. This'll only take a minute." Batty twirled
the keys on one raised finger. "Come on, Mr. Skeptic.
Prepare thyself to be blown away."

Holden followed Batty inside and to the rear of the
building. The door-lined corridor was crowded with
abandoned gurneys and wheelchairs, nests of catheters
and trusses, a crutchless Lourdes. He spotted the black

attaché case he'd worn strapped to his chest, now tossed
onto a collapsed scarecrow of chrome IV-drip stands.
"In here." Batty unlocked the last door, pushed it
open. "All the proof you could ever want." The room
exhaled a chill draft. "At least in this world."
"Great," said Holden as he looked around. "A
morgue." He'd been in enough of them in his time. This
wasn't one of the best maintained he'd ever seen; dag-
gers of frozen condensation had formed on the rows of
metal drawers that made up one wall. "This is it?"
Batty stepped over to the single table, underneath
the light fixture dangling from the ceiling. "You know, I
don't know why, but I just had a *feeling* that this would
come in handy. Good thing I asked 'em to keep it
around." He grabbed the corner of the sheet and pulled
it partway back. "Take a look."
Standing at the table's chrome edge, Holden gazed
down.
And saw himself.
Not a mirror. The eyes were closed. As though
asleep—so far down that there was no breath to raise
the chest beneath the sheet. Unscarred—this body
hadn't caught any rounds to the sternum. *No wonder I
look so peaceful,* he thought.
"Nice, close match, huh?" Hands on hips, Batty
nodded as he admired the corpse on the table. "Say
what you want about those Tyrell people being a crew
of bastards, you gotta admit they do nice work setting
up a production line. They get tolerances down to a
gnat's foreskin. There's probably not a freckle's difference between you and this baby, or any of the rest of
this model. You're all identical. With some . . . *minor*
variations."
With one fingertip, Holden reached down and
touched the forehead of the body. The coldness of the
flesh, flesh the same as his, tingled up his arm like a
small electric shock.
"Who . . ." The morgue smell, the refrigerated

suspension of decay, sat heavy in his mouth. "Who is this?"

"Hey. What does it look like? Maybe it's the twin your mother forgot to tell you about. Slipped her mind." Batty's amused gaze peered closer at him, waiting for a reaction. "Isn't it obvious? It's another David Holden replicant, just like you. It's amazing you haven't run into one before. It may not have been the most popular model that the Tyrell Corporation ever made, but there are still quite a few of them out there."

Holden drew his hand back, rubbing his fingertip against the front of his jacket, as though to wipe off some residue of his own death. The initial shock, that of seeing his own face attached to a body on a morgue table, had passed; now he looked at it with a measure of distaste. "Where did this thing come from?"

"You're sure not displaying much family sympathy. Especially for somebody who came out of the same factory as you." Batty spread his hands above the corpse with Holden's face, as though in benediction. "This 'thing,' as you put it, originally came out of the Tyrell Corporation—just as you did. That's where it died, too. Dust to dust, meat to meat. But between those end points, it went far, far away—to the off-world colonies. This Dave Holden replicant was one of the group of six that escaped and came back here to Earth, back to L.A. and Tyrell. The bunch that your boss Bryant told you to track down and retire. Except that this one was already dead by the time Bryant gave you the assignment. This is the one that got fried in one of the Tyrell Corporation's electrical-field security devices, when they all tried to break into the corporation's headquarters." Batty lifted the sheet corner higher. "There's some burn marks farther down on the abdomen. Do you want to check them out?"

"No, that's okay. I'll take your word on it." He felt oddly relieved that the replicant had gone out in a relatively quick and painless way; the kind of security

devices that were used in places like the Tyrell Corporation had neural-interrupter capabilities, knocking tres-
passers unconscious before killing them. Better that
way—the thought of that face, identical to his own, taking a blade runner slug to the forehead wasn't pleasant,
either. He started to turn away. "I've seen enough."

"Actually, I don't think you have." Batty pulled the
sheet completely away from the table. "Look a little
closer."

Holden glanced over his shoulder. And nearly fell,
surprise triggering a hiccup in his new heart.

The corpse on the table had breasts. Small, an ath-
lete's, but definite. And farther down, the genitalia of a
female.

"Great," muttered Holden. He'd recovered some of
his composure. "They make a double of me, and it goes
out and becomes a transsexual."

"Not quite." Batty redraped the sheet over the table, as though respecting the dead's modesty. "She was
created this way. Another Dave Holden replicant—just
like you—but with one small difference, the chromo-
somal selection for a female rather than male. The Tyrell
Corporation can do that. It's easy enough."

He wasn't quite sure what to think. "What was its
name?"

"Something beginning with a D, I suppose. Deir-
dre? Danielle, perhaps. They're short on imagination
over at the corporation's design labs. And Holden, of
course; they put the same last name on all the units of a
particular model. Like they named the Roy Batty replicants after me."

He really didn't care about the thing's name. Just
giving himself time to think, as he gazed down at the
corpse. Time to sort out the physical evidence—things
didn't get much more factual than a dead body—and
the stuff that wacko Batty kept rattling on about. Which
was considerably less reliable. Somebody saves your life,
gives you a whole new heart and lungs, and they think

they can hand you any old routine. He knew he wasn't buying this one, not without an argument.

"All right," he said. "You got a dead replicant here. And it's obviously a Dave Holden replicant. The female version, at least. That doesn't mean *I'm* a replicant. I could be the human templant for this model."

"Oh?" Batty raised an eyebrow. "You recall getting any royalty checks from the Tyrell Corporation recently? If they based a replicant model on you, they're supposed to pay for that."

"So they screwed me. Christ, I'd rather believe that than . . . than . . . what you're trying to convince me of. That I'm *not* human at all. Hey, you're the one who's been going on about what a bunch of bastards they are over at the Tyrell Corporation. So now I find out that they owe me money; fine, I'll go over there sometime and collect."

He looked down at the corpse again, then back up to Batty. "Besides, what sense would it make? I'm a replicant, and I get put on the squad hunting down escaped replicants? And don't give me that line about setting a particular kind of cat to hunt a particular kind of rat. You'd have a replicant blade runner hanging around with human blade runners—they're not going to figure it out eventually? Even if I didn't get assigned to track down an escaped Dave Holden replicant, one of the other blade runners would. So he'd either let me know I'm a replicant or he'd come back to the police station and blow me away. In either case, it's not going to be much of a secret any longer, about what's been going on."

"You know . . . ." Batty sighed. "Your problem is that you make all these big assumptions. You just sail right into believing stuff that hasn't been shown to be true."

"Such as?"

"Such as there being any *human* blade runners at all."

That shut him up for a moment; he hadn't been expecting that line. When Holden spoke again, his voice was tightened by a barely controlled anger. "I don't have a problem, Batty; *you* do. You're insane. You've got all the classic thought processes of a paranoid schizophrenic."

"Please—" Disgust on Batty's face. "This is what I get for being a nice guy, trying to help people out. Amateur medical advice. You want to believe this or not, fine, it's no skin off my nose. But the truth of the matter is that all the blade runners have *always* been replicants, from day one. Even before there were any replicants being manufactured in the U.S., back when the industry was located in Stuttgart, and the original developers of the technology—people like Paul Derain, and Sudermann and Grozzi, the ones that Eldon Tyrell eventually ripped off—knew they were dealing with dangerous stuff and they put the first safeguards in place."

Holden had to admit that the other man knew his stuff. Those were names from the ancient history of replicant manufacturing.

"From the start," Batty went on, "those companies had replicants on-line whose sole purpose was to keep other replicants from escaping and trying to pass themselves off as human. That's where the name 'blade runner' comes from; those enforcement replicants were originally called *Bleibruhigers*. *Bleib ruhig* is German for 'stay quiet.' And that's what they did, they kept everything nice and quiet; most people around the turn of the century weren't even aware that the replicant technology had been developed. Then when Tyrell and the U.N. brought everything over to the States, and the catching of escaped replicants became a police function, that's when *Bleibruhiger* got Anglicized to *blade runner*. The term doesn't make any sense, otherwise."

"That's a nice etymology lesson, Batty, but it doesn't prove anything. Why use replicants to hunt down other replicants? You'd always be risking them realizing that they had their own interests in common. Then they'd conspire back against you."

"Only if the blade runners knew that they were replicants." Batty pointed a finger at him. "*You* didn't know. And you were one of the best that the LAPD had in the squad. That's the whole point of having replicants do the dirty work. The nature of the blade runner job is nothing but licensed killing—for most thinking, feeling creatures, whether they're human or replicant, that's a corrosive way to live."

Holden shrugged. "I never minded it."

"You know, that's funny, when you think about it—" Batty's eyes glistened in full enjoyment mode. "The whole business of being a blade runner drains the human nature out of the people who do it. People like you. And at the same time, the replicants you're tracking down are trying to be human. Don't you think that's hilarious? The hunter is continuously in the process of turning into a mirror image of the very thing he's hunting. And vice versa. That's what makes it so great . . . from sort of an ironic point of view." He shook his head, still smiling. "I *love* this universe."

"You would." Holden found it easy to resist the other's happy mood. "Right up your alley, obviously."

"Yes, well, the system *does* work, in its own grinding, soul-destroying way. That's why it's so valuable to have the blade runners be replicants themselves. You know that whole bit—Bryant probably told you about it—about these Nexus-6 replicants having only a four-year life span, as a safeguard against their getting away and on their own? That's nothing new. The blade runner replicants have always been built that way. Four years is just about the optimum time that a blade runner can stay on the Curve and operate at max efficiency, before the burnout starts setting in. You got that four-year window of opportunity, you stuff 'em with some implanted memories so they'll think they're human, give some basic hunting and tracking skills . . . bam, you got 'em right at the peak of the Curve. And then—even better—they crap out and die before they go weird on you and become dangerous. Haul the bodies away, bring over some new units of the same models from the Tyrell Corporation, program 'em the same way you did the previous ones, and you're off and running. It's a great system." He shrugged, in a pretense of embarrassed apology. "Except, of course, *you* die. Over and over, actually. But you're usually not aware of that part, so that's okay."

Holden glared at the other. A chill, deeper and more exhausted than before, had started to settle into his bones.

"Like I said before . . ." He turned away from the corpse with his face; it was getting on his nerves. "This is all great talk, but you haven't proven anything. There are other explanations possible for all this. You really haven't shown me any reason to give up believing that I'm the human templant for any Dave Holden replicants. There's no *proof.*"

"There can't be." Batty pulled the sheet back over the dead body. "Not the way you want. That's another problem with you blade runners—you've got it in your head that the difference between human and replicant can be demonstrated. You take it as an article of faith—you couldn't do your job otherwise—that the Voigt-Kampff machine and the empathy tests show who's human and who's not. But at the same time, you've already admitted that we could put the machine on each other, run the tests, and the results would be completely meaningless." He turned an intense, unsmiling gaze on Holden. "You gotta think about what that means. There's a lot of implications. Take that Roy Batty replicant, that copy of me, that you and then Rick Deckard were assigned to retire. Suppose either one of you had managed to catch it, put the Voigt-Kampff machine on it, and run the tests. Would it have flunked because it was a replicant or because it was such a good copy of the human original? If I couldn't pass the empathy tests, and I'm the original, and the copy of me doesn't pass either, *then what's the difference between us?* The whole premise of the blade runners—the whole methodology by which they operate in this world, going around saying this person's human and this one's not— that whole thing is bogus. Fallacious. It doesn't work because it *can't* work." Batty glanced down at the shrouded corpse. "Maybe what you should ask yourself is how much of this you've known to be true all along. And you just chose to ignore it because it would've gotten in your way too much."

He didn't care about that. All this arguing about who or what was human and who or what was not, and how you could tell or could never tell—his brain was starting to ache from the convoluted, seemingly endless labor of picking his way through the branching corridors. *A maze,* thought Holden. *That's what it is.* The basic mental pattern of the clever psychotic. Contagion the danger; Holden knew he had to be careful. In his weakened state, still getting over the effects of having an entire new heart-and-lung set shoved into his chest, it'd be easy to get sucked into Batty's ideational construct. If nothing else, it showed why the Roy Batty replicant had become the leader of the band of escaped replicants: the original was a natural scoutmaster, an organizer of fun and games. Play hard, die hard.

"Let's get out of here." Batty laid a hand on Holden's shoulder, steered him toward the morgue's door. "This can't be all that cheerful for you. I mean, finding out you're a replicant and all—that must be hell on your self-image. I know *I'd* take it hard. Plus seeing some corpse who's the exact same thing as you . . . sort of." He gave a little shudder. "The symbolism is really kind of morbid, you know?"

10

Shift change over, banks of grey steel lockers closed, the wooden benches between them polished to a smooth luster by generations of bare cop buttocks and the black serge of uniform trousers; in the close atmosphere hung the scent of sweat and fungicide. He knew that smell, could remember it from his own tours of duty before he'd promoted up and out. With each panting breath pulled into his lungs, Deckard ran further into his own past, one that he'd rather have forgotten. His shoulders barely cleared the narrow space, the black uniform's sleeves torn by collision with hinges and corners of metal.

"There! Take him down!"

He heard the shout and the clatter of jackboots hitting the bottom of the stairs behind him. Without a glance over his shoulder, he dived with arms reaching out straight, the weight of the gun gripped tight in his fist. He hit the bare, damp concrete as a line of automatic rifle fire stitched across the locker doors. Still sliding, he rolled onto his back, getting his other hand onto

the gun and firing blind, the recoil from three rapid
shots pushing him along another couple of feet.

At least one shot had struck flesh; he heard a gasp of
shock as the auto fire went wild, raking the locker
room's ceiling and bursting the light fixtures into sparks
and glass splinters. In darkness, he scrambled to his feet,
staying low and close to the metal doors to his left. His
hunched shadow leapt in front of him, outlined by each
red muzzle flash back at the stairs.

His own boots splashed into water a quarter-inch
deep. That and the humid air in his nostrils told him
he'd reached the showers. Deckard reached to one side
and touched wet tile; he steadied himself, breath laboring, as his eyes adjusted to the dim illumination from
the one bulb left unbroken. His mind raced, trying to
dredge from memory a way out of the sub-basement
levels below the police station.

"You're not going anywhere, dickhead—"

Before he could lift the gun, a forearm slammed
into his throat, the impact lifting him from his feet and
pinning him against the wall. The back of his skull
cracked against a chrome shower nozzle. His dropped
gun splashed in the thin water, as his hands clawed futilely at the bare, hard-muscled skin pressing under his
chin.

Fragmented light glinted in the eyes and silhouetted
the cop's naked torso, soap residue webbed across his
chest and arms, hair plastered dark and shining on his
broad neck. He must've already been in the showers
when the pursuit had exploded into sight at the far end
of the locker room, then stayed silent and waiting.

"You're the one they're looking for—" A black con-
stellation spun across Deckard's vision as the cop
grinned and jerked him higher against the slick wall.
"Aren't you?"

He couldn't push away the throttling arm. His
hands let go and scrabbled at the tiles behind him. A

blunt-edged X filled one palm; elbow digging into his own ribs, he twisted the handle.

The cop howled as the scalding water shot from the nozzle and into his face. Deckard felt the heat drip across his ear and the side of his jaw, but only for a second—moist oxygen rushed into his lungs as he fell, back sliding against the tiles. In front of him, the naked cop knelt with both hands pressed against the raw, red pulp of his flesh. The water arced over his back, steam billowing as it sprayed onto the floor.

Deckard spotted the gun lying a few feet away; he launched himself forward, scooping up the weapon. A roar of pain and rage echoed off the walls as the cop grabbed him by the front of the uniform and pulled him upright. He brought the edge of his brow against the cop's chest; with one push, Deckard took him to the wall, hard enough to loosen the other's grip for a moment. Long enough to lean back and raise the gun, the black muzzle against the cop's breastbone. He squeezed the trigger.

The tiles cracked, the wall behind crumbling from the impact of the cop's spine and shoulders. Concrete rubble sluiced over Deckard's arms as the exposed pipes bent and snapped. The gun was knocked loose from his grip, as the cop's dead hands let go of him. The corpse sprawled at his feet, the pooled water transformed into a dark red lake.

Through the clouds of steam, he could see the shadowed, indistinct figures of the other cops racing through the locker room's narrow aisles. A darker space had appeared behind the burst pipes and shattered tiles; he braced his shoulder against the concaved section of wall and pushed. He nearly fell as the cement gave way and he stumbled coughing through a burst of white dust. Hot pipes singed his hands as he groped his way through the maze of plumbing.

A quick glance over his shoulder—he spotted the shapes of his pursuers clustered around the ragged opening, the first of them climbing through, brushing aside a tangle of plaster-clotted rebar and the splinters of ancient wooden beams.

Deckard tasted salt seeping into the corners of his mouth, his face sopping with blood and water the exact same temperature. He ducked his head beneath the belly of a sewage conduit and ran as best he could, empty hands clawing a blind passage before him.

Holden had retreated into his head, letting his entropy-laden body get steered outside by the other man.

"Looks like it's going to be another hot one." Outside the Reclamation Center's medical unit, standing in the ragged circle of cigarette butts the doctor had left strewn on the sandy ground, Batty pointed to the horizon. The first coloring of dawn, a purplish-red smear along the tops of the distant mountain range, had crept into the cloudless sky. "Man, everybody bitches about the monsoon season when it's here, but when it's gone, you'd do just about anything to get rained on for twenty-four hours at a clip."

Subterranean heat rose up through Holden's legs. The desert hadn't finished radiating the thermal load it'd absorbed from the day before, and now more would be pounded into it by the sun lifting overhead. Where he gazed past the razor-wired fence, an incipient Santa Ana wind sifted dry dust through the sparse clumps of withered brush.

Everybody says that, he thought. *All the time.* One hot one after another. Someday the cycle wouldn't be broken by the onset of the yearly rains. The heat would go on building up, cumulative, until the sands melted into glass, perfectly smooth and reflective, bouncing a fierce glare back into the sky. Same thing would happen in the city, the streets turning to a black tar lava flow, then hardening to obsidian mirrors. *We could see ourselves that way, all the time*—he could picture it. Everyone looking down and wondering whether the image looking back at them, in that world of permanent night, was human or something else . . .

I should sit down—he felt as old as Batty looked. Or lie down, take the load off his new heart. The doctor was right; if he wasn't careful, the whole setup could give way, like an overstressed motor. And he couldn't allow that to happen, not until he'd moved his own agenda along. He'd have to husband his strength, calculating all of his resources and endurance, to accomplish what he'd have to do.

He glanced from the corner of his eye at Batty. The other—human or replicant; he still wasn't sure—stood silent. The quiet gave Holden the opportunity to start putting together his list of the people who'd screwed him over.

Bryant was on the list, of course. He nodded slowly, gazing toward the red-shaded sunrise. If nothing else, Batty had convinced him of that part, that the head of the blade runner unit had set him up to get blown away by the replicant Kowalski. Why, he didn't know. All of Batty's big talk of high-level anti-blade runner conspiracies hadn't impressed him.

Cops had simpler ways of determining who to go after. Mainly the application of that ancient maxim, *Cui bono?* Who'd benefited from his taking a hit?

The answer came with minimal pondering. *Deckard . . . my old pal. That sonuvabitch.* Deckard had taken over the assignment, to track down the escaped replicants; that was a nice fat bunch of bonuses for retiring each one. Maybe that whole business of his quitting the department had been a ruse, something cooked up between Deckard and Bryant, to make Holden believe that he finally had a clear field, his old rival in the blade runner unit off the scene. Maybe a little kickback arrangement, Bryant and Deckard splitting the bonuses? That was possible as well. Who knew why people did evil shit? Maybe the tests should be redesigned, that determined who was human or not. None of that empathy nonsense. Instead . . . *Would you have any problem sticking a knife in your friend's back? No? Congratulations—you have all the essential qualities of treachery, ingratitude, and two-facedness that marks a real human being. Collect your ID and ammo discount card at Window Five.* That would work.

Holden glanced over again at Batty. He was necessary for the time being; Holden knew he couldn't take care of everything he needed to, not in his present post-op condition. *I'll go along with him for now,* thought Holden. *For as long as I need to.*

The other opened his eyes, bringing his sly gaze around. "You've had a busy night." Batty displayed his psychotic smile again. "Haven't you? All the things you've found out . . ."

Right. He said nothing aloud. He'd already added Batty to the list of things to be taken care of. Whether Batty was human or not—that remained to be seen—he might be the only one who could make that whole pitch about Holden being a replicant. Whether it was true or not, it wasn't a good thing for somebody to be going around talking about.

He'd decided. He smiled back at Batty. If he had to kill the guy to prove that he was human himself . . . or at least keep everyone thinking he was . . .

He didn't have a problem with that.

The space behind the police station's walls had narrowed, a gap through which Deckard had barely been able to squeeze himself, the rough concrete surfaces tearing open the front of the stolen uniform. He left a trail of watered blood on one of the massive pilings that had been sunk into the ground to support the weight of the multileveled structure rearing high above him. The dark gap chilled as it sloped farther underground; a draft smelling of stone and smoldering fires rose into his face and was drawn into his lungs with each straining breath.

Suddenly the constricting pressures against his

shoulders flared apart, the span widening beyond the reach of his raw-scraped hands. The gravel of broken concrete slipped from under his boots, pitching him forward. The only thing that kept him from falling was an angle of pipe that his flailing grasp found a few inches from his head; his fingers tightened upon it as he heard, past the hammering of his pulse, a few dislodged pebbles clatter upon another level beneath. A low rumble moved through the earth itself.

He knew that his pursuers were still working their way down toward him; their muffled voices leaked through the gap, along with the noises of the equipment, hydraulic jacks and hissing acetylene torches, with which they cut a channel through the station's underpinnings. Only a matter of time until they caught up with him, the ratlike escape he'd made coming to an end in some corner of rock and buried steel girder.

A dim glow rose from the space that had opened below, as the rumbling sound grew louder, taking on an insistent mechanical rhythm. Deckard could see now that he had broken through the roof of an arched tunnel, with a parallel ribbon of iron tracks running its length. Some past seismic event had torqued the police station's foundations enough to pry open the cleft through which he'd squirmed; bricks and ragged chunks of concrete lay scattered across the bed of one of the old railway tunnels that ran beneath the massive structure. The glow, rapidly becoming brighter, came from the engine of the rep train approaching around the tunnel's curve. The hot diesel smell, oily and stinging, struck him full in the face, as though the source of all Santa Ana winds had erupted from the earth's core.

The sounds of his pursuers grew closer, perhaps only a few yards back along the gap through which he'd crawled. Those noises were drowned out by the rep train's noise and clatter, now directly beneath him. He squatted down, then got his legs out past the crumbling edge of the hole into the tunnel roof. He held on for a few seconds longer, until the dark shape of the engine was past; then he dropped, pushing himself away from the edge, diving with outstretched hands.

With a jarring impact, he landed on top of one of the freight cars. He clawed for a hold on the wooden slats; through the gaps between them, he could see faces looking up at him. None of the humanlike figures, pressed tight against each other inside the car, raised a voice; their blank gazes regarded him without emotion.

He couldn't hold on. The rattling motion of the train peeled his fingertips, wet with his own blood, away from the slat to which he clung. A hard lurch jolted him loose; in the stink and din, his chest and stomach slipped across the freight car's roof. The rep train took another curve in the tunnel; the swaying motion was enough to throw him over the edge.

One crooked arm caught itself in the angle between a vertical slat and slanting cross-beam. His back and shoulder slammed against the freight car's side, knocking the last of his breath from his aching lungs. The tunnel wall, jagged stone outcroppings and rusting stanchions, screamed a few inches away from his head as he fought with animal desperation to latch his free hand on to any part of the car.

His own weight began dragging his arm from its hold upon the vertical slat. His agonized vision took in the freight car's occupants, their naked forms picked out by the engine light bouncing off the tunnel's arched ceiling. Male and female replicants, packed behind the freight car's sliding door, locked with a single steel bolt.

The other cars behind, stretching into the tunnel's darkness, were the same, filled with the rejects from the Tyrell Corporation's production lines—the replicants whose memory implants hadn't taken, the ones who hadn't passed the mental and physical tests that qualified them to be slaves in the off-world colonies. Their creators routed them through a clearing station administered by the police department, checking them off in numbered lots to make sure all were accounted for prior to disposal. Not retirement—an industrial process, quick asphyxiation and smokestacks belching out the odors of incinerated flesh.

He could no longer tell what things he saw before him, and what fear and exhaustion had pulled from his memory, overlaying the rep train's reality with his own past. A slope-jawed face turned away from him, the male replicant's massive shoulders hunched with a sullen, preverbal resentment; his bare arms glistened with sweat. *Kowalski*—he could remember the face, or one just like it, another unit of the same model. What had the other Kowalski said to him? A long time ago, in another world, up on the streets of the city far above. *Wake up—it's time to die . . .*

Another Nexus-6 looked at him for a moment, her gaze reaching past the other replicants' naked shoulders. Dark-haired, long-limbed . . . her name had been shaken from his skull, leaving only the vision of another one like this, crashing through one plate-glass window after another, blood between her shoulder blades, the bullet from his gun turning her into a wingless angel, a thing that flew amid bright razor crystals . . .

"Help . . ." Deckard couldn't tell if that was his own voice rasping from his throat or the memory of his voice. "Help me . . ." What he had asked of another one of the replicants. His arm dragged farther from its hold, only the crook of his wrist against the cross-beam keeping him from falling under the wheels clashing sparks from the tunnel's iron tracks.

Another woman huddled in the corner of the freight car. The Tyrell Corporation had given her enough knowledge so that she could be afraid; her face, pressed against the paleness of her arms, was wet with tears. The tangled curls of her brown hair fell across her knees.

"Rachael . . ." He didn't know if it was her, or if they would have given this one a name yet. He called to her again. "Please . . ."

The female replicant raised her head and looked at him. And did not know who he was.

He suddenly felt an arm at his back, clutching him and pulling him up against the freight car's side. One of the replicants—he couldn't see which one—had reached through the slats and grabbed him, kept him from falling. He looked down and saw the tracks cutting by, a few inches from his dangling feet.

Brighter light flooded across him, as the rep train burst from the tunnel's mouth and out into the open. The reddish glow of morning slanted across a barren landscape, darkened with years of soot and spattered oil droppings. Abandoned freight cars and rusted-out tankers formed parallel barricades along the rows of tracks to either side.

Deckard managed to get his free hand between his chest and the slats. He pushed himself back against the arm's grasp; the replicant, still unseen by him, sensed what he was trying to do and let go.

He landed on his shoulder, rolling clear of the rep train's wheels. He kept his face down against the stones and rubble, until the noise of the train had passed and faded into the distance. Cautiously he raised his head, enough to see the last of the cars disappearing with its silent cargo.

On his hands and knees, Deckard managed to focus his vision past the tops of the motionless freight cars to his right. The towers and spires of the L.A. skyline carved the advancing daylight into hard-edged segments. He knew that he was out of the city, somewhere in the industrial wastelands ringing its vast sprawl.

A desiccated, blood-temperature wind rolled across his back. He managed to stand up, the rags of the stolen police uniform gaping over his torn and abraded flesh.

Slowly, his feet stumbling against the oil-covered rocks between the tracks, he began walking.

Not north, where his unreasoning heart wanted to start for. But someplace where he knew he could hide. For at least a little while . . .

11

She ascended to the appointed place, at the appointed hour. Without effort, almost without will—thermal sensors had registered her presence within the small space, a disembodied voice had asked if she'd wanted to go up to the building's roof, far above the dense weave of structure and light that formed the static ocean of the city. All Sarah had had to do was say yes.

Thus we rise, she thought as she closed her eyes and leaned the back of her head against the wall of the elevator's vertical coffin. Not as angels, transparent to gravity, buoyant in God's sight, but as inert, gross cargo, hauled aloft by cable and winch, like stones and dust in a box.

What machine would clasp her in its embrace when her death came, bearing her aloft the way the elevator did now? *Nobody*, she thought glumly, self-accusingly. Everything she did, everything she was about to do, was designed by her own intent to bring about that exact lonely result. Fate as programmed as a train's iron rails— she figured she'd wind up like her uncle Eldon, isolate in glacial splendor, brooding over a chessboard like an owl

watching for mice to scurry across the forest's dead
leaves and twigs. Unless . . .

Unless what? She raised a hand, pressing thumb and
forefinger against her eyelids, blue sparks wriggling inside her head. Unless every not-living thing quickened
and breathed, all the earth's graves burst like ripe seed
pods, and the drowned rose with seaweed hair and
pearls in their mouths. *It could happen*—neither thought
nor belief, but what she would have believed if she were
still capable of that. Her own resurrection, or the simulation that was as much of one as she could hope for,
pushed light through her hand and into her eyes as the
elevator came to a stop and the doors slid open.

He was waiting for her. On the building's executive
landing deck, the private one that had been reserved for
Eldon Tyrell, but rarely used. She stepped out of the
elevator and strode toward the unmarked spinner and
the figure lounging against its flank, his arms folded
across his chest.

"How did it go?"

Andersson shrugged. "Oh . . . pretty much as I
expected. He didn't put up a struggle or anything. Not
that it would've made much difference if he had."

"My." She let herself smile. "You're such a professional. Aren't you?"

"I'm paid to be."

"Whatever you indicate will happen, happens. Like
pushing a button . . . on the elevator over there." She
nodded toward the closed doors, the brushed stainless
steel raked by the sun's fierce glare. She turned her own
gaze away from the man. The light and heat would si-
phon away any possible tear. She felt genuinely sorry
about Isidore; the poor little geek's neck, with its wobbling bespectacled head on top, would probably have fit
inside one of Andersson's fists. Perhaps that was how
he'd done it, like twisting and pulling the knobbed cork
out of a bottle of Dom Pérignon. More likely, the obliging Isidore had volunteered, soon as he'd figured out

what was wanted of him. *Wuh-would you like me to kuh-kill myself? Huh-huh-happy to.*

"You're the one who pushes the buttons."

"Am I?" That still seemed an odd concept to Sarah Tyrell. "I suppose so." She remembered being a three-year-old child and looking up at her uncle—the doors of the *Salander 3* had unsealed and popped open; a nurse had led her down the ramp, with the long boxes holding the remains of her parents following right after—and seeing his thick glasses, the lenses shaped like the computer monitors that had been her windows aboard the starship, the cold eyes behind them scanning and assessing, calculating. He had reached down and touched her hair, rubbing a lock of it between his thumb and forefinger, as if gauging its suitability for some new industrial process . . .

"What're you doing?" Her voice, sharp and startled; she felt her spine go rigid, every muscle tensed for flight or attack. The reverie into which she'd sunk had been translated into this reality, the rooftop landing deck of the Tyrell Corporation headquarters, right now. Her uncle's touch had become Andersson's; the man, still leaning back against the spinner, had reached out and stroked the stray wisp of fine brown hair at the nape of her neck. His fingertip stayed there, a fraction of an inch away from her tremulous skin. "What . . . I don't . . ."

"Yes, you do." He leaned forward and kissed her.

Kissed and fell to the landing deck's hard surface, both his hands upon her, as they had been before. She turned her head and saw the undercarriage of the spinner, the extruded landing gear, the vents and air intakes; she could smell the sharp reek of its fuel and the condensation of steam, mixed with the closer scent of his sweat as he reached between them and undid the front of his jumpsuit; she couldn't tell the mingled odors apart anymore, or whether they came from him or the machine. It didn't matter to her.

She closed her eyes. That was part of the payoff, the regular arrangement between herself and Andersson, that kept him working for her, plus the checks drawn upon the Tyrell Corporation's black operations account and made payable to an electronics supply warehouse in Mexico City. The arrangement must have been satisfactory to Andersson; she had lost track of which installment this was. Easy to forget that she wanted this, wanted everything, as much as he did . . .

Something else to be sorry about. That the arrangement had come to an end; she knew it, even if he didn't yet. At the edge of her awareness, she felt her hand remove itself from his back and reach inside her coat pocket, for the object she had taken from the drawer of the *bureau plat* down in her uncle's office.

Andersson gasped—too soon, at least for him; she could feel the shock wave run through his body. He pushed himself back from her, his spine arching. One hand clawed at his back, fingertips smearing through the bright red that had burst open there.

"Goddamn . . ." He'd rolled onto his side, finally having managed to pull out the knife she had inserted, point first, between his shoulder blades. Andersson shook his head ruefully. "I *knew* you were going to do this. I knew it . . ." The knife clattered on the hard surface of the landing deck. He managed to push himself up into a sitting position, propped up against the spinner. His blood shone on the black metal. "It's not like . . ." Voice weaker. ". . . it's unexpected . . ."

"Please don't ask me why." She kept her own voice formal, polite. She had gotten to her feet and was now putting her own disarrayed clothing back in order, reaching down to smooth the skirt of the dress over her knees. "I'd find it tiresome to explain." Sarah straightened up, noticing a spot of his blood on the front of her blouse. Silk, and thus ruined.

He managed to laugh. "Don't bother . . ." He

gazed at her, almost admiringly. "It's pretty much . . . the nature of the business . . ."

Checking the time, as much by glancing up at the sun as looking at the slender watch on her wrist. And waiting; as always, Sarah hoped he wouldn't take too long.

A few minutes later she succeeded in dragging his body to the low parapet surrounding the landing deck, her shoes leaving a triangle and dot pattern in the thin pool of his blood. She was surprised at how light he seemed when dead; she had unexpectedly little trouble in lifting the corpse high enough to topple it over into the empty space at the center of the Tyrell Corporation's slanting towers. *Adrenaline*, she thought; some little surge in her own bloodstream, unnoticed by her cognitive processes, had perhaps given her the extra strength required.

Andersson's body fell of its own accord, arms and legs splayed out in air. Hands braced against the parapet, she watched until it was lost to sight; the corporation's employees, working in the replicant manufacturing units that formed the base and core of the complex, had no doubt already had the surprise of the corpse smashing into one of the reinforced skylights above their heads.

Business to take care of—Sarah straightened up and took her cell phone out of her coat pocket, punched in the security division. "There's been an accident." She smoothed her hair into place as she spoke. "It can be taken care of on an internal basis. There's no need to call in the police." She gave a few more details, some of them true, then disconnected. The corporation's own security people were drones, without Andersson's initiative; she could count on them to do no more than what she wanted. Even the mess up here on the landing deck—they'd all keep their silence, and their jobs.

She started to turn away, to walk back toward the elevator doors, then stopped. A shudder ran through her body; dizzy and nauseous, she had to lean against the spinner for balance. The adrenaline, and whatever other hormones had been released, now seemed to evaporate from her veins. She closed her eyes, her pulse scurrying faster, breath quick and shallow. "I'm sorry," she spoke aloud. As if there were anyone to hear her, as if it would have done any good if there had been. She resisted the impulse to lie back down upon the deck and curl up with her trembling fists and elbows tucked close against herself.

The attack passed. Breath slower and deeper again—she took the few steps back to the parapet and looked across the vast space, to the three other towers of the Tyrell Corporation headquarters. A city in itself, surrounded by the larger compressed mass of Los Angeles. The four towers slanted in toward each other and the truncated pyramid in their midst, like the petals of a cubist flower that hadn't fully opened yet. When she had come back from Zurich, with the corporate minions who now worked for her, she'd been given the grand tour, through all the sectors of the complex, the areas that she'd never been allowed to enter while her uncle had been alive. It'd taken days to complete. They had told her everything, all the secrets. Including what they had called *the red button*, though there wasn't any red button, but an overlapping series of commands that had once been keyed to Eldon Tyrell's voice pattern, but hadn't been keyed over to hers. The one thing beyond her control—even as the minions had been telling her about what would happen if she could have spoken those magic words, a vision had come to her. That had made her heart swell with a fierce gladness.

She looked out now across the landing deck's parapet, that vision overlaying the solid, slanting towers. Fire and force, this world she owned riven by its own private apocalypse. The explosions would start at the base of the structures and continue upward, following the Wag-

nerian sequence of the programming that had been built
into them from the beginning . . .

*Brennt das Holz heilig brünstig und hell, sengt die Glut
sehrend den glänzenden Saal . . .*

" 'If the wood catches fire,' " she murmured, eyes
closed, " 'and solemnly, brightly burns, then the flames
will destroy the glorious hall . . .' "

Wagner had that much right, at least. Not *programming;* she knew that was a stupid word for it. *Fate* was
the true word.

Der ewigen Götter Ende dämmert ewig da auf . . .

" 'The eternal gods' last day then dawns . . .' "

Sarah opened her eyes. The vision had faded, leaving the parallelogram towers of the Tyrell Corporation
still standing.

She turned away and headed for the elevator, to go
back down inside the building's heart.

He'd made his decision. Or, at least, the next step in his
rapidly evolving plans.

What do I need this loony sonuvabitch around for?
Dave Holden glanced over at Batty, sitting beside him in
the cockpit of the freight spinner. They were flying
west, returning from the Reclamation Center out in the
desert, to the sprawl of the city. The same harsh sunlight that darkened the curved glass's photochrome
membrane heated the brown stew of pollutants hanging
in the air above L.A.; he could see it up ahead, like an
old, frayed-edge wool blanket spread over the simmering buildings. Batty's hands moved across the controls,
manually piloting the craft. When he was busy doing
something, he didn't look quite so maniacal. But that
didn't change the situation.

The question didn't need an answer—Holden had
decided that part a while back. But there were other
questions that did.

"So, uh, exactly what is *your* interest in all this?"

"I told you." Batty turned his cracked smile on him again. "The sixth replicant. The one that's still missing."

"What about it?" The smile still had the capacity for making him nervous. "You just want to shake its hand or something? Get an autograph?"

"Don't want anything from it. Except to find it and kill it. And take back the evidence to the people who hired me that I've completed this little job for them."

"And who's that?"

"Can't tell you." Batty's eyes shifted. "It's . . . a secret."

"Bullshit." His inner radar, his honed blade runner senses, flashed on the other's momentary unease. "I can tell you're scamming me." He peered closer at Batty. "You don't know who hired you, do you?"

"Well . . . I got my suspicions about it." Batty gave a minute adjustment to one of the controls. "Might be the LAPD. Or it could be a gov agency. Possibly the feds, maybe even the U.N.—bad replicant business can call down some pretty high-level heat. Whoever it is, they're working outside the official channels, so we're talking cover-up. Ultra-spook stuff; I got the job details and my up-front money through a double-blind courier service, no trace possible on who sent them my way."

"How'd they find you? In the yellow pages?" *Probably under Cannons, Loose*—the thought gave Holden a twist of smug amusement.

"The fact they found me at all just proves these guys're up there. Man, I'd pretty much figured if I was going to be retired against my will, then I was going to be retired all the way—I'd taken every dime I'd saved up, from when those bastards over at the Tyrell Corporation had been still paying me my royalties on their line of Roy Batty replicants, and I'd dug myself in tight into a nice, safe little conapt in one of the Cracow ex-pat zones. I was gonna do nothing but drink gin and listen to Mahler's Second for the rest of my life." He shook his head. "You know, I don't *have* to kill people to have a good time."

"But it helps."

Batty shrugged. "Speak for yourself. I didn't need to take this job—"

"You did, though." Holden's turn to show a thin smile. "So now you gotta go through with it. If these people you're talking about are such heavyweights, they wouldn't like you crapping out on them."

"Tell me about it." His face appearing suddenly older, expression glum. "I've worked these kinds of gigs before. Perform or die's the general rule. Even so," muttered Batty, "I got half a mind to pull the plug on the whole operation. Dealing with an ungrateful little jerk like you—"

"What'd I do?"

"It's what you *didn't* do." Glum to resentful. "I arrange for a whole new heart and lungs to get slapped inside you, and you don't even say thanks."

"Christ . . . give me a break." Holden shook his head. "All right, you have my sincerest appreciation. Satisfied?" He looked ahead to the city approaching on the horizon, then around to Batty again. "Not as if it was all selfless altruism on your part, though, is it? You had some reason for busting me out of the hospital and all."

"True. That's what pisses me off. I need you."

Holden raised an eyebrow. "For what?"

"Come on." A big sigh from Batty. "I've been out of the game for a while now. When I took you out of that hospital, that was the first time I'd been in L.A. in years. It's a whole lot bigger and uglier than when I left it. I need somebody who knows his way around. Otherwise, that sixth replicant could be hiding out in there, and I'd have fuck-all chance of finding it."

"Oh, sure." He gave a snort of disbelief. "So buy a map, already."

"It's not just the lay of the land, pal. It's the connections. You got 'em and I don't. When I took off from L.A., I cut all my ties, all my sources of info, my whole network. I expect that most of the people I used to deal with are dead now, anyway. Places where they were at, things they were into—longevity's not much of an issue there." A shrug. "Wouldn't be such a problem if I'd done anything to replace them. But I don't have time to do that. Replicant number six has gotten a real jump on getting himself safely out of sight. I can't screw around any longer finding it—I need somebody who's already got their systems up and running. Blade runner-type systems. That's you, Dave. That's why you're here."

He didn't say anything in reply. If Batty wanted to believe he was so valuable, he wasn't going to do anything to dissuade him from the notion. A mixed bag regarding the state of his own connections, though. He'd been flat on his back, zoned out on the hospital's IV drip, for the better part of a year; that was a long time to be off the scene, especially in L.A. Batty didn't have a clue about how fast things changed now, compared to his day. Plus he was on the lam himself—his old boss Bryant, and God knew how many other people, had put him on ice for their own reasons, and they weren't likely to be too overjoyed about finding him walking around again. *Though maybe that's a positive,* mused Holden. *If I got taken out by a conspiracy against the blade runners, the rest of them will be on my side.* They'd have to be, for reasons of their own survival. *At least the smart ones will be,* he thought. Which meant that Batty's assessment was correct; he did have resources that he could call upon. The best kind, right inside the LAPD itself, right under the noses of Bryant and the others who'd set him up.

The residue of doubt evaporated, leaving the hard stratum of a blade runner's self-confidence. He still had the edge that came with being human. The spinner had reached the L.A. suburbs, sections of a maze homogenous with that of the city's tight, imploding center.

Somewhere in there was the answer, walking around with someone else's face. Whose?

I'll find out soon enough. Holden glanced over again at the figure beside him. The same question went through his mind, assessing how much further use he had for Batty. Or whether he'd be better off without him, going out on the hunt alone.

"All right," said Holden. "I'll help you out. After all . . . it's only fair."

Batty looked up from the spinner's controls. "We got a little partnership going, then."

"Oh . . . we sure do." And smiled right back at him.

Deckard knew where he was going. He just didn't know how to get there.

It'd been easier when he'd been able to fly straight to the safe-house apartment in an unmarked spinner, at night with the tracking lights switched off, engines throttled back to near silence. *That was when I was a blade runner,* thought Deckard. *A real one.* With all the perks and privileges that accrued thereby. Now he had to creep along on the ground like a civilian or, worse yet, a hunted thing. Whatever transformation Sarah Tyrell promised him had been completed some time ago.

The stolen cop uniform was so torn and shredded as to be unrecognizable as such. His bruises and abraded skin, wounds crusted with dried blood, showed through the ragged gaps. As he climbed over the floes of concrete rubble and twisted rebar, the palms of his hands left small red marks.

At the crest of one long upward pull, Deckard stopped to catch his breath, the dry-heated air scalding the interior of his throat. An exact ninety-degree angle of marble and steel, once vertical and now laid out along the ground, marked where one of the zone's towers had fallen. Some of the buildings had pancaked flat during the long-ago seismic upheavals, but most had toppled

over lengthways, riding out the earth's whip-crack
motion. A knife of freeway cleaved the zone, the lane-
divider dots writing empty, absurd graffiti along the
roadbed turned to wall.

A glance over his shoulder revealed unmarked sky,
no pursuit from the air in sight. Holding on to the tumbled building's ridge, he shielded his eyes with one
hand, scanning across the zone for any other indication
that his laboring progress had been spotted. No one and
nothing—either the cops who'd been on his tail at the
central station had assumed he'd fallen under the wheels
of the rep train, and were still searching the tunnel for
his bits and pieces, or they'd put the chase on hold until
he reemerged in a territory more to their liking. Clusters
of serious-bad criminal types—Sawney Bean dysfunc-
tional families, Dahmer-ized protein fetishists—were
known to make the sideways world their turf; sending a
squadron of fresh uniforms through here would be like
parading a flock of leather-wrapped turkeys into a
wolves' convention. It wasn't worth having a set of
sharp-filed teeth ankle-biting through your jackboots,
when the chances were good that the bones of the person you were looking for were already being gnawed
somewhere else in the zone.

Using the building's broken windows as handholds,
Deckard worked himself down the slope of the other
side. *Just get there*—a message not just to his fatigued
limbs, but from one part of his brain to the other. More
than exhaustion; the rep train and the nightmare vision
it'd held, memories and faces, with the last one the most
disturbing, had rattled him down to his soul. If he had
one left.

He'd have to think about that later. Right now, the
rest of Deckard's functioning cerebral sectors were
mulling over his plan of attack, once he'd reached the
safe-house apartment. There'd be little time to rest, and
the job to do still in front of him. Hooking up with his
old boss Bryant had turned out not only to be a wash,

but worse than that; the task of finding the sixth escaped replicant was now compounded by even darker
mysteries. Somebody had iced Bryant—what the hell
did that mean? *Maybe,* thought Deckard, *the sixth replicant did it. Killed him.* The one whose ID data Bryant
had purged from the police department files. As long as
Bryant had still been alive, the cover-up wasn't complete; there was still at least one person who knew who
the sixth replicant was. With Bryant laid out cold, the
data was purged from its final location, human memory
itself . . .

All of which meant, Deckard knew, that the job of
finding the sixth replicant was going to be that much
harder. Bryant had been his only route into the department's records. The synthesized image of Bryant on the
video monitor, with its glib real-time responses, might
have been lying, stalling him, when it'd said that the
sixth replicant's ID could still be drawn up from some
locked-tight sector of the databases—no way of determining that now. And no way of getting back into the
police station to try accessing the information; the cops
would be on him in two seconds if he were stupid
enough to show his face around there again.

What then? Deckard brooded as he continued his
laborious progress over the sideways world. Dig up an
old Voigt-Kampff machine from the gear stashed at the
safe-house apartment, and start running empathy tests
on everyone in L.A.? That should only take a few centu-
ries to complete.

One possibility had occurred to him. Of trying to
establish some kind of direct comm link with the authorities in the off-world colonies, passing himself off as
a high-level figure in the LAPD—maybe as Bryant, if
the off-worlders didn't know about him being dead—
and getting a repeat transmission of the original data
about all of the escaped replicants. That'd be one way of
getting number six's ID; the only problem was that it'd
be nearly as difficult as bringing Bryant himself back

from the dead and grilling him for the info. The off-
world security agencies weren't exactly on the phone
grid; the U.N. sat on every tight-beam transmission
between Earth and the colonies. Even if he could engi-
neer some way of tapping in and getting on-line to
them, there'd still be the small matter of faking the police department reciprocity codes, convincing the off-
worlders of some bullshit reason for sending the data
again, the whole elaborate ruse—and doing it without
alerting the cops about what he was doing and where he
was doing it from.

He didn't like his chances about pulling all that off,
but at the moment it was the only plan he had. Other
than letting the word get out that he was back in town,
and waiting for the sixth replicant to come looking for
him, with murder on its mind. That was something else
to think about.

Or too much to think about. Deckard gritted his
teeth against the sting of the sun-baked rocks in his
palms and the swirl of plans and possibilities inside
his head. Enough to make him long for the time when
it'd been easier, when he'd hated his job but still knew
what to do. When he could stand with legs braced,
squinting through the rain slashing at his eyes, bringing
the heavy black gun up with both hands locked tight on
its grip, arms extended, aiming as the city's crowds had
parted before him like an ocean with faces . . .

Then firing; the gun's recoil traveling hard into his
chest, then rolling onward, its palpable echo diminish-
ing at the base of his spine, the gun lowering of its own
dead weight. The last had been the female Zhora, one of
that last batch of escaped replicants—and the first of
their number that he'd retired. He could still see the
flight of her body, its energy combined with the bullet's
thrust, crashing through one plate-glass window after
another. Until it had come to rest, blood mingling with
the rain, the bright shards like melting crystals of ice at

his feet as he'd looked down at her. At what it'd become, a dead thing, its quick life over . . .

Deckard pushed the memory loop out of his brain.
Thinking about stuff like that only led to grief. To bitter
meditations about what he'd become. He'd quit the job,
quit being a blade runner, before that time. When he'd
realized that he didn't hate his job . . . but liked it too
much.

With thoughts carefully stilled, Deckard went on
clambering through the rubble. The small bit of luck
he'd had in getting across the sideways world lasted for
the rest of his journey: he spotted no one, human or less
so, though he heard some scurrying noises at various
distances, indicating some of the more timid inhabitants
fleeing his approach. He also managed not to get lost
himself amid the sector's jumble and clutter, even
though he was translating a bird's-eye knowledge of the
route into progress on foot. The fallen freeway served as
a landmark—he knew that if he kept it to his right and
counted off ten up-ended off ramps, he'd arrive more or
less at his destination.

Which was right in front of him, at last; Deckard
managed to get a sigh of relief through his panting for
breath. He stumbled toward the multistoried apartment
building, an early-period Gehry knockoff.

The corridors inside the building were unlit tunnels,
oriented wider than high. Some rudimentary electrical
service still existed in the zone, remnants of some of the
pirate utility grids that had flourished around the turn of
the century. He hoped that no one had tapped out the
conduit that served the safe house's security functions;
it'd been a while since he'd had to use the place.

He found the door, a rectangle on its long side, a
number in the low hundreds barely visible beneath layers of spray paint. A *placa* demon, fuzzy-edged batwings
and Day-Glo fangs, still decorated the inverted hallway.
Deckard knelt down to the small metal grid a few inches
from the plugged keyhole.

"It's me." He tried to keep his voice as level and free of stress tremors as possible. "Come on, open up."

A red LED flashed on behind the grid. "Do I know you?" A canned voice, the emotionless female that resided on most small-device chips. "Please don't violate me. Go away and leave me alone."

He didn't have time to deal with a recalcitrant lock; squeezing his eyes shut in frustration, he banged his fist against the grid. "Open up or I'll take you apart, so help me God." He'd use his fingernails for screwdrivers, if he had to.

"Shame on you."

His forehead came to rest just above the tiny holes. "You want more samples? Fine." He scrabbled through his near-depleted brain for something more to say, to trigger the lock's recognition mode. "Four score and . . . something years ago . . ." He couldn't remember the rest. "Um. Say you're walking along in the desert, and you see a tortoise. You see a tortoise and . . ."

A sharp click sounded inside the grid. He barely caught himself from falling into the room on the other side of the door as it popped open.

He closed the door behind himself, leaning a hand for balance against the wall that had once been a floor. Even darker in here, the windows boarded over and sealed tight. Deckard could make out a few familiar furnishings, remnants of lives led when the building had still stood upright: an overstuffed couch beside a row of framed Keane paintings, footsteps imprinted across the big-eyed waifs, an overhead light fixture that now dangled into one of the inverted corners; through the doorway into the apartment's kitchen could be seen a disconnected refrigerator lying on its avocado-green flank, the magnet-studded door flopped open.

In this small pocket of security—when it'd originally been set up as a safe house, the exterior walls had been injected with both thermal and acoustic sensor-tracker foils—he felt a measure of tension drain out of his cramped shoulders. But only for a moment. He looked down, his eyes having adjusted to the darkness, and saw a miniature Prussian soldier, with a clown's rouged cheeks and an elongated nose, tip broken off, gazing back up at him. The little soldier's eyes went wide in frightened realization.

"I know you!" Its voice was pitched comically high. "I saw you before!" It spun on the heel of its cavalry boot and ran toward the apartment's bedroom door. "Sebastian! Sebastian! There's a man here—a bad man! A killer! Sebastian!"

Before Deckard could react, the door sprang open, its knob whacking the surface on which he stood. Something flew out, knocking the little soldier aside. Something that spun and twisted, and struck him full in the chest before he could get out of its screaming trajectory.

He landed on his back, with a pair of what felt like hands gripping tight around his throat. A white-haired wraith knelt on his chest, its teeth clenched and eyes radiating a murderous fury. He recognized it, even though when he'd seen it before it'd had the face of a young woman, and now wore the skeletal mask of deracinated leather. Its wrists felt like corded bones in his hands as he struggled against its throttling hold.

"Pris!" Another voice, from somewhere else in the tilted room. "Don't do that! You'll hurt him!"

At the edge of his sight, drowning in a red haze, Deckard saw a man with the face of a wrinkled baby, strapped to the back of an animated teddy bear. The man tugged with a single hand at the crazed figure's arm, its tattered leotard tearing open farther. Deckard felt himself falling away from the visions of combined nightmare and memory, the cutoff of his own breath turning red to black.

12

"I'm real sorry about that." Fussy and nervous, a voice that suited the man, or what was left of him. "Sometimes Pris just goes off that way—even with me. She's got like—you know?—a hair-trigger temperament. That probably indicates some sort of deep-seated anger inside her."

"You could say." Lying on a bare mattress inside the safe-house apartment, Deckard watched as Sebastian—a bio-engineer who'd formerly freelanced for the Tyrell Corporation; he remembered the police file on the guy—busied himself making coffee. A complicated process: the teddy bear, eyes tarnished as the buttons on its nineteenth-century waistcoat, had to back up to the sideways-mounted sink, while the triple amputee in the papoose carrier used the end of the counter as a flat surface for the grinder and French press. "Maybe she remembers me." Deckard rubbed his bruised throat. "Maybe she remembers me blowing her away. That might do it."

"Gee . . . I don't know." Sebastian struggled to

press the plunger down. "I can't exactly be sure what Pris *does* remember." Black coffee grounds were scattered all over, from the spilled bag of expensive welfare-drop rations. "Sometimes I wonder if she remembers *me*. And I'm the best friend she ever had—even when she was alive." He finished pouring, then held out the cup on a cracked Meissen dessert plate. "Squeaker, would you take this over to our guest?"

The miniature soldier, the spike-helmeted figure that Deckard had first encountered in the safe-house apartment, grudgingly brought the coffee to him. It gazed balefully past its stretched nose, still regarding him with suspicion; the soldier's memory seemed unimpaired, at least. Deckard pushed himself into a sitting position and took the cup. "How much of her cerebral functioning were you able to save?"

"Oh, most of it, actually." Sebastian sipped from a demitasse. He appeared ancient as a baby bird, almost incapable of feeding itself, the skin of his hand and face translucent, crumpled parchment. "But those Nexus-6 circuits are real fiddly. It's basically an unstable design, with a lot of kludges and work-arounds. I warned Mr. Tyrell about putting 'em out on the market; I told him there'd be trouble. You start havin' to do recalls and boom, your profit margin's all shot to heck. Just the return shipping costs alone, from the off-world colonies . . ." A shudder ran through the abbreviated torso in the papoose carrier. "You can't just stick a postage stamp on 'em and send 'em home, you know."

"That's true." The coffee was hot and bitter on Deckard's tongue. "They tend to get into trouble."

"Yeah . . ." Sebastian took another sip. "But like I said, it's mainly the flaws in the Nexus-6 design. They're susceptible to having visions and stuff. Nearly as bad as real humans."

"Whatever." Didn't seem a point worth discussing. Through the doorway into the even dimmer back sections of the apartment, the mobile scarecrow that'd been the replicant Pris sulked and glared at him, its eyes two red embers somewhere below its albino fright-wig. His skin still prickled tense at the sight of her, a response triggered by the memory of her nearly killing him, riding his shoulders and slamming her fists into the sides of his skull, then twisting his head around like a broken doll's. "You must've moved fast, to get your hands on her at all." The last he'd seen of her, before this encounter in the safe-house apartment, she'd been flopping around on her back, spitting and shrieking in her death throes, the bullet from his gun having torn open her midsection.

"I sure did." Sebastian nodded. "I loaded her up in my van, from the police morgue—I had a pass for doing that. They'd already done their tests on her, so I didn't think they'd mind anyway. Not that I was going to stick around and ask 'em. I figured there'd be an arrest warrant out for me pretty soon. 'Cause I snuck out of a police-custody hospital, my own self—they thought I was dead when I got found up in the Tyrell private suite, most likely since I look so decrepit and stuff, but I'd just kinda passed out, is all; they got my heart started up again, out in the ambulance. But I figured the police probably had me down as having helped Batty get in to kill old Mr. Tyrell. So I just took Pris's body and my little pals, and lit out for this zone. Where they wouldn't be able to find us."

"Good thinking. Accessory to murder's a hard rap in this town. Especially when the evidence is on tape."

"It's a bum rap, is what it is." An indignant expression settled across Sebastian's watery eyes. "I would never have hurt Mr. Tyrell; I know he wasn't a very nice man and all, but he *was* my friend. Sort of. That's why I tried to warn him. That something funny was going on." Sebastian's voice grew excited. "When Roy and I were coming up in the elevator, to Mr. Tyrell's personal suite—I was supposed to tell him that I'd figured out my next moves, in the chess game we'd been playing. Well,

Roy'd figured 'em out; I just repeated what he told me. Only—I bet it's on the security-system tape—when I was supposed to say 'Checkmate,' instead of that I said, 'Checkmate, I think.' That's how I was trying to warn Mr. Tyrell that something was wrong, without letting on to Roy that I was doing it."

The words came out in a babbling rush. "You see, 'cause I didn't know it at the time," Sebastian went on, "but it was like a famous chess game that Mr. Tyrell'd set up—the one that's called the Immortal Game, between a coupla old-time grand masters, way long ago—Roy told me about it, when he showed me the moves I should make. All that chess stuff was part of his memory implant, some of what Mr. Tyrell himself had programmed inside Roy's head. I could never've figured 'em out on my own; Mr. Tyrell knew I couldn't play chess on his level. So when I said *I think*, he should've known I didn't get the moves out of a book, and that somebody else must've told me, and that person was probably with me right then, so he should've called the corporate security folks instead of letting us in, 'cause I knew Roy was up to no good—"

"Okay, okay, I believe you." Deckard held up a hand against the barrage of words. He actually had no idea what the other man was talking about. "Look, it doesn't matter. I didn't come out here to arrest you or anything."

"No?" Sebastian peered closer at him. "I thought maybe you were, because of Mr. Tyrell getting killed, and me breaking in here—I'm sorry about that. I only did it because I found this place with all the locks and everything working, and it didn't look like anybody was living here."

"Don't get into a sweat. You're welcome to it. Just someplace that I used when I was out in the field, hunting down replicants that might've slipped over into this zone. It's nothing special."

" 'Hunting down replicants . . .' " Sebastian's eyes

widened in sudden fright. "You didn't come around looking for Pris, did you? Just 'cause I . . . I *saved* her? She's already been dead once. You're not going to kill her again, are you?"

He doesn't know, thought Deckard. *He still believes she was a replicant.* All that talk about the difficulties with the Nexus-6 neurocerebral wiring confirmed that Sebastian hadn't heard the results of the bone marrow analysis tests on Pris; he'd already cut himself out of any Tyrell Corporation-related loop by then. Hunkered down here in the sideways world, he'd have no way of knowing. And no way of finding out—the bone marrow tests were the only way of determining a physiological difference between a replicant and a human.

Weird how things worked out—in the safe-house apartment, Deckard had found himself in the company of the one person who didn't think he was guilty of murdering a human being. The one person who had the most right to think of him as a murderer.

"You must've loved her." He felt sympathy for the truncated man. "Very much. To . . . put her back together the way you have."

"No . . ." Sebastian shook his head. "I *love* her. Right now, the way she is. Nothing's changed. Not for us, at least. And I know, deep down, Pris loves me."

The wraithlike creature, red-eyed and with a blazing corona of white hair, had heard its name spoken, the name it had answered to when alive. It slid into the apartment's kitchen, keeping its back close to the walls and a wary gaze on Deckard. It stepped next to the animated teddy bear, bending down to be as near as possible to Sebastian, its dried-leather face touching his wrinkled, babyish one. Its idiot eyes remained locked on the figure on the other side of the room.

"You see?" Sebastian couldn't keep from bragging about his own cleverness. "It wasn't easy, but I managed to keep the important parts going—she knows who I am and stuff." With his one hand, he tenderly stroked the

white hair. "She really is inside here. Even though I had
to strip out a lot of the soft tissue from the rest of the
body." He spoke matter-of-factly, as though describing
the repair of a broken radio. "I had a lot of my tools and
spare parts with me already, so I was able to get the
sensor-activator relays and the muscle-surrogate motors
wired in without too much trouble. But she's still pretty
much a high-maintenance item; she can't really take
care of herself. She needs me. So when I was done getting her up and running, I did what I had to, on myself."

He looked down at his own body, what was left of
it, in the papoose carrier. "The doctors back in the city
had told me that this pseudo-progeria I got—accelerated
old age, you know?—that it could be slowed down, even
halted for a while, by reducing the demands on the core
system. It's mainly a progressive collapse of the circula-
tory and nervous systems. So I had to whittle away at
myself, the way I did on Pris. I figured all I really needed
was one hand—as long as I had my little pals to help me
get around." He patted the teddy bear on its woolly
head; it looked over the epaulet on its shoulder and gave
him a steel-toothed smile. "We get along all right, don't
we, Colonel?"

"Did it work?" Deckard used the empty cup to
point to him. "I mean . . . on your condition."

"Don't really know." Strapped to the back of his
button-eyed companion, Sebastian gave a lopsided
shrug. "But I'm still here, aren't I? Surrounded by the
folks who love me." The other of his creations, the miniature soldier with the spike helmet and long nose, had
come into the kitchen and pressed itself close to him,
forming a family tableau. "That's all that matters, isn't
it?"

He supposed it was. There was nothing he could
say to contradict the other man. Carved down to a
one-armed torso, with a couple of toy dwarfs for companions, and the female creature he was in love with
reduced to a murderous skeleton—Deckard envied him.

Loving the dead, loving the bits and pieces left behind, even just memory—maybe that was what defined human. *For the dead,* he wondered, *or for us?* Deckard didn't know.

For a moment, as he had watched Sebastian with the resurrected Pris, a dim spark of hope had flickered inside him. Maybe Sebastian could do the same for Rachael; not keep her from death, but bring her back in some altered but still recognizable form. Just as quickly, the spark had turned to a cold cinder. Even if it were possible, he knew it was nothing that he wanted, nothing that he could endure. Better to have your memories, and your grief, than to be haunted by an animated corpse wearing a mask of the beloved's emptied flesh. *The poor bastard,* he thought as he regarded Sebastian. The little man, or what remained of him, didn't even know how screwed up he was. Just as if some crucial perception of reality had been cut away, along with his other limbs. Just things he'd found he could live without.

Though maybe . . . he could get me off the murder rap. Deckard mused as he sipped the last of the cold coffee. Maybe he could take the Pris-thing, the animated corpse, to the authorities and say that he hadn't killed any human, after all; here it was, still walking around. Or she was, sort of. He discarded the idea. The Pris-thing wouldn't be a very convincing demonstration of his innocence. One look at her, or it—at what she'd become—and they would just take him out and shoot him, throw his body out in the street. From sheer disgust.

He abandoned any more speculations. Deckard supposed it didn't matter, anyway. All that he knew, or cared about, was that he was still a long way from the one whom he loved. And who was dying.

"Here's the deal." The freight spinner swooped in low over the towers of L.A. "First, we find Deckard. We grab him and—"

"What, we have to go all the way up to Oregon?" Holden looked over at Batty in dismay. "What kind of plan is that?"

"Oregon?" The spinner's controls shifted beneath Batty's hand. "What're you talking about?"

He shook his head. More evidence that he was dealing with somebody on the verge of senility. "That's where Deckard went," he explained patiently. "Bryant told me that, while I was still in the hospital."

"That was then. I'm talking about *now*." Batty looked down at the city. "Right now, Deckard's here in L.A."

"Bullshit. Why would he come back?"

"He didn't come back, he was *brought* back. By persons unknown; probably not a police operation. One of my buddies back there at the Reclamation Center heard it on the departmental grapevine and clued me in. Deckard was hauled out of whatever little hiding place he had up north and flown in here."

Holden studied the figure beside him in the cockpit. "Who's got him now?"

"Nobody." The spinner had been put into a big-loop holding pattern; Batty leaned back from the controls. "He either got away or he was let go. One way or the other, we have to find him."

"Why?"

"I thought you were smarter than that." The thin edge of the smile returned to Batty's face. "Haven't you figured it out? Deckard is the sixth replicant. The missing one."

Holden was tempted to say "Bullshit" again, but a thread of doubt slipped into his thoughts. What if Batty was right? "You better give me your logic on this."

"It's simple." Batty's smile broadened. "What's the one kind of replicant that a blade runner replicant—

such as yourself—couldn't be assigned to track down and retire? *Another blade runner replicant.* It would give the whole game away. If you found yourself face-to-face with your own double, or the double of somebody else that you'd always thought was also a human blade runner . . . come on." Batty tapped a finger against his brow. "You wouldn't have to be a genius to start figuring out that something funny was going on. You'd start asking questions, or keeping 'em inside your head, and pretty soon the people in charge are going to run out of bogus answers to fob off on you. Then you're dangerous; that's when they have to pull the plug on smart-ass little replicants who've learned too much."

He might be part right, thought Holden. *Even if Batty's completely cracked regarding my human status . . . he could still be right about Deckard.* That struck him as completely plausible the more he mulled it over. He'd never liked the other blade runner; he'd always found Deckard to be cold and disagreeable, with an irritating batch of moral poses about their jobs. He should've quit the force sooner rather than go as long as he had, bitching about it the whole time.

Or Batty was completely wrong. *Deckard and I might both be human*—that idea had some attractive qualities to it. Simplicity, for one; he could see that as soon as somebody started doubting outward appearances, the surface levels of reality, then that person had entered an infinitely expanding maze, where nothing was really what it seemed to be. That was how people wound up in the same lunatic condition as Batty. Who was probably one step away from thinking that he himself was a replicant. *Of course, if he is,* thought Holden, *then . . .*

He shut off that line with a tight mental clamp. Right now, it didn't matter. Capitalizing on what Batty had just told him was the primary objective he had to keep in view.

"If Deckard's in L.A., then finding him is no prob-

lem." Holden filtered an easy confidence into his voice.
"I know where he'd go."

"Yeah?" Brightening, the other reached for the
spinner's controls. "Lay it on me."

He gave Batty the directions; a moment later they
were hovering over what had once been the city's Los
Feliz district.

"Aw, man." Batty shook his head in disgust. "This
is your big brain wave? You figured Deckard would just
go back to his old apartment? Nobody's that stupid.
Look, you can see the police have already been here and
checked out the area."

Holden glanced out the side of the cockpit and saw
yellow strips of POLICE INVESTIGATION—DO NOT CROSS
strips, now torn and trampled into the windblown dust
by the ground vehicles that had converged on the apartment building, then left. "So?" He shrugged. "The police—those grunt cops—they don't know what I know
about Deckard. He and I were like brothers. Blade runners."

"Spare me."

"Just take this thing down. You'll see."

The locks on Deckard's front door had been
punched through, the tempered steel beneath the numbers 9732 dented and wrenched back. Took Batty a few
minutes to fiddle the police seal without triggering an
alarm signal to LAPD headquarters. He shoved the door
open, and he and Holden stepped inside from the unlit,
silent corridor.

"What'd I tell you?" Batty scanned across the
search wreckage that lapped up against the replicas of
Frank Lloyd Wright's original *faux* Mayan wall panels.
"There's nobody here. If there had been, the cops
would've tweezed him out a long time ago."

Holden said nothing, but walked farther into the
apartment. He knew his way around; he'd been here a
couple of times before, from a period predating his and

Deckard's mutual agreement that two blade runners sitting and drinking in the same room was a bad idea.

The piano bench had been knocked over by the cops who'd ransacked the place. Old brown-edged sheet music lay scattered across the floor, along with the photographs, framed and unframed, from that distant world of the past. Sweet-faced women gazed up with somber understanding from the black-and-white depths.

He found what he'd figured would still be there, what Deckard had shown him once, fastened to the underside of the bench with a strip of wide packing tape. He pulled it free and gripped it tight in his fist.

"Whattya got there?" Batty had had his back turned, but had heard the ripping sound. "Hey—what's that?"

Holden ignored him. He walked toward the bathroom at the rear of the apartment. "I'll show you in a minute."

"You'll show me right now."

He could hear Batty following him. Without switching on the light, he knelt down and snapped one end of the object, Deckard's spare set of handcuffs, onto the metal pipe behind the toilet. He stood back up as Batty appeared in the doorway. "Look right here," said Holden, pointing.

Batty stepped past him, bending down and peering to see. In one quick move Holden stepped back and grabbed the other man's head with both hands. He brought his knee up sharp into Batty's face, knocking him back with a spray of blood from the nose. Dazed, Batty lolled back without resistance as Holden lifted him upright by the padded collar of his jacket. A hard punch to the stomach dropped Batty to the floor.

He found himself panting and dizzy, the biomechanical heart in his chest racing from the sudden flurry of exertion, the new lungs laboring for breath. Taking a step back, out of Batty's reach, he watched as the other man groggily shook his head, blood streaming to his chin. As though a switch had been thrown in his brain, from impaired to full functioning, Batty suddenly snapped into motion, springing from the bathroom floor and instantly being jerked back by the handcuffs fastened to his wrist and the toilet pipe.

"You sonuvabitch!" Kneeling, his face reddening with fury, Batty clawed his free hand a few inches short of where Holden stood. "Get these things off me! Right now!"

"Sorry . . ." Holden retreated to the hallway of Deckard's apartment. "Can't do that. I've got a private appointment to get to." He turned away, striding toward the front of the apartment and the door out to the building's corridor.

"Holden!" Behind him, Batty thrashed and shouted, voice echoing in the bathroom's tiled confines. "I'll fix your ass—"

He could still hear the other man screaming violent curses as he slammed the front door shut. Despite the pounding of the machines inside himself, he broke into a quick trot for the elevator. He didn't know how long the cuffs would hold Batty; the man had looked enraged enough to pull the pipe right out of the wall. Holden punched the ground-floor button and leaned against the elevator's inside wall, a squadron of black spots swarming in front of his eyes.

A couple of minutes later he was aloft in the freight spinner, banking it in a tight curve, then accelerating in a straight line. To where Deckard would actually have gone to hole up.

As the spinner climbed above the city, Holden could see a flash of hot sunlight reflected from the ocean off to the west. At the horizon, a dark mass of clouds had begun to form.

They heard the door being broken in. The teddy bear raised its head as though sniffing the air for the source of the commotion; the spike-helmeted soldier moved in front of Sebastian, a defensive barrier against whatever might come through the kitchen doorway.

From instinct, Deckard reached for a weapon at his hip—and found nothing. Turning, he pulled open one of the counter drawers and extracted from it a paring knife with a cracked handle.

The sounds of someone moving through the front part of the apartment, a passage made more difficult by the rooms being tilted onto their sides—a figure appeared at the doorway, bending down to look in on them.

"Holden . . ." Surprised, Deckard nearly dropped the knife he held. "What're you doing here?"

"You mean, why aren't I stuck in a hospital somewhere, with tubes running in and out of me." The other man ducked his head past the door frame and dropped into the kitchen space. He glanced at the knife in Deckard's hand. "Nice to see you, too." His gaze swept across the figures in the room. "Christ, what a welcoming committee."

"They're a family." Deckard set the knife down on the up-ended section of the counter. "We should be so lucky."

The Pris-thing fastened its red-eyed glare on Holden, then hissed, spine arching catlike. Sebastian's single hand stroked the thing's shoulder. "Now, Pris, there's no call for that. This gentleman's not gonna hurt you—"

"What the hell—" Loathing wonder was visible on Holden's face.

"Don't sweat it," said Deckard. "She's his old girl-friend. One of the escaped replicants. She's been . . . recycled. Sort of." He nodded toward the figure on the back of the teddy bear. "Sebastian's clever that way."

"Pris! Wait! You don't have to—" The voice from the amputated torso rose into a wail as the corpse of his love darted away from him, disappearing into the dark recesses of the safe-house apartment. Sebastian's arm reached futilely for the skeletonized figure, already gone from sight.

"Nice going, Dave." Deckard peered closer at the figure in front of him. "You know . . . I figured you'd probably be dead by now. Or something."

"Yeah, well, that was the plan. But I got a new lease on life." With the flat of his hand, he thumped his chest, turned pale, then recovered. "Feel like a new man. Part of me, at least. No thanks to that pile-of-shit Bryant." Holden's expression darkened to a scowl. "Bastard set me up. I'm going to make sure he goes into major payback mode."

"Wait a minute." He didn't know what exactly his ex-partner was talking about, but one thing was clear. "You don't know, do you? Bryant's dead."

The info rocked Holden back against the wall. Deckard could almost see the gears spinning in the other's head as he tried to incorporate the new datum into his thinking.

"He's dead . . ." Holden lifted his hand, as though there were a veil before him that he had to part in order to see clearly. "Did he just pop off from a heart attack, something like that? The fat pig was overdue for one."

"There was blood all over his office. Or there had been—I saw the stain on the floor. However he went, it didn't look like it'd been an easy process. Or pleasant."

"Jeez . . ." Holden shook his head. "That kind of puts everything in a different light. Because if Bryant got blown away, then . . ." He lifted his gaze, then took a step closer to Deckard. "Look, I realize these people— or whatever they are—might be your friends and all." He kept his voice softened. "But you and I have got some heavy stuff to talk over."

"Hey, you don't have to worry about us." From the other side of the kitchen, Sebastian called over to them. He looked sullen and teary-eyed. "We know when we're not wanted. Come on, fellas. Let's go see what Pris is doing."

"Didn't that guy used to work for Tyrell?" Holden
craned his neck to watch as the animated teddy bear,
with Sebastian in the papoose carrier, clambered toward
the rear of the apartment. The spike-helmeted soldier
gave a dirty look over his shoulder, then disappeared
with his companions. "You shouldn't be hanging around
with people like that—not unless you got them thor-
oughly checked out. What're they doing here, anyway?"
Holden gestured around the tilted walls. "Did you let
'em in here? This place was supposed to be just for
blade runner operations—"

"Simmer down." Deckard leaned against the end of
the counter. The knife was close at hand; his old partner
was starting to sound deranged, and looked agitated
enough to flip out. "They're harmless."

" 'Harmless'—that's a good one." Holden's gaze
narrowed. "Nothing's harmless in this universe. That's
one thing I've learned. You should've learned it by now,
too."

"Maybe I did. Maybe I forgot."

"Well, that's where you went wrong, then. That's
how you got all screwed up, Deckard. Falling in love
with replicants . . ." Another shake of the head.
"Trusting them. You're a fool. What you should've realized a long time ago is that the only person a blade
runner can trust is another blade runner."

"Then I'm off the hook. I'm not a blade runner
anymore."

"Correction. Once a blade runner, always one.
There's no quitting this job—not while you're alive, at
least. Look what happened when you tried."

He could see where this was going. "I get the impression you're about to ask me to trust you."

"As I said—I'm the only one you *can* trust."

"I don't know . . ." Seemed a grim prospect. "If
I'm going to break this trusting habit of mine, maybe I
should go one-hundred-percent cold turkey. Starting
with you."

Holden peered around the edge of the kitchen's doorway, making sure that Sebastian or any of the others wasn't listening in, then turned back to give Deckard a hard stare. "Joke away, asshole. Long as you don't mind laughing in your grave. Because that's what it comes down to. There's somebody who doesn't want us blade runners alive. Probably more than one somebody; a whole conspiracy. High-level and mean. Whoever they are, they've got the resources to take us out, one by one—until they're aren't any more of us."

"Maybe you'd better get that gear inside you checked. Lack of oxygen to the brain can trigger paranoid delusions."

"Equipment's running fine." Holden dug out a pack of cigarettes from his coat pocket, lit up, and took a drag. A moment later blue smoke hung in the kitchen's air; some filtering mechanism inside his chest could be heard revving up. "What needs adjustment is *your* brain. You don't seem to understand yet: somebody's gunning for us. For all the blade runners. They set me up last year for a hit, they got our boss Bryant . . . and this whole business of you being dragged back here to L.A.; that's probably got something to do with it as well." Holden's gaze shifted as he followed that line of thought. "Probably because as long as you're running around alive, even up north in the boonies, you're still a loose end for them. The conspiracy isn't just to kill off the individual blade runners, it's to shut down our whole operation. Wipe it off the books completely."

"Come on." A wearied sigh escaped from Deckard. "Easier ways to do that, Dave. Christ, every year Bryant had to fight to keep our unit alive in the departmental budget. If these conspirators are so high-powered, why couldn't they just pull the money plug on us? Every blade runner in town would've wound up washing dishes down at the nearest noodle bar. Not like we've all got exactly ace job skills."

"Speak for yourself—" The cigarette nearly

dropped from Holden's hand as he started coughing, a nicotine hack that doubled him over for a moment. He looked old and grey when he straightened back up, the pump in his chest visibly laboring for air. "Look, that's all beside the point, anyway. How should I know why they want to kill us rather than just dumping us out on the street? Maybe there's something we all know, something that's part of the job, and as long as we're alive there'd be the possibility of us spilling it. Maybe they want to eradicate the blade runner unit right out of human memory, as though it never existed—they can't leave us walking around, then. Christ, Deckard . . ." The cigarette made a fiery comet trail as Holden angrily gestured. "If I knew *what* they wanted, *why* they're trying to kill us off, I'd goddamn *be* in on the conspiracy."

"There's something else you don't know, Dave." During the other's rant, he'd looked up at what had been one of the kitchen's walls; now he brought his gaze back down. "About me."

"What's that?"

"I don't care." Deckard looked him straight in the eye. "I don't care if there's a conspiracy to kill off all the blade runners. Maybe there is, maybe there isn't; I don't know. But I've got my own business to attend to. I left this city with somebody—and it was easy to do it. Getting killed was just about the only thing left here for me. Somebody's still trying to kill me? I'm shocked, Dave, really shocked. Get real." He folded his arms across his chest. "I've been dragged back here, and I've got one more job to take care of. All I want is to do it and get the hell out of here again. Somebody's waiting for me."

"A job, huh?" Holden studied him. "The only thing somebody would want you to do is to hunt down replicants. That's all you're good for. This little job . . . it wouldn't have something to do with another one of that batch that escaped before, would it? A *sixth* replicant?"

"What do you know about that?"

"Oh . . ." Holden shrugged. "Maybe all kinds of

things. Things that you *don't* know, Deckard. That's
why you should come in with me on this. You don't
stand a chance, otherwise."

"Forget it." He shook his head in disgust. "I've got a
better chance of finding and retiring it than I would have
with a patched-up loser like you hanging around."

"Wait a minute—"

"No, *you* wait. Because I don't have time for your
bullshit, Holden. You're not even interested in finding
any sixth replicant. You've got this conspiracy trip-wired
into your head now, and you can't get it out. That's not
my problem. I'm not interested in breaking up conspiracies, saving the blade runner unit, whatever. That's all
stuff in *your* world. Mine's not big enough for that sort
of thing. Not anymore."

"You stupid sonuvabitch." A carrier wave of pity,
mixed with a higher cutting frequency of loathing, radiated from Holden. "It's not as if you have a choice
about what world you live in. What makes you think
they'll *let* you go crawling back to whatever hole you've
dug in the ground? Even if you manage to ice their missing replicant for them. You'll know too much; they
won't let you go."

Deckard hesitated, then pulled back from the needle that the other man had inserted into his thoughts.
"I'll make it. Whether they want me to or not. Like I
said: somebody's waiting for me."

"Big talk, Deckard." A sneer twisted the corner of
Holden's mouth. "And a long walk. The only spinner
outside is the one I came here in. Don't—" His hand
darted into the same coat pocket that'd held his cigarettes, this time extracting a small chrome gun. He
smiled. "Just in case you had some idea about—shall we
say?—*borrowing* it from me."

"Thought had crossed my mind." Deckard looked
closer at the weapon in the other's hand. "Where'd you
get that? Not your regular piece."

"I'm making do with whatever I can find these days.

It belongs to a mutual acquaintance of ours—the same one I got the spinner from. He left it in the cockpit." Holden nodded slowly. "You'd be amazed if I told you who it is."

"Don't bother. I told you already. I'm not interested in this stuff."

"You're screwing it up, Deckard. For all of us." Holden's voice tightened. "We've got a chance if we stick together. If we don't, we'll get picked off, one by one."

He shrugged. "You look out for your ass. And I'll look out for mine."

"Okay, jerk—" The machinery that'd been stuck inside Holden sent an angry surge of blood into the man's face. "Don't say I didn't warn you."

Eyes closed, leaning back against the up-ended kitchen counter, Deckard listened to the other's racketing exit from the safe-house apartment. A few minutes later he heard the distant noise of a spinner lifting from the rubble outside the building. Then everything was quiet again.

For only a moment. The silence was broken by a knock at the apartment's front door.

No one came inside. Deckard waited until the knock sounded again. He pushed himself away from the counter. Making his way through the tilted rooms, he grasped the doorknob and pulled.

Rachael stood in the corridor outside, bending her head down to look past the top side of the doorway.

No— He pushed the memory trip out of his brain. *It's not Rachael.*

"I thought he'd never leave." Sarah Tyrell turned her head to look down the dark, empty corridor, then brought her gaze back to his. She smiled. "May I come in?"

13

They came to burn.

Nothing fancy; wood and rags didn't require anything more than a simple flammable liquid, an accelerant to get things started. "Put them over there—" The leader of the team pointed to a clear space several yards away from the cabin. "There's some other things we have to take care of first."

The other men, in coveralls marked on the shoulders and breast pockets with the Tyrell Corporation logo, began stacking the red canisters on the ground, their boots crunching through the layers of dead pine needles. An owl, startled from its diurnal slumber, flapped noisily away, its broad wings drawing a curtain across the sun for a moment.

Shading his eyes with one hand, the team leader watched the bird's flight; the creature disappeared under the denser canopy of the forest farther down the mountain ridge. The trio of spinners in which he and the others had come up from the south reflected sunlight from their metal flanks. No effort had been made to conceal the corporation's emblems; up here, there was no need for a covert operation. The one person who might have seen, and noted their identities, was engaged elsewhere, down in the city where they had received their orders.

"Should we go in?"

A voice beside him; the team leader turned and saw his second-in-command, patiently waiting. The gasoline cans had been arranged in a neat, shiny pyramid. *We brought too much*, thought the team leader. He'd known how small the ramshackle cabin was, but hadn't worked out in his head the practical consequences of that fact. A tiny space, bound by thin, mossy walls and a sagging roof; barely large enough for the lives it'd held. The plural was somewhat inexact, he knew. A life, the man's, and a partial one, the woman's, constricted by sleep and death intertwined. A single can of gas and a match would've been enough. Like torching a doll house, a fragile plaything, a bubble in the great, hard world that surrounded it.

The inside of the cabin's window was covered by a tattered cloth. He'd already gone up to it, right after they'd first brought the spinners down from the sky, and brought his face close enough to the cold glass to catch a glimpse of the interior darkness. And the objects therein: an out-of-date calendar on the rough-splintered wall, a wooden chair toppled over on its back, an ancient stove black with soot. And something else, even blacker, an oblong shape resting on crude, low trestles: a glass-lidded coffin, its occupant unviewable from the window's angle.

He knew she was there, though; he had seen her the last time he'd been in this place, when he'd been the second-in-command and Andersson had been the team leader. They'd all worn unmarked gear then, just their name tags, no Tyrell logos on themselves or the spinners. And they'd come at night, shadowy predators, waiting until their employer had finished her business with the man inside the cabin, then swooping in and carrying him away, as the owl did with the mouse in its claws.

"There's nothing left to do out here," said the second-in-command. The other men stood around, waiting. Patiently—they were regular Tyrell employees, security division, paid by the hour and not by the mile.

"All right." For a while, it'd seemed to him as if this place, the small forest clearing with the cabin at its edge, were deep in some sort of magic time, without clock or event. Suspended, like the living and dying of the woman in the transport module, between one sleeping breath and another, this day's heartbeat and tomorrow's. "Might as well get it over." Maybe if he'd come here alone—he could've taken care of everything that needed to be done, by himself. As it was, with all these others around him, there was no way the spell could remain unbroken. "Come on."

The team leader pushed the cabin door open, letting the afternoon sunlight spill across the bare planks of the floor. He stepped inside, letting the rest follow him.

Now he could forget their presence. In hers; he stood beside the black coffin, looking down at the woman who rested there. Under the glass, the curls of her dark hair spread out across the silken pillow. Eyes closed; lips slightly parted, as though waiting for the few molecules of oxygen that sustained her or a kiss; hands pale with stilled blood, folded beneath her breasts.

He could have kissed her. The impulse to do just that, to lean down and press his lips against the cold glass, a few inches away from hers, had moved inside him before. When he'd come up here with Andersson on that other job, just a couple of days ago, when they'd taken the sleeping woman's true lover away with them and back to L.A. He hadn't done it then, because he'd known that Andersson wouldn't have understood. Or worse, would have—he knew that Andersson had loved this woman, but in another form; the same face, but not mired in death.

That'd been while Andersson himself had still been alive, of course; he'd been among the security detail back at the Tyrell Corporation headquarters who'd scraped Andersson's broken body from the base of the slanting towers. He knew what had happened, though it wouldn't be mentioned in the official explanation. Andersson had loved the living woman, and had died for that sin. That mistake. Maybe those who loved the dying, the dead, would find eternal life thereby. In his own motionless heart, the team leader wondered how poor Deckard was doing.

For a moment longer he stood gazing down at her. Then he stepped back and gestured to the other men. "All right. Pick her up and take her out of here." It was what he wanted, but it was also part of the orders he'd received from the sleeping woman's double. He watched as they picked up the black coffin by its recessed handles, lifting it from the knocked-together wooden trestles. "Careful . . ."

They carried her outside, away from the cabin, toward the spinners. A moment later the men returned, this time with the canisters of gasoline in their hands; the team leader hadn't had to tell them to do that. Or the rest; they were on program now.

When the cabin's interior was soaked, the men splashed more gasoline on the outside, then poured a trail on the ground to where the team leader stood. He lit a match and dropped it at his feet. The fire, a hot shimmer in the daylight, ran from him and dived into the darkness behind the cabin's open door. A moment later the fire shouted from the single window, its bright fingers spreading apart the walls and roof.

They watched the cabin burn, until the charred boards collapsed in upon each other. It took only a few blasts from the extinguishers they brought out from the spinners to end the fire's short life, grey smoke unfolding into the sky. Then they finished up the rest of what they had to do.

From the cockpit of one of the spinners, the team leader looked down at the black mark on the earth's surface. The spinner lifted higher, and the cabin's burned remains were lost among the surrounding trees. He turned around in the seat, closing his eyes, keeping them that way until he could see the sleeping, dying woman's face again. All the way back to Los Angeles.

"Quite a place you've got here." She looked around, as though completing a realtor's assessment of a valuable property, estimating its worth on today's market. Sarah had stepped into the room, the disorder of its sideways condition having no visible effect on her. She radiated a cool assurance, money more powerful than gravity. "Distinctive."

"We like it." Deckard as gracious host. "It's those homey touches that're so important."

"I can imagine." Swathed in her coat, the fur collar turned up against her bound hair, she seemed insulated from the still heat collected between the safe-house apartment's inverted walls. She turned her inspecting gaze toward him. "For Christ's sake, Deckard—you look like a scarecrow." She reached over and fingered the torn sleeve of the stolen uniform. "If the LAPD decided to go into beanfield management, they could stick you on a cross out there. You could frighten off the birds all day long."

"There are worse jobs."

She followed him into another section of the apartment, ducking her head to get past the sides of the doors. To one of the bedrooms; it must've been a child's at one time, before the seismic events that had turned everything around. Faded curtains with a still visible pattern of baby ducks and chicks hung askew over the boarded-up window. He felt Sarah watching him as he lowered the door of the closet and dug out some of the clothes he'd stashed there. Spares; operations in this zone had often taken days to complete. Holden had kept some clothes here as well, his finicky tailored suits carefully hung in a plastic garment bag smelling of cedar extract. He didn't see the bag now; he pulled himself back out of the closet, his own things draped over one arm.

Keeping his back to her, he stripped off the uniform jacket and the shirt beneath, things of cloth and leather, stained with his own blood. He didn't flinch, as though the nerve endings were already dead, when he felt her hand touch the wounds across his shoulders.

"You should take care of those." Sarah's voice had softened just a little. "You wouldn't want them to get infected."

Somehow the apartment's bathroom had wound up not just tilted onto one side, but turned 180 degrees around, the ceiling light fixture now in the middle of what had become the new floor. Deckard knelt down by the remains of the sink, letting a trickle of water fall away from the cracked porcelain and into his cupped hands. Carefully he sponged away the dried blood from his torso and arms, using the wadded-up rag of the cop's shirt to dry himself. A piece of the broken mirror was large enough to see himself in: a face made lined and older-looking by exhaustion, eyes even older by witnessing. The water was translucent pink on his hands when he took them away from his brow and deepened sockets.

He dressed in the bedroom, knowing that she was still watching him. The new clothes were only slightly musty from their long stay in the closet; he buttoned the tight-checked shirt's collar up against his throat, the top button digging at his abraded fingertips. The long coat was identical to the one he'd worn before; he'd bought them both at the same time, from a Paraguayan haberdasher working out of the dense warren of linty cubbyholes in the old Cooper Building downtown. He slipped it on, though he knew how stifling hot the safe-house apartment, and all the Santa Ana-battered world out-

side, was right now. The blood he'd lost from all the tiny
marks on his skin might have been enough to take his
core body temperature down a couple of degrees. *Or
else it's from her,* thought Deckard. The woman brought
her own winter along.

"Very nice." Sarah spoke from behind him. He
glanced over his shoulder and saw her leaning back
against the bedroom wall, arms folded across her
breasts, a judgmental smile. "Is this the man I fell in
love with? The other I, that is. Rachael. Is this the way
she first saw you?"

"I don't know. Maybe she did." He picked up the
last of the things he'd taken out of the closet. "Maybe
she didn't see anything at all. Just a cop." His hands
worked the rough wool necktie under his collar, then
started fumbling the knot together. He could feel Sarah
watching him. "Why did you come here?"

She regarded him for a moment. "I thought I
should check up on you, Deckard. See how you were
doing."

That was the problem with working for other people. She probably wanted the head of her sixth replicant
on a stick. "How'd you find this place?"

"It was easy. Your old friend Holden—he has a nice
new heart-and-lung set pumping away inside his chest.
The unit was manufactured by one of the Tyrell Corporation's medical subsidiaries; there's a lot of crossover
work between manufacturing replicants and human
prosthetics." A smile. "We knew for whom that particular one was intended. They're all custom jobs; they
have to be. So a miniature transmitter was put in it, way
down inside where the valves go clickity-click. Anywhere Dave Holden goes, we know about it. *I* know
about it. That's all that matters. That's why I wasn't
worried about being able to find you again. No matter
where you got to. I figured Holden would always be able
to find you. Blade runners know each other, don't they?
Your minds work the same way."

"Maybe," said Deckard. "Up to a certain point. But I didn't go with him—did I? He had business with me, too. An offer; like being partners again. But I didn't pick up on it."

"Why not?"

"Nothing I was interested in. Besides—" A shrug. "I already have a job."

"Oh?" Sarah raised an eyebrow. "I appreciate your loyalty. But then . . . you're motivated. Aren't you?"

Something caught his eye. He turned his gaze away from her and saw that it was the broken mirror inside what had been the apartment's bathroom. He could see his own splintered, fragmented reflection, an image that'd been cut up, pieces scrambled together, then sorted out and poorly reassembled.

His brooding was interrupted by a sudden noise, a hissing intake of breath, pitched high and loud enough to be a cry of dismay. At the same time, something grabbed his arm, two hands squeezing tight into the heavier fabric of the coat's sleeve. He looked beside him and saw Sarah, drawing behind him as though for protection, an expression of loathing and disgust on her face.

"What the hell is *that*?" She took one of her hands away from his arm and pointed.

In the bedroom doorway, the rectangular opening turned on its side, crouched Pris. Or what remained of her, what her lover Sebastian had been able to salvage. The emaciated figure, flensed to the bare minimum inside the ragged leotard, balanced itself with one bony hand against the door frame; the red eyes, dots of fire beneath the uncontrolled shock of white hair, had already scanned across the bedroom space. And fastened onto the other female creature held by it.

"Don't worry." Deckard watched as the Pris-thing unfolded itself spiderlike into the bedroom. "It won't hurt you." The head stayed low, the stare of the red eyes sweeping to either side as it cautiously advanced, as though looking for any possible threat, before returning to Sarah.

"You're right about that." Her other hand let go of his arm, and she began rummaging in the deep pockets of her own coat for something.

"Pris! *Pris!*" Sebastian's piping voice echoed down the hallway outside. "Don't go in there! Leave those folks alone—"

Beside him, Sarah raised her arms, both hands locked together. He saw what she had pulled out of her coat, the black metal filling her doubled grip.

At the same time the Pris-thing rose up in front of Sarah, spine telescoping like a machine rearing into place. The hissing breath changed into a gasp of wondering surprise, eyes widening to reveal more of the fiery lenses inside the skull. A trembling arm, a skeletal hand reaching its white fingertips toward the face of the woman, drawn back by instinctive aversion. Its mouth opened wider, a word, a name, struggling to bridge some fragile synapse and emerge onto the rattling leather tongue . . .

He tried to stop Sarah, to grab her arm and pull it away, but he was too late. The smallest motion of one of her fingers was all that was required. The recoil pulsed through her braced stance, pushing her back against his side for a moment. Muzzle flash eclipsed the Pris-thing's ravaged face, only inches away from the black hole at the end of the gun. Even before the afterimage had begun to fade from his sight, he could see the lightweight creature hoisted by the bullet's impact, desiccated splinters spraying from the shattered cheekbones and brow, the spinal column arching into a bow as its shoulders were flung back onto a bed of empty air.

In the doorway, Sebastian screamed. His single hand and forearm had lifted him higher onto the back of the teddy bear, so he'd been able to see everything that'd happened. The toy soldier shoved past the bear, then stood rooted in place, eyes and nose following the

Pris-thing's trajectory as it slammed into the angle of two walls.

Nausea rose in Deckard's throat. The last time Pris had died, when he had killed her, the body with its ripped-open gut had flopped and spasmed on the floor, shrieking not so much with pain as with the release of the fierce energy unspent. This time around, the twice-dead Pris lay crumpled like a rag doll, torso folded at the hinge of the lower back, disjointed hands sprawled behind, head bowed forward as though to reveal the red fissure beneath the albino golliwog hair. The red eyes had already dimmed to black dots, any remaining battery cells shorted out.

"You didn't have to do that." The nausea had mutated to a heavy sadness, a stone in his chest, as he'd watched Sebastian crawl from the back of the kneeling teddy bear toward the broken corpse.

Sarah turned a level gaze at him. "Yes, I did."

On the other side of the room, Sebastian had reached the dead thing, had gathered it into the embrace of his single arm, and now rocked back and forth with it. Tears ran along the wrinkles of his face as an anguished keening issued from low in his throat. One of the teddy bear's paws stroked Sebastian's shoulder in a futile effort at comforting him. The toy soldier completed the *pietà* arrangement, the point of its antique helmet bending low over the corpse's blood-spattered feet.

Deckard crossed the room and looked down at the other man. "Can you . . ." He gestured at the body. "You know . . . put her back together?"

"Don't be stupid—" Sebastian gulped back his sobs, enough to speak. "Look. Her brain . . . it's all tore up. I can't fix that. Nobody can." He leaned the side of his face against what remained of hers. "She's dead. All dead." His tears mingled with her drying blood. A blind gaze swept across the room, a spark of red showing far inside the unfocused eyes. The corpse's clawlike fingers scrabbled at the wall beneath, as though some residual life force had dribbled out of one of its batteries.

"How touching." Sarah's voice, her cold words. Glancing over his shoulder, Deckard saw her returning the dark bulk of the gun to her coat pocket. "Perhaps now we could get back to business."

He stood in front of her. "It recognized you. Didn't it?" He peered into her eyes, as though trying to catch some betraying response without benefit of a Voigt-Kampff machine. "What was that about? When it saw you, it knew who you were."

"I doubt it." No blush response, no flutter of the pupil. "It probably thought I was Rachael. It must've thought it had spotted another replicant like itself."

No. Like she'd thought herself to be. He'd started to correct Sarah, to remind her of what she already knew— that Pris had been human—but had stopped himself from speaking. The distinctions were blurring again. He'd killed, murdered a human being named Pris, who'd convinced herself that she was a replicant; if he'd had a chance to run the empathy tests on her, she probably would've failed them. What had she been after Sebastian had kept a spark going in her addled brain, made her capable of moving again? Alive or dead, human or replicant? He didn't know. He supposed he had arrived at that state Isidore had talked about, back at the Van Nuys Pet Hospital. Of not even being able to see the difference anymore.

Other thoughts remained unspoken, barely formed. If it'd been Rachael, not Sarah, that the Pris-thing had recognized . . . where would that have been from? Maybe some memory of the assembly line at the Tyrell Corporation's headquarters, all the Nexus-6 models, the Prisses and the Zhoras and the Roy Battys, all warehoused together before being shipped off-world. That was wrong, he knew immediately; there had never been any Pris model replicants. Only in her mind. *Maybe it'd been out there*, thought Deckard, *in the U.N. colonies.* Maybe Pris had managed to convince other human beings that she was a replicant, and had served time along with a Rachael model in a sanctioned military brothel. The image made him squeeze his eyes shut tight, as though he could blot it out from his own brain. It might not be true, anyway; hadn't Sarah told him that Rachael hadn't been a production model, but a one-off, a single creation for Eldon Tyrell's purposes? She could've been lying about that; there was no way of knowing . . .

Out of the darkness behind his eyelids, a memory flash. Not that long ago—*I saw her.* He saw her again now, the face in the rep train, that other darkness beneath the central police station. Huddled with the other replicants, the discards of the industrial process that had created them. Weeping with a terror that'd had no way of expressing itself except the trembling of her naked shoulders, the tears leaking salt into the corners of her mouth. So there were others like her, like Rachael. There had to be. If what he'd seen was true, and not just some fevered vision drawn from his own exhaustion and fear.

"So what's it going to be, Deckard?" A knife or Sarah's voice. "Shall we talk?"

He opened his eyes. And looked at her. Or at Rachael, or the one who had wept behind the locked gates of the rep train's rattling freight car. The memory overlays faded, one veil after another. Until he saw clearly again.

"No . . ." A sigh, indicator of the weariness that had wrapped itself around him again. "I don't have time. I've got a job to do." Behind him, he sensed Sebastian's and the others' presence, the various living and not-living forms, the dead tucked close in its lover's embrace. "We don't have anything to talk about."

"You're wrong. We have everything to talk about. At last." She regarded him with the same flat, level gaze. "I'm trying to make it easier for you, Deckard. I

want you to come with me, right now. Outside, to my
spinner. As charming as the hospitality here has been,
I'd really prefer to have our little discussion elsewhere."

"Why should I?"

"Because you don't have a choice." Head tilted
against her coat's fur collar, Sarah Tyrell regarded him.
"You come with me now, or I leave by myself. And I
notify the police of where you're hiding out. I could do
it from the phone in the spinner—it wouldn't be more
than a few minutes until they got here." She glanced at
the figures on the other side of the room. "I imagine
they'll clean up the rest of this mess here as well."

"Come on." He returned her gaze with distaste.
"This poor bastard hasn't done anything."

"That doesn't matter. He can be picked up and
screwed with until he might as well be guilty. You know
how it works, Deckard; you've done the same. Of
course, if you don't want that to happen . . ."

She had him, and he knew it. The time when he
would've been able to tell her to go to hell, when the
threat of bad shit happening to other people wouldn't
have mattered to him—that was long past. *She's trading
on that fact*, thought Deckard. He could almost admire
the accuracy of her perception. She knew that he'd already become less of a blade runner . . . and more of a
human being. Which made him, to her, more exploit-
able.

"All right." He glanced over at Sebastian, then decided against saying anything to him. There wasn't anything. He thrust his hands deep into the pockets of the
long coat. "Let's go."

Holden had rummaged through the freight spinner's
cockpit until he'd found what he wanted, needed, had
known would be there. The gun had been the first find,
and the best; it'd come in handy talking with that idiot
bastard Deckard.

I should've killed him, thought Holden. *Right then*

and there. That had been his original intention; disgust at what a pussy Deckard was being had overwhelmed him, though. Plus, there'd been others inside the safe-house apartment, like that sawed-off Sebastian, riding around on the back of his wind-up teddy bear. Who knew whether the little basket case might be packing something? Holden shook his head; he knew he'd still have to be extra cautious, at least until he got his full strength back.

And his regular gun. The one he'd found in the freight spinner was all right for now. It was smaller and didn't weigh as much as the big black cannon that served as standard blade runner equipment. Which was a good thing; he'd started to feel a little weak and breathless, as though the implanted heart-and-lungs set was crapping out under the load he'd been putting it through. All this running around, adrenaline jazz, couldn't be good for a man in his condition. His old gun would've pulled him over like an anvil strapped to his shoulders.

The other handy thing he'd found, underneath the pilot's seat, was a pair of Zeiss binoculars with resolution-enhanced optic-feedback circuits. The help screens at the upper right corner of the vision field had all been in German, but he'd still managed to get the device up and running. And focused on the toppled building that contained the safe-house apartment.

Behind a low rise of concrete rubble, he'd stashed the freight spinner safely out of sight. Inside the apartment, his former partner Deckard probably thought he'd gone on, winging back into the center of L.A. His pissed-off-and-shouting behavior, that'd concluded their little conference, had been at least partially an act, designed to make Deckard believe that all he wanted to do was lay down as much distance as possible between the two of them. He wasn't through with Deckard yet, not by a long shot. And from the looks of it, neither were some other people.

No sooner had he gotten the freight spinner hidden than he'd spotted the next visitor. *She must've been there all the time, waiting for me to leave*—lying on his stomach, elbows braced against the ragged concrete edge, Holden trained the binoculars on the woman as she went into the sideways apartment building. Too late to get a glimpse of her face, but the sleek arrangement of her dark hair, and the fur coat—in this heat? It must've had one of those cryonic linings—all spoke of money. *Like I'm surprised*, he thought bitterly. It would be just like that weasel Deckard to have belatedly learned the art of selling out to the highest bidder.

He'd searched through all the bins and equipment caches of the freight spinner's cockpit, looking for some kind of long-range microphone, something he could've used to eavesdrop on what was going on inside the safehouse apartment, but had come up empty-handed. It would've taken powerful, professional quality gear to get anything, he knew; when the place had been taken over for use by the blade runners, with no connection to the LAPD, they'd all chipped in to trick out the windows and exterior walls with sound-deadening insulation. So creeping up and laying his ear on the building wouldn't have done any good, either.

They're up to something in there. Frustrated, Holden rolled onto his back, setting the binoculars on his chest and trying to get the mechanical heart's pulse back down by sheer force of will. It wasn't obliging. "Goddamn," he muttered aloud, glaring at the empty sky. He might've strained the equipment, perhaps irrevocably; he felt worse now than when he'd left the Reclamation Center out in the desert with Roy Batty. *Miserable cheap gizmos*—he wondered what bargain-basement gear the LAPD had requisitioned for cases like this. For all he knew that quack doctor-*cum*-garage mechanic had implanted a rusting tin can and a couple of balloons left over from some kid's birthday party.

Taking deep breaths, he managed to get the black

spots wandering in his sight—bad warning sign of an-
oxia, brain strangulation—to fade to grey and even dis-
appear. Mostly. He turned back onto his elbows and
swept the binoculars' view toward the other spinner,
the one the woman, whoever she was, had arrived in.
She'd left it in plain view on the other side of the apartment building.

The bar code on the spinner's fuselage came into
focus. He tripped the binoculars' reader function; a few
seconds later the LED display flashed the minuscule
words SECURED REGISTRATION; NO INFO AVAILABLE ON THIS
VEHICLE. He wasn't surprised; a late-model, high-thrust
job like this one had to belong to somebody who could
buy the pull to keep it off the databases.

Invariably a way; words of wisdom. Holden dialed
in higher and higher rez levels, until he was looking
right into the intake manifolds of the expensive after-
market turbos that'd been mounted on the spinner. The
sunlight slanted into the curved titanium mouths, just
enough for the binoculars to pick out the manufac-
turer's serial numbers. Repeating the string to himself,
he slithered back to the freight spinner and keyed up the
control panel's computer. A moment later he had the
info he'd wanted: the after-market gear had been pur-
chased with the appropriate U.N. acquisition order by
Ad Astra Transport Services. He didn't need to look
them up; he knew that the company was the shipping
wing of the Tyrell Corporation. Its logo, a tacky Soviet
Realist image of a stylized male figure lifting a ribbon-
tied package to an anonymous planetoid, was on the
sides of all the container trucks taking sleep-frozen
replicants to the San Pedro docks, for delivery to the off-
world colonies.

So, Tyrell . . . that's interesting. Holden tried to
dredge up what he could from his own, pre-Kowalski
memory banks. Eldon Tyrell was dead—Bryant had told
him that while he'd been in the hospital, bubbling and
gurgling away—but wasn't there a daughter or some-

thing, who would've been his heir? No, a niece; that was it. Maybe this was Ms. Tyrell, the new head of the replicant-manufacturing industry, who'd zipped out here in the company spinner to talk with Deckard. She'd known where Deckard was; so he must've gotten in touch with her and told her to meet him here, or she'd met him before. No way she would've been able to find the hiding place by herself.

So that meant this woman—and by extension the Tyrell Corporation itself—was in cahoots with Deckard. Who was supposedly an ex–blade runner, or at least had previously been represented to be a blade runner— Holden wasn't sure anymore about that. The Tyrell Corporation and the blade runner unit had always been two mutually antagonistic forces, inasmuch as the corporation was always engaged in creating replicants that were increasingly closer to passing for human—how much longer would it have been until there'd been Nexus-7 or Nexus-8 models running around?—and the blade runners were just as dedicated to finding them and exposing them as replicants. One of those locked-in predator-and-prey relationships, where each side could take turns being either the wolves or the sheep. *So what's Deckard up to now?* wondered Holden. *Sleeping with the enemy?*

His musing was cut short by a sound he didn't need high-powered eavesdropping equipment for, loud enough to penetrate through the safe-house apartment's acoustic insulation. He ducked instinctively as the gunshot reverberated over the concrete rubble on all sides of the freight spinner. One shot, then silence again; Holden cautiously raised his head above the level of the cockpit panel and looked out toward the toppled building in the distance.

Even more interesting—he speculated as to who had shot whom. Deckard didn't have a gun, he was fairly sure, but that didn't matter. He could have gotten whatever weapon the woman had been carrying away from her. Unless she'd come here with the specific intent of plugging Deckard, and had just done so. *Conspirators falling out?*—it wouldn't be the first time.

Whatever had gone down inside the safe-house apartment, he knew the smart thing for him to do was to lie low and go on watching. There was *somebody* walking around in there with a loaded gun. He had one as well, but in his present physically depleted state, he wasn't sure he'd be able to lift it up and get a shot off without a disastrous wobble to his double-handed grip. Even the binoculars seemed to weigh a ton, as he crawled back out to the top of the ridge and aimed them at the building.

What the . . . He peered harder into the eyepieces, as he spotted two figures coming out. Deckard *and* the dark-haired young woman he figured was the new owner of the Tyrell Corporation. Neither one had shot the other—they both looked reasonably intact. What the hell did *that* mean? Still conspirators? Hard to tell from the habitually sour expression on Deckard's face what the degree of cosiness between the two people was . . . though the woman looked somewhat satisfied with herself. Deckard had taken on the appearance of his old self, a memory flashback to his days of officially being a blade runner, having changed from that ratted-out cop uniform to plainclothes, including another one of those long coats he'd always been so fond of.

He watched through the binoculars as Deckard and the Tyrell woman got into the hot-rodded spinner and took off. The temptation hit him, to scramble into the freight spinner and tail the other craft, but he thought better of it—they'd have spotted him right off.

For a moment longer he watched the spinner, a black speck at the head of a fiery trail, fading from view above the mirror-radiant towers of the city. The Santa Ana winds had died away, leaving the atmosphere still desert-hot, but hushed with an almost subliminal, subcutaneous trembling, as though charged with some urgency beyond verbalization.

Balancing himself with one hand against the ground, Holden got to his feet, then straightened up. And immediately regretted it; a wave of dizziness washed across him, as unsettling as if another earthquake had struck the zone. Artificial heart pounding in his chest, he bent over, palms against his knees; something had lodged in his throat, around which he could barely breathe. It seemed to take the last of his strength to cough it up. When he opened his eyes, he saw a wet red spot on the concrete rubble in front of him.

"Goddamn . . ." Tentatively he poked at his breastbone with the fingertips of one hand, trying to determine if he had broken something loose on the implants inside him. He swallowed the salt taste in his mouth rather than risk spitting it out. Everything seemed to be working; he could breathe, and the heart was still beating. He tried to remember whether a particular loose, rattling noise was something he was imagining, or whether it had always been there and he just hadn't noticed it before.

One thing was certain. He felt weaker than before, closer to the edge of collapse. *Great timing*, he thought bitterly. What he needed to do—what his stressed-out body told him he should do—was go lie down in some dark quiet place, until his new heart and lungs had finished knitting themselves into his corporeal fabric. But there was no time for that. Things were happening too fast for him to take a break, no matter how badly he required one. The spinner carrying Deckard and the Tyrell woman had vanished from sight, taking them to another locus of conspiracy. Maybe they'd finished up here, the two of them having cooperated on the shooting of some third party in the safe-house apartment . . .

He forced a deep breath into the lungs' machinery, trying to get his brain clear and functioning again. *Work it out,* he commanded himself. Who had Deckard and the Tyrell woman killed in there? The only other human being had been that little geek with all but one of his limbs sawn off—Holden tried to remember the guy's name, but couldn't. Granted, the triple amputee had seemed to be an annoying little bastard, but that by itself wouldn't have been sufficient motivation for icing him. There must've been another, more compelling reason. What?

The little guy had worked for the Tyrell Corporation; that much he remembered for sure. Doing . . . bio-engineering. Holden nodded, as if he could suddenly see the guy's entire police file in front of him. Specifically, replicant design. Even more specifically: *work on the Tyrell Corporation's Nexus-6 models.* That was it.

So he must've known something. Not just something, but a lot. The little one-limbed guy had been up to his weepy-looking eyeballs in the design and production—every detail—of the Nexus-6 replicants. Knowing too much about something like that—something that other people wanted to remain a secret—was always a good way of getting yourself eliminated.

It came to him then, a sudden illumination, as though the dark clouds he'd seen massing over the Pacific had sent down a sudden bolt of lightning. *Of course,* thought Holden. *That's what the little guy in there knew. And that's why they had to kill him* . . .

The problem was, the realization didn't do him any good if he was in no shape to act upon it. Another realization, not quite as welcome, shoved aside his other thoughts. He needed help; he couldn't go it alone, as much as he would've wanted to.

Holden glanced upward. The sky was empty again, the spinner with Deckard and the Tyrell woman long gone, its red trail evaporated. He turned and walked toward the freight spinner, carefully and slowly, husbanding his strength for the confrontation he'd already set his mind upon.

14

"Come on, fellas." He gazed around at the empty rooms, the spaces that were silent now but had held as much of a real life as he'd ever known. "We should be just about all packed up now." He and the others, the companions left to him, had done what they could to clean up the blood smeared on the angle of the walls and the remainder of the mess caused by his true love's death. *Her second one,* Sebastian reminded himself. That made him even sadder, thinking that poor little Pris had had to go through all that twice. It wasn't fair; she'd never hurt anyone, or at least not much.

Right now, he didn't even know where she was. He hadn't had the heart to pull the batteries from Pris's brain-damaged corpse, shut off the various switches and relays that had kept her moving feebly around. *She must've crept away,* he thought sadly. Out into the zone's rubble, to lie down with the other broken and unfunctional things, debris among debris. Whatever blind spark that had remained inside her would die out in the ashes and rags and splintered, scrappy bones of the world.

Colonel Fuzzy and Squeaker Hussar came back over to where they had left him in the sideways apartment. They bent down low, their faces coming close to his; he had to turn his own slightly away, to avoid getting poked in the eye by Squeaker's elongated nose. He knew what they were doing. With every sense organ he'd built into them—mainly optical, though the teddy bear's round, fleece-lined ears were more finely tuned than a human's, and Squeaker actually did have some extra olfactory receptors built into that thing—they were trying to assess what condition he was in, physically and mentally. They knew some great tragedy had occurred, devastating every fiber of his being. He felt as though the one appendage he couldn't sacrifice, his heart, had been scooped out of his frail chest. Squeaker and the Colonel were aware that death had visited them in their home, she'd come swaggering in on spike heels, and with a big noise had removed one of their number, from the world of the living to that other place where all one's batteries were run down flat and the light behind one's button eyes went out. They were worried and fearful that that was where he was going, too.

"It's okay." Sebastian reached up and scratched behind the teddy bear's ears. Squeaker was less given to intimate body contact; he knew that for him to come this near, the circuits inside the spiked helmet must be in a considerable state of distress. "You don't have to worry about me. I'll be fine."

He had to wonder where they'd gotten that behavior from; it wasn't anything he'd programmed into them. From the beginning, they were supposed to have been jolly little fellows, happy creations, rays of sunshine in his gloomy life. He'd wired in logic paths by which the teddy bear and the toy soldier were able to learn new aspects of their environment and modify their behaviors based on that data—a basic feedback loop—

but all this tender-hearted fussing and crooning was something different. Or was it? He'd have to think about that, when they got to wherever they were going to next.

Squeaker helped strap him into the papoose carrier on Colonel Fuzzy's back. Food and batteries and other survival necessities had already been piled into the drag sling they used for scavenging the welfare drops.

"Wait a minute, fellas. I gotta leave a message."

The teddy bear, impatient to start traveling before dark set in, stamped its feet. "Just hold your horses," soothed Sebastian. "This'll only take a minute."

He had the colonel back up toward the biggest bare wall in the apartment. That would make a nice canvas, he'd decided; those other folks were so busy and rushed, coming and going and killing other people, that he didn't want to risk having his words overlooked. Using the black spray can from a Chaka Signature Model Li'l Graffitster Kit, part of the art supplies that'd come in a drop several months ago, he carefully spelled out what he had to say.

DEAR MR. DECKER . . . That was what he'd overheard the woman calling the man. Biting down on his tongue, Sebastian sprayed out the next words. MY FRIENDS AND I ARE MOVING ON. THERE ARE TOO MANY PAINFUL MEMORIES FOR US TO STAY HERE. That was putting it mildly. He flinched every time the tape ran through his thoughts again, of poor Pris flying through the air with her head shot open. THANKS FOR NOT KILLING US AS WELL. As soon as he saw those blurry-edged words on the wall, he regretted them. The logic seemed a little whacked; people should try not to kill you, just as a matter of course. There wasn't time to do the message over; the teddy bear was getting restive. He hurried to finish up. I HOPE YOU FIND WHAT YOU ARE LOOKING FOR. VERY BEST REGARDS, SEBASTIAN.

That would have to do; the spray can was nearly exhausted. He'd gotten some of the black paint on his single hand; tossing the can aside, he rubbed the smear against his coveralls with its pinned-up sleeve and trouser legs.

"Okay, okay. We're ready to leave now." He jounced up and down in the papoose carrier as Colonel Fuzzy hurried for the door. "Take it easy, you're gonna shake my head off!"

Outside, the three friends headed east, their shadows racing before them. Sebastian glanced over his shoulder as the teddy bear marched along. In the distance he could just make out the skyline of Los Angeles, the sunset bleeding red light around the dark towers. He supposed things had worked out fifty-fifty for him in this corner of the universe. He'd found true love, his heart's desire, but had had it taken away from him again. *Still,* he thought. *Least I had it for a little while.*

He turned away, setting his cheek against the back of the teddy bear's head. Closing his eyes but not sleeping. Not for a long while.

Darkness and life; both had begun again, the city moving into the nocturnal portion of its cycle. *When everything comes crawling out,* thought Holden, looking down from the freight spinner's cockpit at the lights carpeting the earth.

He'd decided, when he'd left the sideways zone, upon the general outline of his course of action. Circumstances—his own failing strength; the overtaxed artificial heart and lungs inside his chest had begun to sputter and wheeze alarmingly, complete with fuzzy-edged blackout dots hitting his sight like negative snowflakes—dictated that he needed assistance. Not later, when events had settled out, but *now.* So they would be determined as he wished, as an active agent in the historical process, or at least this little part of it, and not some breathing vegetable strapped by tubes to a hospital bed.

A terrible vision had come to him as the freight

spinner completed another circle above L.A's downtown core, of his bio-mechanical innards reaching their
stress limit and going into some half-powered, partially
shut-down mode, just enough to keep him alive in the
pilot's seat, but not conscious. Even worse off than he'd
been in the hospital. No longer human, a thing kept
alive by pumps and artificially inflated bladders, wearing
his face and his clothes, riding around forever in the sky
on the course he'd set when his brain had still been
functioning. Through the rotation of day and night, the
progress of the seasons, the manifestations of dry and
monsoon beating against the transparent cockpit dome,
the curved glass shielding his blank, unseeing eyes . . .

Well, not exactly forever, thought Holden with glum
relief. He supposed the police would have eventually
shot the freight spinner out of the sky, just for violating
air-space regulations. Or else they would've let it go on,
and it would've eventually run out of fuel, plunging
down into the streets. He could just see some by-the-
manual uniformed cop with one jackboot up on a
fender-high piece of the wreckage, writing out a ticket
for parking in a restricted zone.

The night had settled in complete, the somberly
violet line at the horizon, the last vestige of sun slicing
extinguished beneath the cliff front of mounting clouds.
Dark enough now for him to move further into the spe-
cifics of the plan upon which he'd decided. If he needed
assistance, to keep from either dying or blacking out,
there was only one place he could go, one person to
whom he could turn. The police department, either on
an official basis or by getting hold of his old friends and
acquaintances on the force, was out of the question. No
telling how rotted out the whole structure of the central
station was with conspiracy; anybody he talked to there
could be one of the bastards who'd determined, for their
own malevolent reasons, that the only good blade runner was a dead one. And as for Deckard, who was pre-
sumably as much a target as anyone else . . . that was a

no-go as well. For a lot of reasons, some of which Holden had spent the time up in the air mulling over. He reached out to the control panel and switched off the freight spinner's autopilot. Another looping circuit had been completed, bringing him back over the dense, poorly lit warrens of the city's Los Feliz district. Holden took over the freight spinner's manual controls, steering it down toward the building in which his expartner had once lived.

On the building's rooftop landing deck, he sat frozen in the pilot's seat, a layer of perspiration forming between his palms and the rudder's inert metal. *Go on,* one part of him nagged all the rest. *What're you waiting for? Don't crap out now.* He ascribed the knot of fear festering in his gut to the malfunctioning of his new lungs, the brain they fed reacting to partial oxygen deprivation with innate animal terror. But he knew that the cowardly body was in league with his own cold rationality. He'd left Roy Batty in the apartment below, handcuffed to the pipe behind the toilet; just replaying the tape in his head, of Batty cursing and flailing around at the limit of the short chain, like some baleful genetic cross between a bull and an enraged hornet, sent a squirt of adrenaline through his heart's polyethylene valves. And now he was going to go back in there and tell Batty that the two of them should be pals again? *Good luck,* whispered a lobe of doubt.

"Might as well get it over with." His own voice, speaking out loud. Holden opened the freight spinner's cockpit and climbed out.

In the apartment, a puzzle: the handcuffs were there, bright chrome dangling beneath white porcelain, but Roy Batty was gone. Holden stood up from his kneeling inspection of the cuffs, seeing his own puzzled face in the mirror above the sink. The fluorescent tube's partial spectrum gave the skin of his cheeks and brow an even more death-approaching, cheesy appearance.

He got away, thought Holden. He must have,

though there was no indication of how. The building was constructed so shabbily—parts of it, those that looked like concrete, actually were embossed styrofoam—that even an old man like Batty could possibly have yanked the plumbing free from the bathroom wall. But he surely wouldn't have bothered putting the pipe back into place, mortaring it with toothpaste and soap. Plus, the handcuffs would've still been dangling from Batty's wrist, not there on the pipe.

Turning the mystery over in his thoughts, Holden flicked off the bathroom light and wandered out into the apartment's corridor. Immediately he was slammed up against the wall, the impact against his spine sufficient to knock the air from his lungs, the new heart twitching through a spasm of rapid fibrillation.

"You stupid sonuvabitch. I oughtta kill you." Batty's face, its crevices reddened with a fierce energy, pushed itself nose-to-nose with Holden's. "Matter of fact, I'm *planning* on it. I hope that doesn't come as a surprise to you."

He got his hands onto Batty's wrists, trying to pull them far enough away from his throat to suck in air. A detached fragment of his mind noted that the handcuffs were gone. "Wait . . . wait a minute . . ." He gasped out the words as his feet dangled clear of the hallway's floor. "I have . . . to talk with you . . ."

"No, you don't." Batty pushed him up higher against the wall. "You and I have talked plenty already. I'm so on your pitiful wavelength, I don't *have* to talk to you anymore. I knew you were going to come back here, looking for me. Once you figured out that you're too screwed up to get by on your own." A shark's grin floated into Holden's fuzzed vision. "So you see, I know what you're going to say before you do."

A thread of oxygen flowed down his throat. The other man was tiring, not visibly so, but detectable by the slight weakening of his arms, the weight dragging them down. The black spots in front of Holden's eyes, that had interposed a drifting polka-dotted veil between his face and Batty's, faded a little.

"Look . . . it's important . . ." The words scraped through his constricted larynx. "I wouldn't have come back here . . . if I just needed help . . ."

"Yeah, right." Batty followed the words with a scornful grunt.

"Really . . . I figured it out . . ." He tugged at the other's wrists. "*I figured out . . . who the sixth replicant is . . .*"

Batty tilted his head to one side, studying the pinned figure in front of him. "What're you talking about?"

"Put me down . . . and I'll tell you . . ."

Through narrowed eyes, Batty regarded him for a moment longer. "All right." He lowered Holden to the floor, letting go of the front of his shirt. Batty stood back, arms folded across his chest. "This better be good."

Holden doubled over, gasping to fill his lungs, head level with his artificial heart to increase the passage of blood between the two organs. Weakly, he straightened back up, balancing himself against the wall with one hand. He stumbled toward the apartment's living room, with Batty following after.

"It's simple. Really." He flopped down into one of Deckard's overstuffed chairs. With his foot, he nudged aside the toppled piano bench, so he could stretch out his legs. "Once you think about it." The numbness in his limbs had changed to prickling as his circulation rattled back to normal. Or what passed for that. "The sixth replicant . . . the one that's still missing. It's Deckard."

"You idiot." Batty looked down at him with contempt. "I'm the one who told *you* that." He sat down heavily on the padded bench, his elbows knocking two atonal chords from the piano as he leaned back against the keyboard. Disgusted, he shook his head. "Jesus

Christ. I can't believe this. If you've been worrying about whether that new pump of yours is starving your brain of oxygen—and you should be; I can hear it wheezing all the way over here—then you don't have to worry anymore. Your brain's obviously gone to mush."

Unruffled, Holden smoothed his hands out along the rounded arms of the chair. He managed a smile. "Sure—you said something about Deckard being the sixth replicant. But I know how *your* mind works. You'd never have made it as a blade runner. You're too sloppy. The whole modus operandi of someone like you is to kill someone else, and then if it turns out to have been the wrong person, do another. Until you finally get it right." He paused for a moment, to regain his breath. "Blade runners, on the other hand, try to be a little more precise about who we kill."

"Piss off."

He knew he'd nailed him. Holden leaned forward, relishing the small measure of control he'd gained, the shift of power between himself and the other man. "There; you see?" It'd been worth coming back here, taking the risk, just to screw with Batty's mind. In the best way possible, by feeding his own words back to him. But with a difference. "You know I'm right. When you said Deckard was the sixth replicant, that was just an idea you had. You didn't know for sure. Did you?"

Batty shifted uncomfortably on the piano bench, but made no reply.

"Whereas I can say that Deckard is the sixth replicant—*and I can prove it.*" He leaned back into the deep upholstery. In triumph.

"Go ahead." Batty had reassembled his own composure. "I'm listening."

"There's a safe-house apartment, out in the sideways world—you know, all that toppled-over seismic zone—that Deckard and myself and some of the other guys in the blade runner unit set up. Without any departmental connection; we used it for stakeouts, remote

operations, all that sort of thing. That's where I knew
Deckard would go. And I was right." Holden forced
down a deep breath. "After I took care of you, I went
out there and found him, talked to him—"

"You should've plugged him. And if you were so
friggin' smart, you wouldn't have left me where I could
get hold of dental floss and a razor blade. Those handcuffs ain't shit, when you know what you're doing."

Holden rolled past the comment. "At any rate, I
didn't get very far with him. I'd figured that between
the two of us, he and I could locate the sixth replicant
and retire it—but Deckard wouldn't buy into that plan.
Turned me down flat. So I left . . . but I didn't go
away. I kept an eye on the place, from outside. And sure
enough, Holden had a visitor. A woman—"

"Oh?" Batty raised an eyebrow. "Young, dark-
haired? Expensive-looking?"

"Pretty much." He nodded. "I figured that it was
the one who owns the Tyrell Corporation now—"

"Sarah Tyrell. Good guess."

"They were both inside the safe-house apartment
for a while, then there was a gunshot. Then both Deckard and the woman came out, climbed into a Tyrell Corporation spinner, and flew off. The person who *didn't*
come out of the apartment was this little weird guy,
who was also there. Used to be one of the corporation's
top bio-engineers, name of Sebastian."

"Yeah, I know about him. Big involvement in the
design of the Nexus-6 models. I met him when they
were putting together the prototypes for the Roy Batty
replicant model."

"That's my whole point." The artificial heart in
Holden's chest revved with excitement. "Deckard and
this Sarah Tyrell iced one of the few people—hell,
maybe the only one left—who could identify the
Nexus-6 replicants. Why would they do that, unless
they wanted to make sure that there wasn't anybody
around who could put the finger on the missing sixth

replicant? And who'd be more concerned about that then the sixth replicant itself? So it *has* to be Deckard. All that stuff about him having run off up north, that was all a ruse, an alibi to make it look like he wasn't on the scene down here. But he was, and he was busy taking care of anybody who could identify him. Like Bryant. It's obvious—Deckard killed the one guy who'd seen the original escape report from the off-world authorities, after Bryant had already purged the info on him from the police files. Just goes to show what a thorough bastard Deckard is; he's not leaving any loose ends."

Batty musingly stroked his chin. "Why didn't Deckard kill you? Out at this safe-house apartment."

"Because I had a gun, and he didn't—at that time. The Tyrell woman must've brought out the one they shot Sebastian with."

"Huh." Slowly Batty nodded. "That makes sense, I guess." He gave a shrug. "Look, I'm glad you've come around to my way of thinking about this—"

" 'Thinking,' hell."

"All right, all right." Batty held both his palms outward. "I admit I operate more on instinct than reason—so sue me. But what you've come up with just confirms what I'd felt was the case about Deckard. So it must be true, right?"

Holden relaxed a bit. He'd managed to push the other man into a mellower portion of whatever manic cycle he operated on. Like a mollified wolf, it struck him. Important to not display any fear, to show the wild animal who was really in charge.

"Now that we know," said Holden, "who the sixth replicant is, we just have to calculate what we're going to do about it . . ."

He leaned forward, as Batty did the same from the piano bench, bringing their heads closer together. Breathing together; a back part of his mind recalled that that was what the word *conspiracy* meant.

Fires at night put some people in a holiday mood. Or
some creatures, he corrected himself. The one below
him had actually broken into a little stubby-legged jig,
more enthusiasm than dance skill, at the sight up ahead,
flickering incendiary glow and sparks threading through
mounting columns of smoke.

"Whoa!" Sebastian clung to the teddy bear's neck,
to keep himself from being jounced out of the papoose
carrier. "Steady on there, will ya? You're going to make
me seasick."

Squeaker Hussar had spotted the fires as well.
"What's that? What's that?" He jumped up and down,
pointing. "What the heckety-heck is *that*, Sebastian?"

"I don't rightly know." A pirate-style brass tele-
scope was packed somewhere in the gear that the animated teddy bear and the toy soldier had been dragging
along between them. Out here in the dark, he didn't
feel like rooting around for it. "People, I guess." He let
himself slip back down into the papoose carrier. "A lot
of 'em, actually. I can see their shadows and all."

"Hmmm . . ." Subdued, Squeaker tilted his nose
into the air, as though trying to sniff out the nature of
the unseen others. "Gotta think!"

The toy soldier didn't really think, not on a deep
analytical level—Sebastian hadn't programmed him for
that—but he did a good imitation of the process, something he'd probably picked up from observing his
maker. Sebastian knew he'd have to do the thinking for
all three of them, as he'd always done before. *Not that I
ever did such a good job at it.* Maybe it was time to give
Squeaker and Colonel Fuzzy a crack at these necessary
tasks. Once, just a little while ago, he'd done the thinking for a group of four, counting in Pris; though even
when she'd been alive, really alive, she hadn't been the
sort of girl for whom thinking had been a preferred
mode of making one's way through the rigors of existence. And all that his thinking had accomplished, at

least for her, had been death, utter and final. And his own, inasmuch as he was now a one-limbed, withered husklike thing, the core of his life having been extinguished along with Pris's feverish, constantly scanning red eyes. A toy soldier with a Pinocchio nose couldn't screw it up any worse.

He waited, but Squeaker didn't say anything more. Colonel Fuzzy looked over its shoulder at him, the expression held in its button eyes apprehensive.

"Okay . . ." He sighed, aware that they were depending upon him. "Let's figure it out. Out here, at night, the things you gotta be afraid of are the ones you can't see. Right?" The teddy bear and the toy soldier nodded. "These folks, whoever they are—" He pointed to the radiant distance with his one hand. "They don't seem to care if we see 'em. I mean, they built those fires and stuff. So it seems only logical that we *shouldn't* be afraid of them. You follow?"

"Maybe they're savages!" Eyes wide, Squeaker had already spooked himself. "Cannibubbles!"

"Oh, shoot. That's only in bad movies. Postapocalypse tootie-frootie jive." Sebastian had found his own logic convincing enough. He urged Colonel Fuzzy forward. "Come on, let's go check 'em out. Maybe they got a barbecue going. Welfare weenies and marshmallows—you guys like that, don't you?" They didn't actually eat, but they enjoyed using their ceremonial dress swords to hold things in the flames.

That notion motivated his companions. They left their supplies, food and water and batteries, tucked into a crevice they'd be able to find later. Clambering over the flank of a Neutra-derived retail pavilion, they made their way toward the fires.

Even before they could clearly make out the human figures, they heard the single raised voice, loud and stentorian. Colonel Fuzzy's round ears twitched at either side of his head; Squeaker looked genuinely perplexed. "Sounds like church!"

The toy soldier's notions were derived from old televangelical broadcasts, but he was right; it did sound like that. Sebastian couldn't make out the words, not until they had actually come through the line of wavering shadows and near enough to feel the heat of the fires against their own faces.

" 'With this wisdom, enlightened disciples will be able to master every inordinate desire!' " A man dressed in a white jumpsuit—one of the sleeves was torn, and there were black char marks across the front, as though he'd wandered too close to the fire, or been in some kind of explosion—stood on a box, reading from a battered old paperback book. " 'Every kind of living creature, whether hatched from an egg, grown in a womb, evolved or brought forth by metamorphosis, whether it has form or knowing, whether it possesses or lacks natural feeling—from this constantly shifting state of existence, I command you to seek deliverance!' " The man's voice grew stronger and more fervent. " 'Then you shall be released from the sentient world, a world without number or limit. In reality, no sentient world even exists; for in the minds of enlightened disciples, such arbitrary notions have ceased . . .' "

Perhaps a couple dozen other people stood around in a circle, listening; regular, full-size humans, not like what he'd become. They were all a little on the ragged side; in this territory, it was impossible to stay exactly spiff. A few curious faces turned toward Sebastian and his diminutive pals.

"Sorry." He raised an apologetic hand above the teddy bear's head. "Don't let me interrupt you." The sermon, if that's what it was, had ended; he didn't know whether it was supposed to have or not. "Just go ahead."

The man stepped down from the box and walked over toward them. He looked to be some kind of spiritual leader; he had the sort of craggy, God-haunted face for it, complete with a straggly, greying beard, also slightly singed.

"Have you come to roust us?" The evidently holy man leaned down to peer into Sebastian's face. "Perhaps you are an advance scout of the law-enforcement agencies, specifically those in charge of stamping out heresies such as represented by our little group. Would that be the case?"

"Um, no . . ." He shrank back from the other's piercing gaze. "We're more like private-individual types."

"I see." The man straightened back up. A number of the others had collected behind him, following the discourse. A sigh came from their leader. "In some ways—many ways—that's a pity. Inasmuch as the doctrines of our faith invite martyrdom. The final sacrament, as it were. Without which, many of our activities, if not all, seem to be in vain."

"Well . . ." He didn't know what to say. "You gotta hang in there, I suppose."

"Easy for you to say. Come here." The bearded leader took one of Colonel Fuzzy's mittenlike paws, as though it were an actual extension of Sebastian's body, and led him toward the center of the circle of fires. Where the rest of the people were—he shifted uneasily in the papoose carrier, aware of having become the focus of their attention. "That is the purpose of our gatherings out in the open air, in fields and pastures as it were. Similar to the early free-thinkers, those who had rejected the wicked doctrines of the ruling elites. Of their time. Though, of course, wickedness is an eternal thing, the great deceiver merely shifting from behind one mask to another."

"Oh." With a sinking feeling in the pit of his stomach, Sebastian realized he had stumbled into a nest of lunatics. *Just my luck*, he thought glumly. When things started going bad for you, they went on that way for a long time. That was the real nature of the universe.

"The better to oppress the righteous." The leader sank into the ongoing currents of his own thoughts, though he continued to speak aloud. His frail shoulders slumped inside the white jumpsuit, like an insect folding itself into a semi-resting posture. "Though in reality, the Masked One, the deceiver and oppressor, does the righteous a service through its cruelty. A paradox. Inasmuch as it is only through the experience of oppression, of suffering, that one becomes human. Through suffering, one becomes the object of compassion. You know all this, don't you? That is how the one who sees only suffering, the Eye of Compassion, becomes aware of your existence; she sees no other thing, is blind to all except those who suffer."

The leader ran elongated, skeletal fingers through his beard, the undertones of his voice skewing toward the speculative. "Once, humans—humans such as us— suffered; that was the bread and salt of our existence. That was a long time ago. Now we have become that which *causes* suffering—not on an individual basis, but as a species; we have become one of the masks behind which the great deceiver and oppressor manifests itself in this universe. The question then becomes . . ." One of the others, a young man, hollow-cheeked and febrile, stood nearby, transcribing the leader's words into an old-fashioned manual steno pad. "Whether the Masked One, by causing suffering, acts as a necessary precursive agent of its compassionate opposite?" The bearded man looked round from the corner of his eye.

The glance, and its accompanying expectant silence, made Sebastian nervous. "I wouldn't know." He tightened the hold of his forearm around Colonel Fuzzy's shoulder.

"Are you sure," the leader inquired hopefully, "that you're not with the police?"

"Positive."

"Well . . . we shall 'hang in there,' as you advise.

For the sake of those more human than us. Those blessed ones."

It suddenly dawned on him who these people were. *Hell's bells*, thought Sebastian. *They're rep-symps.* He'd heard rumors, before he'd first come out to the sideways world, that certain congregations of the true believers frequented the zone. Living a basically reclusive life, he hadn't encountered them before.

"Look, it seems to me that you're going about it all wrong." He could afford to be helpful; he had nothing against them. He let go of the teddy bear long enough to wave off the smoke that was getting into his nose and making him sneeze. "If you *want* to get busted by the police, you oughtta go where the police mainly are. It's no good being out in nowheresville. The cops probably don't even want to bother with you, long as you stay someplace like this. You should go into the city—"

"We've done that." A younger, darker-bearded version of the leader spoke up. He had fanatic eyes, whites showing all around the pupils. "We have our uses for the *city.*" A dirty word, the way he spat it out. "And we have taken our message there. Not just in words, but in deed as well. We brought down in flames one of the voices of the deceiver, and upon its carcass we gave forth our testimony."

"Gosh." It sounded scary, even though he had no idea of what the man was exactly talking about. Though he was pretty sure it involved criminal activity of some kind; these people were religiously obsessive types, after all, capable of anything. Morally, if not in terms of actual accomplishment. He was beginning to have second thoughts about keeping company with them; the police *might* come all the way out here, to kick ass and take names, as the saying went. If they'd been sufficiently provoked.

"If you really want my opinion, I'd say you should

rethink just what it is you're going for," he said. "This martyrdom thing, and all." Sebastian wished that he and his companions had just circled around the fires and continued on their way, instead of poking their noses in here. "I just don't see where it gets you anything." *Except in your crackpot heads*, he thought to himself. "Bringing the heat down on yourselves is not something you should care to have happen. Or any kind of bad shit. Suffering's not all that great; believe me, I should know."

The assembled people glanced at one another. Significant glances, indicating a measure of worry about the strangers that had wandered into their midst.

"Listen to me." Sebastian heard his own voice, louder and more fervent. As though he were the one testifying now. "I know what I'm talking about. Suffering *sucks*. I just lost the woman I love—again, for the second time. She was shot right in front of me. And she was a replicant, too; or at least she'd been one—"

The bearded leader peered closer at him. "Yes," he said after a moment's inspection, during which Colonel Fuzzy had hissed and drawn back. "I can see that you speak the truth." He laid a wrinkled, cordite-smelling hand on top of Sebastian's head. "You have the aspect of the blessed about you. Suffering has given you that. You are nearly human, yourself."

"Well . . . thanks. I guess." What the hell was this old doozer talking about?

"But there is more for you to suffer." The leader raised his hand in a gesture of benediction. "For you to complete your journey."

"Rats." He didn't even know where he was going.

"Come with me. I have something to give you."

Mounted on the back of the teddy bear, Sebastian followed after the old man. Squeaker trailed behind, glancing over his shoulder at the other people, his elongated nose twitching with suspicion.

"You can't stay with us." At the flickering limit of the fires' glow, the old man rummaged through a duffel bag he'd drawn out of a military-surplus canvas tent. "You have your own destiny. But this might help you. It's a holy relic." He turned and laid a rectangular object in Sebastian's hand.

Something metal, lightweight aluminum, with a few dents and scratches, indicators of age. Smaller things, of metal and possibly glass, rattled inside as Sebastian turned it around. He held it up so the faint orangish light hit it. On the box's lid was a prominent mark in the form of a red cross. "It's a first-aid kit." That could be helpful, actually; he didn't have one in the supplies they'd dragged along with them.

"Look closer."

He did, nose almost touching the metal. Smaller words, stamped into the surface. Sebastian spelled them out. "Salamander . . . no, that's not right." Sebastian squinted. "*Salander.* That's it. *Salander 3.*" He supposed it was the name of the ship that the kit had come from. It sounded vaguely familiar. Maybe a star ship, one of the old explorer types that'd gone out past the limits of the solar system.

The old man nodded. "I was there . . . when it came back to us. Bearing its message. Written in the eyes of its dead." The grey-streaked beard lifted from the front of the jumpsuit, as he raised his eyes to the night sky. "They were the first to know. What all shall know someday. They traveled, and returned. They saw. And brought back the message . . ."

"What message?"

For a moment, it seemed as if the leader hadn't heard him. "Of our damnation," he spoke at last. "Or our salvation." He turned a wan smile on the figures before him. "We're still not quite sure yet."

Maybe you should work on that, thought Sebastian. He didn't look up at the old man, but concentrated on fiddling with the metal box.

"There is one who knows . . ." The bearded leader's voice drifted into deep musing. "One who should know, who *must* know . . . but may not even know that she does."

"That doesn't sound too smart." The box's catch was rusted tight; Sebastian frowned at it.

"She was but a child," the old man spoke softly, "when the revelations were made. A child in the stars, a little girl . . . poor thing." He shook his head. "The things she must have seen, that she could not understand. Perhaps it was best that she couldn't. Her mother and her father . . . I helped carry their coffins from the ship. They died from too much knowledge. Too much of the light."

"Knowledge, huh?" Sebastian wedged the box against the rim of the papoose carrier and jabbed his thumb at it. "What about?"

"That way in which things change, in which they become other than what they were." The old man lifted his rheumy gaze toward the sky. "That which was human shall not be. And that which was not . . ." His voice sank to a whisper, before he turned and looked again at Sebastian with a wan smile. "It's all very confusing. Perhaps *she* will remember one day . . . those things she saw as a child. The revelations. That which she has forgotten. And then she will tell us of them."

Sebastian didn't bother asking who *she* might be. He had finally managed to pry the first-aid kit's lid open. The various little bottles and ampules, simple disinfectants and antibiotics, looked dried-up and innocuous; he supposed there wasn't much risk in carrying the thing around. And he didn't want to hurt the old man's feelings. "Um, thanks." He snapped the lid shut and held up the box. "For this, and all."

"Go in peace."

Back where they had left their things, he had Squeaker stow the box away in the wrapped-up sup-

plies. The rep-symps' distant fires had died down, leaving Squeaker to redo the bungee cords by starlight.

And not much of it. Sebastian looked up and saw
the blunt fingers of silver-tinged clouds moving east-
ward. He wondered what that meant.

15

"I'll need transportation." Deckard tilted his head toward the vehicle they'd left on the Tyrell Corporation's landing deck. "Your spinner will do."

"All right." Sarah gave him a knowledgeable smile. "After all . . . you can't just go walking around on the streets, can you? As we've learned."

He turned away from the view of the city's lights spread out below the headquarters complex. "You're the one who put me out there. You knew that was what that Isidore person would do." He studied her reaction. "I can't figure out why you'd want that to happen."

Her smile deepened. "Let's just say that we both learned something. That we might not have, otherwise. You survived, didn't you? So now I can be certain that finding our missing replicant won't be beyond you." Sarah's manner became brusque, businesslike. "Go ahead and take the spinner—I figured you'd need it, so I had it . . . *prepared* for you. Don't try to leave, to get out of the city. That wouldn't be advisable. The spinner has a perimeter choke. A circle with its center here."

She didn't need to make a gesture; Deckard knew she meant the Tyrell Corporation headquarters itself. "Try going farther and you'll get a red warning light on the instrument panel. Keep going, and you'll fall from the sky in little flaming pieces."

It had been pretty much what he'd expected. Why should she trust him? A small, irrational hope flicked off inside him. If the spinner had had no spatial limit, he would've hotfooted it straight north. To Rachael, sleeping and dying and waiting for him. Screw L.A. and Sarah Tyrell and any missing sixth replicant.

"Don't worry," said Deckard. "I'll return all your company property to you in good shape. Except for the sixth replicant. It might be a little beat-up when I dump it at your feet."

"Really?" She raised an eyebrow. "I'm glad to see you showing such . . . enthusiasm for your job." Sarah turned away and began walking toward the elevator that would carry her down into the corporation's bowels. She stopped and glanced over her shoulder. "I'll be waiting. I had you coded through the security systems. So you can come straight in . . . when you're ready."

He called after her. "Is that it? I thought you wanted to talk about something."

"Please . . ." She pressed the control and the silvery doors parted. "Let me have a few pretenses, Deckard. I just wanted to see you. That's all." Sarah stepped inside the elevator and with the palm of her hand kept its doors from closing. "You were on my mind. Perhaps I just wanted to find out if I were on yours." She pulled her hand away; the doors slid shut, and she was gone.

A moment later Deckard traversed the night sky, the bright pinprick carpet of the city's lights rolling below him. To either side, police spinners shot by on their own errands, either not picking him up on their radars or getting a VIP readout on their computer screens high enough to keep them sailing past.

The city's towers were well behind him. Deckard

looked out the side of the spinner's cockpit and down, and saw darkness, more complete than the cloud-mottled sky. The sideways world, with its fallen build-ings and edge-tipped empty freeway, seemed to be within the spinner's circle. That made it easier; he still needed some place where he could pull his act together, think everything through—as he'd been doing before Sarah Tyrell had shown up and spirited him away, for no good reason other than to lay the spinner on him. Off in the distance, a red glow shone, a flickering apparition; somewhere else in the zone, a fire apparently had bro-ken out.

Just beyond the knife blade of steel and concrete that ran a diagonal through the sideways world was the familiar aspect of the safe-house apartment's toppled building. He brought the spinner down low, hovering and then descending vertical into the small cleared space beside it. Once he'd gotten out, boots crunching into the cement fragments and bits of rusted metal that constituted the zone's surface layer, he activated all the spinner's security devices, sealing the cockpit down tight. Parts scavengers were always active at this dark hour, along with randomly motivated vandal types; he didn't want to come back out here and find his transpor-tation stripped. He pocketed the small remote that Sarah had given him, and headed into the unlit apart-ment building.

The safe-house apartment still smelled like death, an odor that connected with receptors off the olfactory net. A reverse seepage into the walls, like electrical ser-vice shut off for failure to pay the bill. That was more or less what'd happened to Pris; not even retired, that bad-faith euphemism, but forcibly unplugged. All the bat-teries removed, or a new one put in the socket above her eyes, a cold shiny one that sucked up pseudo-life rather than bestowing it. That image weighed on Deckard's thoughts; it made him feel as if he'd spent his whole blade runner career as more of a sinister electrician than anything else.

Former blade runner, he reminded himself as he straightened back up after ducking beneath the apartment's front doorway. That hadn't changed, despite his having been recruited for one more job. He reached behind himself and lifted the door closed. The resistance to becoming a murderer again was even more final than when Bryant had put the pressure on him. Plus there wasn't a big open-ended prospect ahead, of searching and killing and searching and killing, until he'd gone through the whole list of escaped replicants. There was only the one to deal with. *And I already know*, thought Deckard, standing still to let his eyes adjust to the darkness. *Who it is.*

He stepped through the apartment, hand outstretched to find any of the generator-powered lights. That little geek Sebastian and his friends had moved everything around; Deckard supposed they had as much right to do it as anyone. He halted, as the sound of something beside his own breathing and stumbling progress hit his ears.

"You make this too easy." He recognized the voice—it hadn't been that long ago—but had no chance to reply. Another sound, that of something hard and narrow whipping through the air; he doubled over in pain when the object hit him in the gut. Another poke knocked him off his feet.

The lights came on. He found himself, as he gasped for breath, looking up at Dave Holden, standing above him, the leg from the kitchen table in his hands. "Goddamn it . . ." Deckard managed to squeeze the words out. "What the hell . . . was that for . . ."

"*That* was for jerking me around for so long." Holden put the end of the table leg against Deckard's shoulder, pinning him back down to the wall beneath. "Not just the last time I was out here talking to you, but all the times before as well." He jabbed the table leg harder. "You must've been laughing your ass off, when I walked out of here before."

Getting onto his knees, Deckard knocked the table leg away with the back of his hand. "I don't know what the hell you're talking about."

"Oh? You will." Taking a step backward, Holden called out over his shoulder. "Hey, come on out here. I've had my fun." He brought his smug gaze around to Deckard. "This is going to trip you out, buddy. A real blast from your past."

As he stood up, Deckard could hear someone else emerging from the farther sections of the safe-house apartment. That could be a problem, dealing with two people; he would've been able to take Holden, with or without the table leg between them. His ex-partner looked as frail as he'd had during their last confrontation, with the bio-mechanical heart in his chest audibly clicking and laboring to perform its functions. Whoever it was that'd come out here with Holden, the person had given him a shot of confidence; smiling, Holden threw away his crude but minimally effective weapon.

"Say hello." Holden tilted his head toward the doorway at the other side of the room. "I think you know each other. In a way, at least."

Deckard glanced away from him, in the direction indicated . . .

And felt the world drop out from beneath himself.

"Jesus Christ—" A shock wave of adrenaline pulsed through him, drawing his spine rigid. Deckard's startled brain spun gearless for a moment.

Ducking underneath the side of the door, a dead thing stepped through, finishing the zipping up of his fly. "Visitors always come around, you know, when you're indisposed." Roy Batty straightened up and flashed his manic smile, eyes bright. "Hey, it's good to see you, too."

"No . . ." He took an involuntary step away from the smiling, hands reaching behind himself for balance.

"You're dead . . . I *know* it. I saw it happen . . ." An entire memory reel fast-forwarded through his head, a jumble of water sluicing blood over rusted metal, then a scruffy white pigeon, a winged city rat, climbing into the sky from hands that had fallen open and would never close upon anything again. "You're dead, Batty . . ."

"Well, yes and no." Batty's image—Deckard wasn't sure yet whether it was real or an hallucination—gave a judicious shrug. "A *copy* of me is dead—hell, *lots* of copies are—but I'm not. The original has proven to be somewhat more durable."

"That's the truth, Deckard." With his hands free of the table leg, Holden had dug into his jacket pocket and come up with the same gun he'd had before. "Or at least I think it is. For the time being. This guy's the templant for all the Roy Batty replicants. Including the one you met up with before."

The explanation made sense, of a sort. Looking closer at the figure standing before him, Deckard could see that the man appeared older than the one that existed in his own memory banks. Both bio- and chronologically older, hands bonier, a little loose flesh around the tendons of his neck, lines that came with the passage of time set into his face. A Batty replicant would never have reached this stage; the built-in limitation of a four-year life span precluded it. Unless—he supposed it was a possibility—something had been done to prolong its existence past that hard cutoff point.

Whether the Roy Batty in the tilted room was human or not—that wasn't something he was worried about now. The shock of again seeing that smiling face had passed. What concerned him was the gun in Holden's hand, and the cooperative air between the two men.

"What's the deal?" He looked from one to the other. "I have a feeling you didn't come out here just to say hello."

"That's the truth as well." Holden kept the gun pointed at him. "We're taking you in, Deckard. We're going to hand you over at the police station downtown."

"On what? Administrative charges?" If these two didn't know about Pris having been human, and his being tagged for her murder, he wasn't going to tell them. He couldn't believe that these two loose cannons were in on the LAPD loop; maybe they could be bluffed. "So I made unauthorized use of a department spinner when I split town—that's not a hanging offense. They can reimburse themselves out of the money I left in the pension plan."

"Can the bullshit." Holden shook his head in evident disgust. "Replicants don't have 401-k's."

"What're you talking about?"

The two men shared glances and a smile between them, then looked back at Deckard. "You're a replicant. You know it, and now *we* know it. Retirement for you is a whole different sort of thing."

"Actually, Roy, I'm not entirely sure how we should proceed here." With his free hand, Holden scratched his chin. "Why are we bothering to talk with this schmuck? He's a replicant—we've already established that—so why don't we just ice him now? We can drag his dead carcass into the station just as easily. Easier, as a matter of fact."

"Don't be stupid." Batty looked annoyed. "It's not just that he's an escaped replicant here on Earth. He's the only lead we've got on the conspiracy against the blade runner unit. If we snuff him before we can shake him down for what he knows, how're we going to find out who was behind setting you up, and killing Bryant, and all the rest of that stuff?"

"Oh, yeah. Right . . ." Holden appeared confused, his gaze wandering to some abstract point near the apartment's uppermost wall. His face and throat had drained white, as though whatever repair work the doctors might have done on him was now beginning to come apart. "Wait a minute."

"We can't even take him *in* to the station until we find out more shit." Even more insistent, Batty's voice prodded the other. "We have to find out who in the police is tied up in this. Otherwise, we could be walking into there and handing him right over to the people he's been working with. Then they'd ice *our* asses."

"I said, *wait* . . ." With his trembling, upraised hand, Holden tried to ward off the other's arguments.

Deckard looked from one to the other. *Geriatrics*, he realized. Like having been captured by a mobile wing of the nearest old folks' home. "You people are completely screwed up." He took a quick couple of steps and picked up the wooden table leg that Holden had tossed aside. Before the other man could react, he turned around and knocked the gun from his hand. The partial impact was enough to send the enfeebled Holden sprawling.

The other one was faster. He sensed Batty launching himself from across the room; a split second later a forearm was against his throat and the man's weight on his back. Locked together, they toppled and crashed into the wall beside the door.

A hand brought up by his chin was enough to peel Batty's choke-hold away. The lined visage snarled at Deckard as he got his palms against the other's shoulders and pushed him away. Deckard shook his head. "You're too old for this nonsense." He raised his knee against Batty's abdomen, prying away the clawing grasp of the withered hands and throwing him on top of Holden's dazed, prostrate form.

"Fuck you—" Batty scrabbled toward the gun a few feet away.

In an instant he'd estimated his chances of reaching the gun before the other man or getting it away from him. Deckard turned and dived for the apartment's entranceway, yanking open the door and tumbling out into the unlit hallway just as a bullet ripped out a section of plaster above him. He got to his feet and ran.

"Shit—" Outside the building, he discovered that the pocket of his long coat had been ripped loose in the struggle with Batty. The remote for the spinner's security devices was gone, probably somewhere back inside the safe-house apartment. He slammed his fist against the curved glass of the cockpit, but nothing happened.

Noises came from the front of the building. He glanced behind himself and saw that both Holden and Batty had emerged. Some kind of scuffle had broken out between the two of them; Deckard could hear them shouting, faces close to each other. As he moved around to the other side of the spinner, he saw Holden grab for the gun in Batty's hand; they wrestled briefly, before a shot snapped through the night air. Holden fell against the side of the building, clutching at the bright smear of blood that had erupted through the torn shoulder of his jacket.

"Deckard! Stop!" He heard Batty shouting as he pushed himself away from the locked spinner, turned, and ran. Another shot kicked up a spray of concrete chips and dust at his feet. "Come back here!"

Your ass. He kept running, picking his way as quickly as possible across the jagged terrain. Fragments of starlight penetrated the clouds overhead, turning the low jumble of broken shapes to tarnished silver.

Perhaps he was dying. It was hard to tell. Right now, his head felt as though it were about to explode, not with pain, but with the rush of energy that had welled inside him, from the moment he'd stood back up in the safe-house apartment. *That bastard knocked something loose,* thought Holden as he lay against the wall of the deserted apartment building, one hand clutched to his bleeding shoulder. Some governor mechanism for the clattering heart in his chest had gone awry; his pulse seemed to be racing twice as fast as it ever had before.

The wound was more of an annoyance than anything else; Holden managed to get to his feet, swaying a little. But it would serve his ex-partner right if the blow from the table leg and its consequences were what enabled him to catch up and nab Deckard, beat his head a few times against the stony ground before deciding what to do with him next. If his own heart didn't swell up and burst before then, like an overheated engine flying to pieces with its internal violence. Deckard had taken advantage of him during a temporary moment of weakness, when the bio-mechanical heart and lungs had been chugging through a low point in their cycles; now the sonuvabitch would have to deal with the old Dave Holden. *Better than old*, he thought grimly.

Bracing himself against the wall for balance, he spotted something on the ground before him; his artificial heart surged when he saw what it was. The gun— he'd gotten it away from Batty, but the other man had twisted it around and squeezed off the single round that had dropped him. Then the sonuvabitch must have been in too much of a hurry, chasing after Deckard, to stop and search around here for it.

Holden bent down to pick up the gun. And realized his mistake immediately. When his head went below the level of his heart, the amped-up wave of blood dizzied him. To blackout: he fell, fist grasping tight around the gun's handle.

On the spinning earth, he could feel the gun sweating against his palm. He managed to lift his head for a moment; the edges of his gaze turned red as he scanned the limits of the angular landscape.

Motion against stillness. He'd sighted Deckard; even better, he saw that there was no place farther to which the replicant and ex–blade runner could get to. Deckard had traversed enough of the rubble-strewn ground to hit smack against the abandoned freeway, turned onto its side by the long-ago earthquakes. A blank wall trisected by lane divider dashes reared up against the night sky, with a humanlike figure small against its base.

Another figure appeared, running, quickly eating up the distance between Deckard and itself. The shock of white hair was enough to identify Batty.

"Don't bother, Deckard—you're not going anywhere!" Batty's gloating call cut through the night air.

As Holden watched, vision wavering, the figure in the long coat started climbing, hands clawing at cracks in the freeway's vertical surface, boots scrabbling at crumbling projections of cement or ends of metal reinforcement rods. Deckard had already worked himself up to the center lane by the time Batty sprinted across the last few yards.

"Don't . . . kill him . . ." Holden's voice came out as an agonized whisper. "You've got to keep him . . . alive . . ." Gun in hand, he pushed himself up from the ground, to his knees.

That was his last effort. Holden sprawled forward, seeing nothing. Feeling only the cold weight of the gun under his fingertips and the razor-edged stones pressing against his face.

Into his eyes fell dust and grit, knocked loose from above by Deckard's progress toward the freeway's upper edge. Batty reached for the next hold and pulled himself up, threads of blood trickling from his abraded fingertips to the tautened cords of his wrists.

Against the clouds that had shrouded the night sky, he'd momentarily lost track of Deckard; only when he got his hands onto the top edge, scrabbling one knee and then the other up onto the horizontal surface, did he catch sight of him again. As Batty crouched, he spotted Deckard running along the narrow ribbon. The freeway's understructure had broken away during the original quake, leaving a sheer drop into darkness on either side of a meter-wide span.

Batty saw a dark space open up before the figure in

the long coat. A section of the freeway wall had previously disintegrated, leaving an abrupt cliff front on either side of the gap. Deckard halted, nearly toppling from the crumbling brink; he glanced over his shoulder at Batty, then drew back for a running leap.

That hesitation was enough; Batty dived, one outstretched hand grappling Deckard's foot just as it lifted from the edge's flat surface. They fell together, Batty's shoulder hitting the concrete as he crooked his gun arm around Deckard's knee. Rolling onto his back, Deckard shoved the butt of his hand against Batty's forehead, pushing him back and toward the edge's limit.

From beneath them came snapping and grinding noises. The impact of their bodies was more than the freeway section could withstand; the network of cracks along the vertical surface suddenly widened, boulders of cement crumbling away from the mesh of rusted metal beneath. Batty felt the gulf open beneath, the dark air made tangible with the grey dust filling his mouth and nostrils. The collapse of the freeway section yanked Deckard's ankle from his grasp; he rolled onto his shoulder, his arm desperately reaching, hand locking on to an angled stub of rebar sticking out from the ragged precipice above him. Twisting his neck, he saw the concrete and interwoven metal tumbling to the ground below with a crescendoing, bass-heavy roar.

Batty held on, his other hand reaching up and grasping the freeway's narrow edge. He pulled himself onto it, chest scraping across the rough surface. The collapse of the middle section had peeled with it another layer of the remaining vertical wall, leaving a tightropelike span only a few inches wide. Kneeling, with one hand gripping the edge for balance, he looked across the now wider gap as the dust sifted out of the moon's thin radiance.

He could see that Deckard had managed to hold on as well, catching on to the far edge of the gap and scrambling up onto the ribbon of horizontal, empty space falling away to either side. He watched as Deckard got to his feet, one behind the other, arms outstretched to darkness, carefully backing away from the gap, then halting.

There was nowhere else for Deckard to go. The section of freeway edge on which he stood was less than two meters long, a narrow island rearing up from the rubble and ancient debris below. He looked over his shoulder at the sharp drop behind him, one heel right at the crumbling rim, then back across the unbridgeable gap between himself and his pursuer.

Another rumbling noise moved through the air, the monsoon clouds gathered so low as to almost press upon Batty's shoulders. He could taste the electricity discharged and crackling in the atmosphere.

"Don't go away, Deckard—" A shout, and then a smile that Batty knew would be even more disturbing to the trapped figure opposite. "I'll be right there."

Dragging himself up the side of the crevice, after the vertical wall had given way beneath him, left Deckard gasping for breath. His pulse hammered in his throat as he looked across the breach of empty space, toward the figure on the opposite freeway section. A few drops of rain, warmed to the temperature of the blood in his veins, spattered against his face as he watched Batty take a few careful steps backward.

He can't . . . impossible. Fragments of thoughts were all that Deckard's brain produced. *It's too far—*

Batty stripped off his leather jacket and tossed it away. The sparse, hot rain mingled with the sweat on his shoulders and chest; the smile diminished as Batty's gaze narrowed, seeking out and locking on to Deckard's. The face was still ancient, lined and chiseled by time, even as the revealed body seemed to grow larger, the corded and veined muscles swelling with some deep vital influx. The drops of water collected in the hollows beneath Batty's cheekbones, then curved along the angles of his jaw and into his throat as he leaned forward, one hand reaching before him, as though the untremored fingers could grip the humid air itself.

Thoughts dissolved to wordless memory flash inside Deckard's skull, as he saw Batty running toward him. Another time, another place. In the city's depths, far above its darkly luminous streets; another vault of empty space carved out of the night by the lashing rain. The past merged without seam into the present as he watched, his own breath lodged fistlike in his throat, as the glistening form, human yet not, sprinted along the concrete ribbon. A last footfall at the crumbling rim, then Batty launched himself across the dark gap.

The past moment and the present, and none at all, time halting with Deckard's pulse. Sudden lightning lit up the heavy undersides of the storm clouds, the blue-white illumination transforming Batty into an angel of steel and diamond, held aloft from the dull earth's gravity by its own fierce, eternal falling.

Deckard shook himself from the image's spell, scrambling backward, one foot misplaced and slipping off the edge. Pebbles of cement pattered down the wall as he caught himself hard on one knee, both hands clutching at the horizontal surface beneath his chest.

"Got you—" Batty's voice sounded from above him; at the same moment the other's hands grabbed the front of Deckard's shirt. Rain oozed from the wadded cloth and ran over the knuckles of Batty's fists as he lifted Deckard from the narrow concrete. He smiled, his bright gaze shining up into Deckard's dazed eyes. "You weren't expecting that." Batty jerked his arms, wrists pressed against each other, his doubled fists knocking Deckard's chin back. "Am I right?"

He made no answer, but rammed one knee against Batty's gut, hard enough to break the hold at his throat. Batty staggered backward, arms flailing, catching himself just before the crevice gaping behind him.

Deckard twisted as he fell, his spine hitting the edge

of the concrete, shoulders leaning back onto empty air. Before he could scrabble away, Batty was on top of him. "Good job—" The words slid through Batty's clenched teeth. "You know . . . you really are one of the best." His hand gripped tight on Deckard's throat. "I hate to have to kill you."

Blindly, Deckard clawed at the concrete edge pressing into his back. A stone weight fell into his fist; he whipped his arm up in a roundhouse arc, the chunk of cement slamming into the corner of Batty's temple.

The blow rocked the other man back, his grip loosening on Deckard's throat. He took one hand away and touched the rain-diluted blood streaming down the side of his face. Batty nodded appreciatively. "That . . . really hurt . . ."

Deckard managed to push his shoulder blades a few inches farther along the edge. He cradled the cement chunk in his fist, warily eyeing the figure crouching above him. The realization had rushed upon him. "You're . . . you're the sixth replicant . . ." He saw it now; there must've been two Roy Batty replicants among the escapees. "Aren't you? You'd have to be . . ."

The oozing blood leaked into the corner of Batty's smile. "No . . ." He slowly shook his head. "I don't think I am."

"But . . . the way you jumped . . ." Raising his head, Deckard pawed the rain away from his eyes. "It was too far. That was the way *he* did it . . . the other Batty. The one . . . that died." He peered closer at the face, the white hair plastered onto its wounded brow. Impossible to tell if the appearance of age had been a shuck, something to lull his quarry into complacency, or whether a deep reserve of energy and will had surged up inside Batty, transforming him to some ancient, maddened glory. "So you must be another replicant . . . just like it was . . ."

"No." Another shake of the head. "It's like I told

your friend. I'm just very, *very* good at what I do. That's why I was hired for this job." Batty's smile faded. He turned his head, gaze shifting toward the dark. "Besides . . . if I were a replicant . . ." His voice grew low and brooding. "That would mean . . . that certain people had lied to me. That they had been lying to me all along. And I wouldn't be at all happy about that." He looked back around at Deckard. One sly corner of the smile reappeared. "It doesn't matter, anyway. Whether I'm the replicant . . . or *you* are. I'm still going to kill you. Then I'll turn you in—what's left of you—and get paid." He leaned forward, hand reaching for Deckard's throat. "That's all there is to it."

Deckard whipped the cement chunk toward the side of Batty's head; the other blocked it with his forearm, the impact dislodging the stone from Deckard's grasp and sending it clattering down the wall of the abandoned freeway. At the same moment the sharp ridge beneath them crumbled; Deckard slid a few inches farther out into empty space, with Batty's fists locked onto his throat.

"Go ahead, Deckard!" Batty had shot a glance down to where Deckard's hands had shoved themselves against the top of the wall. A push from his braced arms would send them both toppling toward the jagged ground below. "Maybe I'll make it—" A mad spark flared in Batty's eyes. "But you won't!"

The other's grinning face wavered behind a haze of red as Deckard's throttled breath swelled to the bursting point in his lungs. He could feel his own hands pushing at the crumbling stone, the tiny stones and grit digging into his flesh. His spine scraped raw across the edge, trapped blood rushing into his skull as he dangled backward . . .

Rain spattered on the roof of his mouth as the night's air suddenly rushed into his lungs. Batty's grip had loosened on his throat. The blinding haze faded; above him, the fierce intent in the other's eyes had been replaced by uncomprehending wonder. Red seeped through Batty's eyebrows, spidering out from the concave ruin of his shattered forehead. From a black hole, its diameter that of a high-caliber bullet, a finger of blood reached down and gently touched Deckard between his own eyes. The echo of the gunshot was swallowed by the rumbling thunder of the clouds masking the sky overhead.

Batty fell, his body collapsing on top of Deckard, then tumbling, arms outstretched, down the freeway's wall. Deckard scrambled to grab hold of the edge of concrete, to keep from being pulled after the dead thing.

Gasping in exhaustion, Deckard crawled full-length onto the narrow horizontal space. With his chest and the side of his face flat against the concrete, fingertips dug tighter holds. Sheets of rain lashed across his back.

One of the corpse's heels had caught in an angle of rusted steel, leaving it dangling a few feet above the sideways world's rubble-strewn surface. Batty's arms flopped back in an inverted crucifix, the face gaping upward so the rain could sluice the blood from the head wound, pink rivulets thinning upon the ground beneath.

Holden lowered the gun, bullet heat seeping from the metal into his hand. The artificial heart staggered in his chest; he drew one cautious breath after another, trying to keep from passing out again. He'd barely been able to make it this far, creeping and stumbling from where he'd fallen in front of the empty apartment building. He knew he'd almost been too late; it had taken nearly all of his strength to wrap both hands around the gun and lift its crushing tonnage above his head. The rain had pounded into his face as he'd sucked in his breath, aimed, and fired.

He heard other noises now; he looked up again and saw Deckard slowly clambering down the cracked and gouged surface of the freeway.

With the gun's weight dragging his arm, he hobbled over to where the other man now stood. *Looks worse than me*, thought Holden. That sonuvabitch Batty had really worked him over.

"Deckard . . . I heard . . ." Holden gulped air into his wheezing bio-mechanical lungs. "I heard . . . what you said up there." He nodded, his own wet shirt collar rubbing against his neck. "You're right—Batty was the sixth replicant. He had to be . . ." It all seemed so clear to him now. "That's how he was disguising himself . . . trying to get away with it. As somebody else hunting down the sixth replicant . . ."

A cold gaze came from Deckard's wearied eyes. "Maybe." He shrugged. "But it's like Batty said. It doesn't matter." Deckard turned and started walking away.

Holden grabbed on to his arm. "But . . . we still don't *know!*" He held on desperately, both to keep from falling and so that Deckard would have to listen to him. "We don't know . . . who was gunning for us. Who was trying to get rid of all the blade runners . . ."

Deckard shook him off. "You'll have to worry about all that. I've got other business to take care of."

"You don't understand—" Lungs straining for oxygen, Holden shouted after him, "We have to stick together—"

He heard something behind him, back by the wall of the tilted freeway. As did Deckard; they both turned and looked.

A figure almost human had crept out of the shadows behind the vertical stone and exposed lacework of metal reinforcement. A thing with darkened eye sockets and a tangled mat of hair, white as that of the dangling corpse. Sinews and skeletal joints poked through the gaping holes of a ragged leotard; the creature's flesh was pallid leather beneath.

Arrhythmic heartbeats passed before Holden recognized the thing. *It's that other replicant*, he thought, appalled. *The female one.* He couldn't remember what its name had been. Blood had seeped into the colorless hair, the dried-black spikes melting into red as the monsoon rains tangled sticky tendrils along the thing's neck. It was the one, he knew, that the little geek Sebastian had been in love with, that he'd been able to make move around in a bad parody of living things. Something had happened to it, a wound similar to Batty's; white bone fragments and jellied brain tissue showed through the catastrophic damage to the skull.

Dead, but still moving. Holden watched in distaste and dread as some blind instinct drew the once-living thing toward the other corpse. Its hands reached up and tremulously stroked the hollowed angles of Batty's jaw. It laid its own ravaged cheek against his, as though the gaping mouth were still capable of bestowing a kiss. Blood and rain mingled together, weeping along the faces of the dead.

Holden shuddered as he raised the gun and aimed. He couldn't stand it any longer. Before he could squeeze the trigger, another's hand stayed his, pushing the weapon aside. "Don't," said Deckard. "Just leave them alone."

He let the gun dangle at his side as he watched Deckard walk back toward the empty apartment building. The sustaining trickle of adrenaline ebbed from Holden's veins; he sank down upon the ground's wet stones. He breathed and listened to his own erratic heartbeat under the rain's slashing counterpoint.

16

The wall underfoot ran at enough of an angle that everything loose collected at one side of the safe-house apartment. A few moments of searching yielded the remote for the spinner's security devices; Deckard scooped it up and went back outside the building to the spinner.

He looked out the side of the cockpit as the spinner rose and banked over the wall of freeway, and saw the small figure of Holden, and farther away the dead Batty and Pris. Then they were lost to his sight; the spinner gained speed and altitude, its straight-line trajectory already set. The dark shapes of the sideways world fell behind as the city's bright-specked towers loomed ahead.

As the Tyrell Corporation headquarters approached, the blue-lit rectangle on top of one of the slanting towers flashed on, the landing deck's sensors responding to the spinner's coded signals. The guide beam locked on, bringing him down in the spiral of falling angels.

I should've taken the gun, he thought. Would've
been easy to get it away from Holden. Eyes closed,
Deckard leaned his head back against the cold wall of
the elevator. Another descent, maybe the last one. But
he also knew there had been no need. That anything he
had to do here, he could accomplish just as well with his
bare hands.

The metal doors slid open, revealing the private
suite of Sarah Tyrell. The vast, columned spaces
stretched out before him, shadows chased into the far
corners by the ranks of flickering candles. He didn't
know whether she had lit them, or if it was part of some
corporate flunky's evening duties, to go around with a
sacristan's taper, touching each black wick with the
small flame. It didn't matter. There was no one else here
now; the interlocking rooms held only her presence. He
could feel it, like the shift in the night atmosphere's
pressure on his skin.

Deckard stepped out of the elevator, letting the silvery doors close behind him. Stillness so complete that
the motion of his breath made the flames of the candles
on the nearest wrought-iron stand tremble.

Another's breath; he heard it, a sigh, as of one
dreaming. He turned toward the bed and saw her, face
against the silken pillow, dark hair loosened along the
curve of her shoulders. For a moment his heart stopped
between one beat and the next as he gazed down at the
sleeping woman, his hand reaching out and then hesitat-
ing, fingertips trembling an inch away from her pale
cheek . . .

There was something else on the bed, smaller and
darker. A weight of metal, one part molded to fit the
human hand, his hand. He picked the gun up, balancing
it in his palm. It was either his old one or another just
like it. He could tell, just by the few ounces difference,
that a full clip was loaded inside. Ready to go.

That was thoughtful of her. Deckard brought his index finger around the thin crescent inside the gun's trig-

ger guard. He straightened his arm, bringing the muzzle's cold circle of metal to the brow of the sleeping Sarah Tyrell . . .

"Would you really do that?" A voice, her voice, spoke from behind him.

He turned, looking over his shoulder. A different light from the massed candles shone toward him. He saw now that the ornate antique desk from the office suite had been pulled closer, between the columns that marked the bedchamber. Thick cables snaked back from a large-screen video monitor to the wall cabinet that had previously held it. A remote-controlled camera, red dot blinking above the lens, focused on him. On the monitor's screen was Sarah's image, her hair smoothed and bound, a thin smile at her lips as she regarded the scene before her.

He said nothing. But slowly, carefully, drew the gun away from the sleeping woman on the bed. The other one . . .

"I wasn't sure if you would or not." Sarah's voice came again from the monitor's speaker. "So I thought it best to be careful. You've been through some rough experiences just recently. That could make anybody . . . unpredictable."

"You brought her here." A simple statement of fact, that which he now saw to be true. "You sent somebody up north, to get her." He looked down again at the sleeping woman. At Rachael, sleeping . . . and dying. "You shouldn't have taken her out of the transport module." The last time he had seen her, she'd been beneath the black coffin's transparent lid. There, the interval between each breath had been measurable in hours; here, he could see the pulse in her soft throat ticking away the seconds, the minutes. He turned a fierce glare at the mirror image on the monitor screen. "She doesn't have that much time left."

"A relative concept." Sarah's image smiled. "I expect she has more time than I would have, if I'd been so foolish as to make myself physically present during this little conversation. So I hope you'll excuse this contrivance, this . . . electronic separation between us. As I said, I don't know what you're capable of doing now." She regarded him almost with pity. "We've grown apart, haven't we?"

He knew she was mocking him. The urge to raise the gun, aim, and put a bullet through the monitor was almost irresistible. Anything to silence her. "Why did you do it? Have her brought here?"

"Why are you so angry?" The camera on top of the monitor shifted, the lens focusing on the bed's sleeping figure, then returning to him. "Isn't that what you wanted? To see *her* again—perhaps I thought that would make you happy. Isn't that the most a woman can do? Really, Deckard . . . there's no abasement greater than that. Even if she *is* the exact duplicate of me. It's still not quite the same thing, is it?"

He regarded her image for a moment. "And the gun? What was that for?"

"I didn't know what you'd do . . . but I wanted to find out. It's important to know these things." One of the image's eyebrows raised. "You've found out quite a few things as well. Haven't you?"

"Everything you wanted me to."

"Oh? Such as?"

He stood in a room lit by candles, with a sleeping woman on the bed behind him, and the same woman's image, phosphor dots and radiant glass, inside a metal box. As though the living and the dying had somehow exchanged places. He had to close his eyes, shut out everything, reassembling the component elements of his thoughts, before he could go on.

"There's no sixth replicant." Deckard opened his eyes and looked straight into the monitor.

"Perhaps." Sarah's image gave a noncommittal shrug.

"There never was. That was just Bryant screwing

up, a misfired brain cell. A slip of the tongue, too much alcohol. He couldn't keep track of the nose on his face when he was sloshed."

A shake of the image's head. "What about the information he purged from the police files? The off-world authorities' report about the escape?"

"I never saw those things. *You* told me about them." He let the gun dangle at his side. "And you were lying. Simple as that."

"Ah." Sarah's image slowly nodded. "If that were the case . . . it would explain a lot. Wouldn't it? I suppose it's too late, after all I've put you through, to say that I've been completely honest with you."

"You're right. It's too late."

The image gazed sadly, pityingly, at him. "Then it doesn't matter whether I tell you there actually is a sixth missing replicant or not. You won't believe me. About that or anything else."

"Maybe not. But you could start by telling me some other things. Like why you set Dave Holden out looking for your sixth replicant, too."

"That . . . was someone else's idea. The person I hired before was Roy Batty. The original, the human one, not a replicant—or at least as far as I know. I believe he brought Holden in on the project. But that's unimportant."

"I agree." Deckard glanced over his shoulder; Rachael had stirred in her sleep, but not woken. "Especially now that Batty's dead. Again."

"Of course he is." Sarah's image smiled. "I knew as soon as it happened. I had ways of monitoring the state of his health."

"I bet you did."

The image regarded him. "And is that when you knew?"

Deckard nodded. "I saw him die. It wasn't the same as the other one. I saw right in Batty's eyes. I could tell

that he wasn't a replicant . . . that he was human. And
that it didn't matter either way."

"Ah." A smile formed on the image's face. "How
very mystical of you. Then what does? Matter, that is."

"Just the question," said Deckard. "Why you've
done any of this. With me, or anybody else. And why
you killed Bryant."

"Yes . . ." The image nodded, apparently pleased.
"I knew you'd figure that out. Let's face it; you've accurately described him just now. An alcoholic, losing track
of the details . . . not very reliable. Not for my purposes, at least. I prefer having my secrets well kept. Bryant was necessary, at one time, to set things up. And
then he became . . . less than necessary. A liability.
And he had to be eliminated." Another small shrug.
"And I had to do it. Not because it's the sort of thing I
enjoy doing. But just because he knew me. His defenses
were down, so to speak."

"All right . . ." Deckard nodded. "I'm not exactly
crying for him. Now answer the other question. Why
would you put together a conspiracy to eliminate the
blade runners? Just to make sure nobody could track
down your precious replicants when they get loose?"

The pitying gaze returned to the image's face.
"You're not thinking clearly, are you? I've told you before—you just don't know how things work in this
world. If the blade runners were eliminated—and it appeared that a mysterious, unidentifiable Nexus-6 replicant had not only eluded them, but had killed them
rather than letting itself be killed—then the U.N. authorities would shut down the Tyrell Corporation.
They'd push that little red button, the one that ensures
the destruction of our dangerous technology."

He gave another single nod. "You told me that."

"You were right, Deckard, when you said I'd lied to
you. I have to admit that now. I told you I wanted you
to track down the sixth replicant, and save the Tyrell
Corporation . . ." The image leaned forward on the

monitor screen, its gaze sharpening and fastening tighter upon him. "That was the lie, Deckard. *I wanted you to fail.* I wanted all of you—Batty and Holden as well—to not only fail, but to kill each other off. What else could you do? With no missing replicant to find, you'd turn on each other. Not just the blade runners, but anyone else capable of tracking down escaped replicants, such as Roy Batty, would be eliminated. And the U.N. authorities would know about it. Not how it happened, but that it did. And that would be enough. For my purposes."

He understood now. "You want them to destroy the Tyrell Corporation."

"I've wanted that for a long time. And before that . . . I wanted to kill Eldon Tyrell. My uncle. The way he'd killed me; slowly, from the inside out. A little bit at a time. I knew there was still something like a soul inside him. Not much of one, but something that could love and grieve and mourn—just a little bit. All that was left inside him . . . but that would have been enough. He'd loved Ruth—my mother—but he'd lost her. To his own brother." A smile that was like a razored wound appeared on the image's face. "Rather biblical, don't you think? At this level of money and power, this world that I've lived in, there are no real complications. Everything is reduced to its simplest elements. The oldest stories. Complications are for little people . . . like you, Deckard. That's what you were, for Eldon Tyrell. And for me. Nothing more."

"And what were you . . . you and your uncle . . . to each other?"

"If I said *lovers*, that wouldn't be correct. Not really." The voice from the monitor softened. "Perhaps as some euphemism for the mechanics of incest. But I didn't *love* him . . . and he didn't love *me*. He loved the dead . . . the way you do. Because the dead are memories. Where moth and rust doth not corrupt— isn't that the way it is, Deckard? Look behind you."

He did as the image ordered. He saw the sleeping, dying woman on the bed. The same face as on the monitor screen, but with eyes closed, a flush of pink to the skin across her cheekbones, a line creased in her brow, as though she were fighting off some nightmare evoked by the words tangling in the still air above her head. One of Rachael's hands was closed into a trembling fist upon the pillow.

"You see?" Rachael's voice, but not Rachael's voice; Sarah's voice, a whisper from the monitor. "She's as good as dead. You know that, don't you? All that keeps her here is time . . . and that's such a little thing, Deckard. And memory is so much . . . truer." The whisper lowered, gentler, almost a kiss at his ear. "I made you this offer before. I could be for you . . . what I was for my uncle. Not the real thing . . . not the woman you loved . . . not the dead. But close enough."

He said nothing. As if he had heard nothing. He reached down and stroked Rachael's brow, soothing away the bad dreams that had troubled her long sleep. He laid his hand, softly, against the side of her face, and her lashes trembled against his fingertips.

"I knew you wouldn't." Bitterness etched the voice that came from the monitor. "Nothing can change your mind."

"No . . ." He spoke without turning to look at Sarah's image.

"I knew it would be this way. You prefer the dead to the living, the fake to the real. The memory . . . to me." The voice became harsher and more grating. "The same as *he* did. That's why I've had to do these things. Perhaps if I became the dead . . . if I became a memory . . . then I'd have a chance."

Another voice spoke. The same, but another. A whisper: "Deckard . . ."

He looked down and saw that Rachael had opened her eyes. She gazed at him, calmly and unafraid, as she

had done once before, a long time ago. When he had
woken her from a deathlike sleep.

Do you love me? Memory, his own words.

I love you . . .

Do you trust me?

He bent down and kissed her. "Don't worry . . ."
He placed his fingertips against her lips before she could
say anything. "We'll be leaving here soon."

I trust you . . .

"That's very touching." Sarah's voice came from
the monitor. "I admire your faithfulness. I'm not lying
when I say that. What I wouldn't give . . ." The voice
broke off for a moment, then spoke flat and harsh again.
"You're right. It is time to leave. Time to finish . . .
everything."

Deckard glanced over his shoulder, to the image on
the screen. "Where are you?"

"I'm right here in the building with you." She
laughed, short and humorless. "I wouldn't miss this for
the world. I've waited too long for it."

Outside, visible through the high windows at the
far end of the suite, jagged lightning shot down from
clouds pressing lower with their own weight. A low
rumbling noise, almost beneath the limits of human au-
dibility, trembled through the expectant air.

"Did you hear that?" On the monitor screen, the
image looked away, listening.

"It's the thunder." He spoke to both the image and
to Rachael near him. "That's all it is."

"Oh, no—" The image looked back at him. Sarah
slowly shook her head, eyes widening. As though with
delight. "It's starting. The end of everything . . ."

"What are you talking about?" A cold fingertip
touched his spine.

"You never remember. I tell you things . . . but it
seems you just don't *want* to remember." Pity in the
gaze of Sarah's image, in her voice. "The red button . . . though there is no button, nothing to be

pushed. If it were that easy, I would have done it myself
. . . a long time ago. There's a command series, transmitted by the U.N. authorities, to initiate the auto-
destruct sequence, the explosive charges that were built
into and throughout the Tyrell Corporation headquarters. Right here."

Another low-pitched noise rolled through the
building; the candle flames shivered. Deckard reached
down, his arm around Rachael's shoulder, pulling her
closer to him.

"They must have made their decision." The image
spoke as though savoring its own words. "The U.N. authorities have been monitoring your progress all along;
not as closely as I have, but enough to be aware of the
results. Of yours and Batty's and Holden's futile quests.
The fact that none of you were able to track down this
missing sixth replicant. That you were, in essence, de-
feated by it."

"But they also know—they'd have to—that it's all
lies." He tightened his grip on Rachael's upper arm. "It
was all concocted by you, for your own reasons—"

"That doesn't matter to them. The U.N. has been
looking for a pretext to shut down—to eliminate—the
Tyrell Corporation. Now they have it. Why it came
about is of no concern to them. They'll be able to make
the changes to the off-world colonization program that
they've wanted to for a long time. No Tyrell Corporation . . . and no replicants." The image smiled. "As
has been shown now—they're just too dangerous. Too
much . . . like us."

A stronger shock wave traveled through the building. He felt the floor buckle beneath his feet as the columns running the length of the suite cracked around
their bases. There was no use for the gun now, if there
ever had been; he tossed it aside. Rachael made no resistance as he drew her from the bed and got her to her
feet.

"So now you'll have what you want." Through the

far windows, he could see a roiling light, flames, and smoke-churning explosions, advancing up the sides of the other slanted towers. "Nothing that Eldon Tyrell created will be left. That should make you happy."

"No . . ." Sarah's image shook its head. "Not *happy*. Satisfied, perhaps. In this little time we have left together—"

Harder, and deafening; he was barely able to stay upright, stumbling backward a step, with Rachael pressed close against himself. Columns toppled and crashed to the floor, as the walls were torn apart, raw-edged darkness showing through the chasms splitting wider. Glass fragments sprayed across the rooms as the tall windows twisted in their frames and shattered.

Immediately before him, the antique desk reared and fell, the monitor snapping free of its cables. The monitor struck the floor, the screen bursting into bright shards, the voice struck silent.

"Come on—" Deckard pulled Rachael toward the suite's doors. The carved wooden panels had flown open, hinges wrenched loose, and thick smoke pouring across the ceiling.

The corridor beyond was a racketing hell, alarm sirens shrieking as red light pulsed through the churning black. The elevator shaft gaped open, a torrent of fire leaping from the levels below. As they ran, the floor suddenly tilted beneath them; he landed on his shoulder, skidding and drawing Rachael down against himself. A steel girder, twisted loose of its anchorings, ripped through the ceiling panels like a massive scythe, gouging a ragged trench a few inches away from them.

He couldn't tell if Rachael had screamed in fright and shock; the noise of the explosions climbing through the buildings obliterated his hearing. She might have thought it was part of the same nightmare in which she'd been mired before he woke her—he didn't know. Taking her around the shoulders, he tottered upright, stumbling through the spark-laced smoke toward the stairwell door, barely visible at the corridor's far end.

There, below him; Holden could see them, small human figures surrounded by the larger forms billowing toward the night sky's darker clouds. The other towers had already collapsed, their flank torn open by the sequenced charges, steel frames twisting apart section by section, then falling toward the flame-engulfed center of what had been the Tyrell Corporation headquarters.

Rain lashed across the freight spinner's cockpit, the heavy monsoon gouts hissing into steam as they battered wavelike against the inferno that had burst from the city's heart. Holden gasped for breath, the pulse inside himself staggering in the wash of heat, as he leaned against the controls, willing the spinner through the updraft's coiling hurricane.

He had flown straight here from the sideways world, only to find one even more chaotic. Whatever was going on, it looked terminal; even as he forced the freight spinner down, another series of explosions rolled through the remaining tower, bringing it even closer to the point of toppling into the molten center of the compound.

The building's sudden lurch knocked the two figures from their feet—looking out the side of the cockpit, he recognized his ex-partner Deckard, with a dark-haired woman. They had been trying to reach the spinner parked on the roof's landing deck, but the last shock wave had put an end to that: the empty spinner toppled off the tower's brink, pinwheeling down into the flames, then adding another, smaller explosion to the ones already shaking the surrounding city.

With the flat of his palm, Holden hit the control for the cargo hatchway. A nearly solid gust of heat and smoke slammed against his back as the freight spinner's midsection slid open. He could see Deckard, one arm supporting the woman, looking up at him as he brought

the craft down closer to them. He punched the autopilot into proximity hover, then pushed himself up from
the seat and made his way to the rear section, grabbing
one bulkhead strut after another to keep from falling.

"Deckard!" He held on to the side of the hatch,
reaching down. "Give me her hand!" The dark-haired
woman looked barely conscious, as though asphyxiated
by the smoke churning upward. He could hear, through
the roar of the flames, his own artificial lungs wheezing
for oxygen. Deckard managed to lift the woman, his
arm around her waist, high enough that he could grab
her by the wrist and elbow, and draw her up and into
the freight spinner. She wasn't unconscious; when
Holden lowered her to the tilting floor of the cargo area,
she was able to grasp the metal ribs and pull herself
away from the bottom of the hatch.

He reached back down for Deckard's outstretched
hand. Their fingertips had almost touched, when another explosion, the loudest and nearest of all, ripped
open the last remaining panels of the roof. Holden saw
the surge of glaring light a split second before its impact
concussed the spinner; he was thrown backward, catching a flash of Deckard leaping desperately for the hatchway.

The spinner tumbled nose downward. Holden's
spine hit the back of the pilot's seat; he twisted about,
hands pressed against the controls, a fireball like the interior of the sun welling up to engulf the craft. Over his
shoulder, he saw the hatchway door sliding shut; Deckard, teeth clenched in agony, fought to claw his way
inside. The woman screamed his name, reached, and
grabbed his hand and forearm; the door's edge scraped
open Deckard's shirt and the skin beneath as she pulled
him toward herself. Deckard got one foot on the doorway's rim and gave a final convulsive push. He and the
dark-haired woman slid together against the opposite
bulkhead.

In the same moment the fireball was cleft in two by

the fall of the last tower. The updraft swung the freight spinner around in a dizzying loop as Holden struggled to keep from being torn away from the controls. Suddenly he found himself looking at the dark storm clouds above, the monsoon's torrents pounding the curved glass of the cockpit; with a single lunge he hit the throttle full-on. He clung to the pilot's chair against the mounting g-forces as the freight spinner shot skyward.

Then stars, a diamond sweep from one horizon rim to the other, and silence, the storm left below. Holden managed to claw his way up to the control panel and pull the spinner's ascent into a level flight.

"Here—let me take over." Deckard came forward from the cargo area. Gasping in exhaustion, Holden watched as his ex-partner climbed into the pilot's seat. The bio-mechanical heart in his chest staggered and lurched, then settled into a slower and more stable rhythm.

The craft banked into a slow turn as Deckard's hands moved across the controls. The rain had plastered his hair black against his forehead, a cut along one cheekbone diluting pink down his throat. The sodden coat hung on him like a wet shroud. Watching the navigation screen, he brought the freight spinner slicing back down through the clouds.

Deckard cut the throttle to a slow crawl as they came directly above the Tyrell Corporation headquarters. Or what had been the corporation; a gigantic square section had been cut from the center of L.A. and transformed into what now looked like the mouth of a ground-level volcano. The wind gusts and saturating Pacific rains drove the flames far enough back to reveal the twisted skeletal girders, the distorted structural webs all that remained of the towers.

Black specks, what humans looked like from this altitude, and the larger shapes of emergency vehicles, clustered around the apocalypse perimeter, the ululating wail of their sirens piercing the night.

Holden gazed down through the snakelike rivulets coursing over the cockpit glass. "What the hell brought all that on?"

Reaching again for the controls, Deckard lifted his hard-set gaze from the scene underneath them. "Bad attitudes." He punched the throttle.

A few minutes later—or hours; Holden had lost track of time, closing his eyes while the freight spinner had shot above the city—he felt the craft slowing and descending again. To a landing; he looked out and saw a bleak desert landscape, silvered by the moon and stars. The monsoons' seasonal return hadn't extended this far inland yet. No buildings or fences nearby; the Reclamation Center that Batty had brought him to was obviously miles away.

Deckard cut the engines as the freight spinner settled into the loose gravel and sand. The quiet of the empty landscape penetrated the cockpit glass. He glanced over toward Holden. "We gotta talk." He pushed another control and the side panels swiveled open.

As they walked away from the spinner, leaving prints in the sand, Holden dug the gun out of his jacket. "You know . . . I could take you in. To the police station. And turn you over."

"Sure." Deckard glanced at him. "But you won't."

"I guess not." He put the gun away. "That Batty guy . . . he screwed up my brain. Right now, I don't know whether I'm a replicant or not." He shook his head, still trying to make the pieces come together. "The way it works out for people like us—it comes with the territory, I suppose—a certain leap of faith is required. To assume that we're human at all."

"It's not just for us." A dark edge moved through Deckard's voice, as though it were the product of long, deep brooding. "That's the way it is for everybody. Human or not."

"Yeah, well . . . maybe." Holden wasn't sure he

understood what his ex-partner was talking about. "Right now, though, what I think I'll do is, I'll turn *myself* over to the police. Maybe they'll be able to tell me what I am. Not that it really matters, of course."

"Suit yourself."

"What're you going to do?" He stopped and tilted his head back toward the freight spinner. "The woman in there. Is that . . ."

"Rachael. She's Rachael." Deckard closed his eyes for a moment, then slowly nodded. "The other one— Sarah—is dead. Back at the Tyrell Corporation. That's what she wanted."

The black clouds had massed higher to the west, blotting out the stars close to the horizon. It wouldn't be long before the storms swept across the desert, all the way to the mountain ranges. And beyond.

"Are you going to try to get away? The two of you?" Holden felt a chill creeping in toward his artificial heart. "If you go north again . . . I won't tell them. They'll come looking for you, and they'll find you, but it won't happen because of anything I said."

"No . . ." Deckard shook his head. "We won't go north. That's not far enough . . ."

Holden watched him tilt his head back, eyes barely open. A blue needle of light touched the drop of water that inched along the corner of his brow.

"We'll have to go farther . . ." Deckard's voice a murmur, taken by the wind sifting the desert. "As far as we can . . ."

After

The official behind the counter returned the blue leath-
erette folder, smiling as he handed it back. "I hope you
have a pleasant journey, Mr. and Mrs. Niemand." He
gazed upon them kindly, though that was merely part of
his job. "And that you find everything you're looking
for."

"Thanks." Deckard tucked the folder—it had the
seal of the U.N. emigration services on it, along with
gold-embossed letters spelling out A NEW LIFE!—inside
his jacket. "I'm sure we will."

He picked up the carry-on bag beside him. A knot
in his stomach unclenched—getting the forged ID cards
and other documents stamped had been the last barrier
they'd needed to get past. He turned away from the
counter. "Come on, sweetheart. We don't want to miss
the flight."

Rachael held on to his arm all the way through the
corridors of the San Pedro off-world terminal. Scenes of
happy life in the colonies—Norman Rockwell mixed
with early Soviet Realism, laughing children and fields
of grain—lined the gleaming chrome walls. Even when

Deckard and Rachael were seated aboard the ship, she leaned her head against his shoulder, as though she were already fatigued from the rigors of flight.

Rachael kept her eyes closed all through a lecture from a pair of uniformed attendants, on the various safety procedures. She might have been asleep. He let her hand rest in his; he could just feel the flicker of pulse at her wrist.

Eventually, a low-pitched vibration shivered through the cabin. He looked across the tops of the seats; there were only a few other passengers— emigrants—besides themselves.

"I was dreaming . . ." Rachael's eyelids had fluttered open. She gazed upward.

"Of what?"

She shook her head. "I don't remember." She glanced out the small round window at her side. Not really a window, but a simulation, a video feed from one of the ship's exterior cameras. The slate-grey Pacific extended to the horizon, its curvature visible now.

" 'From Earth we shall quickly remove . . .' " Her voice a murmur. " 'And mount to our native abode . . .' "

An old song—a moment passed before he recognized the Protestant hymn. It called forth a memory; not of childhood, but of another world, the one that had been enclosed by the rough wooden walls of the cabin far to the north. And of that other moment, when a woman had leaned down to look through the glass of a black coffin, at the face that had been a sleeping mirror image of her own. She had spoken the words of a different hymn then. But he had known it, as he knew this one.

He spoke its title aloud: " 'Away with our sorrow and fear . . .' "

Rachael turned and looked at him. Her eyes widened, as though in sudden realization. Of what her own words had disclosed.

"Don't worry." He leaned his head back against the
seat. "It's not important." More of the ancient words
came to him.

We soon shall recover our home; the city of saints shall
appear, the day of eternity come . . .

He closed his eyes, her hand still in his.

They gave him a new heart—a newer one, top of the
line, better than the one he'd been born with. And a
new job, an easy one, at least for a while. Wrapping up
loose ends, more or less. For the department files.

He checked his pulse and blood pressure, the oxygen mixture in his artificial lungs, with a glance at the
miniaturized LEDs that had been implanted in his wrist.
Everything in order—Dave Holden felt no strain as he
walked up the path from where he'd left the police
spinner. The dry pine needles shifted beneath his boots
with each step. Small living things scurried away, into
the forest's deep and dark shade.

The cabin was ashes and charred boards, as he'd
expected it to be. The men who'd worked for Sarah
Tyrell had given all the details about their assignment
here, the last they had gotten from her. What they had
done, and what they had left. He raised the camera and
took a few photographs, for documentation.

Holden stepped across what had been the sill of the
cabin's door and looked around the black rectangle.
Glass in the ashes, the remains of a heat-cracked window, an iron stove toppled onto its side, shapes of what
might have been a wooden chair and table before the
fire had been set around them . . .

And something else, untouched. In perfect condition—the men had done that, as they had been told to.
Taken the black coffin, the transport sleep module, out
of the cabin and a safe distance away; then returned it to
where it had been before. Complete with that which it
held. No longer sleeping; no longer dying. Beyond all
that.

He looked down through the coffin's glass lid, at the woman's face. Eyes closed, dark hair spread across the silken pillow. *Rachael,* he thought. He knew it was her. The one that his ex-partner Deckard had loved. It had always been.

A glance at the transport module's control panel had shown that all life processes had ceased, vital signs at zero. The coffin's sustaining mechanisms had been switched off. Not murder, not technically, but an authorized procedure on Tyrell Corporation property.

He didn't take any photos of the black coffin. He didn't need to. In the picture in his memory, she could still be sleeping.

Walking slowly back to the spinner, he wondered. Why had Rachael been left there? Like that, untouched. He knew, or could guess, why Sarah had done everything else. The whole charade of pretending to be Rachael, asleep on the bed in the Tyrell private suite. While the persynth—the real-time, computer-generated replica of herself, a talking, responding simulation of herself—had shown on the screen of the video monitor. There had been enough evidence in the smoldering remains of the Tyrell Corporation headquarters to reveal what she had done. The same trick that the police had used before on Deckard, set up in the shabby office in the central station, to make him believe that Bryant had still been alive. Deckard had seen through that one. Strange that he hadn't seen through Sarah's little joke as well.

He supposed it was all a matter of getting what you wanted. A hawk wheeled across the sky and was gone. Sarah had done that, gotten what she wanted. To become Rachael. To be loved . . .

Maybe Deckard had as well. Something that Holden had thought about before, back when he'd first figured out what had happened. Maybe Deckard hadn't been fooled at all.

He got back into the police spinner and let the

cockpit glass seal around him. *Maybe,* thought Holden, *he got what he wanted. Somehow. Maybe he did.* Not that it really mattered.

A moment later the spinner mounted into the sky, banking south and toward Los Angeles.

About the Author

K. W. JETER is one of the most respected sf writers working today. His first novel, *Dr. Adder*, was described by Philip K. Dick as "a stunning novel . . . it destroys once and for all your conception of the limitations of science fiction." *The Edge of Human* resolves many discrepancies between the movie *Blade Runner* and the novel upon which it was based, Dick's *Do Androids Dream of Electric Sheep?* Jeter's other books have been described as having a "brain-burning intensity" *(The Village Voice)*, as being "hard-edged and believable" *(Locus)* and "a joy from first word to last" *(San Francisco Chronicle)*. He is the author of twelve novels, including *Farewell Horizontal* and *Wolf Flow*.

Turn the page for
a special preview of

**BLADE RUNNER:
REPLICANT NIGHT**

by K. W. Jeter

The enthralling story of Rick Deckard and his "more human than human" quarry continues in *Blade Runner: Replicant Night,* in which a critical character from Deckard's past returns for an unknown purpose. But, in true *Blade Runner* tradition, nothing is what it seems. Here is a special preview of the opening scene, which vaults readers back into the action of the original movie.

**Look for *Blade Runner: Replicant Night,*
available now in paperback
wherever Bantam Books are sold.**

1

Wake up . . .

He'd heard those words, that voice, before.
Deckard wondered, for a moment, if he were
dreaming. But if he were dreaming *I'd be able to
breathe,* he thought. And right now, in this segment
of time, all he could feel were the doubled fists at
his throat, the tight grip on the front of his jacket
that lifted him clear of the Los Angeles street's
mirror-wet and rubbled surface. In his vision, as he
dangled from the choking hook of factory-made
bone and flesh, all that remained was the face of
Leon Kowalski and his brown-toothed grin of
fierce, delighted triumph.

The other's stiff-haired knuckles thrust right
up under Deckard's chin, forcing his head back,

enough to make him dizzily imagine the passage of air snapping free from the straining lungs in his chest. He could just make out, at the lower limit of his vision, his own hands grabbing onto Kowalski's wrists, thick and sinew-taut, more like the armatures of a lethal machine than anything human. His hands were powerless, unable to force apart the replicant's clench.

"Wake up . . ."

The same words, a loop of past event repeating inside Deckard's head. An echo, perhaps; because he knew the other replicant, his murderer had only said it once. But he'd known it was coming. Those words . . . and his own death. Everything had to happen, just as it had before. Just as he knew it would.

Echo, dream, memory . . . or vision; it didn't matter. What was important was that there had been a gun in Deckard's hands, in the hands that were now clawing to let desperate air into his throat. His gun, the heavy black piece that was standard issue in the LAPD's blade runner unit, a piece that could blow a hole through the back of a fleeing replicant and an even larger, ragged-edged hole through its front.

And that had happened as well. Echo of time, echo of sound, the impact of the gun's roaring explosion travelling up Deckard's outstretched arms, locked and aimed, as it had so many times and so many replicants before. While the sound of death itself had slammed off the city's close-pressed walls, the intricate neon of *kanji* and corporate logos shivering as though with a sympathetic fear, the honed leading edge of the shot and its lower-pitched trail rolling over the street's crowded, incurious faces. All of them as used to death as Deckard was, just from living in L.A.; he knew they could watch him being pulled apart by Kowalski with the same indifferent gazes they had swung toward the replicant Zhora's bullet-driven terminal arc.

When he'd still had the gun, he'd walked with the black piece dangling at his side, its weight pulling down his hand the same way it'd dragged rock-like the shoulder holster strapped beneath his long coat. Rivulets of L.A.'s monsoon rains and his own sweat had oozed beneath his shirt cuff, across the back of his hand, into the checked, death-heated grip inside the aching curve of his palm. He'd walked across spear-like shards of glass crunching under his shoes. The frames of the store windows through which Zhora's dying body had crashed were transformed into gaping mouths ringed with transparent, blood-flecked teeth. He'd walked and stood over her, his sight framing a vision of empty hands and empty face, eyes void as photo-receptors unplugged from any power source. All life fled, leaked from the raw hole between her hidden breasts, dead replicant flesh looking just the same as human. The furious energy, the animal grace and fear, that had impelled her dodging and running through the streets' closing trap, spent and diluted by the drops of tear-warm rain spattering across the pavement's red lace. Deckard's energy, that of the hunter, also gone. The chase, from the moment Zhora had wheeled about in her dressing room at Taffy Lewis's club down in China-town's First Sector and nailed him with a hard blow to the forehead, then all the weaving among crowds and dead-run stalking over the metal roofs of the traffic-stalled cars—that hadn't exhausted him. It'd been the end of the chase, the shot, his own will inside the bullet. That had struck and killed, a red kiss centered on her naked shoulder blades. That had seemed, for a moment, to kill him as well.

Exhaustion had made it possible for the other escaped replicant to get the drop on Deckard, to pull him between two segmented refuse haulers, then smack the gun out of his grip like swatting a fly and send it spinning out toward the street. So exhausted that he hadn't been surprised at all when Kowalski, eyes maddened by the witnessing of the female's death, had picked him up like a rag doll and slammed him against the side of one hauler, spine leaving a buckled indentation in the carapace-like metal. And words, spat out angry and sneering, something with which Kowalski could hammer the killer.

How old am I? Then *My birthday's April 10, 2017. How long do I live?*

Deckard had told him the answer, gasped it out with the last of his breath. *Four years.* That was how long all the Nexus-6 replicants had been given. They carried their own clock-ticking deaths inside their cells, more certain than any blade runner's gun.

The answer hadn't been to Leon Kowalski's liking, though he must have known it already. His eyes had gone wider and even more crazed. *More than you.* More than the man dangling from his fists had to live . . .

"Wake up!"

But that's wrong, thought Deckard. The other's face, mottled in his sight with the black swirling dots of oxygen starvation, grinned up at him. The operating remnants of his brain could remember what had happened before. Kowalski hadn't shouted the words, not that loud; he'd mouthed them softly, as though savoring their taste between his teeth. Those words, and the words that'd come after. *And he didn't lift me so far off the ground . . .*

"Wake up! Time to die!"

He could feel himself dangling in air, could hear the replicant's voice, the words shouted or whispered—it didn't matter now. It hadn't mattered before. All that mattered was the crushing pressure on his throat, the weight of his own body against Kowalski's fists squeezing off the city's humid air from his lungs. The other's words roared inside his head, each syllable a pulse of blood against his skull's thin shell of bone. Now the voice, the shout, seemed to hammer right at his ears. *Maybe that's why it sounds so loud,* thought a cold, abstracted part of Deckard, watching himself die. *Because I know . . .*

He knew what happened next. What would happen, had already happened; foreordained, scripted, bolted to the iron rails of the past, unswerving as those of the rep train that rolled in the darkness beneath the dark city.

Time to die . . .

He wondered what was taking so long. *Where is she?* wondered Deckard. *She was supposed to have been here by now* . . .

Kowalski's fists lifted him higher, his spine arching backward. The sky wheeled in Deckard's sight, needles of stars and gouts of flame penetrating the storm clouds above the L.A. towers. Police spinners drew distant, slow-motion traces of light, while the hectoring U.N. advert blimp cruised lower, seemingly within reach of his hand if he could've taken it away from the replicant's choking grasp. Emigrant vistas swam across the giant screen embedded in the midst of the blimp's spiked antennae; an even larger voice boomingly cajoled him to seek a new life in the off-world colonies. *What a good idea,* that other part of him mused. His old life was almost gone.

The city's faces roiled across his sight; all of them, indifferent or hostile, eyes hidden behind black visor strips or magnified and glittering behind chrome-ringed fish-eye lenses. Chemical-laced tears ran down pallid cheeks, laughter broke past doubled ranks of filed teeth; a row of Taiwanese Schwinn clones jangled the bells on their handlebars, to cut through and then be swallowed up by the two-way rivers of foot and motor traffic. The black dots in Deckard's vision had grown larger and started to coalesce. Beyond them, he could see another face, made of a grid of photons. A woman in *geisha*-lite drag, Euro-ized kabukoid make-up and perfect black-shellac hair; she smiled with ancient suavity at the Swiss pharmaceutical capsule on her fingertips, then swallowed it, her coquette smile and glance turning even more mysterious. He didn't know her name, or even what she was selling; he had never known, during all the time he had walked and lived and killed inside the trap-like city, and the woman had floated above him like some anonymous, disdainful angel. In his anoxic delirium, he could imagine that she was about to lean down from the adscreen and bestow a kiss upon him . . .

The Asian woman's face disappeared, replaced by the only one that mattered. Kowalski pulled him close, not for a kiss but to snap the vertebrae at the hinge of Deckard's neck. He'd be paralyzed before he was dead, but only for a few seconds, until Kowalski finished him off.

"Wake up! Time to die . . ."

Deckard heard the words again, but knew it was only memory. He saw Kowalski's smile and nothing else, as the replicant jabbed two fingers toward Deckard's eye sockets.

Maybe they finally got it right, he thought. *This time it'll be different . . .*

But it wasn't. Even as he looked down at the other's face, time started up again, the loop running as it had before. As it had so long ago. The replicant's expression changed to one of stunned bewilderment. The light behind Kowalski's eyes dwindled to a spark, then died out, as the life that the Tyrell Corporation had given him now rushed from the red flower, torn flesh and white thorns of bone splinters, that had burst from his forehead. The bullet had passed all the way through and vanished tumbling somewhere beyond Deckard's shoulder.

The thing that had been Kowalski crumpled forward, falling onto Deckard and trapping him against the shining wet pavement. Deckard clawed out from beneath him and stood upright again, regaining his balance and his breath. His vision shifted, from blurred to focussed, close to medium distance; Rachael stood at the mouth of the alley, swathed in high-collared fur, the gun that Kowalski had knocked away now clasped in both her hands—it must have landed right at her feet—and trembling from the shock of its firing, the slight motion of the trigger that had placed the steel-jacketed bullet like a quick finger-tap at the back of Kowalski's head. She looked dazed, lips parted to draw in her own held breath; just as though she had never killed anyone before. As though this were the first time this had happened.

His gaze went back down to the dead replicant at his feet. Or supposedly dead. *He's doing a good job,* thought Deckard. Kowalski looked as dead as a real corpse.

"Come on, get up." Deckard kept his voice lowered, so that none of the on-set microphones would pick it up. "It's a wrap, they got it all on tape. You can get up now."

Blood welled from the hole in Kowalski's shattered brow.

Then Deckard knew it was real.

"What the hell . . ." At the edge of the sound stage, where the fake streets, the re-created Los Angeles, gave way to bare dry concrete and steel, the flooring laced with thick power cables and data conduits like black snakes. Deckard stood up, angrily ripping the headphones away from his ears. The folding chair toppled over as he threw the 'phones at the central monitor, the one that had shown the view from the eyes of the other Deckard, the fake one, the one that had been dangling from the now-dead replicant's fists. Across the smaller screens, the angles of all the other videocams unfolded like a magician's pack of cards.

"Now what?" The close-up on the fake Rachael showed her dropping out of character, the look of shock on her face transmuted to that of a disgusted professional, as she let the heavy gun hang at the end of her arm. She sighed wearily. "Christ, this shoot's taking *forever.*"

Deckard ignored her, striding past the cameras on their automated tracking booms, the skeletal apparatuses of light and event. The drizzle from the overhead rain gantry ran off his jacket sleeves; the grid underneath the sound stage sucking away the excess from the glossily photogenic puddles. He pushed aside the *faux* Deckard, the actor playing him, and stood looking down at Kowalski. At what was left of the replicant, the bleeding artificial flesh.

"Please . . ." A hand clutched ineffectually at his elbow. "Mister Deckard . . . you can't just—"

He turned angrily upon the production assistant, a tiny androgynous figure with heavy *retro* black-framed glasses. "It wasn't supposed to happen this way!" He jabbed his finger at the assistant, who fended it off with an upraised clipboard. "I was told you weren't going to kill anyone!" The circumference of his gaze tinged with red as he looked back toward the crew ringing the sound stage. "Where's Urbenton?"

That was the name of the director. Who was conspicuously missing, the folding chair that had usually supported his pudgy frame now unoccupied. *Chickenshit sonuvabitch*—Deckard felt his teeth grinding together. The director must've snuck out after the video recorders had started rolling, while Deckard had been wrapped in the view from the cam monitors, watching the re-creation of his own past. Urbenton would've known that Deckard would go ballistic when a real bullet, from a real gun, wound up churning through someone's brain.

"Come on, man . . ." The actor playing him—not a replicant like the dead Kowalski, but an actual human—tried out as peace-maker. "It can't all be special effects, you know. Sometimes you gotta go for *realism.*"

"Get away from me." Revulsion worked its way up Deckard's throat, choking him as though the replicant's big hands had been around his own neck instead of the other man's. The actor didn't even look that much like him, or at least not yet. Like most of the talent in the video industry, in addition to the remote cam implanted behind one eye, the actor also had barely visible tracker dots sewn under his skin, so that in post-production another's face could be ceegee'd over the one he'd been born with.

The new face would've been the real Deckard's. *But not now,* he fumed. *Not if I can help it.*

"So where is he?" Deckard stopped just short of gathering up the front of the assistant's collar in his hand and squeezing tight, the way the dead Kowalski had done to the human actor. "Where's Urbenton?"

"I . . . don't know . . ." The assistant retreated, sweating hands clasped to the clipboard. "He got called away . . ."

"Yeah, right. I bet." He stepped over the corpse and started toward the soundstage's big rolling doors and the interlocking corridors and spaces of the studio complex beyond. "I'll find him myself. He's got one hell of a lot of explaining to do."

He didn't look over his shoulder as he strode away. But he could sense the fake L.A. dying its own death, the constant artificial rain stopping, the vehicles halting and being shut off in the middle of the crowded street, the actors and extras walking off the set. The replica blimp, a tenth the size of the one that had once actually floated above the city, dangled inert from the overhead rigging, ad-screen blank and faceless.

The city's walls parted as the grips moved the scenery back. There was nothing behind them except dust and stubbed-out cigarettes, and a few scattered drops of blood.

Printed in the United States
by Baker & Taylor Publisher Services